Praise for Ali...

Winner of Best Romantic Read, ...
(Festival of Romantic Fiction)

'**Brave and beautiful**' Bear Grylls

'This book **made me cry**, which no other book has
done before' Lucy Walton-Lange, *Female First*

'A book that **won't fade easily** from your memory'
Daniela Sacerdoti, author of *Watch Over Me*

'**Moving, sensitive**, thought-provoking' Alison Mercer,
author of *After I Left You*

'It's not often that I fall **in love** with a book **within
the first few pages**, but it happened to me with this
one' *The Bookbag*

'A **touching love story** . . . all very
engaging and delivered in spades!'
Tom Williams, screenwriter of *Kajaki* and *Chalet Girl*

'Driven by some **compelling** characters, **rich**
storylines and **powerful** issues, Peterson's latest novel
is a real **tour de force**' *www.chicklitclub.com*

'I am **incapable of not loving** anything
Alice Peterson writes'
Sophie Hedley, *www.reviewedthebook.co.uk*

'**Inspiring** and **warm** hearted' *Glamour Must Read*

'Alice Peterson has a **tremendous gift of
characterisation** and of gentle plots that grapple with
some **surprisingly gritty** issues . . . often **deeply
moving** and **thought-provoking**' *Goodreads*

'As it was the **favourite book of the year** to date for
my reader in this field, I had to read it too before carrying
her enthusiasm forward. I loved it. It's **character-led,
warm and sensitive**' *The Bookseller*

Also by Alice Peterson

Another Alice
M'Coben, Place of Ghosts
You, Me and Him
Letters From My Sister
Monday to Friday Man
Ten Years On
By My Side
One Step Closer to You

THE
THINGS
WE DO FOR
LOVE

ALICE PETERSON

Quercus

First published in Great Britain in 2015 by
Quercus Publishing Ltd
Carmelite House
50 Victoria Embankment
London EC4Y 0DZ

An Hachette UK company

A CIP catalogue record for this book is available
from the British Library

ISBN 978 1 84866 901 7
EBOOK ISBN 978 1 78429 050 4

10 9 8 7 6 5 4 3 2 1

Typeset by CC Book Production

Printed and bound in Great Britain by Clays Ltd, St Ives plc

To Kim, Steve and Charlotte Edwards
And to my friend and cousin, SJ
Thank you for bringing this book to life

PROLOGUE

A beautifully presented two-bedroom garden flat in a popular street, only a stone's throw away from excellent local shops and restaurants . . .

Finally I stand outside the front door of Flat 4a, 23 Priory Road. I catch my breath, handbag dropping to the pavement, my back aching, puffy ankles throbbing. I reread the estate agent's blurb. I'm sure I've only passed a twenty-four-hour shop, tattoo parlour and a Tesco Express. No sign of any restaurants. Surely they can't mean that old hut across the road that sells kebabs? I sigh. Course they do. They're full of bullshit.

I glance at my watch. It's coming up to half past one. I congratulate myself on being only ten minutes late when these days I can't get anywhere quickly; I'm like a bus without wheels. What's his excuse? I need to be back at work for a two thirty meeting. I'm bursting too.

Ten excruciatingly long minutes later, after leaving

Alex Whyte a couple of messages, I'm about to give up when I see a tomato ketchup-coloured car zooming into a tight space on the opposite side of the street. Out comes a stocky man whom I guess to be about my age – early twenties – with short blond hair, chest puffed out, clearly proud of his parking skills. Must be him, he looks like an estate agent. I pick up my bag, thinking this place had better be worth the journey. I can't face walking round any more depressing damp-ridden flats, agents advising me to strike while the iron is hot. This Alex guy is new so with any luck he'll get what I'm looking for: a simple, small two-bedroom flat in West London, modern, a flat that needs no work . . .

I watch as Alex strides across the road in a dark suit and tie, talking on his mobile, his voice so loud that surely the whole street can hear his business. He raises an eyebrow in my direction and looks me up and down, keys jangling. The first one he locates doesn't unlock the door and he's *still* on his phone, no sign of an apology for keeping me waiting. I feel like grabbing his mobile, throwing it on to the ground and stamping on it. Oh the pleasure! 'Yeah, mate, bang on,' he's saying as he tries another key. 'Can't, mate, the missus wants me back tonight.' He rolls his eyes at me as finally we enter the building that . . . I sniff . . . smells of cat pee.

'Okey-dokey!' Alex hangs up and opens the front door to Flat 4a. 'I'm all yours! I'm Alex by the way and I'm assuming you must be January. Cool name. How you doing? Having a good day so far?'

'Not bad,' I mutter, stepping into the hallway, painted olive green with an ivy-trellised border. I glance down the dark and narrow corridor, already feeling disappointed. It's like dating. All your hopes are built up and then you meet a man who tucks his jumper into his trousers and wears white socks.

'This is the hallway,' Alex says, before walking a few steps and turning left, 'and this is the kitchen.'

Why do they always say that? Makes me want to snap back, 'No, really Sherlock? You don't say.' My bladder reminds me I need the loo.

'As you can see, this property has a great feeling of light and space,' says Alex, repeating word for word what is on my sheet, 'and could make a terrific investment.'

I open one of the cupboard doors. A hinge is loose and the door swings.

'Nothing that a bit of DIY can't sort out,' claims Alex, attempting to come to the rescue. 'I'm sure your hubby or partner is a whizz with the screwdriver and hammer, hey.' He slams the door shut and it falls off its hinge again. 'Okey-dokey, moving on.'

'Yes, let's,' I say, before asking him if I can go to the loo.

'So, how many months are you?' Alex calls through the bathroom door.

'Er, hang on,' I call back.

'My girlfriend always says I should never ask if a woman is preggers just in case they're, you know, partial to one too many doughnuts, but . . .'

Oh go away. You're too close for comfort.

I flush the chain. 'Seven,' I say, spotting mould around the bath. 'Two months to go.' I unlock the door and Alex steps inside immediately, asking, 'Is it safe or do I need to hold my nose?' Another chuckle.

Is there a special school for estate agents, where they get gold stars for being the biggest knobs?

'Anyway, as you can see,' Alex continues, 'this is the bathroom with the power shower.'

I nod, staring at an old white hose attached to one of the taps.

'Okey-dokes.' Next he's leading me down the corridor and into a decent-sized room. 'This,' he says, as if it's the *pièce de résistance*, 'is the master bedroom with its own en-suite.'

The yellow walls look suspiciously as if the previous owner smoked in bed and a white shower curtain separates the shower from the loo. If I was brave enough I'd tell him not to waste any more time, this isn't for me, but clearly I'm too polite because I'm now following him through the double doors and out into the garden, which says in the blurb is well kept and west facing. 'It's not exactly well kept, is it?' I can't help saying, pointing at the weeds sprouting through the paving stones and peering into a pot of dead herbs. I wish my flatmate, Lizzie, was with me. Right now we'd be trying hard not to get the giggles. She was my closest school friend and the first person I lived with when I moved to London at eighteen. During this past year I don't know what I would have done without her. Lizzie has stood by me every step of the way since, well, since everything began to go so horribly wrong.

'Sure, sure,' he says. 'But you know what, all this place needs is a lick of paint and a woman's touch . . .' he winks at me, 'and Bob's your uncle, you've got a great little family pad that ticks all the boxes. So, how do you feel? Do you think your husband . . . ?'

'How many years are left on the lease?' I ask, my skin burning.

'Not sure, but I can find out,' he suggests, placing an arm around my shoulder and leading me back into the musty-smelling sitting room with its two plastic-leather sofas, the walls painted in lilac. 'I was going to say, do you think your other half might want to take a look?' He registers my face, but continues, 'I'm only asking because we've had serious interest and I can imagine you want to move . . .' he stares at my bump, '*pronto.*'

You hate it. Tell him you hate it and he needs to do a whole lot better next time if he wants to get a juicy commission.

'You're a first-time buyer, right?' Alex carries on before I have a chance to reply.

I nod.

'You're pretty young.'

I'm twenty-three. 'Uh-huh. Anyway, thanks Alex, but . . .'

'Lucky old you on the property ladder, hey? Is your husband a banker or something? Or let me guess, you guys won the lottery?'

'No, no, nothing like that.' I struggle for the right words. 'Unfortunate circumstances,' is what I come up with.

He clicks his tongue against the roof of his mouth. 'Nothing unfortunate about being on the property ladder. A million people would *kill* to be in your shoes.'

'Would they.'

'Are you kidding me? I'm nowhere near buying my own place.'

As Alex continues, I see myself aged five, holding my toy rabbit as my grandparents told me the news about my parents' death, Granny holding me in her arms. I remember going to an antiques fair for my tenth birthday and choosing a gold locket, Granddad telling me I could put a photograph of Mum and Dad on either side, reminding me that they were always close, inside my heart. I recall my grandparents telling Lucas and me, when we were eighteen, that they'd invested the money from the sale of my parents' house, for us. It was our inheritance. Then I hear Dan's voice inside my head and the pain deepens. When will it go away? They say time heals, but how can it when I have his child growing inside me? I'm in a dark place, a place that sometimes I don't want to be. I touch my bump, feeling guilty that I am plagued by doubt with the choices I have made. How can I raise a child without his or her father? Am I mad thinking I can do this on my own? Will he come back? Where is he?

'January?' I feel someone touching my shoulder.

'I have to go,' I say, heading towards the front door.

'So, give us a tinkle once you've had a chance to think about it and—'

'I've thought about it,' I cut him off, before reinforcing with increasing frustration that this flat doesn't tick any of my boxes.

He must sense my mood as outside, in the cold and drizzle, he says, 'Can I give you a lift anywhere?'

'I'm fine, thanks,' I reply. Catching a bus back to work is infinitely preferable to another minute spent with Alex and his wild assumptions.

But then I see something out of the corner of my eye and Alex follows my gaze.

'Oh shit!' He races across the road just as a traffic warden plants a ticket behind his windscreen wipers.

On my way back to the office I can't stop smiling. There was something so funny about watching Alex argue in vain about his ticket, saying he'd only parked for one lousy minute. One minute! If only.

So, I didn't find my dream house, and time is against me, but it will be out there somewhere; it's just hiding well. Perhaps finding the right house is like finding the right man. Just as you have to kiss a lot of frogs to find your prince, clearly sometimes you have to visit many places like Flat 4a, 23 Priory Road before you find the right match.

I take a deep breath and stare out of the window, wiping a tear from my eye, my emotions all over the place these days. I touch my locket. It doesn't matter how often I tell myself that I have many friends and I have my wonderful grandparents and I have Lizzie – the thing is, I don't have *him* anymore. Dan's face haunts me every single day. Every waking hour I fantasise that this is a dream and soon I'll wake up and see his face.

I wish I didn't feel this way. How weak I am. I should hate him for being such a coward, shouldn't I? And I do, but there is a fine line between love and hate.

As the bus pulls into the next stop, I sit up, promising myself to stop thinking about him all the time. I have my baby now; he or she is my priority. Perhaps, one day, he will regret the choices he has made. Maybe it's better to be on my own than with the wrong man. Lizzie tells me there is nothing lonelier than being with the wrong person. I will raise my child and give it all the love I have. I *can* do it. I know I can. Just watch me, Dan Gregory.

I know, in many ways, that Alex is right. I am in a fortunate position. I find myself smiling again recalling him laying into the traffic warden, calling him the scum of the earth, so angry spit was flying out of his mouth. Imagine being with a man like him. I think I'd rather have pins stuck in my eyes than go out with a man who says 'okey-dokey'. Life could be worse. Life could be so much worse.

I can't stop smiling now.

'*Your mother loved to laugh, January,*' Granny once said to me when she was teaching me how to plant seeds in her greenhouse. '*Her glass was always half full. As a child she used to love watching the* Carry On *films. I could hear her laughter coming all the way from the other side of the house.*'

I must be laughing now as my neighbour is looking at me strangely, as if I'm mad. Maybe I am.

All I can think is I could be married to an Alex.

I could be married to an estate agent.

1

Eight years later, 2011

I stand in front of my bedroom mirror, holding my stomach in. I don't remember my navy suit trousers being *this* tight . . . but then again I haven't worn them for *years*. But still, surely not? The drycleaners *must* have shrunk them.

'Are you wearing the shoes that make your feet go up?' Isla asks me. She has always described high heels this way. She's sitting on the end of my bed, stroking Spud, our Jack Russell rescue dog. His coat is snow-white with a light brown circular patch on his back and sturdy little chest. I shove my feet into my shoes. 'Yep! Ta-dah!' I give her a twirl, trying to disguise my nerves.

Isla sticks her thumbs up. 'She looks pretty, doesn't she, Spud?' She pats him on the top of his head before cocking her head to one side. 'But your hair is funny.' She shrugs. 'Doesn't matter, ha ha ha!' Isla has a naughty contagious laugh.

'Ha ha ha!' I repeat before glancing in the mirror and noticing how static my hair is after washing it this morning. 'Come on,' I say, 'breakfast.'

I couldn't eat a thing.

This morning I'm having my second interview for Sherwoods, a property firm in Mayfair that specialises in selling country houses and estates. I have applied for the PA position, working for the chairman of the London office, Jeremy North. I don't know a thing about property, except that I don't like estate agents. I still can't believe I'm applying to work for one. Clearly I'm not only desperate but insane too. I think back to the agent who sold me this place in Hammersmith, pound signs bulging out of his eyes. But surely not all estate agents are tossers, are they? After weeks of circling job adverts and nothing materialising, Lizzie, who works for a travel company, told me she'd heard about this job through a friend. 'Don't worry about having no experience,' she'd reassured me, 'you just need to be able to run an office.' But that's the trouble. I'm seriously rusty. I haven't worked in an office since Isla was born. I had every intention of going back to my old job at a literary agency in Notting Hill, but when I sat down and really worked out the sums, I struggled to see how my salary could cover full-time care. It couldn't. And then Isla needed all that extra attention, and suddenly I wasn't sure I'd ever be able to have a job or lead anything close to a normal life ever again. A lot has happened over the past eight years to chip away at my confidence.

Things used to be simple. I moved to London when I was eighteen, ready to throw myself into any job. Unlike my older brother Lucas (he managed to get away with a more conservative name), who knew he'd always wanted to be a banker and earn serious money, I had no idea what I wanted to do except to earn enough to pay my rent and enjoy my freedom. My first job was waitressing in a bar and then over the next three years I shampooed hair at Toni&Guy, worked in the toy department at Harrods where I met my first love, Billy, who worked in the men's toiletries department. He used to pick me up for dates on his motorbike, wearing his hot leather jacket. When I heard the sound of the engine I'd rush out of the front door and he'd whip his helmet off for a kiss before I hopped on to the back, Billy telling me to hold on tight. It was like being with Tom Cruise in *Top Gun*! Then I sold silver heart necklaces and engagement rings in Tiffany's, worked for a courier company and, finally, a secretarial job for a literary agency. I've enjoyed each job in a different way, but it hasn't exactly been a career ladder or whatever you call it. Given half the chance I'd read books for a living, so my last job was the most fulfilling. I was not only doing secretarial work but also reading scripts and learning about the contract side. At last I'd found something that gave me a kick in my stride. I didn't want to have cigarette and coffee breaks every minute of the day. And then I met Dan and . . .

well, everything changed and . . . I stop, not wanting to live in the past. Focus on this morning, January. I need this job to help pay my bills and mortgage. However, it's not just about the money. These past eight years have been some of my most challenging yet, and I have no regrets. I love being Isla's mother. But somewhere along the way I've lost a part of me that I need to find again.

Deep breath. I can do this. Be professional. I can work for an estate agent, as long as he doesn't say okey-dokey . . .

Isla and I head into the kitchen and I try to ignore the mess of bills and paperwork littering the worktop. Isla lifts herself on to the stool; she's as light as a sparrow and short for her age, with rich chestnut-coloured hair like my own and my mother's and grandmother's, except Isla's hair is cut in a cute bob with a blunt fringe that highlights her almond-shaped eyes. I have grey-green eyes, like my mother's. Granny often hugs me tightly, saying she can't believe how alike we are, that I have grown up to be a beautiful woman. 'Although you might be a tiny bit biased,' I add.

I pour Isla a glass of milk before switching on the coffee machine and radio, sticking some bread into the toaster and mashing some vile-smelling tinned meat into Spud's bowl. Next Isla is off the stool and singing 'Edelweiss' with Spud, Spud's head tilted to one side, tail wagging as he howls along to the music. It's one of his party tricks and normally I find it endearing . . . 'Isla! Will you sit down otherwise we'll be late.'

'Doesn't matter.'

Her favourite expression, said with a shrug. This morning I butter and cut her toast. I know I shouldn't do it for her but I don't have the time or energy to argue. I think back to my teens and early twenties, the job interviews that I had. I don't remember feeling this nervous, but then I didn't have anything to lose, nor care so deeply about rejection. Now there's this part of me screaming, '*Who the hell would want to employ you? You're just a mum. You haven't been in the job market for years! You won't even know how to work the photocopier!*' The knife slips from my fingers.

'Isla! That's enough!' I force her on to the stool before plonking Spud's bowl on to the floor for him.

'You'll be all right, Mummy,' she says, looking up at me with that soulful expression.

It's only a job. I drop my shoulders. 'Sorry, darling.'

'They liked you the first time,' she reasons, 'so I'm sure they'll like you again.'

I think back to my first interview. I'd arrived at Green Park with plenty of time to spare so decided to have a coffee. I was in a queue in Starbucks and the young woman standing in front of me was constantly looking at her watch. She had long fair hair and patterned tights and I could see a packet of cigarettes in her jacket pocket. When the time finally came for her to order a double espresso she rummaged in her handbag before explaining to the indifferent man behind the counter that she'd left her wallet in the office and could she pay later? Everyone in the queue began to tut because the manager needed to be called. Sensing her stress I tapped her on the shoulder and said I'd be happy to pay, and no, she didn't need to pay me back. It was only a coffee. My grandmother always says do kind things for people; what goes around comes around. When I was shown into the boardroom later that morning there she was, sitting at the table. 'Lucie Henshaw, Jeremy North's number two,' she said, shaking my hand and telling me to sit down, and that she'd never come across the name January before. She then looked at me again, narrowing her eyes and said with a small smile, 'Can I get *you* a coffee?'

School is thankfully only a five-minute walk from home. I like this part of west London. It's where Lizzie and I rented our first flat together on Hammersmith Grove. Isla, Spud and I live close to Ravenscourt Park; we're only minutes away from cafes, the Lyric theatre, the rundown cinema and pubs along the river. As Isla rushes on ahead with Spud I tell her to keep her right foot flat on the ground. 'No Miss Tippy Toes!' I call out, ignoring another passer-by looking at us. We're fairly immune now to stares. Walking in a straight line has never been Isla's strong point.

My mobile rings. It's Granny. 'Sock it to him, darling.'

Granddad comes on to the line. 'And if you get nervous imagine the old chairman starkers.'

I smile. 'What are you doing today?'

'Sleeping,' he says, 'in between eating cheese.'

Granny comes back on to the line. 'Call us, won't you, when it's over.' She sounds breathless.

'Granny, are you all right?' Granny is seventy-four. 'You haven't had any more of your giddy spells? Isla, not too fast!'

'I'm as right as rain. Now good luck, you can do it.'

At the school gates I receive many admiring glances since my school-mum friends are so used to seeing me in jeans, a sloppy jumper and boots. As everyone wishes me good luck I'm beginning to regret telling them all about this interview. It reminds me of announcing the date of my driving test to all my friends, only to go and mount the kerb the moment I left the driving test centre. Isla dawdles. She hates saying goodbye to Spud and me; normally she heads off with her friends, no glance over her shoulder, but today she's clingy. 'If you get the job,' she says, 'you'll still be my mum, won't you?'

I bend down and wrap my arms around her, feeling guilty for snapping earlier this morning. 'I love you more than any job. You will always come first.'

She nods as if that answer will do. As I watch her walk through the school gates, I can't help comparing her spaghetti-thin legs to the sturdy legs of her friends. I overhear her telling them Mummy is trying to get a job, which is why I am wearing shoes that make my feet go up.

*

Sherwoods is on Dover Street, close to Berkeley Square, in the heart of Mayfair. Next door to a modern art gallery is a shoe shop, a pair of silver heels mounted in the window as if they are jewels.

The office building is two-toned, white and charcoal-grey, with long sash windows and a little black balcony. As I approach the front door I remind myself of all the things not to say or do during my interview. Don't chew nails. Don't ramble, no going off on tangents. Remember my W.A.I.T. tactic – it stands for 'Why Am I Talking?' Lizzie tipped me off about this one. Often we have this need, driven either by insecurity or some warped sense of responsibility that it's always up to us to fill an awkward silence, but it's dangerous since it can lead to waffling. W.A.I.T. is useful to remember on first dates too; you don't want to give away your whole life story. Not that I've had huge success lately on the date front . . . don't think about that right now . . . concentrate . . .

Don't say 'you know' a lot. Impress Mr North with your knowledge about the company. There are twelve offices in the country and roughly two hundred staff. It was founded in 1875 or was it 1895? Say late nineteenth century. Their rival is Barker & Goulding, a much bigger property firm. I thrive in smaller set-ups. I press the buzzer. 'I can do this,' I mutter for the millionth time. The reason for the eight-year gap on my CV, well that's a long story . . . W.A.I.T. He doesn't need to know all about my private life . . . Lucie will have told him that I have a child, just say no plans to have any more and . . . 'Oh hello, it's January Wild,' I say through the intercom, straightening my jacket and brushing one of Spud's hairs off my trousers. 'I'm here for . . .'

They buzz me in. 'My ten o'clock interview,' I say to myself, touching my locket.

The receptionist greets me again, soaked in Chanel scent. She's called Nadine and looks as if she's in her late forties, short honey-blonde dyed hair, top-heavy but great legs, I notice, as she totters in front of me in a skirt and purple suede boots. Sherwoods is based in a private house on two levels. The reception is in the hallway, a wide wooden-floored corridor, big enough to fit a desk, a couple of chairs and a glass coffee table scattered with *Country Life* maga-zines. Downstairs is the open-plan office that everyone shares, except for Jeremy who has his own private room upstairs, next to the boardroom. Nadine comments on how quiet it is since everyone is out on a pitch.

As I walk into Jeremy North's spacious office the first things I take in are the tailored suit, silvery-grey hair and old-fashioned spectacles perched precariously close to the end of his nose. I shake his hand firmly before sitting down.

He shuffles some paperwork in front of me. 'So, January, your name certainly stands out.'

'I'm often teased. People say to me, "What's your sur-name? Let me guess. *February*?" Or I tell you another one . . .' W.A.I.T. I laugh nervously and shut up.

He skims through my CV. I want to tell him I'm a hard worker, that had it not been for Isla's complications, my qualifications would be more impressive. But I remain quiet. 'I see you have no actual work experience in property, but obviously you know the difference between when a property is for sale, when it's under offer and when it's exchanged contracts?'

'I do,' comes my solemn reply, as if answering vows in a church.

'This role requires someone who is organised. I travel a fair amount, mainly meeting colleagues at the other offices or I'm doing pitches across the country. I need someone here to manage my time and my diary.'

'Absolutely.'

'What's your geography like?'

'My geography? Very fine.' *Very fine?*

'My last PA was charming, but her geography. She didn't know where Princes Risborough was. Fancy that. She thought it was a person, that I was meeting a Prince Risborough.'

'Fancy that,' I say, clocking on the wall behind him a framed print of a map of Britain, but drat, I'm too far away. I didn't reckon on having to be a geography whizz. My grandfather once asked me the capital of Turkey and I said 'Bernard Matthews'.

'You see, if I'm going from Norfolk to Cheshire in a day,' Jeremy continues, 'I need more than an hour to get there, unless my name is Obama and I fly by private jet.' His light-blue eyes twinkle. I imagine he had fair hair when he was young. Looking at him now makes me think of my father. They would have been roughly the same age.

'How long would you give me to travel from Norfolk to Cheshire, January?'

'Norfolk to Cheshire,' I repeat, indiscreetly trying to place both on the map. Why isn't he asking me what my strengths are and all that? 'Well, that depends on all sorts of things.' I give him one of my megawatt smiles, hoping that will be enough for him.

'Such as?' He peers at me from behind his round-framed glasses.

'The traffic and . . . the weather, you know, flooding or, you know, wind . . .'

'Wind?'

'Yes, howling gales that can, you know, rock your car side to side and if your satnav doesn't send you on, you know, a little detour . . .' W.A.I.T. 'Three hours, maybe a little more,' I add when I see his face.

'I'd say at least four to be on the safe side. In this business you cannot afford to be late for pitches.'

'Yes. Always best to be cautious.'

'It's essential to be professional and on time.'

'Absolutely. Normally I'm far too early. I once turned up at a wedding before the groom, ha ha . . .' I stop; fold my hands on to my lap. 'Anyway, as you were saying . . .'

'Yes, right. Some of your work will involve advertising and brochure design, booking photographers and researching the area to get key selling points across in the text. You'll get the hang of the property blurb.' He pauses. 'Lucie mentioned that you have family commitments?'

I nod. 'I have a little girl, Isla.' I go on to tell him that I have provisionally made arrangements for her, but without going into the detail of interviewing a Romanian woman called Ruki, who wants to work part-time in between cutting people's hair from home.

'I have a dog too,' I say, glancing at the photograph of two golden Labradors on the bookcase behind his desk.

'Oh, do you? What kind?' For the first time Jeremy looks interested, as if a dark room suddenly has light.

'A Jack Russell. He's called Spud.'

'I have two.' He swings round to pick up the photograph. 'Albert, named after Albert Bridge, and Elvis because my wife loves . . .' He begins to sing 'I'm Dreaming of a White Christmas', Elvis Presley style. 'I tell you, it's exceptionally handy to be a dog lover in this job. I was once at a house and happened to know that the woman's four-legged friend was a Spinone Italiano. That got me the pitch immediately.'

I laugh with him.

With renewed energy Jeremy goes on to tell me about how one of the most important aspects of the job is to keep the clients happy. 'Some are charming; others you want to poke in the eye with a dirty stick, but the thing is, without clients we have nothing to sell.'

He picks up his telephone, calls down to Nadine to ask for a pot of coffee. 'And some of those *biscuits au gingembre*,' he says in a French accent as he winks at me. 'So, as I was saying . . .' He trails off.

'You were saying how important your clients are.'

'That's right. Often we sell houses to the rich and famous, or the rich and famous *are* our clients, so one needs a degree in discretion.'

'I have that.'

He drums his fingers against the desk. 'What people tend to forget is that selling a house can be emotional. I am dealing with someone's most prized possession. It's not like selling British Telecom shares. There are tears, especially from my older clients and it's important to respect what they're going through. These are people who have often spent forty plus years in their home and finally they have to move because they can't manage or one of them is gravely ill. They have to say goodbye to a home filled with memories, a place where they raised their children. Where do your parents live?'

'Cornwall.'

'Lovely. Which part?'

'South coast, near St Austell.' From my bedroom window is a blanket of green lawn and blue sea. I picture my grandmother now, sitting by the telephone, waiting for me to call as she distracts herself with the crossword or some sewing. She used to knit cardigans and smock dresses for Isla. Or maybe she's practising the piano. She took it up when I left home aged eighteen. She doesn't do as much gardening or walking as she used to. I feel emotional as I picture her weekly pillbox, Granny laughing that unless she sticks her tablets into each little compartment she forgets if she's taken them.

'Have they lived there all their life?'

'We moved when I was nine,' I say, recalling how unhappy my brother Lucas had been when we'd left London. 'You've ruined my life!' he'd tell our grandparents, slamming the door behind him. 'I hate it here!' I'm brought back to reality when Nadine comes in carrying a tray that she puts down on his desk, and I'm hoping that will stop Jeremy asking any more personal questions.

'Thank you, Nadine.' He pours the coffee and offers me a biscuit before going on. 'I'm sure that when they eventually do sell your parents will remember all those rainy afternoons when you did your maths homework at the kitchen table, or the times you camped in the garden. My children loved to dress up and perform plays in front of our long-suffering friends.'

Please don't go on. It's beginning physically to hurt not to cry. My parents didn't have the chance to see me learn to ride a bike. They didn't teach Lucas and me to swim, or read our school reports. All their hopes and dreams for the future . . . maybe they had wanted a third child . . . everything gone, taken away in one instant . . . my grandparents picking up the shattered pieces . . .

'I bet your mother even remembers . . . Oh no, oh January, what's wrong?' Frantic, he opens the top drawer of his desk and hands me a small packet of tissues.

'It's not your fault. I'm sorry.' I pluck one out of the packet. I haven't cried or thought about my parents for some time, so why now? 'I'm fine,' I assure Jeremy, wiping my eyes. Don't muck up, January. I've got to get out of my rut and back into the real world again. These last eight years have been taken up with Isla's hospital appointments, one after another, and I'm lonely, so lonely, because now that Isla's at school I have all this time to fill, time that stretches like a long empty road leading nowhere.

I'm lost.

'Shall I call a doctor?' Jeremy asks when the tears come again.

There's a knock. 'Not now, Nadine!'

She pokes her head round the door and winces. 'It's just Mr Parish is on the line, he wants to put in an offer . . .'

'Later!'

Nadine backs away.

'I'm sorry.' I sneeze. 'Please take the call.'

'It can wait. Was it something I said?' There is genuine concern in Jeremy's voice.

'My parents died when I was a baby.'

Jeremy looks vexed. 'How insensitive of me.'

'You weren't to know. My grandparents raised my brother and me. I'm lucky. They *are* my parents. I had everything a child could possibly want.'

'Except your mum and dad.' There's a long pause. 'You have your own family now? A daughter,' he continues, clearly hoping that will ease my pain.

I feel a lump in my throat. *'If you get the job you'll still be my mum, won't you?'*

And I'm off again. The tears won't stop. What was I thinking believing I could sit here in my stupid old suit that's too tight pretending everything is normal?

There's a further tentative knock on the door. Nadine comes in, 'I'm sorry, Jeremy, but Mr Parish is insisting . . .' She stops when she sees me. 'I'll come back later.' The door slams shut.

'I'm so sorry,' I say to Jeremy. 'I've wasted enough of your time, I'll . . .'

He raises a hand to stop me. 'Would you like to start the interview again?'

Stunned, I nod. He gives me time to gather myself and dry my eyes. Ask me about Sherwoods, ask me anything that's easy to answer.

'How old is your daughter?'

Surprised, 'Eight,' I reply.

'And you're a single mum? That must be tough.'

'Isla's father, Daniel . . .' I stop, unsure how to begin

telling Jeremy that messed-up story. 'He's around. He's a good father, but we're not together anymore.' I see Dan giving Isla a piggyback in the park, both of them laughing as Dan chases Spud across the field, Isla saying, 'Faster, Daddy!'

Jeremy picks up his telephone. 'Nadine, cancel all my appointments for this morning and tell Mr Parish I'm unavailable for the next hour, that there's been an emergency.' He looks at me with kindness in his eyes. 'What's Isla like?'

'Goodness, where do I start?'

'At the beginning.'

2

Six years ago, 2005

Isla is two years old. After seeing the doctor, I leave the hospital, numb, pushing her buggy down the corridor and towards the lifts. A blast of fresh air hits me when we exit the building. I watch the traffic, hear an ambulance siren and see people rushing down the street with cups of coffee talking on their mobiles. How can life carry on when my world has been turned upside down?

As we wait at the bus stop I keep reminding myself that Isla is the same girl she was twenty minutes ago. Nothing has changed. I look down at her, sitting in her pram, chestnut curls, podgy cheeks and big round eyes. Except everything *has* changed. On the bus on our way home, 'What shall we have for our tea?' I ask, adopting that cheerful voice when inside my head all I can hear is the doctor saying those dreaded words, '*Isla has cerebral palsy.*'

I dig my thumbnail into the palm of my hand.

'Nana,' she says, holding her teddy.

'How about I make us a banana smoothie!' I dig my nail even deeper. Of course it was obvious. Isla can't stand straight or still, she has little or no balance. She is still crawling and when she does manage to stand, she can only walk on tiptoe.

I stare out of the window. I see the doctor sitting in front of his computer screen.

'*Often we don't pick up on spasticity in the early months . . .*'

I shift in my seat.

'*The damage to Isla's brain has occurred in the area that controls the muscle tone. This is why she has that tightness in her legs.*'

'*So you're saying Isla's brain can't give the right messages to her body?*'

'*Indeed. The command from the muscle itself overwhelms her spinal cord and as a result the muscle is too dense, or spastic.*'

That 's' word again. I wish I'd had the nerve to ask him to stop using it.

'*Of course patients have varying degrees,*' he'd continued. '*I see Isla has some tightness in her hands too, but it's mild. I think her walking could be significantly affected and she could possibly have learning difficulties, linked with the brain damage . . .*'

I feel sick. Helpless.

'*But in her case, I don't believe it's severe. Isla's a bright girl. Treatment is important. We don't want to see her get any worse . . . she'll need splints for her feet and I'll refer her for hydrotherapy. She must carry on with her stretching exercises.*'

I watch another mother with her young fair-haired son. He looks as if he's about three or four, dressed in dungarees and a cap. He presses the button before he runs down the aisle, towards the exit doors. All I can think is, why did this happen to Isla and me? Is it something I did during my pregnancy? Tears sting my eyes. Is this *my* fault?

Back at home it's deathly quiet. I turn on the television, anything to have some mindless noise. I stick the kettle on, before deciding to scrap tea and open a bottle of wine instead. Isla is playing with her toys next door, scattering them across the sitting-room floor. I sit down at the kitchen table and glance at the blue hospital information pack the doctor had given me at the end of our appointment. '*There are three types of CP,*' I read. Isla has spastic diplegia cerebral palsy. I had no idea there were different kinds. They all sound equally bad. I'd always pictured people in wheelchairs with contorted limbs, barely able to speak.

'*It's almost impossible to say why part of a baby's brain has been injured or failed to develop, there could be a number of reasons . . . Muscles must have enough tone to be healthy. The command to tense or increase muscle tone goes to the spinal cord via nerves from the muscle itself . . .*'

There's a diagram of half a body with lots of arrows sticking out of it. I remember the doctor saying something about 'sensory neurons' and 'motor neurons'. I glance at the text again, the words blurring on the page. It's another language I don't want to learn.

I should be cooking Isla's tea.

I press my head into my hands, strength draining from my body. Please, dear God, let this be a dream. Then I sit up, knowing exactly what I have to do. I reach into my handbag, take out my mobile. I will track Dan down once and for all. I call his old office. Dan is a journalist. Well, he used to be. Who knows what he's up to now? I'm determined not to hang up until I have some information. Somebody has to know *something*. He can't just vanish into thin air. 'Hi, can I speak to someone who used to work with Dan Gregory?'

'Who's calling?'

'A friend.'

She hesitates, before putting me through to his old boss.

'Haven't I spoken to you before?' He sounds abrupt.

'Yes, but does anyone have his contact details?'

'Nope.'

'It's important . . .' I say with a trembling voice. 'I need to—'

'He didn't let us know,' he interrupts. 'As I told you before, Dan left pretty suddenly, packed his desk . . . I think he went abroad.'

Clearly I wasn't the only one let down by him. 'Do you know anyone who might know where he is?'

'Sorry.'

'It's urgent. *Please*.'

'Can't help.'

I slam the mobile down on the table, anger coursing through my veins. Dan and I went out for such a short time that I didn't meet his friends or his family. It's as if he has erased his past, changed his mobile number, his address; he has completely reinvented himself.

I look through the glass doors and watch Isla picking up a piece of jigsaw puzzle, tapping it against her mouth, before throwing it across the room, giggling.

I gulp down some more wine before I call home. Granny picks up immediately. 'What news?'

My silence says it all. 'Oh January.'

Just the sound of her voice makes me tearful. 'I can't do this, Granny. I'm scared.' I tell her I tried to contact Dan again, that I'm desperate.

'Come and stay with us,' she pleads.

After I finish our call I don't know how long I sit at the kitchen table, staring into space, until I feel a tug on my leg.

'Mummy?' Isla looks up at me and gives me one of her best smiles, as if to say 'we'll be all right.' I pick her up and rock her in my arms.

'It's you and me, Isla, and we're going to be fine,' I say, my heart breaking inside.

3

Spring, 2014

I'm in the cocktail bar of the Royal Overseas League in central London, ordering a glass of champagne before Jeremy's retirement party begins in . . . I glance at my watch . . . approximately half an hour. Jeremy is a member of this club, so it made sense to have his leaving party here. It's an old-fashioned venue with rich red-and-gold carpets, chandeliers, a restaurant with white linen table-cloths and spacious rooms that members can hire for conferences and events. Nadine and I came early to help set things up. We've hired a room on the top floor, easily big enough for a hundred and fifty guests. Nadine is still up there, making sure everything is in order. 'Chill, J,' she'd said five minutes ago. 'Have a drink and look out for Jeremy arriving.'

Virtually everyone from Sherwoods wanted to come tonight. We have some staff travelling all the way from the Hexham office in Northumberland. Jeremy touched people's lives; his clients loved him because he cared.

Jeremy's retirement has caused ripples of anxiety within the company. Nadine has been at Sherwoods for sixteen years and thinks of him as a favourite uncle. I may have only worked for him for three, but he has been a father figure to me. Sure, he has a few annoying habits, especially the breaking out into French mid-sentence. But, along with Granddad, he's one of the kindest men I know and a real gentleman. When I think back to my first interview, I can't believe he gave me the job given my tearful Oscar-winning performance. Most people would have shown me the door. They certainly would not have been handing me handkerchiefs as they listened to me talking about Isla's diagnosis and how Dan was absent from our lives. I recall Jeremy asking if Isla went to a special needs school and I'd told him that she went to a mainstream one, describing how the ethos was about inclusion now, not exclusion. I confided that Isla was lucky in that she had no physical look of CP but people did stare when she was out and about because her legs were so thin and her walking unsteady.

A few months into my role, I was brave enough to ask Jeremy what had possessed him to give me the PA position in the first place. 'I felt you needed a break,' he'd said. 'And besides, anyone who loves dogs . . .'

Over the past three years Spud has become the company

mascot. He's even included on the website, sitting at the head of the table in the boardroom.

I'll never have a boss like Jeremy again. He's one in a million. When my grandmother did die, thankfully peacefully in her sleep two years ago, he took me into his arms and hugged me until my crying had stopped.

Feet aching, I take my glass and sit down at the only free table in the corner of the room to go over my notes. I was surprised when Jeremy asked me to give the speech, but he'd asked especially, so how could I refuse? I'm so anxious to do Jeremy justice that I don't even notice Spencer Hunt, off-the-scale handsome, who works at our major rival firm, Barker & Goulding, entering the bar. He surprises me with a kiss on the cheek, eyes playful as he clocks my crumpled notes.

'You're looking beautiful, Jan, love the red dress.' He drops his mobile on to the table and sits down opposite me. I look at him, in his white shirt, suit and tie – tall, fit, broad; blond hair and blue eyes framing chiselled features – wishing he didn't reduce me to a simpering schoolgirl. 'But I love what's underneath even more,' he carries on.

'Spencer. No, not tonight.'

'How about you and me go somewhere private when this party's finished?' he says, raising an eyebrow.

'Can't. Busy,' I reply, promising myself to be strong.

I've known Spencer for about eighteen months. Before he secured a job at Barker & Goulding he was based in

New York working for a commercial property firm. Often Jeremy and Spencer have joined forces as double agents, and while Jeremy likes him he did once warn me that if I ever succumbed to Spencer's advances he'd never forgive me. Which is why Jeremy must never know that I have already succumbed. Not once, not twice, but three times. First time was at the Christmas party. I was a fresh audience for Spencer. We sat at the bar laughing, downing shots, laughing some more, me unable to believe my luck at being the centre of his attention. Isla was on a sleepover so I was determined to let my hair down, even though I knew it wasn't wise to sleep with someone who worked in our rival firm. But wisdom flew out the window that night. It almost returned the following morning, me insisting to Spencer it was a one-off.

'Why?' he'd asked, watching me get dressed before grabbing my arm and pulling me back into bed, his fingers deftly unbuttoning my top.

'I have to collect Isla,' I murmured.

'Call the mother, say you're stuck in traffic,' he was saying, his lips pressed against my neck, my body melting into his.

Second (well, technically, third) time was when Jeremy had treated our office to a day out at Wimbledon to watch the tennis, and who should I happen to bump into queuing up for champagne? It had been six months since we'd slept together, but Spencer was always calling, texting, asking me to meet him after work for just one drink. I knew he was trouble and that it was leading nowhere. I reminded him I was a single mum, but each time I said no his attention went up another notch. 'Screw the tennis,' he'd whispered in my ear, his hand against my back making me weak with longing. After the best sex I've ever had I began to think that maybe Spencer and I did have this amazing connection and chemistry, so why was I always turning him down? Over the next few days I began to fantasise that I was special, that maybe I could be 'the one' who stopped him from being the notorious playboy. I almost convinced myself until I saw him one evening, heading towards the tube, his wandering hands all over another woman. I was angry, but not with Spencer: with myself.

Third time, well third time was recently. I was feeling down, exhausted. I love Isla with all my heart, but I'd been having a hard week with her, nothing was going right and I wasn't coping. I needed to be touched . . . it's damaging not to be touched, isn't it? But that's no excuse.

'Spence, I can't do this.' I shake my notes in front of him.

'Sure you can. Trick of a good speech is don't go on for too long.' He leans towards me with that seductive hint of a smile. 'Seven minutes is the max before guests nod off, their head in a plate of canapés.'

I scan the room once more. Everyone will arrive soon, including my new boss-to-be, Ward Metcalfe. All our team met him briefly last week. According to Jeremy, Ward had sold his own property company six months ago, wanting a new challenge instead. Well, he's got that in Sherwoods. We've been underperforming this past year; there's no doubt we've lost our way. After Jeremy's rave reports of Ward being driven, passionate and a natural born leader, I didn't warm to him as much as I'd hoped. He appeared cold and distant, as if his mind were on something far more important than meeting us. Spencer knows him well because he used to work for his old company. Sadly Spencer's opinion of him isn't glowing either. His mobile rings and I see the name, 'Alicia' lighting up the screen. Only last week it was Jemima. You see, that's why I turn him down. Who wants to be another name?

'Gotta go,' he says with a wink, before glancing, if you can believe it, at the blonde sitting at the next table.

I stare at my notes again, rereading the bit about Emma being in such a bad mood with Jeremy one morning that she'd sent him off to work with a chicken and gravy dog-meat sandwich, only to call me at twelve to say she was getting cold feet about the whole idea and could I make sure he didn't eat it. I knocked on the door, only to find Jeremy sitting behind his desk polishing off the last bite, exclaiming how delicious it was, and that he must ask his wife where she bought *le pâté*.

I must have laughed out loud as the woman Spencer had noticed is now looking at me curiously. She's alone, drinking a glass of white wine, a delicate gold chain sliding up and down her slender wrist.

I can't begin to tell her about the dog-meat sandwich, so instead I confide it's nervous laughter, that's all, ignore me. But she doesn't look away, her gaze questioning.

'I'm meeting my new boss tonight,' I say, noticing how good-looking she is in that English rose kind of way. Her fair hair is cut in a stylish bob, not a single strand out of place.

'Oh, right. What do you do?'

That dreaded question. 'I'm an estate agent,' I reply in an apologetic tone. 'Well, I'm not really one. I work for one, in the country house and estate department. Sounds so much more glamorous than it is! Anyway, it doesn't help that I've heard nothing good about the new boss.' I take another sip of champagne. 'Heard he's a bit of a shit actually. According to Spencer, the guy who was here a minute ago.'

She nods. Clearly she'd noticed him.

'Well, he says Ward is a real slave driver with no sense of humour.' I take another swig of champagne, already feeling light-headed. That's what happens when you have a child and rarely go out. 'Spencer says he's a real womaniser too, even though I think he's married.'

'Bastard.' Carefully she circles the rim of her glass, without taking her eyes off mine.

'Exactly. Although Spencer is a fine one to talk! Anyway, Ward,' I continue, enjoying the distraction. 'Ward? I mean, what kind of name is that?'

'I'd sue the parents.'

Her stare is disarming, making me babble on. 'Mind you,

I'm January. You should hear some of the surnames people come up with. Sales. January *Sales!*'

She stands up, eyes now glazed over. 'Excuse me,' she says, walking away, dressed in elegant cream trousers and a gold waterfall cardigan. She has the figure of a ballerina and I notice many men at the bar looking over their shoulder to admire her.

As she leaves the bar I catch Nadine in the doorway, beckoning me over. She's wearing a purple dress with a homemade macramé belt. I gather my notes and touch my locket, whispering, 'Wish me luck.'

'Jeremy was a ray of sunshine,' I say to a sea of faces, my throat already dry, my sheets of paper shaking like jelly and my knees about to give way. I pick up my glass of water. 'Only rarely was he angry.' I spot Jeremy's wife, Emma, near the front, standing next to Graham who shares an office with me. Emma is on the plump side with a warm, open face, and though only in her fifties, she's not afraid of going grey. 'I didn't enjoy working for him the day Emma put diesel into the car instead of unleaded . . .' I get a few laughs for that which gives me a boost. 'He was old-fashioned in many ways; he hated mobile phones in meetings; he hates them full stop.' Jeremy, standing by my side, claps. 'In fact he is the opposite of how I used to imagine estate agents.' Lots of laughs as I catch Spencer's eye. He's standing near the back, talking to the blonde who was in the bar. Unbelievable. How many women can he chat up in a week? Hang on. I think of all the things I said to her. Who is she?

'I can safely say on behalf of everyone here you'll be missed,' I continue, my mind still wandering. 'Thank you for being the best boss and friend.' Relief overwhelms me as I hand him a rectangular package wrapped in brown parcel paper. It's a watercolour of Jeremy's favourite fishing spot on the Brora: a fisherman casting.

As Jeremy goes on to thank the entire team, making a special mention of Nadine who has been the face of our London office for many years, I notice Ward edging towards the front, talking to a dark-haired woman in an orange dress who must be his wife.

'Jeremy!' I grab him the moment the applause has died down. 'Who's that woman over . . . ?' I stop. She's gone.

'January.' He takes my arm, leads me away. 'Can I say, in private you have made my last three years so very special.'

'That's lovely.' Out of the corner of my eye I catch Ward speaking to Spencer.

'Your interview was . . . let's say it was one of the most memorable I've ever had in my career, but I knew the moment you walked through that door that I'd be a fool not to hire you. It's about trust and integrity.'

'Really?' Where has she gone?

'Your parents would be proud and so would your granny.'

'What?'

'You haven't heard a word I've said, have you?'

'I'm sorry, so sorry.' I turn towards him, kissing his cheek and clutching his hand. 'Thank you.'

'I promise I've left you in good hands,' Jeremy says, before being distracted by another well-wisher patting him on the back.

Alone, I notice Ward approaching me. Like Spencer he's tall and slim and models a suit and tie, but he appears older than his age – Jeremy told me he's forty-one. 'Good speech.' He runs a hand through his thick dark hair.

'Thanks.'

'I gather you were rather nervous beforehand.'

'Public speaking was never my strong point.'

I stop smiling abruptly, wondering how he knew.

Ward scans the crowd. 'Darling, this way.' He turns back to me. 'I'd like you to meet my wife, Marina. She was keen to meet my new PA tonight.'

I take another glass of champagne from the waiter and knock it back in one go. It really would be colossally unlucky if the one person I happened to talk to in the bar was . . . She's now standing in front of me. Please don't stop here. Move on. Go on, off you go.

But of course she stops, placing a hand on Ward's arm and looking me in the eye, clearly sensing my discomfort.

'I gather you've already met,' Ward says, 'and had a good old *chat*.'

For a moment everything in the room stops. I can't breathe.

Ward appears completely unruffled, as does Marina. 'It's lovely to meet you,' she says with unblinking eyes as she shakes my hand. I have lost my voice.

'I'll see you in the office tomorrow,' Ward says. My skin burns as I watch them leave, Marina glancing over her shoulder at me, her gaze cold.

'I can't believe how stupid I am.' I'm on the mobile to Granddad on the way home in the cab.

Already I've called Lizzie, but she was out, so I left a garbled message asking her to call me back. 'That is if I'm not busy digging my own grave.'

'What if Ward sacks me?'

'He won't do that. Calm down.'

'But Granddad, it was career suicide! What shall I do?' Already I'm thinking about meeting him in the office tomorrow. *I've heard he's a bit of a shit actually. A real slave driver.* How will I be able to look him in the eye? I'll call in sick. But then again, he'll know it's a hangover, he'll think me a coward and besides, I'd only have to face him the day after tomorrow. I could pretend I've been struck down with a mysterious bug.

'Granddad? Are you still there?'

'I'm thinking.'

'Well don't think too long.'

Spencer says he's a bit of a womaniser too, even though I think he's married.

Maybe she hasn't told him everything I said? But she had. He knew all right.

'Jan, you go into work tomorrow with your head held high and you say sorry for any misunderstanding. If he's half decent he'll accept your apology and you can both move on.'

I chew my lip. 'You're right.'

'I'm always right. Now, can I get back to watching *Frankenstein*?'

Since Granny died, he stays up late most nights watching old black-and-white movies. Sometimes I'm not sure he even goes to bed. 'I'm coming home this weekend,' I remind him as I ask the cab driver to take a left at the lights, 'for someone's special birthday.' Granddad is going to be eighty-six. Coincidentally, he shares his birthday with my mother too, so we always mark it as an anniversary for my parents. It's an important weekend.

'Is Lucas coming?' Granddad asks, hope in his voice.

'I think so,' I say, unsure. 'Hasn't he called you?'

Lucas had rung me earlier in the week to warn me that he may have to work over the weekend, and that he won't know until right up to the last minute. He didn't come last year either. Sensing my disapproval he'd added, 'Don't give me a hard time, Jan.' Lucas is a financial adviser for a leading UK merchant banking group and I understand it's stressful with long hours, but still I wish he could occasionally prioritise Granddad over his career. Granddad doesn't complain that he rarely visits, but deep down I know it hurts.

When I see Isla in bed, one arm hanging out of the duvet, soft silky hair falling down her cheek, instantly I feel calmer about Lucas, Granddad and Ward. OK, it was a disaster, but I've come through a lot worse. Countries are being devastated by civil wars. Some perspective would help here. Badly done, January, but it's not the end of the world. I kiss her goodnight. 'When things go wrong you pick yourself up and dust yourself down,' I hear Granny's voice saying inside my head as I leave the room. 'Things always look brighter in the morning.'

4

1988

'First one who sees the sea gets an ice cream on the beach,' says Granny, just as she does each time we set off to Cornwall for our summer holiday. We go to St Austell. It's on the south coast, close to Bodmin.

I glance at Lucas, his yellow Walkman on his lap. I'm nine; Lucas is twelve.

'I can see the sea!' I say.

Lucas whips his headphones off. 'We're miles away, moron.'

Granny turns round to us. 'Now now! No argy-bargy.' She offers me a tin filled with powdered sweets.

Granddad puts on his opera music and mutters something about how the delivery men had better not break anything. All our stuff is being shipped over in vans later today. You see, we're not going on holiday to Cornwall this time; we're moving there. Granddad's dad, my

Great-granddad Mick died and left us his house. It's called Beach House because it's by the sea, obviously. Lucas didn't want to leave London; repeatedly he threatened to stay behind. 'Now listen here,' Granny had said to him, finally losing her patience, 'while we look after you, you have to live by our rules. When you're eighteen you can do what you like.'

'I can't wait till I'm eighteen,' Lucas had said, staring at me with those dark unforgiving eyes.

I look down at my bruised hand. I close my eyes and see Toby Brown's face as he slams one of his gym shoes on to it. I am trying not to cry when he laughs; I don't want to give him the satisfaction. He presses his face right up to mine and says, 'I'm glad your parents are dead!' Mum and Dad were killed in a car accident when I was one and Lucas was nearly four. Another time he stole my cardigan and I found it at the end of the day, hung up on my cloakroom peg, wet and smelling of urine. 'Why does he do it, Granny?' I'd asked, feeling ashamed as I watched her put my cardigan into the washing machine.

'People like Toby, they pick out a person and if it wasn't you, it would only be someone else.' She held me in her arms and rubbed my back. 'But that doesn't make it all right. I promise you I'm never going to let this happen again.'

A new start, Granny keeps on saying, for all of us. Granddad had told me that they had always wanted to move out of London because they'd lived in the city for over forty years. For the past nine we'd been living in Hampstead. 'Sad as Dad's death is, change is good.'

I'm glad to be leaving London and Toby Brown behind. Besides, Beach House has always felt like home to me. My bedroom has a blue patchwork duvet and a kidney-shaped dressing table with a three-tiered mirror and a set of silver hairbrushes. I love falling asleep in my big bed and waking up to the sound of the waves. First thing I do is look out of the window to see if it's sunny because sunshine means a day on the beach. Rain means a day inside playing board games and Lucas throwing a tantrum if I beat him.

The one thing Lucas and I can spend hours doing together, with no cross words spoken, is fishing. Granddad sometimes takes us out in his small boat and we fish for mackerel. Lucas and I also see what we can catch in the rock pools with our buckets and nets. We've caught crabs, shrimps and prawns and quite a lot of seaweed too, which usually ends up in a seaweed fight. My brother can be all right when he wants to be.

After hours and hours of travelling, finally we turn right, down a narrow winding lane decorated with camellias. Our house is at the bottom of a steep hill, through a dark green wooden gate. My heart begins to race when I see the sea, a big blue blanket stretching into the horizon. It's odd not to see Great-granddad Mick standing outside the front door, waving like the Pope, before hobbling towards the car leaning on his stick. After each holiday it was sad to say goodbye to him, knowing he would retreat back inside, alone. Granddad said how stubborn his father was; he wouldn't go into a nursing home until he couldn't look after himself. He wanted to end his life surrounded by memories of where he'd spent so many happy years.

The following day, after the removal men have left and we have been unpacking boxes for far too long, Granny suggests a picnic on the beach.

How I love the smell of the sea, the sound of the seagulls and the sight of boats bobbing in and out of the bay. I run across the front lawn and clamber down a couple of steep steps, swing open the gate and head down a wooded path. 'Slow down!' I hear Granny calling, 'Your laces!'

I laugh. Granny is always fussing.

Then I scream.

'It was this long!' I make a wide gap between my hands, 'and it shot right out at me.' I stare at the grass. I caught a glimpse of scales, a dark stripe and a beady eye.

'Yeah, right.' Lucas crosses his arms. 'Anyway, even if it was, grass snakes aren't poisonous.'

'Do your laces up,' Granny commands, 'and then on we go, no more dramas.' She holds out her hand and this time I take it.

The beach is small and not too crowded today. As Granny arranges the picnic on the rug Granddad won't sit down.

'Our revels now are ended ...' he's saying, his eyes shut, as if on stage.

'Uh-oh. He's off again.' Granny rolls her eyes.

Granddad loves to act. He is a theatre director and ran the theatre in Hampstead, and always has his nose in a script or a play. He ran his first theatre in west London aged twenty-six and remembers that year well because it was the year he met Granny. He told Lucas and me that fate had brought her to a performance of *The Taming of the Shrew*. Granny's best friend was playing the leading role. 'You must meet Tim,' she'd said to her in her dressing room that evening after the performance, 'he's so handsome.'

Granny shook her head, saying she didn't recall the handsome part.

'There she was, in this long black dress with her striking chestnut hair, hair just like yours, January. I asked her out there and then. You see if I hadn't, someone else would have beaten me to it. Remember that tip, Lucas.'

'I don't like girls,' he'd said, looking at me.

'We married six months later.' Granny had been twenty-one.

I think Granddad will miss his job in London, but he's not going to retire just yet. He'll work from home instead, approaching theatre companies with ideas and stories. He also wants the time to write his own play and he might get in touch with some local schools here: 'To see if they need a crusty old drama teacher.'

I remember Granddad coming home telling us what wonderful creatures actors were, vulnerable and magnificent, all rolled into one. Sometimes Lucas and I would mimic him at the kitchen table, Lucas pretending his maths homework book was a play he'd written. '*Darling!*' I'd gasp, waving the book in the air. '*It's simply marvellous. We must do it!*' Or I'd cross my legs dramatically, sigh and hand the book back with a, '*It sounds simply ghastly!*' and we'd all laugh, especially Granddad who said it often was like that.

Granny unwraps sandwiches. 'Lucas, egg or cheese?'

'Not hungry.'

I sense Lucas blames me for moving; he knows part of the reason is because I was bullied at school, yet he was happy. Why does he have to been torn away from his friends? I notice Granny gesturing to Granddad that Lucas has barely said a word since we arrived. It's as if there is a black cloud over his head. She looks out to the sea, wrapping her arms closely around her. 'Even in the winter Mick used to come out in his old blue trunks and swim before breakfast. I wouldn't like to get in, would you, Lucas?'

'Wimp,' Granddad says to her, making me laugh.

'You can talk. You never swim.'

'I swim.'

'Since when? I dare you,' Granny says, and at last Lucas looks up, though he's still pretending not to be interested.

'How much will you pay me?' Granddad flexes his muscles.

'If you go in I'll buy some lobster from the fish man for your supper.'

Granddad whips off his navy jumper (he always wears jumpers, even in the summer), kicks off his shoes and pulls down his trousers and I laugh at his skinny white legs.

As he runs towards the sea in his baggy underpants, Granny and I clap our hands. A few other families stop to point and watch. Next we hear a giant groan and splashing.

'You have to stay in for at least three minutes!' Granny calls out.

And we share a secret smile when we hear Lucas laughing as Granddad says, 'Bugger! It's freezing! How much longer?'

'Are we daft old bats?' I overhear Granddad say. I'm outside the sitting-room door, a glass of milk in one hand. It's late, but I can't sleep.

'We're not daft and we're not *that* old. I'm still in my fifties.'

Granddad laughs. 'Not for long.' Granny is fifty-nine. 'This house needs so much work.'

'We'll be all right,' Granny says. 'Mick left us some money and if things get tight we can heat only part of the house and live off baked beans on toast.'

There's a silence.

'We've made the right choice,' Granny goes on. 'I know it's hard leaving London, but what would your father have said if we'd sold up and someone had turned this place into a seaside hotel? This house has been in your family for *generations*. And I keep on thinking . . .'

'What?' Granddad asks.

'This is what Ellie would have wanted.' Eleanor was my mother, always called Ellie for short. I've seen pictures of her. She was beautiful, her thick chestnut hair tied back in a scarf, her full lips painted red. Granny told me that she loved to dye her hair. One time she'd dyed it turquoise and pink. She had a small heart tattoo on her ankle and in her early twenties she was rarely seen without a roll-up and a drink in her hand. 'She was a wild thing who swept your father off his feet.' When I asked why my father's parents didn't see us Granny used to get fidgety saying, 'You're too young to understand, but they're the ones losing out.' But now Lucas and I understand. Lucas had demanded answers on his last birthday because one of his friend's granddads always slipped a ten-quid note inside his card. 'Why don't they send us presents?' he had asked.

'The sad thing is your father's parents didn't approve of their engagement,' Granny had replied, exchanging a look with Granddad as if to make sure we were ready for the truth. 'They threatened that if he married her, they'd disown him.' And they did. They cut him out of their lives overnight. My grandparents only met my other set of grandparents at Mum and Dad's funeral. Granny said it was terrible in every way. Their remorse was too late.

'Ellie loved her summer holidays here,' Granny says. 'I

know she would have wanted us to get Jan away from that school. I swear if anyone lays a hand on her again I'll call the police . . .'

'Our local school here promises zero tolerance.'

'Heard that one before. What these teachers should be doing is working out *why* the Toby Browns are bullying and re-educate them. And it can't just be because she's different. I'm not the only granny at the gates, and touch wood Lucas has been all right.'

'He's a different kettle of fish,' Granddad says.

'You're telling me. When I read his last school report I thought I must be reading about another kid the way the teachers said how polite and hard-working he is, a joy to teach and all that. I mean, I was proud, of course I was, but . . .'

'He's bright.'

Lucas is top of his class in most subjects and excels in maths.

'Clearly he saves his bad moods for us.'

'Lucas will be all right, but any sign of trouble with Jan and I'll come down on them like a ton of bricks. I'll tutor her from home if need be.'

Granny laughs gently.

'I can wear a gown and you can call me sir.'

'January is softer, not as rebellious as Ellie, but sometimes when I look at her I see my little girl . . .'

'Come here.'

'Timothy, I've been thinking.'

'Uh-oh.'

'Do you think we should join a gym?'

Granddad bursts out laughing now. His idea of exercise is turning a page or getting up and down off the sofa.

'We are all those children have and we have to stay fit. Any lump or bump we go straight to the doc. You promise?'

'Promise.'

Finally I open the door and see them huddled together on the sofa. Granny sits up. 'I thought you'd gone to bed, love.' She wipes her eyes on the sleeve of her cardigan.

They make space for me to sit between them. 'I was saying to Granddad how happy we're going to be here.' She's putting on that cheerful voice.

'Granny, what happens if you and Granddad die? Who will look after Lucas and me then?'

They exchange glances. 'There's lots of life in us oldies yet,' Granddad says.

'But what happens—'

'Nothing will happen.' Granny strokes my hair; it's something she has always done since I was tiny. 'Do you want to know something, January?' she says. 'I held you in my arms twenty minutes after you were born. I can see your mother's face now, exhausted but so happy. "Look, Mum, I have a daughter, a baby girl," she'd said in her flowery hospital gown, before asking me if I wanted to hold you. I couldn't wait to get my mitts on you.' Granny nudges me with affection. 'So I introduced myself. I said, "Hello you," because we didn't have a name for you at that stage. And I said, "I'm your Granny and I will always be here for you."'

They tell me to go to bed and hope for another sunny day tomorrow. 'Get a good night's sleep, my angel. Things always look brighter in the morning,' Granny promises.

As I leave the room, I hear footsteps and see the back of Lucas, rushing down the hallway before he heads back upstairs. Maybe he couldn't sleep either? How long had he been listening outside? Why didn't he join us? Sometimes I wish I understood my brother.

5

2014

My alarm clock shrills and Spud jumps on to the bed, lands on my head and dives off again. Reluctantly I stir. It's the morning after Jeremy's party and slowly I'm remembering why I have a sinking feeling in the pit of my stomach. I wish I could cancel today and spend it under the duvet. It's a myth that things look brighter in the morning. They look just the same. Or worse.

As I head towards Isla's bedroom, ready to put on my happy 'time to get up!' face, I marvel at how my grandparents managed to keep so upbeat with Lucas and me when they suffered much worse than my humiliating fate last night.

'One more stretch,' I say, after breakfast. Isla is lying down in her bedroom, on her exercise mat. Gold stars are stencilled on the wall behind her bed; her desk in the corner, by the window, is scattered with artwork, books and a bubble-gum pink CD machine blasting out Katy Perry's 'Last Friday Night'.

Isla wriggles as I catch her leg. 'No more! Why do I have to do them like *all* the time?'

'You know why.' Isla's muscles get so stiff and tight if she doesn't do her exercises. I hold her right foot and then place my other hand over her fragile knee and stretch the leg, understanding why physiotherapists are often as unpopular as estate agents. Isla is now eleven and still as slight as a bird, her legs painfully thin, but she's taller and has grown up hugely over the past year. She screws up her face as I straighten the other leg.

'One more.'

'You said that last time.'

I pretend not to hear her as I say, 'On your side now, knees together.' I wait. 'If you don't I'll feed you mushy peas for the rest of your life.'

We laugh as we sing along with Katy Perry and for a moment I forget having to face Ward and Isla forgets the discomfort.

'Hello, Sherwoods! Nadine speaking, how can I *help* you?' she sings down the telephone as Spud and I walk past her desk, my heart thumping when I hear Ward's voice coming from upstairs. When I see him pacing the corridor I dive into my office, tripping over a box of brochures. I hop about on one foot, desperately trying to keep the burning pain inside when all I want to do is swear. I let Spud off the lead and immediately he trots off to Nadine and her treat jar. If Ward comes in look busy and efficient. Hang on, I *am* busy and efficient, I think, sifting through a pile of photographs on my desk of the house in Suffolk that's going into *Country Life* magazine next month. My computer whirs into action. I sit down and rub my foot. I also have thirty-one new messages, most of them brochure requests. My heart sinks further when I see an email from Mrs Hook with that paperclip attachment icon. Oh please not more historical notes on your house. Nadine totters into the room, Spud close behind her, telling me that Lucie is already up in the boardroom. 'Ward wants a meeting. You left pretty quickly last night.'

'Isla,' I mutter, scratching my head.

'Ward's a dish, isn't he,' she whispers, fanning her face, 'in that kind of Heathcliff way.' I gather my notepad before hesitantly looking down at Spud, nostalgically picturing the good old days. 'No other dog smiles like our little Spud,' Jeremy used to say with Spud perched on his lap being fed bacon tidbits. 'Shall I take him up?' I ask Nadine.

The boardroom is next to Jeremy's old office, now Ward's. A wooden table runs down the middle that can seat eight people comfortably and architectural prints decorate the walls. Up one end of the room is a television that doubles up as a computer screen for our weekly meetings. I take a seat alongside Lucie, Jeremy's number two. I've always got on with her, ever since my interview. She's hardworking but also great fun and I enjoy the spark between her and Graham. Ward is still on the telephone. Lucie whispers, 'It's his wife. Think he was late home last night. Spencer says—'

'Don't listen to Spencer,' I cut her off, before saying, 'What?'

'Apparently they fight a lot.' Lucie is now in her early forties, slim, with long fair hair that she wears either loose or in a ponytail. She smokes like a chimney, drinks coffee like water, and is on tenterhooks waiting for her long-term boyfriend, computer programmer Jim, to propose. Each time they go away for a holiday or weekend break we wait with baited breath to hear the announcement on Monday morning, but when she comes into the office and heads straight to her desk, avoiding eye contact, we know not to ask any questions. Initially she worked in finance, but hated everything to do with money and balance sheets, nor did she get on with the long hours, so, reluctantly, she followed in the footsteps of her parents who were both estate agents. 'At home the word "exchange" was either accompanied by a bottle of fizz or a massive headache and stressed calls to the solicitors. I swore I'd never do the same job as them,' she'd once confided. 'That went well. What did your parents do?'

Everyday someone says something that reminds me of my childhood, those gaps where Mum and Dad should have been.

'Great speech, Jan.' She strokes Spud under the table. 'I'd forgotten the dog-meat sandwich. Hilarious.'

Nadine bustles in with a tray of coffee and a packet of chocolate biscuits, saying the bacon sandwiches are on their way. A bacon sandwich is the only decent thing about having a meeting first thing, but no wonder my trousers are tight.

'Right,' Ward says, entering the room and sitting at the head of the table. He's wearing a suit with a pale-blue shirt and stripy tie and dark-rimmed glasses. 'Where's . . .' He stares at the empty chair. 'Graham?'

Graham is Jeremy's number three, a maverick who does his own thing, chatting up wealthy people and getting this firm virtually half its business.

'Oh, you know Graham!' chirps Nadine. 'We don't normally have a meeting on a Thursday so I suspect he's—'

'Everyone needs to be at the office on time, meeting or not.'

Spud barks, making Ward jump. 'Well, let's crack on without him.'

Spud barks again, wagging his tail, wanting Ward's attention and perhaps a treat.

'January, it can stay here,' he says, staring right through me, 'but can you keep it under control.'

I nod. It? *It?*

Nadine pours the coffee and hands mugs round. If Jeremy were here we'd have talked about the weather by now and did anyone see *EastEnders* or *Borgen* last night.

'Right, it's good to meet you properly.' Ward adjusts his

tie before Graham flies into the room eating a banana, half his shirt hanging out of his trousers.

'Sorry, darlings! Acute chest pain this morning, and I was getting this bizarre tingling in my right hand.' He shakes his hand in front of us. 'So I googled . . .'

Graham stops when he notices the hushed atmosphere.

Ward coughs. 'Morning, Graham.'

Graham slams his briefcase and banana on to the table before shaking Ward's hand. 'Good morning, *Boss.*' Graham is in his mid-forties, freakishly thin given he eats all day, light-brown floppy hair, a wayward strand always getting in his eye. He looks as if he belongs in an artist's studio much more than a boardroom.

'As I was saying,' Ward continues, 'Jeremy has appointed me to get Sherwoods back on track.'

'We're not doing that badly.' Graham frowns.

'From the look of the financial spreadsheets I think you've taken your eye off the ball.'

Spud barks at the word 'ball'. I glance at him relegated to sitting on the floor. He's staring at me as if to say, why aren't I on Jeremy's knee being fed bacon?

'Barker & Goulding, even Andersons are miles ahead.' Andersons is another rival firm, similar in size to us, but recently they too have been performing better than us. 'So I'm here to look at our strategy moving forward and make some changes.' Briefly I catch his eye and look away.

'After the meeting I'd like some one-on-one sessions.'

Oh God! I stare at my pad of paper as Ward taps some keys on his laptop and a list of houses come up on to the monitor screen.

'First things first, let's go through the current houses that are available for sale. Lucie, can you get the ball rolling?'

Spud barks, making Ward jump again. If he could just stop saying 'ball'.

'Absolutely. Well, we've got a couple of houses launched in Hampshire, one in Middle Wallop.'

'The goldfish pond!' Graham laughs, leaning back in his chair, only to be met with a stony look from Ward. 'Sorry, Ward, it's just I fell into it. It wasn't quite the Mr Darcy white shirt moment, but the owner was delighted . . .'

I have tried to teach Graham the W.A.I.T. tip. Unsuccessfully.

'. . . and asked me to whip off my shirt and trousers, said she'd warm them on the Aga. Sorry, sorry,' Graham says, finally picking up on Ward's impatience.

'The other in Broughton,' Lucie goes on, 'a Georgian red-brick house, perfect family home. We have six viewings lined up this coming weekend, and someone looked at it yesterday.'

'Good work, Lucie.' I notice her blushing as Nadine enters the room with a plate piled high with bacon sandwiches.

'Look, can we all focus?' snaps Ward, who looks just as hungover as I feel. 'Take them away,' he orders Nadine. Graham's face crumples with disappointment as he watches her leave the room. 'If you're getting acute chest pain, Graham, maybe you need to keep an eye on your cholesterol,' adds Ward. 'Any follow-up, Lucie?'

'I'll call her tomorrow.'

'What's wrong with today?'

'Jeremy always thinks—' She stops. I imagine she was about to say Jeremy thought potential buyers should be given time to sleep on it. 'I'll call straight after the meeting.'

Ward nods. 'Get her feedback and mention there's a lot of interest in the house. What else?' He clicks his fingers at us.

Lucie and Graham take it in turns to reel off more properties we have on the market along with viewings, before discussing the houses that are under offer.

'Has the survey taken place?' Ward asks Graham.

'Yes. Let's pray we see no words like '*riddled*' or—'

'Let's not worry about something that might or might not happen.' Ward attempts a smile, but it looks more like a grimace. 'Next!' he goes on, as if whipping a tired horse.

At the end of the meeting I want to flee downstairs. Sending brochures or even wading through the historical notes is preferable to being alone with Ward.

'Hang on,' he says, catching Lucie, Graham and me halfway out of the door, Graham probably determined to get his hands on his bacon sandwich. 'I want fifteen minutes with each of you, time for me to get to know you, time for you to get to know me, although some people,' Ward looks my way, 'already have a head start.'

*

I sit down opposite Ward, noticing a framed picture of Marina on the bookshelf behind his desk. I clear my throat, already dry. 'Ward, about last night.'

He pours us both a glass of water. 'How's the head this morning?'

'Fine.' Spud jumps up against my thighs, sensing I'm in trouble. Flustered, I push him down. 'Um. I wanted to say, well, I wanted to say how sorry I am for—'

'Calling me a bit of a shit?' Is that a glimmer of a smile behind his dark eyes?

'Obviously I was wrong to talk to your wife, but the thing is I didn't know who I was talking to, not that that's any excuse, and I was nervous, and when I'm nervous I say stupid things.'

'I'm not interested in gossip, January, and nor should you be.'

'I'm not, I'm -'

'I've heard a lot about you too, although I tend to make up my own mind about people.'

I look at him, still feeling ashamed.

'I can be tough.' He shrugs. 'You don't get to the top of the game being Mr Softy.' I sense he wants to add, 'like Jeremy.' 'But I'm happy to put it behind us if you are?'

I nod, suddenly wishing Jeremy was opposite talking to me about the dogs or how he's just discovered a delicious granola with pecan nuts.

'I'm planning on visiting some of our country offices next week,' Ward informs me.

'So I need you to sort out some appointments.' The way Sherwoods works is that we deal with selling houses within seventy-five to one hundred miles of London, but we are often called in to help with the high-profile valuable properties further afield.

'I'd like to visit Marlborough, Princes Risborough . . .'

Hearing that name reminds me of my first interview with Jeremy and makes me miss him even more. I scan the list of various offices and partners he wants to meet. 'I imagine you don't want accommodation.'

'That won't be necessary.' He takes off his glasses, rubs his eyes. 'So, Jeremy mentioned you have a daughter. How old is she?'

'Eleven,' I reply, taken aback by the change of subject.

'She hasn't reached the teenage slam the door, you have ruined my life phase yet?'

'With any luck I have all that to come. Do you have children?' I look at the picture of his wife again.

'One day, I hope. Jeremy also mentioned . . .' His mobile rings. He looks at the screen, sighs. 'Thanks, January,' he says, as if that will be all, although our fifteen minutes is barely up. 'Shut the door on your way out.'

I walk away strangely disappointed, before hearing an ominous trickling sound, and glancing over my shoulder see Spud cocking his leg on the corner of Ward's desk.

*

Later that morning, after scrubbing Ward's carpet with soda water – talk about *yet* more humiliation – I'm back at my desk dealing with his appointments. At least we cleared the air. I look at Spud again and picture Ward's face as he'd realised exactly what was happening, glancing down at the golden puddle on the floor.

Graham crouches down beside me, his knees clicking. 'Arthritis. So, Ward wants a few changes around here. He banged on about how he accepts that I can do my own thing but he won't tolerate me being late to meetings, blah blah blah. What did he say to you?'

I tell Graham he's planning on visiting some of our offices next week.

'Great, we'll have the place to ourselves for a few days.' He breathes in deeply. 'I called my GP a minute ago, told him that it feels like there's this knife in my chest.'

'Ouch.'

'Do you know what he said? He said, "Graham, you're not dead. Go and visit a cemetery and you'll soon feel much better." It's not funny, Jan!'

'Shush!' Lucie gestures to us, still on the telephone to the woman who viewed the house in Broughton yesterday.

'Oh, that's terrible,' she's saying. 'No, of *course* I understand.' They say their goodbyes and she hangs up.

'So?' Graham asks as we hear footsteps coming downstairs and towards our office. Quickly I tie Spud's lead around my chair leg.

'Ward,' Lucie addresses him, 'I've just heard from—'

'Broughton House. And?'

'She's been in hospital. Her husband tripped over the garden hosepipe. She tried to help him up, but then fell over herself and all her fingers were like this.'

There's a snort of laughter from Graham as Lucie bends her own fingers back to ninety degrees.

'Then when their daughter saw her fingers she fainted,' Lucie continues, 'and if you can believe it, she then goes and knocks her head on the marble mantelpiece.'

Ward's eyes glaze over. 'Is she interested or not?'

There's an awkward pause. 'No,' Lucie says.

He leaves the room, telling Nadine he's heading out for a minute.

When we hear the front door slam Graham bursts into laughter. Nadine rushes in to see what's going on. 'And then what happened?' Graham swivels his chair round to Lucie's.

She presses her head into her hands. 'Did you see Ward's face? He thinks we're a bunch of losers.'

Graham crosses his arms. 'Listen, sweetie, we can't make people fall in love with the houses we show them, we're not magicians. Ward might think he knows it all . . .'

'Graham!' Nadine says, all of us still laughing nervously. Even Spud gets the joke, his little squashed nose wrinkling as he looks up at me with a smile.

'. . . but seriously, that man has a charisma bypass.'

6

As Isla and I drive to Granddad's for his birthday weekend, I only wish that when we drove through the gate we'd see Granny waving. I picture her standing by the door, dressed in her muddy gardening trousers, carrying a basket filled with flowers, carrots or spuds. That's where we got the name for Spud. Isla loved Granny's roast spuds.

Her absence is like a hole in my heart. During the first year following her death, I felt as if I were in a permanent traffic jam. I realise now grief is a sort of madness, in the same way that falling in love is. When I fell in love with Isla's father, Daniel, I didn't notice the world around me, only him. When Granny died it seemed grotesque that the world should carry on. When someone you love dies, the stars and sun disappear and it takes a long time to see light again, to look out of the window and see a blue sky.

She was my mother, best friend, the first person I'd ring when I needed to hear a familiar voice. I think of all those times I sought her advice. I also knew that everything I asked Granny was also put to Granddad. They were a formidable team. Granny was my rock; he was hers. When I told Granny what Dan had done, Granny had to physically stop Granddad from getting in the car in the battering winds and rain and driving to London to give this man a piece of his mind. I have learned from my grandparents that in life I have to stand up for myself, but more importantly, I have to stand up for others.

I look across at Isla, now fast asleep. We stayed up late last night, talking as we iced Granddad's chocolate sponge. So far Isla has escaped the likes of the Toby Browns, but I'm worried about her going to secondary school this autumn. When we moved to Cornwall and I went to secondary school, Granny advised me not to tell friends about my past. 'What they don't know they can't hurt you with,' she'd said. 'All you need to do is make one friend, find that one person in your tribe.' She was right. I found Lizzie. Lizzie was different from all the rest with her long straggly hair and nose ring that the teachers made her take out during term time. She paid no attention to the cliques and cool girls. She was also the only person curious enough to ask me why I lived with my granny and granddad and I knew I could trust her with my secret.

As I continue driving I smile, remembering how funny Granny could be. She never used to let Lucas and me get away with not doing the washing-up. 'Why should I cook *and* clear up?' she'd ask, chasing us around the table with the drying-up cloths, a game that usually ended in laughter. 'You pick a husband, January, who will dry the dishes.'

Lucas and I used to wonder what Granny did when she was young. 'Hush-hush,' she'd reply, pressing a finger against her lips.

'Were you a spy?' asked Lucas, his brown eyes shining with curiosity.

'Not exactly, but I worked in an organisation where there were spies.' I could feel Lucas's excitement rise like a bird soaring to the sky. I was picturing Granny sitting on a park bench dressed in a wig and shades, hiding her face behind a newspaper.

'Tell us more,' Lucas insisted.

I think Granny was so pleased to have his rapt attention that she did. I recall her reinforcing that the work was so hush-hush that if they had typed a letter with a mistake they had to tear the piece of paper into tiny little shreds before casting it into the bin. One morning one of her colleagues had been so angry with their boss that she'd hurled her bin out of the window, secret scraps of paper littering the road and pavement. She had been fired on the spot. 'That's how top secret it was,' Granny had said.

I am jolted from my thoughts when my mobile rings. It's Lucas. I pray he'll say he's jumping on a train and will be with us later. 'How are you?' he asks.

'Fine. I can't speak long, I'm driving.'

'Sure. Listen, I just called Granddad.' I know from his tone he's not coming. 'Don't give me a hard time, J.'

'I didn't say a thing.'

'You didn't have to.'

He's right. Anger is rising in my chest. When the worst imaginable thing happened to us, our grandparents gave us a home; they sacrificed their lives just when they should have been retiring and skipping off hand-in-hand to Benidorm. It's only because of them that Lucas and I have a roof over our heads. They sold Mum and Dad's flat in north London and invested the money for us, not one penny went into their own pockets. Without Granny, Granddad is alone in that big house, rattling around like an old coin in a large tin. He depends on us to visit. He looks forward to seeing his family, and Lucas could be part of that if he wanted. Yet, he's making the same old choice not to be involved. Despite Lucas and I resolving our many differences some years ago, I still find his behaviour deeply frustrating. I know he loves Granddad, if only he could show it more. Equally Isla doesn't really know her Uncle Lucas. To her, he's a shadowy figure who is always working. Why does he remain on the outside?

'I didn't get round to posting his iPad so I wondered if you could swing by a service station and grab him some chocolates or those shortbread biscuits he loves.'

'Fine.'

There's a loaded silence that Lucas finally breaks. 'I would have driven down, Jan, but I can't. It's just not possible.' Another long pause. 'Granddad understands.'

'Fine.'

'If only he'd move back to London, J! It would make life so much easier.'

And then I hear a female voice. 'Lucas, sweetheart,' she says in a soft seductive tone. 'The bed's getting cold.'

'Who's that?'

'No one,' he says, knowing he's been caught out. I hear shushing noises. 'A colleague, OK.'

The selfish bastard. I take a deep breath.

'Jan . . .'

I look across to Isla, wanting to say so much more than I can. 'Granddad isn't going to be around forever, you know.'

'I know,' he says. But I can't. Don't make me feel guilty.' There is a long pause. 'Remember everything I've done for you.'

As if I could forget.

After we hang up I want to wind down the window and scream, but instead I keep my frustration locked inside. I see Lucas as a child, always resisting help from my grandparents. He hated Granny trying to button up his coat. He wasn't cold. He didn't want Granddad reading to him. Books were boring. He didn't need tucking up in bed. He wasn't a baby. He acted out the orphaned child. I know now that he was hurting, he was unhappy and missed our mother and father so much that he withdrew into his own world, but I wish we could be closer now. He is the only brother I have, and I need him.

As we grew older I began to ask him more about our mum and dad. Our grandparents positively encouraged us to talk about them. What did he remember? He'd shrug and say 'not much.' I could see pain in his eyes; I longed for him to let me in. But I do recall one time when Lucas was in bed with a raging cold. He would have been about fourteen; I was eleven. Granny had asked me to run upstairs to check on him. Tentatively I knocked on his door. He looked pale and weak, propped up against the pillows, his eyes red and sore. When I sat down on the edge of his bed, to my surprise he didn't tell me to go away. He said, with a croaky voice, 'I remember this one time, Jan, being really ill and Dad wrapping a blanket around me and showing me the stars.'

Whenever I feel like hating Lucas I remember him saying that, and it makes me love him and forgive him.

7

Isla, Spud and I arrive at Granddad's in time for a late lunch of sausages in baps, Isla's favourite. In the afternoon we head down to the beach. I find the sea and the sound of the waves helps me clear my head and calm down about Lucas.

Early evening, Bella, an actress friend of Granddad's, joins us to celebrate his birthday. She's in her mid-sixties and lives in Fowey, a small town roughly five miles east of St Austell, where Lucas and I went to school. When we first visited Cornwall, I recall thinking Fowey was a world away from London. Everyone was relaxed; cars could park in the high street; people enjoyed barbecues on the beach; the sea was a brilliant blue.

Bella knew Granddad had been a successful theatre director, so when we moved, she approached him with her own idea for a play written by one of her many ex-lovers. I see her sweeping into this sitting room twenty years ago. The sofas weren't quite so sunken as they are now; the photograph frames weren't collecting dust. She would have been in her mid-forties then, tall and chic, her jet-black hair striking with her red lipstick. She left the script on Granddad's desk; the pages smelt of rose perfume. We didn't see Granddad for the next two days. He sat glued in his chair, paper scattered across the floor like confetti. Bella and Granddad have remained close ever since. Granddad has always respected actors. 'The only important things in my job are the audience and the actors,' he used to say. 'You don't need the writer. If you get a group of actors in a room they'll have the imagination to put on their own show.' But he could never have married one. 'What a desperate way to live, being out of work fifty out of fifty-two weeks; only a tiny percentage make it to the top.' Bella would have been too highly charged for Granddad, but she is undoubtedly kind. She is one of the first people on his list whom he calls if he has an emergency.

Granddad opens his cards and presents. Bella praises Isla's drawing of Granddad with his bushy white hair and thick eyebrows. Old age and grief have not diminished his looks. He remains handsome, his sharp eyes still full of curiosity. Bella rocks her head back with laughter when she reads the caption, 'Granddad, it's a disgrace! At eighty-six you should be in a wheelchair, but you're not!' Underneath Granddad is a picture of an empty wheelchair.

As Granddad finishes unwrapping his presents I remember he has one more, although I'm almost reluctant to give it to him. 'From Lucas,' I say, handing him a box of chocolates.

'Bendicks. My favourite,' Granddad says, unable to hide the sadness in his voice. 'It was a shame he had to work but you young people have to work so hard these days.'

'It's not your real present,' I reassure him, touching his knee.

'No. This is,' says Lucas, standing at the door, holding a small brown parcel.

I can't believe he's here. Nor can Granddad from the look of surprise on his face. Granddad stands up, unsteady on his feet, and opens his arms wide. 'How wonderful to see you, dear Lucas.'

'Well I couldn't miss your birthday again,' he says, before glancing at me. 'I knew I wouldn't be forgiven.'

After supper Granddad lights a fire and we settle back in the sitting room, Isla in her pyjamas, promising to go to bed in a minute. Since it's Granddad's birthday I let her stay up later than usual, especially as she's helping Granddad set up the iPad that Lucas gave him. 'My new toy,' he calls it. I watch Lucas take out one of our old family albums from the bookshelf.

I look over his shoulder at the newspaper cutting with the faded picture of Mum and Dad, dated 1979, the year I was born. In the photo, I'm perched on my mother's lap, chubby-cheeked and smiling, my father is standing behind us in a shirt and tie, looking proud. Dad looks so like Lucas, with his light-brown hair, broad shoulders and lean figure. I remember Granddad telling us how much our father used to exercise; he was paranoid about keeping fit and had loved cycling and running. 'Unlike me,' Granddad had laughed. Lucas is sitting on the floor in dungarees with his head resting against Mum's knee. Mum is wearing a black polo-neck dress and knee-high boots. The headline reads:

TREACHEROUS ROAD CONDITIONS ROB TWO YOUNG CHILDREN OF THEIR PARENTS . . .

A young couple were tragically killed in a car crash on New Year's Day. Dr Michael Wild and his wife, Eleanor, were travelling back from Gloucestershire to London, when their car hit black ice . . . they leave behind their four-year-old boy, Lucas, and their baby girl, January . . .

I sit down next to Lucas, his expression giving little away.

'They suffered no pain,' Granny had told me when I was five, Lucas eight. Lucas was shuffling from one foot to the other, head down. 'People die all the time, January,' he said darkly.

'Lucas.' Granddad touched his arm, tried to steady him on his feet.

'Where are they now?' I asked, confused. Where had my parents gone? Were they in the sky? Sitting in the clouds?

'Well . . .' Granny had looked at Granddad.

'When people die they go to heaven,' Granddad said. 'Heaven is a good place, where your mum and dad are happy and at peace.'

I remember Granny trying to comfort Lucas, but he'd pushed her away saying, 'I hate heaven!' He snatched my toy rabbit from my hands and tossed it across the room. I rushed into Granny's arms, scared. Granddad went after my brother and I overheard him saying, 'Come here Lucas, *please* come here.' I heard Lucas crying, Granddad saying, 'It's all right, it's all right.'

I wipe a tear from my eye, before we carry on looking at the photograph albums filled with black-and-white pictures of my grandparents when they were younger, with Mum as a baby and Mum growing up. I feel sad when I look at these albums, but I need to see them from time to time, especially on my mother's birthday. It's important never to forget their faces. I see my mother in me. I have the same high cheekbones, thick chestnut-coloured hair, full lips and freckles scattered over my nose. My father has my green eyes, tinged with grey. He was more serious in his expression, like Lucas, but when he did smile the world smiled back at him.

We come across a telegram to my mother, Eleanor Barry, tourist passenger, Southampton Docks, sent from Granny with the message, 'Come back soon, Mummy'.

'Ah, she went to New York,' says Granddad, looking at a

picture of Mum and Dad huddled closely together on a park bench, Mum's long hair blowing in the wind. Granddad peers at Isla over the top of his glasses. 'You know the story of how your parents met, don't you?'

'Tell me again,' she says.

I have heard this story many times too, but love it no less. Granddad recalls how my mother had returned from a ski resort in Stowe, Vermont, where she'd been working as a waitress. She had hated being back in England so much that she'd taken the first flight out of the country again, to America. An old school friend was living in New York, so she was able to stay with their family. 'Ellie was working for some fashion company. Her boss was a tiny woman who tottered about on heels, her bangles jangling as she walked. Ellie told us that she never had anything to do, except type the odd boring letter. Anyway, one day she decided to skive and took herself off to Soho.'

'What's Soho?' Isla asks.

'It's a fun part of the city,' Lucas tells her, 'with art galleries and coffee bars.'

'Anyway, she was sitting in a cafe reading, when who should come in but her boss, Miss Jangle Bangles.'

Isla giggles at the name. Even Lucas smiles.

'Ellie grabbed the man sitting next to her.' Granddad grabs my arm. 'And she buried her head behind his newspaper muttering, "Get me out of here."'

We all laugh now, more at Granddad's acting skills.

He goes on to explain how my father had wrapped his coat round her shoulders and, keeping her head down, they had shuffled towards the door. Outside, my mother had burst into relieved laughter, before noticing with great joy how handsome he was. They spent the rest of the morning together. She discovered his name was Michael. He was training to be a doctor, and the reason he'd been in the cafe alone was that he'd been taking some time off from shopping with his lawyer girlfriend. 'Well, that was the end of their relationship, I'm afraid. When Michael flew back home he tracked Ellie down and that was that. They were madly, deeply in love.'

'Will you get married, Uncle Lucas?' Isla asks him.

'Crikey. Not any time soon.'

'Why not? I can be your bridesmaid!'

'Long way off,' Lucas says, clearly wanting to nip this conversation right in the bud. Intimacy and commitment are alien to him. I don't think Lucas has ever been in love. He's had a few flings, the odd six-month relationship, but I've never sensed anyone has come close to stealing even a small piece of his heart. They'd have to be prepared to do a lot of digging to find it. It makes me think of Dan too. Was I in love with him? I thought it was real at the time. I don't regret meeting him; how can I when he gave me Isla? Falling in love hurts and you can pay for it. My father didn't, of course, realise back then that his decision to marry my mother would cost him his parents. How cruel of my other set of grandparents to disown him, thinking my mother too flighty, too bohemian for him, in contrast to the lawyer girlfriend with better career prospects. All that time they wasted; they never woke up to their foolishness until it was too late.

I look at the album again and stop when I see a picture of my mother holding Lucas. He's wrapped in a pale-blue blanket. 'Our baby boy', Mum had written underneath.

I catch Lucas touching the photograph briefly.

'How can it be that here I am, a doddery old man of eighty-six,' Granddad says, looking at both Lucas and me. 'Growing old isn't a right. Age is an honour.'

'Let's change the subject,' Lucas suggests, firmly snapping the photograph album shut, as if he's done enough looking back to the past.

'Yes!' claps Isla. 'Chocolate cake!' Before long she is marching into the sitting room with the birthday cake she baked with Ruki. Spud follows close behind, sniffing the air with hope, since luckily for him Isla often falls or trips. But not this time as the cake makes it safely on to Granddad's lap.

He claps his hands before we sing Happy Birthday, Isla taking a photograph.

In between mouthfuls of chocolate cake, Lucas says, 'So come on, Jan, what's the new boss like?'

Granddad roars with laughter as I recall the catalogue of disasters, ending in Spud peeing against his desk. Soon we're all laughing, Granddad saying it would make a great scene in a film. If only Ward could hear us.

'You came,' I say quietly to Lucas as we head upstairs to bed.

'You were right.'

'What did you say? I was right?'

'Don't push it J.' He is almost smiling back.

'I didn't know you had a girlfriend.'

'I don't. Am I in my old room?' he asks. Clearly he doesn't want to elaborate on his love life.

I nod.

'Night then.' He kisses me on the cheek.

'It means the world to him, you being here.' I hesitate. 'And to me.'

The following afternoon Granddad takes me into his arms as we say goodbye. Lucas had to leave soon after breakfast, but even a glimpse of him improved Granddad's spirits. I can feel how thin he is, even under his many layers of jumpers. 'Don't you worry, Jan. I have my new toy and chocolate cake. Now go. You don't want to hit rush hour.' I hug him even more tightly.

As I drive off, Isla is excited about the photographs she has taken over the weekend, whereas I am fighting hard not to cry. I hate leaving him. For a moment I see myself nearly seventeen years ago smoking a cigarette out of my bedroom window, my bags and suitcases packed. Lizzie was picking me up that afternoon to drive us to our new flat in west London. I was nervous, unlike Lizzie who saw adventure in everything. 'We're going to set the Thames on fire!' she'd say. Lizzie was used to change because her parents could never settle in one place. By the time I met her in Cornwall she was fourteen and attending her sixth school. It was lucky for me that her parents fell in love with Fowey enough to stay put for a few years. I remember many children in our class saying Lizzie was a 'weirdo and a thickie.' 'Two for the price of one,' Lizzie would reply, appearing unaffected on the surface but I know it hurt deep down. 'Everyone bullied me except for you, Jan,' she once said. 'Even the teachers thought I was stupid, but I didn't get the time to learn anything because we were always moving on.' Lizzie became part of our family. She loved my grandparents because they were kind and welcoming, always inviting her for sleepovers and picnics on the beach. Our family provided stability. Granny adored Lizzie because she knew she looked out for me just as I did for her.

Lizzie was headstrong, wild, confident and ambitious. She used to tell my grandparents that she was going to be a famous chef and travel across the world. 'She will too,' Granddad said, loving her spirit. During those last few hours, waiting to go, thoughts were racing through my mind. Maybe I should stay? I wasn't like Lucas, who couldn't wait to get away to earn his fortune and prove that he didn't need anyone, least of all our grandparents and me. Nor was I like Lizzie. I heard Granny's footsteps approaching and threw the cigarette butt out of the window.

As I drive on, I can see her now, so vividly.

'I'd be nervous too,' she said, standing at my door. She looked around the bare room with my wardrobe doors swinging open, nothing inside except for hangers and an old coat, along with a stripy hexagonal hatbox on the top shelf. 'It's going to be strange without you,' she said, perching on the bed.

'I'll miss the sound of the sea.'

'But it's always here for you. The sea, me, your granddad.' She stared ahead. 'My first flat, January, was in Wilton Street, smart location but grotty. There was no plumbing in the kitchen so when you let the water out you had to catch it in a bucket, then throw it down the loo.' She chuckled. 'But the thing is, I loved being independent. There's a whole world out there, waiting for you, so you grab it.'

Our goodbye was brief. Granny hated them as much as me. So Lizzie and I set off in her old Mini. Ten minutes later she was flicking through radio stations when I realised I had to go back. 'I forgot something.'

Lizzie looked at me suspiciously. 'We can't get anything else in the car, Jan.'

'*Please*,' I urged.

I left Lizzie in the car as I raced into the hallway. I was

about to call out for them, maybe Granny was in the kitchen garden, but I stopped when I heard their voices in the sitting room.

'We knew this day would come,' Granddad said.

'But it . . . it . . . makes it . . . it makes it . . . no easier.' Granny was choking on the words.

'Come here. Those children are a credit to us, to you.'

'When we lost our little girl we had no time to grieve, didn't have that luxury with a baby and Lucas. I had to learn to be a mother again. But now . . .' She gasped, trying to catch her breath. 'We don't have *anyone*, only an empty house.'

'We have each other.'

'I feel . . .' Granny was still struggling to talk. 'Somehow it was easier saying goodbye to Lucas, but with Jan – I feel as if I'm losing my baby girl all over again.'

I burst in. 'January!' Granddad said as Granny wiped her eyes and attempted to compose herself.

'Did you leave—?' She sneezed.

When her tears began to flow again, I rushed to her side and wrapped my arms around her, inhaling her lily of the valley scent, kissing her damp powdery cheek.

She tucked a strand of hair behind my ear. 'Did you forget something?'

'I forgot to say thank you,' I turned to Granddad too, 'for all the things you have done for me. I couldn't have had better parents.'

She pulled me into her arms. 'Don't be sad,' I pleaded with them. 'Promise me you'll dust off your passports and go somewhere you've always wanted to go.'

They went to Fontainebleau in France, close to Paris. I remember Granny sending me a postcard. I pinned it to the fridge and smiled each time I saw it, realising that just as I had a new life in London, they too had a new life without Lucas and me.

'Mum?' Isla hits my arm, bringing me back to the present. 'Daddy wants to talk to you.' She hands me her telephone. It's one of my old mobiles.

'I can't chat, Dan. I'm driving.'

'Sure. This can wait.'

'What?' I sense there's a problem.

'It can wait.'

'Quickly.'

'OK, I was wondering – how do you feel about Isla meeting my new girlfriend soon?' Clocking my hesitation he continues, 'We've been going out for some time now and . . .'

I glance at Isla. 'Can we talk about this tonight?'

'Sure. Drive safe.'

I hang up, already dreading meeting her.

Dan came back into our lives seven years ago. I told Isla about him when she was old enough to understand. 'If he's my dad why doesn't he live here?' was one of her first questions. 'Will you get married?' and 'Why not?' Isla asked a lot of 'why' questions, most of which I struggled to answer.

I like the way things are between Dan and me. Over the years Dan has gradually spent more time with his daughter and now has Isla to stay every other weekend. He has become a good, stable, positive influence, and Isla is happy with our arrangement. Dan's financial help has also meant I can afford to pay Ruki, plus it helps with the bills and pays for most of her activities after school. My mind fast-forwards to Dan marrying this woman and having a child, dropping all his responsibilities towards us. I don't want her getting in the way. Oh, how did life get so complicated?

Sometimes I wonder what might have happened if Dan and I had met five years later. We'd have been in our late twenties. Our timing was lousy.

What if, what if . . . ?

As I drive on I think about the day I met Daniel Gregory. The day that changed my life.

8

2002

It's my lunch hour and I'm in a crowded cafe off the Portobello Road, in Notting Hill, close to my office. I've been living in London for four years and am currently working for a literary agency, Green & Noel, on Westbourne Grove. I'm PA to Rachel Noel, and one of my jobs is reading submissions. Each week hundreds of unsolicited scripts land with a thud on my desk – we call it the slush pile – and it's my responsibility to pass on to Rachel any script that has potential.

This is my favourite lunchtime haunt. The cafe is set on two levels. Black-and-white prints of celebrities decorate the walls, bottles of wine line the shelves and there's always a mouth-watering display of cakes and biscuits on the counter. Westlife is playing in the background. I glance at my watch. Where's Lizzie? After ordering my second cup of coffee I reach down into my handbag and pull out a script, deciding it's better to look busy and alone than just alone. I scan the covering letter – the story is a thriller; it's called *The Man with Hollow Eyes*.

Unable to concentrate, I leave Lizzie another text message. Recently she's been scattier than ever because she's broken up with her Greek boyfriend. Lizzie definitely wins the gold medal when it comes to complicated love lives, not that we're competing or anything. When we first moved to London she went on a two-year catering course. She rebelled against the routine and structure, said it was like being back at school again. However, she stuck it out, determined to get a decent qualification. And in the meantime, to make it more interesting, she dated, in secret, one of the hottest-looking teachers on the course. Often I had to wear earplugs in bed. Lizzie has shoulder-length dark-brown hair that she ties back in a ponytail, accentuating her blue eyes, which are usually smudged with kohl eyeliner. But it's her openness, free spirit and huge heart that make her so magnetic to both men and women. She also has this deep gravelly voice; she says she's had it since she was a child. After catering college she was longing to travel again, so found work cooking for rich Americans in Nantucket, spent a season being a chalet girl in France and briefly dated one of the skiing instructors. 'It's sex and black runs, Jan,' she'd say. After France she moved to Scotland to cook for a bunch of politicians, but hated it so much that she quit and found a job in Greece instead, working in a villa in Paxos. I remember her sending me postcards saying how much she loved it there, although she could do without being chased around the kitchen by dirty old Greek men. Lizzie has packed so much into the last few years because, like her parents, she can't stay in one place for long. Lizzie can't stay with one man either; it's as if she is anxious that they will leave her, so she ends it before they can even try. But this time her tactic didn't work. She fell in love. It all seemed so perfect until Lizzie discovered he was married with three kids. Out of the blue his wife had turned up at the villa when Lizzie and Andreas were in bed and, put it this way, they weren't sleeping. Objects were thrown, names were called and Lizzie's heart was broken. Since returning to England six weeks ago she's been avidly reading self-help manuals. Despite her raciness and sense of fun, Lizzie hates the idea of hurting anyone. She feels tormented with guilt that she slept with a married man. It doesn't matter how many times I point out to her that he was the one who hid his wedding ring from her, that he was the one who had deceived his wife, she is still at war with herself.

I don't envy Lizzie's heartache, but her deep pain has made me realise my love life has been tame by comparison. I was positively relieved when my last relationship came to an end a few months ago. I'd been going out with Christian Gibbons for five months. Christian worked in finance, like my brother – a bad start. 'At least he's a *hot* banker,' Lizzie had said. Even more strange, he was incredibly kind and in touch with his emotions. When I'd told him about my parents' death it brought tears to his eyes. He said he loved his mother with all his heart and couldn't imagine a world without her, which I found touching. Another bonus, he was generous, never allowing me to pay for a thing, which was lucky because I could barely afford a starter at the restaurants he chose.

It was bliss at first. The sex was great, conversation lively, we partied all night and he was a good dancer. When he introduced me to his mother and father after only a month, I assumed it was serious. Christian's mother wore the trousers in their family. Her husband could barely get a word in edgeways, and when I asked why their fridge was padlocked Christian explained that his mother had put Dad on a strict diet. Alarm bells began to ring when Christian wanted to visit his parents every weekend for Sunday roast. They lived in Islington. 'No one makes bread sauce like Mummy,' he'd say. I began to dread these lunches, Christian's older sister staring at me from across the table (I think she believed I was only after Christian for his money) and Christian's mother slapping her husband's wrist when he tried to steal a roast potato without her looking. 'A moment on the lips, a lifetime on the hips,' she'd say. I wanted the father to kick the table over and tell her to stop treating him like a child, but he was so submissive and weak. When I suggested to Christian that maybe one weekend we could go away or do something different, he'd say, 'But Mummy's expecting us.'

Over the next few months, much to my friends' annoyance, and mine, my weekends were tied up with his parents; even my birthday was spent with them. I became increasingly unhappy, but the final straw came nine months into our relationship, when he wanted us to go on holiday with them. 'No, we need space,' I'd said, determined not to give way this time. I also wanted to tell him that being a mummy's boy was a massive turn-off. We were in his flat, in his bedroom. I'd walked up to him and slowly begun unbuttoning his shirt. 'I want it to be you and me, alone, wandering around naked in our apartment,' I said, now running a hand slowly down his chest. 'I want to go out and get drunk and behave very *very badly*.'

'But, Jan, Mummy's already booked the hotel in the Algarve.'

I withdrew my hand. That was it. I couldn't make him choose, and even if I had, he wouldn't have chosen me.

My grandparents have raised the bar when it comes to relationships. I want what they had; someone who makes me laugh, cry, someone for whom I will go to the ends of the earth and back.

I glance outside. It's still grey and pouring with rain. Come on, Lizzie. You could at least call me. A tall man enters the cafe, light-brown hair and brown eyes to match. Fit. Good figure. I notice a couple of women gaze at him, before whispering to one another across the table. He scans the room before clocking the free table next to mine and pouncing on it before anyone else can, taking off his jacket and hanging it on the back of his chair. He calls the waitress and asks for a black coffee, sits down and picks up the mini blackboard with the specials. He's tapping his foot against the floor as if he's had one too many cups of coffee already.

'Lizzie, it's Jan,' I say when I'm put through to her voicemail yet again. 'I'm worried. Call me.'

As I hang up I'm intensely aware of his presence. He's now reading the sports section of his newspaper. I return to my script, pretending to read, but then a terrifying thought occurs to me. What if Lizzie has done something stupid? No, she wouldn't have – would she? The most likely explanation is she's forgotten about our lunch date, she's at my flat watching *Loose Women* and her mobile isn't charged. Since returning to London she hasn't found a permanent job. She's been sleeping on my sofabed and working night shifts in our local pub while she circles ads during the day.

The man sitting next to me is on his mobile now. 'He's cancelled?' Pause. 'Why?' Pause. 'Fine, I'll be back later.'

I can't help stealing a look. He is impossibly handsome. His coffee arrives. 'Thanks,' he says, flashing an easy smile at the waitress. He looks my way and I feel heat creeping up my neck. 'Hello.' His eyes light up. 'Are you an actress?' He gestures to my script.

'Oh no. No.'

'Why do you say "no" like that?' There's a sparkle in his eyes, an air of mischief in his expression. Next thing I know he's getting up and sitting opposite me. 'Have you been stood up like me?'

Flustered, I shuffle the script into a neater pile. 'Yep.'

He opens a packet of brown sugar, pours it into his coffee. 'His loss my gain.'

I decide against correcting him.

'So, if you're not an actress, what do you do?'

Briefly I tell him about my work. 'Trying to find the next John Grisham.'

He tries to get a good look at the script. '*The Man with Hollow Eyes*,' he reads out loud. 'Any good?' He's so close to me now that I can hardly concentrate.

'I haven't got into it yet,' I mutter.

'Another coffee?' he says, registering my empty cup. As he calls the waitress over I notice a patch of eczema on his hand before he looks at me again with that angelic smile, as if he's just found a fifty-quid note in his pocket. This man has put some fizz into my otherwise bubble-free lunch hour. 'I'm Dan by the way.' He holds my hand for a second too long, his skin warm.

He waits. 'And you are?'

Concentrate, January. Yet all I can think about is how edible this man is. Can I order him for lunch? 'Er, January.'

The corners of his mouth curl into a smile. 'I didn't ask which month we're in.'

'It's not a joke.'

He cocks his head to one side. 'Did your mother hate you?'

I don't answer that, never sure when it's a good time

to kill a conversation by telling someone I never knew my mother or father.

'My parents met in January,' I explain. I'm aware that he's tall since his legs are stretched underneath the table and his foot just brushed against mine, either by mistake or not. Either way, I don't mind.

'My parents met in . . .' he narrows his eyes, as if working it out, 'in June, but I'm glad they didn't call me that.'

I laugh, enjoying his undivided attention, so much so that when I see a blonde woman entering the cafe I'm relieved it's not Lizzie.

'So, what do you do?' I ask him.

'Dan.' The blonde-haired woman is now standing at our table. She's stylish, wearing a pencil skirt and a blouse that shows off her figure. 'I've been calling you.'

'Sorry, sorry,' he says to her, scratching his hand.

'Looks like you've been distracted.' She stares at me.

'Anyway, I'd better go.' I fight hard not to show my disappointment as I gather my script and jacket. 'I'll see you around,' I say, heading out of the cafe as soon as I've paid my bill.

I walk back to work, deciding to take my time and stop by at the newsagent's for some chocolate. Are they together? She looked older than him. All the decent guys are taken, aren't they? Oh, why did she have to turn up? He was so, well, so *lovely*. We didn't even have a chance to exchange numbers. Although I guess if he has a girlfriend . . . I unwrap my chocolate bar and take a big bite.

Green & Noel is located in the basement of Rachel's private home; my small office looks out on to her back garden, which is filled with plants in large pots, a children's climbing frame, and often a plump ginger cat too. It's pretty higgledy-piggledy, but somehow it works. Tess, the receptionist, lives in the corridor. I stomp past her desk. 'What's up with you?' she calls.

'Nothing.'

In my office, I drop my bag under the desk and plonk myself down in front of my computer. I press my head into my hands, unable even to think about tackling my overflowing in tray or finish checking the royalty statements. I get the script out of my bag, before Tess transfers a call to me. 'Oh hello, it's John Turner,' he says. 'I was wondering if you'd received my script, *The Man with Hollow Eyes*?'

Dan has an open and innocent face, yet he must know the effect he has on women. I sigh. And he asks questions! Lizzie and I were complaining just the other day that men so often don't ask you a thing, it's all me, me, and how about some more me?

'Hello?' a voice says.

'Yes, thanks, Mr Turner, we'll get back to you shortly.'

After I hang up, my mobile rings and for a second my heart lifts before I realise it would be impossible for Dan to call unless he has a unique gift for guessing mobile numbers. 'I'm sorry, Jan,' Lizzie says. 'I crashed out and the next thing I know, it's two o'clock. I hope you didn't hang around for me?'

I'm about to tell her about my lunch when Tess shouts, 'Jan, visitor!'

Surprised, I head out of my office only to see Dan leaning against the photocopying machine. Tess gets up, pretends to be busy filing.

'You left quickly,' he says, as I try to wipe the smile off my face.

'You had company.'

He steps towards me. 'Well, you left this behind.' He hands me a piece of paper with his mobile number scribbled on it, along with a note: *Meet me this Saturday, front entrance of the Royal Festival Hall, 4 p.m.'*

'Hang on a minute, wasn't she . . . ? Don't you have . . . a girlfriend?'

Tess slams the drawer, catching her finger.

Aware we have an audience, Dan whispers into my ear, 'She's a work colleague and way too bossy for me.' He walks away, glancing over his shoulder. 'Until Saturday,' he says.

'*Ooh lá lá!*' Tess says when he's gone. 'Where did you find him?'

If this office were big enough I'd be doing cartwheels and somersaults down the corridor. Instead I do a little dance round her desk, waving the piece of paper in the air as if it's my winning lottery ticket.

9

2014

Spud and I sit on the tube as it rattles its way towards Green Park. I make a mental list of the things I need to do when I get to work. I glance at my watch; 8.28. Our meeting starts at nine. Ward has returned from his trip visiting a selection of our country offices. I stop when I see Daniel Gregory's name at the top of an article in the sports section of my next-door neighbour's newspaper. I hear his voice inside my head, saying, '*One day, January, you're going to see my name out there in bold.*' I must be staring since the man touches the corner of the page, saying, 'Ready?'

It's two minutes before nine. Lucie and I are waiting for Ward in the boardroom. Spud is downstairs, tied to the leg of my chair (and furious about it) and Lucie and I are praying that Graham isn't going to be late. A spreadsheet of prices, property and contact names is already fired up on the monitor screen. As we continue waiting I glance at Ward's slick silver laptop and find myself missing Jeremy again. I picture him in this room, standing over his ancient computer. 'Just waiting for it to warm up,' he says, rubbing his chubby hands together, dressed in his blue shirt, silver cufflinks and sleeveless fleece jacket.

'We'll come back in half an hour, shall we?' I tease.

'Who was last on this bloody machine?' He's stabbing the buttons in vain.

'Scroll down,' I tell him, 'minimise everything.'

'Minimise? I don't want to minimise!' He punches another key.

'Do as I say, Jeremy, or else.'

'I don't need another bloody wife, January,' he snaps, before finally obeying and locating the right program on his desktop. 'Ah, there we are! Eureka!'

'Gordon Bennett, Grandpa,' Graham sighs.

Jeremy turns to him, saying, 'Less of the Grandpa. Besides, you're a fine one to talk with your orthopaedic chair.'

'When you have severe back pain,' Graham retaliates, 'you'll understand. Sitting still isn't easy.'

'Except when you're watching *Les Mis*,' I quip. *Les Misérables* is Graham's favourite musical of all time. He's seen it close to twenty times.

I snort with laughter, recalling us all singing 'I Dreamed a Dream' around the table.

'Something you'd like to share with us, January?' Ward

asks me, tapping his pen against his diary and bringing me back to the moment with a bump.

'No, no, nothing.'

'Anyone know where Graham is?' Ward stares at the empty chair opposite mine just as Graham flies into the room eating a muesli bar. 'Sorry folks, on the phone to a Russian oligarch.'

'The Clock House, Mr Sparrow,' Ward kicks off barely giving Graham time to sit down. 'Did that lady call back?'

'Yes.' I nod. 'She left a message. Nadine's set up a viewing for this Saturday.'

'May I add,' Graham says, 'Mr Sparrow has cancer. Prostate. Strictly confidential.'

Ward clicks the top of his ballpoint pen up and down, up and down. 'Your point?'

Jeremy had always impressed on us that if our clients were selling, it was highly likely to be because of change. 'It's the 3D effect: death, divorce or debt, and there is nothing funny about any of those. Often we're moving people's lives from one point to another. Sometimes that change is exciting; sometimes terrifying and our clients need our support.'

'Well, I thought it worth mentioning,' Graham says defensively, 'because we want the sale to go through as smoothly as possible, with no added stress for Mr Sparrow.'

I put my hand up, as if at school.

Ward sighs. 'January?'

'I agree. It's important to be aware of what's going on.' I catch Graham's eye and he mouths, 'Thank you.'

'We want the sale to go through smoothly, prostate cancer or not.' Ward stops pacing the room for a second. 'Though I get your drift,' he concedes.

'Take the Old Rectory off the list,' Lucie says when Ward reaches it. 'The clients are getting back together.'

'Are they?' exclaims Graham. 'I'm amazed! They were at each other hammer and tongs when I pitched.'

'Graham,' Ward warns.

'The husband thought she was having an affair with me! Can you imagine it?'

'No,' Ward mutters.

'Demanded he saw my ID. You see, they weren't communicating at all so he didn't even know we'd made an appointment. You should have heard him charging up the stairs shouting, "Where is the bastard?" I—'

'Enough,' Ward interrupts, 'great they've worked it out, but we've lost a deal,' he says, striking the Old Rectory off the list. 'Toad Hall?'

Graham crosses his arms. 'No one likes the house. Can't say I'd like to live on a main road either, with a party of gnomes, but he won't lower the price.'

Ward runs a hand through his hair. 'Graham, you need to be tougher with him if he wants to sell the place. Balldown Farmhouse?'

'Under offer,' Lucie says with another flick of the hair. 'Survey happening today.'

Graham scribbles something in his diary, passes it my way. 'Does L fancy pants off him?'

I look at Lucie, noticing she is wearing more make-up than usual.

Ward hits a few keys on his laptop and a fresh list of properties comes on to the screen. 'As you know I visited all the offices recently, some aren't doing as well as others.'

'Sevenoaks,' says Graham, followed by a cough and a rub on his back.

'Exactly. What's going on with the Vine?' Ward asks. It's a house in Sevenoaks that hasn't sold for over six months.

'Nothing,' says Graham. 'I suggested tactfully to the owner that we reduce the asking price. She set her terriers on me and showed me the door. She's loop the loop.' Graham pulls a dotty face.

Even Ward smiles now. 'For once, Graham, I agree.'

'Right, we're almost done,' says Ward, an hour later. 'But before you go,' Ward takes off his glasses, 'I've been going through the books.'

Graham twitches. 'Uh-oh.'

'We had fourteen pitches in March and out of those fourteen we won only six.'

'Mine,' claims Graham, pouting. 'Well, five of them.'

Lucie shoots him a death stare.

'Yes yes, Graham, without you the ship would sink, but we're a *team*,' Ward says. 'So, come on you lot, we're well into April now and spring is the best time to sell so we should be doing twenty to twenty-five pitches and winning over half. What's going wrong? And you can't tell me the market's dead. Our competitors wouldn't agree. Barker & Goulding are doing a hell of a lot better than us right now.'

'They're bigger,' Graham whines.

Ward raises an eyebrow. 'Size isn't everything.'

As he reinforces how much we need to improve our pitch-to-win ratio my mind drifts to Jeremy again. About a year ago Jeremy had to have keyhole surgery on his knee. After returning to work one of his first pitches was at two o'clock in Reigate Heath, between Dorking and Reigate. He had returned to the office much earlier than expected. 'What happened?' I'd asked, watching him furiously pop painkillers out of a silver packet. 'You won't believe it, Jan. I thought I'd try and do the pitch without my stick, looks more professional. So I begin to walk down the garden path, lose my balance and almost fall when this little man rushes out and shouts, "Stop right there! Off my property! I know the likes of you!" He thought I'd had one too many down the pub.'

'Didn't he give you the chance to explain?'

'Oh, I explained all right. I went back to the car and showed him my stick, felt like hitting him over the head with it. Sometimes, January, I wonder why estate agents get such a raw deal. It's the owners who treat us as if we're nobodies.'

'So what happened when he realised you weren't drunk?'

'He tried to apologise, but I didn't want to set foot inside his poxy little house.'

It was a five-million-pound mansion that went straight into the hands of our rival, Spencer Hunt, the 1.5 per cent commission lining Barker & Goulding's pockets instead.

'January?' Ward is standing next to me. 'Any ideas why this company has slowed down over the last year?'

'Who does that man think he is?' Graham says downstairs in our office. 'The Mary Portas of property?'

'I think he has a point,' I say, letting Spud off the lead.

'So do I,' Lucie backs me up.

Graham frowns. 'Well of course *you* would.'

'Meaning?'

'You just want to jump into bed with him.'

'In case you haven't noticed, Graham, I have a boyfriend.'

'Ah yes, Jim, who won't put a ring on your finger.'

'And Ward is married,' she continues, ignoring his unkind remark. Criticism never brings out the best in Graham.

'You've got to admit, we have slowed down,' I say.

Graham gets up. 'Well, I know I'm pulling *my* weight.' He gathers his jacket and diary, and leaves.

'How does his boyfriend put up with him?' Lucie asks,

before telling me she's heading out for a fag. On her way out I hear her talking to Spencer.

Spencer Hunt's office at Barker & Goulding is only a fifteen-minute walk away, and my workmates have guessed why he pops in more than he should do. 'It's your boyfriend, Jan,' calls Nadine. He strides into the office, suit jacket flung over his shoulders as if he's modelling for Paul Smith on a catwalk, grabs Graham's chair and slides across the floor, positioning himself right next to me. 'You're looking particularly spring-like this morning, Jan.'

I'm wearing my navy trousers, white fitted shirt and a mandarin-coloured flower in my hair that matches my shoes. After Mum died Granny used to dress in bright colours, refusing to wear black and brown. 'Your mother loved colour, Jan, the brighter the better.' I stop typing, hiding some paperwork under a brochure. I turn to him, narrow my eyes. 'What do you want?'

'Depends on what you're offering. A croissant and latte would be nice.'

'There's a cafe over the road.'

I turn away, wishing I wasn't attracted to this man. He has an air of arrogance, even in the way he sits with one leg crossed casually over his knee.

'When will you go out on another date with me, J?'

'We haven't really ever had a date, have we?'

'Well now's our chance. How long must a man wait?'

'A long time.' I could sleep with Spencer again. He's sexy,

good in bed – but I want more than that. Besides, I can't fool around. Maybe if I was on my own, with no responsibility, things might be different. Stakes are higher with Isla.

He sighs, picks up one of our brochures and turns the page. 'This charming, one of a kind property . . .' He winks at me, 'like that phrase, might nick it.'

'I nicked it off you, ha ha.'

He laughs. 'Full of character . . . So basically this house needs a shit load of work.'

I watch his lips as he talks, wishing I didn't fancy him.

'We didn't want this one.' He tosses the brochure back on to my desk. 'Too small fry for us.'

'Spence, unless you've got something interesting to say, get lost.'

'She loves me really, doesn't she, Spud?' He scoops him up and tickles his tummy, Spud in heaven. 'So, how are you getting on with the new boss?'

'Fine,' I pretend, considering . . . And then I whisper what happened in the bar the night of Jeremy's leaving party.

'You didn't,' Spencer keeps on saying, our faces close as I recount me telling Ward's wife that he was a bit of a shit and a womaniser.

'I was tipsy. Anyway, it's your fault for gossiping.'

He holds his hands up. 'Everything I said is true, your honour.'

'Please don't tell anyone, not even Nadine.' I lean back in my chair and stretch, aware Spencer is watching me. 'So we're not the best of friends. And then to top it off Spud peed against his desk.'

Spencer roars with laughter, lifts Spud's paw to do a doggy high five. 'You see, dogs are a fine judge of character.'

'You used to work together for years, didn't you?' I ask quietly.

'Yeah. We go back a long way. No love lost between us, I'm afraid.'

'Why?' My telephone rings. 'Hang on.' I pick up. 'Oh hello, Mrs Macintosh.'

'I want a meeting,' she demands. 'The photos in the kitchen don't capture the new oven.'

'Your oven is great,' I roll my eyes at Spencer, 'but since you'll be taking it with you . . .' I hold out the telephone as Mrs Macintosh continues to complain that we didn't zoom in on any of her appliances. Spencer touches my shoulder in solidarity before leaving the room.

Twenty minutes later, engrossed in a telephone call with our printer, discussing floor plans and photographs, I hear footsteps in the corridor before our front door slams. I look through the shutters and see Spencer heading down the street. 'January,' Ward calls from upstairs, 'my office, now!'

Lucie glances at me, almost as if she wishes he'd called her into his room instead. Spud follows me protectively, but I give him a pat before closing the door behind me. I can't afford to have any repeat performances.

I take a deep breath before entering the room. 'Spencer paid me a visit,' Ward says in that maddeningly calm way of his, when I sense he's feeling anything but.

I take a seat opposite him. 'Oh, right.'

'He can't invite himself over whenever he feels like it. In future he makes an appointment.'

'I'm sorry, but—'

'Maybe that was fine when Jeremy was here, but not under my roof. Is that clear?'

I nod.

'Fine. You can go.' I can't get out of here quickly enough. 'Actually, January,' he says, when I reach the door. My heart sinks. 'Our Thursday meeting needs to start at eight.'

I swing round. 'But . . .'

'No buts.' His stare is cold.

How will I leave the house by 7.15? How will I get Isla to school? Before I can open my mouth, 'End of discussion,' he says.

As I leave I realise Spencer was right. He isn't a bit of a shit, he's a royal one, and in my roundabout way I'm so glad I told him.

'How's my little girl?' I say, dropping my supermarket bags on to the kitchen table, covered with pens and crayons and a bowl of tired-looking bananas and grapes. I head straight for the bottle of wine in the fridge.

'I'm not little. I'm eleven,' she states, more interested in greeting Spud, 'and I'm going to a proper school soon.'

Ruki is frying mince and onions. She's dressed in a scarlet skirt and cream mohair jumper, her dark brown hair coiled into a bun and tied with a navy bow. As she tells me about their afternoon I am reminded of how lucky Isla and I are to have had her in our lives for the past three and a half years. I met many more qualified child minders, but the moment I set eyes on Ruki I felt sure she was the right fit. During the interview, I discovered she'd just turned twenty-seven. She came from Medias, a small town in Romania, and had been a qualified civil engineer. 'People always look surprised when I tell them that,' she said, making me wish I hadn't looked that way too. 'I had a job in a multinational company. I worked for four years in the industry. I had the fast car and the money, but I felt like a stranger in that environment. I saved money, sold my car and studied in a hair academy for a year. My friends thought I was mad, but . . .' She shrugged. 'Here I don't feel out of place. London makes me happy.'

'We went for a walk in the park,' Ruki tells me, 'and we've done some maths homework haven't we?' Isla is top of the class in art, but needs extra help at school with her maths and science. 'And we've been drawing.'

'Look, Mum,' says Isla, 'this is where Ruki lived.' It's a picture of a farm with cows, chickens and ducks, and Isla has drawn mountains in the background with a bright yellow sun.

'I didn't know you grew up on a farm.'

'My grandparents did. I used to spend the summer holidays there. Granny taught me to sew and milk the cows. She was special. I was telling Isla she never put us to work, she showed us how to do things instead.'

'Isla, shall I show you how to scrub the floor and do the washing-up?'

'Ha ha,' she says. 'Not funny, Mum.'

'Anyway, how was your day?' Ruki asks, as she does each evening, like my surrogate husband.

'I'm glad it's over. Ruki, can you start work early on a Thursday?'

'How early?'

'Be here by seven and get Isla to school?'

'Why did the Mexican man push his wife off the cliff?' Isla asks.

'Hang on a sec, Isla. Could you?' I look at Ruki beseechingly.

'Tequila!' Isla falls about laughing.

The telephone rings. 'Hello,' Isla says, picking up, 'the Wild household. Oh hi, Dad. Why did the Mexican man push his wife off the cliff?'

'Can you talk?' Dan asks me when I come on to the line.

I dread what he wants to talk about. I've been putting off the conversation all week, hoping it would go away. I pour myself another glass of wine before taking the call upstairs in my bedroom. 'Who is she, Dan? Why haven't you mentioned her before?'

'I didn't want to introduce you until I knew she was going to stick around.'

'Is she CRB checked?'

'For fuck's sake, January.'

'What does she do?'

'She's a teacher.'

'Are you sure you're ready?'

'You know what, forget it.'

'It's fine. Let's meet her and get it over with,' I snap.

'This isn't about me being ready, is it? Sometimes, January, I think you *still* haven't forgiven me.' The line goes dead.

I sit down on the edge of my bed, staring at the phone. What did I expect? That Dan would never meet anyone ever again? Neither of us has had a serious relationship since we've been back in touch. I had a short and sweet relationship with one of Lucas's friends, Tom, a lawyer. I met him at my brother's flat. Isla was staying, for the first time, with Dan for a long weekend and I was feeling strange without her. I kept on looking over my shoulder, expecting to see her face or hear her voice. I couldn't get used to not having to get her an orange juice or help her to walk upstairs. Then Lucas had called unexpectedly; he'd wanted something, can't remember what. He asked if I could pop round and I was only too pleased to get out of my house.

That night I ended up getting so drunk with Lucas and his friend that I can't even remember taking a cab home with Tom. The following morning I woke up disorientated, dressed in a T-shirt that had that unmistakable man smell, a smell I'd missed. I expected Isla to come into the room and hop on to the bed. Instead I rolled over to face Tom. 'We didn't do anything, did we?' I asked, self-consciously, but nevertheless thinking it was a shame.

'Nothing. Which is why we have to make up for it now.'

I smile, remembering us ending up on his bedroom floor, naked, laughing breathlessly. 'Well, I haven't done that for a while,' I told him.

He grinned. 'Which is why we have to do it all over again.'

Each time Isla went to see Dan for the weekend Tom and I hooked up. It was perfect; he didn't want commitment; I wanted distraction from being alone. It went on for six months until finally he met Isla. I think we were both unsure if this thing between us was more than a thing, so I broached the subject of him coming over one weekend. Isla didn't stop us from making a go of it, but she did burst the bubble. She didn't like him or the attention he gave me. 'She's *MY* mum,' she shouted, throwing chocolate cake mixture in his face and down his shirt. Tom had a sense of humour failure (I don't blame him for that – it was an expensive shirt), but he was desperately awkward around her. When we tried to pick up from where we'd left off it didn't work. Sex can take you only so far. We had nothing else to keep us going. His last communication was to send me a bill for the dry-cleaning. Since then I have invested practically all my energy and emotion into Isla and I've been happy in so far as it keeps everything simple. Although sometimes . . .

I think about Dan's new girlfriend again. I imagine he's had many flings, but maybe now, finally, he has met 'the one' who will fit into our lopsided triangle. But the truth is, I've felt comfortable with our routine, I've loved the way we have co-parented Isla these past few years. Despite everything that has happened between Dan and me, I'm proud that we have become friends again.

I head back into the kitchen. 'Is something wrong?' Ruki asks.

I confide that Dan has a serious girlfriend. 'I want her to be nice,' I say quietly, 'of course I want Isla to like her, but . . .'

'You still have feelings for him?'

'I don't think so.' *I don't think so?* Confused I say, 'No.'

'Perhaps it's time *you* went out on some dates,' Ruki suggests, taking a seat at the kitchen table, next to me.

'I'm fine,' I pretend, hearing all my friends, even Graham, Lucie and Jeremy asking why I chose to be on my own. Yet I only have to think of Dan and how wrong everything turned out between us not to want to complicate my life again. I'm better off on my own. At least I'm in control and no one can hurt Isla and me.

'You're fine,' Ruki says dubiously.

I touch my locket. 'I have a beautiful daughter and Spud.

I have no one snoring in bed. I have you. We have cottage pie in the oven.'

Ruki smiles, but I sense she can see my loneliness. She wants to understand exactly what happened between Isla's father and me to make me feel this way. All she understands is that Dan and I parted ways, as millions of couples do.

She knows I have told her only half the story.

'I had a terrible relationship back home,' Ruki confides. 'He left me when I needed him most, broke my heart. But I won't give up on love. Love may hurt, but not loving hurts more.'

10

2002

My bedroom floor is strewn with discarded clothes.

'Prefer the white one,' says Lizzie, sitting on my bed, flicking through a magazine. The white shirt was the top I tried on first, about an hour ago.

I turn towards her. 'Hair up?' I scoop my long hair into a ponytail. 'Or down?'

'Down.' Lizzie looks out of my bedroom window. 'Well, whatever you're doing, you've got a nice day for it.'

I am trying to tone down my Dan fever in front of Lizzie. These last few days have been spent in a cloud. I've achieved nothing at work except daydreaming and fast-forwarding to today, 4 p.m. at the Royal Festival Hall. What will we be doing? It's a funny time to meet. I don't know a thing about Dan, or what he does. All I know is he makes my heart race. Lizzie says she's happy for me and that the world can't stop because her love life is in ruins, but still, I don't want to rub it in her face.

As I apply some make-up we reminisce over first dates. 'How about that time when you went out with that guy, Jan, in your sexy old turquoise Puffa jacket.'

'It was freezing cold,' I insist, both of us laughing. I'd come home with a date and had told him to make himself comfortable while I freshened up. I rushed into the bathroom, brushed my teeth before trying to take my coat off. I gave the zip a good yank. I tried again and again. Normal people get trapped in lifts. I get trapped in my Puffa. Desperate, I unlocked the door and fled to Lizzie's bedroom. She was lying on her bed listening to Oasis. 'Help!' She tried but the zip was having none of it. My date had walked in on us when Lizzie was cutting the jacket off me with a pair of scissors.

There was this awkward silence that eventually I filled, saying, 'Saving you the job of undressing me.' He left. Thought we were weird.

'We are a bit weird,' Lizzie concedes. 'At least you got a free meal.'

'Didn't. He'd forgotten his wallet. You know, all I want is someone normal, kind, funny, sexy, someone who gets the joke.' Basically, someone like Dan. I sit down next to Lizzie and ask how she's doing since her break-up.

'Keeping busy. Should hear about the travel company job next week. It's time I stopped moping around your flat.'

I nudge her affectionately. 'I like having you here.' For the past few weeks I've been feeding Lizzie chicken soup and keeping a close eye on her. I gather my handbag and coat. 'You sure you'll be OK?'

'I'll be fine, Mum. Text me, won't you?' She hugs her knees to her chest. 'Let me know how it's going.'

I blow her a kiss goodbye. 'See you later.'

She smiles. 'Or maybe not – I've got a good feeling about this.'

Dan is standing amongst the crowds, smoking a cigarette, wearing jeans, a dark jacket and pale-pink shirt. He's on his mobile and hasn't noticed me yet. I head over, heart in my mouth, feeling faintly sick, partly because I haven't eaten much all day. 'Hi,' I say, unsure whether we kiss or shake hands, feeling shy since we'd met only four days ago. He chucks his cigarette on the ground, stubs it out against the heel of his boot. When he smiles my heart melts all over again.

I must be dreaming as we walk hand-in-hand along the South Bank. We stop and watch some of the street entertainers. There's a tiny woman, standing on a raised platform, painted entirely in gold. Children tiptoe towards her or pull silly faces but still she doesn't blink or move. Dan decides to drop a few coins into her pot. Magically she comes to life, taking a bow and fluttering her golden eyelashes at him.

We watch children being sketched by a caricature artist. A child is screaming because his mother won't buy him any popcorn. We laugh at a man dressed as a dog, his head trapped under the pretend roof of a kennel, his body under the table, covered with a black cloth. Children point at his furry black ears and wet squidgy nose, giggle when he licks his lips and says, 'Give us a treat.' We head past the fairground horses and street dancers in lime-green and red striped tops but I'm finding it impossible to concentrate as I look his way and he looks mine. All the noise and the crowds soon fade to nothing. It's just him and me. Our eyes exchange that understanding look that something is going to happen between us, but we want to take our time.

Dan holds his champagne flute up to mine. Our glasses chink as slowly we ascend into the sky.

'This is amazing,' I say. When Dan had mentioned the South Bank, I did have a sneaking suspicion we might be going on the London Eye. We're sharing a pod with a couple of tourists and what looks like a trio of hen-party girls dressed in pink and silver, wearing matching hats. Dan and I sit down on the wooden bench running down the middle of the pod. 'So,' we say at the same time. I notice Dan rubbing his hand again. Perhaps he's just as nervous as I am, although it's hard to imagine him ever feeling nervous about anything.

'You go,' we both say again.

'Me first,' I suggest. 'What do you do?'

'What do you think I do?'

'TV? Maybe radio?'

He turns to me. 'Are you saying I'm too ugly to be on screen?' He tries to pull an ugly face, but doesn't succeed.

'City?' Please don't be like Lucas. Or Christian for that matter.

'No good with my own money let alone other people's.'

'Estate agent?'

'Do you want me to throw you out of this pod?'

I laugh. 'Traffic warden?'

He nudges me saying, 'Or drown you in the Thames?'

I'm still laughing, enjoying his touch. 'I give up.'

'Fine. I'm a journalist.'

'Close. I thought it was something in the media.'

'You said an estate agent.'

'Hoping to rule it out.'

'I'm not a proper journalist, not yet, more like an apprentice, but I will be.'

I discover he wanted to be a sports reporter since the age of ten; his dream was to present *Match of the Day*. 'Deep down I'm a real nerd, Jan. At school I was a major swot. During the summer holidays, when my friends were hanging out in the town, I found work experience at one of the local newspapers, which basically meant I became a qualified tea and coffee maker, but I'm glad I did it because I made contacts.' Dan tells me he went on to read English at Reading University where he ran the student union paper there. After Reading he became an undergraduate trainee at one of the nationals, which is where he is now. He's twenty-two, a year younger than me. 'I've been doing the rounds of different desks, you know: lifestyle, health, politics. It's tough and I hate my boss. He always axes my ideas and puts me down. I've applied for a place on this course, unlikely I'll get it, but . . .'

'You might. Someone has to.'

'Yeah, that's what I keep on telling myself. So many guys want to be sports journalists and jetset around the world watching football and golf and be paid for it. Thing is, it's much more than just watching a game.'

'In what way?'

'A good reporter goes into why someone won. I've always been interested in why some of us have that killer instinct and others don't. What makes someone good at his or her game and what makes another a champion. You can relate that to anything too, not just sport,' he says, trying to keep my interest. 'It's about what goes on up here.' He points to his forehead. 'It's about human emotion, the drive to be number one, to survive.'

'I hadn't thought about it like that.'

'Do you like racing driving?'

'Men in fast cars going round and round in circles?'

'Fine, but come on, surely what makes it interesting is why these men risk their lives? What makes them want to be so close to death each time they get into that car? Is it just for the thrill and the speed? Is it that basic?'

'Probably.'

'Yeah, you're probably right.' He laughs. 'Us men, we are pretty basic. What about you? Do you like sport?'

'I was always the girl who was picked last for the team. Me and sport, we never got on.' I jump up and stand in front of him. 'This is how I catch a ball, right.' I hold my arms out wide and pretend a ball is flying my way; I act as if it has dropped to the ground and now I dance around it in a state of panic. Lacrosse was the worst game. I once came home with a black eye and Granny was convinced the bullying had started again.

'Catch,' Dan says, tossing his wallet over and to my amazement it's now in my hands.

I shrug. 'I can catch credit cards.'

He laughs, warmth in his eyes. I sit back down next to him. 'Thanks for this. It's the perfect date.'

He runs a hand through his hair. 'I wasn't sure if it was a bit of a cliché.'

'It's perfect,' I assure him, hopping up again, telling Dan I enjoy being near to the water, to the Thames with its barges. I gaze at the handsome Houses of Parliament and the Ministry of Defence building with its green roofs. There's Buckingham Palace in the distance, along with so many buildings and towers I can't put a name to, but I love all their different colours, textures and shapes. 'Big Ben doesn't look quite so big next to the London Eye, does he?' I say, shivering when I feel an arm wrapping itself round my waist. He rests his chin on my shoulder. 'When I come here, I understand why I live in London,' he says. 'There's so much to see and do. I want to have an office on the top floor of one of those skyscrapers, sit in a leather padded seat, drink scotch and have people running around after me.'

'You want to rule the world.'

'Yeah, or maybe just a tiny part of it.' He turns me round to face him.

'You don't ask for a lot,' I say.

'What do *you* want?' Our faces are only inches away now.

Before I can answer his lips are on mine and we don't pull apart until our pod comes to a halt, an assistant telling us to hop off, 'And do us a favour,' he adds, 'get a room.'

It's Saturday morning and I'm at the supermarket trying to remember the ingredients for lasagne and chocolate tart because stupidly I forgot my list.

Tonight I'm cooking supper for Dan. It'll be our first night alone in my flat. Since our afternoon on the London Eye we've had a couple more dates. He has been the perfect gentleman, taking it slowly, but I'm hoping he'll drop the act soon and bring a toothbrush.

Dan makes me feel like a schoolgirl who writes all over her pencil case 'January 4 Dan, 4ever' accompanied by little love hearts. When I think of him my body fires up with desire. I can't switch him off; can't eat, can't sleep. He is driving me insane. I try to visualise my list and shove in another packet of dark cooking chocolate just in case.

I've let my reading slip at work. I begin on a script, only to replay our first date again, remembering how he'd walked me home. We'd spent hours strolling across London. 'Why get the tube and be underground when you can see all this?' Dan had said, gesturing to the Albert Bridge lit up in the night sky. When we reached my front door hesitation hung between us. 'I've had a great time,' I said, before asking if he wanted to come in for a coffee. 'No,' he said, giving me his hand instead. 'I want your number.'

I dug into my handbag to find a pen.

'Now I've got no excuse,' he'd said, glancing at his hand tattooed with my email address, mobile and phone number. He pulled me towards him, hooked an arm round my neck, his forehead pressed against mine. 'Not that I want to make any.'

As I stand dreamily in the checkout queue, I find myself thinking about how my mother and father had met by accident in that cafe in New York. My grandparents told me how happy they'd been together, despite the opposition from my father's parents. Granny said that their disapproval of Mum had deepened her insecurity that she hadn't been to university like his previous girlfriend. 'She didn't want him to have to choose. She went to his parents, urged them to reconsider, she couldn't bear to see your dad so hurt, but it was all in vain. Oh, I could have killed those parents for being so stubborn and making her feel she wasn't good enough for their son. OK, she didn't have a long list of qualifications, but so what? What she did have, January, was an abundance of fun and kindness, and she brought it out in your father too. He was an academic you see, and could be on the serious side, rather like Lucas.' My father must have been devastated by their rejection. How I would have loved to hold him in my arms and tell him how proud I was that he'd stood up for my mother and had had such belief in their love.

Later that day, I flick between the radio channels before I make my lasagne. There's a programme dedicated to the Queen Mother, who died last month. More than a million people lined the streets outside Westminster Abbey. There's news on the forthcoming election for the presidency in Pakistan . . . gossip about Britney Spears after her split from Justin Timberlake . . . 'January Wild is cooking for her new man,' I say, making up my own headline, 'and hoping food is the way to a man's heart. Tune in to find out what happens later.'

Music playing in the background, I tackle the white sauce for the lasagne. 'Melt the butter.' I pop a creamy lump into the pan and read the next instruction: 'Add plain flour.' I decide to pour myself a glass of wine first. Let's get priorities right. 'Stir in the milk.' Oh I love this song, I think, turning up the volume to Kylie.

'Granny!' I say five minutes later on the telephone. 'It's gone lumpy.'

'What has?'

'My white sauce!'

'You stirred it continuously?'

'Yes,' I pretend, rereading the recipe and cursing under my breath. 'I'll have to start again.'

'Just calm down and whisk it.'

Time is running on and Dan will be here in an hour. My hands are sticky; my T-shirt stained with tomato sauce. I need to phone Granny again.

'It says here put the butter and chocolate into a bain-marie – what the hell is that?'

She's trying not to laugh. 'It's a basin of hot water. You—'

'Well, why don't they say that?' I hang up.

Granny calls me back five seconds later. 'January, this Daniel chap hasn't come round to test you on your culinary skills, darling.'

'Just as well.'

'He's come round for a bit of nooky, hasn't he?'

'Oh, Granny!' Embarrassed I hang up.

'Something smells good,' Dan says after I have given him a quick tour of the flat, kicking my T-shirt and jeans under my bed before showing him into my bedroom. Now we're back in the kitchen, the table laid with candles and wine glasses.

'We should eat soon,' I say as he stands so close to me. His hair is washed, his skin fresh and I breathe in the intoxicating smell of his aftershave. 'Here,' he says with a hint of a smile, 'you've got a bit of chocolate.' Gently he wipes his finger across my cheek ... next he's taking my face into his hands and we're kissing quickly, passionately, Dan lifting me on to the countertop, me coiling my legs around him, not caring when the pinger for the chocolate tart rings.

Dan and I lie in bed, a tangle of limbs, both of us out of breath, our clothes strewn across the floor. 'Beats going to the gym.' Dan strokes my arm that rests over his chest. 'Fancy another workout?' he says just as we hear a thud against the wall.

'That's Morag,' I whisper, holding my breath and trying not to laugh. 'Grumpy old neighbour.'

'Yes,' Dan groans, trying not to laugh. 'Do it to me baby! Yes, yes, *yes!*'

We wait, only to hear her hit the paper-thin wall again with her stick.

The following afternoon Dan and I are eating lasagne in bed. My chocolate tart sadly didn't make it. Burnt to a frazzle. Dan and I set off the smoke alarm. 'You should have seen the effort I went to,' I tell him. 'Melting the chocolate and butter in a bain-marie.'

'In a what?'

'Exactly. The effort.'

He feeds me another comforting mouthful of tomatoey mince and cheese sauce. Suddenly I am ravenous, and by the looks of it, so is Dan. We practically lick the plates clean. I'm drawn to his hands again. 'They look sore.' I touch his skin.

'Eczema. I've had it since I was a child. Mum used to find me sitting on the stairs in the middle of the night, scratching. It gets worse when I'm stressed.'

'I'm sorry.'

He shrugs. 'It's no big deal. People have much worse problems. Anyway . . .' he runs a hand through my hair. 'why are we talking about scratching and skin – it's deeply unsexy.'

I laugh, jumping out of bed to draw the curtains. The sun streams in. I look down at the main road. 'Morag's off on her scooter,' I say, watching her zoom down the street, her squat mongrel dog running alongside her on the pavement. I turn back to Dan. 'What shall we do for the rest of the day?'

He puts our plates on to the floor, sits up and looks at me, that air of naughtiness back in his eyes. 'Well, I don't know about you, but if the old witch is out . . .'

I walk towards him, peeling off my T-shirt. Without words I push him down against the mattress, climb on to his lap, one leg either side of him. Already he's hard. I hold on to his shoulders and lower myself down, slowly, teasingly. Soon he's inside me, deeper and deeper.

I don't hear the telephone ringing until I hear Granny's loud, distinctive voice on the answerphone.

'I'm sure you're out and about as it's such a lovely day. I've just been in the kitchen garden. The agapanthus is looking heavenly.'

'Don't stop,' Dan murmurs, pulling me into him.

'Anyway, I just wanted to hear how last night went with your nice young man. I hope it was fun and the chocolate tart was yummy.'

11

2014

As Ward kicks off the boardroom meeting I'm still thinking about Dan. It's been a week since our fateful telephone conversation when I'd asked if his new girlfriend was CRB checked. No wonder Dan was angry. I called him last night to say I was sorry. If he was ready to introduce Isla to his girlfriend this weekend, then I was ready too. I promised him I'd talk to Isla. 'You'll like her,' he'd said awkwardly. I didn't reply.

My thoughts are interrupted when Graham enters the room. 'It's only six minutes past eight, Ward,' he says as he dives into his seat. 'Sorry, but I do have to get up *so* early.'

'Well, there is the option of moving,' Lucie suggests. Graham lives in Holyport, close to Maidenhead in Berkshire. Each morning he hops on a train from Reading to Paddington and don't we know about it. Often there aren't seats and his back is hurting, or there are leaves on the line, or the buffet cart has run out of flapjacks – I feel as if I'm on the train with him.

'I can't move to London,' Graham points out. 'There isn't a real tennis club here.'

'Queen's Club,' Ward says like a shot, keen not to waste any more time.

Twenty minutes into the meeting, after doing a round-up of the houses on the market, we run through last week's pitches.

'We didn't get The Farmhouse,' Ward says. 'Barker & G bought the instruction.'

Spud barks. He's downstairs. Ward has asked me if he could remain downstairs at all times from now on.

'They won't get three million for it,' Ward states. 'January, can you send Mrs Lewis some flowers?'

Mrs Lewis is the owner.

'Why get her flowers?' Graham asks, as puzzled as me.

'Because when B & G fail to sell it I want Sherwoods to be the first company she comes back to. The Convent?'

'B & G,' says Lucie apologetically.

'Why? Was it the value? The fees? Often it can be a chemistry thing.'

'I bet Spencer chatted up the nuns,' Graham murmurs.

'He wouldn't have got far,' I say, but then reflect that if anyone can convert a nun . . .

'Talk about confusing,' Graham goes on. 'They were all in their habits, spinning round and round in circles *and* they were all called Sister Mary Jane or Sister Mary Josephine. Insane.'

On the rare occasion when Ward smiles he looks ten years younger.

'I think B & G valued it for more,' admits Graham.

'How much more?' Ward fires back.

'Two hundred and fifty grand,' I come in.

'Well, maybe we undervalued,' Ward suggests, 'and it's time to revise, be more optimistic in this market. Keep an eye on it. Send the Sister Marys some flowers too.'

'What, all of them?' Graham shakes his head. 'We'll be going bust at this rate, Ward.'

'Well, we'd better not lose any more pitches, had we?'

'We did win the Grange,' Lucie tells him. 'That was a big one.'

'Good. We need a lot more of them.'

Next, Ward asks Lucie and me to talk us through the applicants who have called this week along with those who have registered their details. I look at the screen. 'Mrs Tennant called again. She's the one that's looking for a six-bedroom house in Chichester. The family love sailing.'

'We've got nothing down that way at the moment.' Graham sighs. 'I keep on telling her that there's nothing.'

'All I'm hearing is nothing.' Ward is getting increasingly frustrated.

Spud begins to bark furiously.

'When will that dog shut up?' Ward shouts.

'When he's allowed to be back in the boardroom,' says Graham bravely.

Ward shoots him a warning look.

I can't believe Graham continues, hand on his chin, 'If things could just go back to the way they used to be. Jeremy—'

Ward thumps his fist against the table, making me almost jump out of my seat. 'Things *change*, Graham. We can't go back to the good old days. I was hired to save this fucking company, don't you understand that? Don't you . . .' As Ward continues to shout I try to blot out the noise, but instead see Toby Brown thumping my hand with his fist and laughing in my face. 'Stop shouting,' I say. 'Stop it. Stop it! I can't listen, I can't!' I put my hands over my ears, wishing the noise would go away.

The room is silent. All I can hear is the sound of my heavy breathing. Why is everyone staring at me? I realise then that the noise is coming from me.

After the various outbursts, the meeting continues, but awkwardness lingers in the air. Ward taps a few keys on his laptop. 'If the Tennants are keen sailors they might like that house in Salcombe.' Ward brings up the image on to the screen.

Graham coughs. 'Salcombe is a million miles from Chichester.'

'I know that,' Ward says, trying to keep a lid on his

temper this time. 'But what I don't know is if Mrs Tennant might consider living somewhere further away if the house is perfect. This is what I mean. We've got to think laterally,' says Ward as he snaps down the lid of his laptop to signal the end of the meeting. 'Right, before you all go.' Graham is already at the door. 'We will get there,' Ward says. 'In a year's time Barker & Goulding will be sitting round their boardroom table asking why they lost the pitch to us.'

'Nadine, you are looking hot,' I overhear Spencer saying. 'Am loving that top—'

Nadine cuts him off with, 'January's in her office, Spencer.'

'But I only have eyes for you, Nadders.'

'What are you doing here?' I call from my desk, thankful that Ward is out. I'm reading a postcard from Jeremy who is currently on holiday in the south of France. Spencer strolls into the office and I'm almost knocked out by a cocktail of deodorant and aftershave.

I turn round in my chair. 'Seriously, what are you doing here? Ward says—'

'Oh, Ward says does he?' Spencer strokes Spud. 'What does Ward say?'

'You can't just turn up when you feel like it. You need to make an appointment.'

'Well, that's very unfriendly.' He's tickling Spud under the chin now. 'Where is everyone? It's hardly busy round here.'

Graham has gone to do a viewing. Ward is accompanying Lucie on a pitch. 'They're all out,' I say, ignoring his goading.

'Out where?'

'None of your business.'

'Touchy. Why are you buying yourself flowers?' He glances at my computer screen just as the telephone rings. Nadine sings down the line, 'Good morning, Sherwoods! Nadine speaking, how can I help you?'

Spencer glances at my scribbled note to send flowers to Mrs Lewis. 'Why are you sending her flowers? In case you didn't know, we won the pitch.' He perches himself on the corner of my desk, glances at a piece of our headed paper. 'We've got the photographers going round there tomorrow. I think Ward seriously undervalued it.'

'Ward was being honest.'

He gets up, walks away. 'Drinks later, J?'

'Can't. Hang on,' I stop him. 'How did you know what Ward valued it at?'

He turns to me with that megawatt smile. 'Let's just say your new logo stands out beautifully and I have a canny knack of reading upside down.'

Later on that afternoon I knock on Ward's door.

'Come in.'

'Have you got a minute?'

Surprised, he looks up from his computer screen. 'Take a seat.'

I picture Jeremy tucking into his packed lunch or playing with Spud, but then stop myself. As Ward pointed out, we can't go back to the old days.

'About the meeting this morning,' I begin. 'I'm sorry I, you know, lost it.'

'I lost it too, January.'

'The thing is, the thing is . . .' Restless, I hop up from my seat.

'What's the thing?'

I pace the room. 'You're right. We have become stuck in a rut and we do need you to help us get out of it.'

Ward takes off his glasses, gives them a wipe.

'I hope you like a challenge,' I say, sitting down again.

He raises an eyebrow. 'Graham is quite a challenge.' He puts his glasses back on.

'I can't pretend sharing an office with him is easy.'

'He's never in the office, January.'

'His working methods are different,' I admit, 'but he's not shopping and eating fancy lunches. He's networking.'

'Ah, that's what he calls it.'

'Deep down Graham's passionate about his work and he's loyal to this company.'

'Hmm.'

'We will trust you, but you kind of need to trust us too.'

Ward looks at me curiously. 'We got off to a rocky start, didn't we?' There's a flicker of a smile between us. 'Jeremy said I was lucky to have you on my team.'

I enjoy that compliment until I remind myself why I'm really here. But what if I'm wrong? Spencer loves to boast and tease. Yet there's something clearly not right between Ward and Spencer.

Ward leans in closer towards me. 'Is there something else, January?'

Tell him. 'I've sent some flowers to Mrs Lewis. Peonies.'

'Right. Thanks.' He waits. His telephone rings. 'It's my wife. I'd better . . .'

'It's Spencer,' I say before he picks up.

He lets it ring.

'He came in today.'

Ward notices me touching my locket. 'I've told him he needs to make an appointment, but . . . Anyway, I think he saw your letter to Mrs Lewis. He read it and upped the value.'

'How did he see it?'

'Mrs Lewis must have left it lying around somewhere,' I say, 'and when he was out on the pitch . . .'

I can feel Ward's fury envelop the room. 'That man would sell his own Granny,' he mutters.

'I thought you should know.'

'I'm glad you told me.'

I'm about to leave, but something preys on my mind. 'Ward, I thought you two were friends?'

There's rage in his eyes, yet he says so calmly, 'We were. But we're rivals now.'

'Right.' It's clear he doesn't wish to discuss it any further. Whatever happened between them remains between them.

As I'm heading out of his office I sense he's watching me. I turn. His eyes are icy. 'This is war,' he says.

That evening, over sausages and mash, I broach the subject of Dan's new girlfriend. Isla stops eating. 'Do you want to meet her, Mum?'

I nod. 'I'm sure we'll become friends. So what do you say? Can I call him and say we're cool to meet this weekend?'

She thinks about it. 'We will still go swimming, won't we? Dad said he was going to take me on the slides.'

'Of course.'

'Why don't you stay with Dad too?'

'Don't let your carrots get cold.' Spud sits underneath Isla's seat, waiting patiently for something to drop on to the floor.

'You could come swimming with us.'

'I can't, sweetheart,' I say, touched by Isla's innocence and her protectiveness towards me.

'Why not?'

'Because it's *your* time with Dad. Now, we've got plums for pudding.'

I watch as Isla counts the stones left in her bowl, saying, 'Tinker, tailor, soldier . . .'

My grandparents taught Lucas and me this childhood

fortune game, but you can only play after eating things with stones. 'Poor man.' She stops, looks dismayed. 'Beggar man,' she says, before we both dissolve into laughter. 'I'm going to marry a beggar man!'

'The game had different meanings for boys and girls,' I tell Isla, clearing out plates. 'For Uncle Lucas it told him what he would become in later life, so he always ate five plums on purpose. For me, it was all about who I was going to marry.' Feminists would hate the game now, I think to myself.

'Is Dad going to marry Fiona?'

'It's too soon to say.'

'I could be bridesmaid.'

'Grab a cloth, please. Washing-up time.'

'Will you ever marry again, Mum?'

'I never married your father, Isla.'

'Do you want more children? I could have a brother or sister.'

'I'm not sure I'll have more, and anyway, I'd need to meet someone first.' I look at her, wondering if she ever feels lonely, like me. 'Would you like a brother or sister?'

'You could adopt a husband,' Isla suggests, still thinking about my plight.

I smile at that. 'Oh Isla, come here.'

'Why not?' She pulls away from me far too quickly these days. 'You can adopt children.'

'It's not a bad idea.' I shrug. 'Adopt a husband scheme. I

could pick Colin Firth, Mr Darcy.' I ruffle her hair and she jerks her head away. 'I think you should suggest it to the prime minister.'

Lying in bed later that night, Spud curled up in his basket beside me, thoughts crowd my head. One moment I see Spencer's face as he boasts that he can read upside-down; then I hear Ward's voice, 'This is war,' and feel a wave of unease, knowing there is going to be a battle ahead. I stretch across the bed, toss and turn in the darkness, unable to stop thinking about the weekend too. I need to keep busy; I don't want to be alone, imagining Dan, Isla and Fiona playing happy families. I picture Fiona sliding down the swimming pool flume, Isla close behind, and hear their laughter when they reach the bottom.

When I spoke to Dan earlier tonight he was clearly relieved that I'd come round to the idea. 'I wouldn't suggest this unless I was sure,' he'd said quietly.

'I know.'

It's serious. Dan is almost thirty-four. Let's face it, he's had his time playing the field, he's now settled in a great job, a sports journalist for the *Guardian*, he's climbing the career ladder, he'll be looking to settle down soon. Maybe he wants to start another family? Isla was right to ask all those questions. Perhaps they will get married. I turn on to my other side. Isla will have a brother or sister, maybe both. I squeeze my eyes shut. 'I miss you, Granny,' I whisper, desperately trying to picture her face. I lie still, imagining she's by my side, stroking my hair, telling me everything will be all right.

I see Dan and me in the early days of our relationship. I picture us on the London Eye, recall us taking hours to walk back home before he'd kissed me goodnight. He didn't want to come inside. 'All good things come to those who wait,' he'd said. I see him running down the street, waving an arm in the air as if he'd just scored a goal in the World Cup. I'd lent out of my bedroom window and wolf-whistled. He'd turned, waved, called out, 'Until next time.' It made me think of Granddad taking Granny to the ballet on their first date. 'I'd skipped home, January. When you're in love it's like walking on air.'

Twelve years on, all I feel is a deep ache inside, an ache for what could have been, and in the darkness I can't escape the shadow of my past and the deep fear that I will be left behind.

12

2002

It's a warm summer's morning in June and I'm jogging along Chiswick Mall, a road that runs alongside the Thames; the surrounding area is filled with riverside pubs, a boat club, schools, and houses with blue plaques beside their front doors, celebrating the lives of famous painters and novelists. It's one of my favourite parts of London, almost like another part of the city, with its long line of colourful houses that overlook the river, their fronts adorned with window boxes, geraniums, bay trees or statues of lions. Handsome gates lead into gardens that lie close to the water, lawns surrounded by trees and flowerbeds. I love the smell of the river and watching the birds, boats and canoes; it makes me feel closer to home. On a hot day I feel as if I am in another country, far away from my cluttered flat in Hammersmith.

I jog past dog walkers, mothers pushing prams and fellow

runners in their fluorescent tops and black leggings. A plane soars high in the sky. I'm on top of the world just anticipating meeting Dan tonight.

We've been together for six weeks now and the time has flown by. I've confided in Dan about my parents dying when I was little. I also told him about Lucas and how different we are, and that sadly our parents' death hasn't brought us close together. Dan is strangely private about his own family; I haven't met any of his close circle of friends yet and he won't let me stay in his flat; he says it's too messy and his roommate is weird. But we've begun to talk about arranging a weekend so he can introduce me to his set. I sense it's a big deal for Dan to do this. Despite his confident manner, I'm beginning to see another side to him too, a side that isn't so sure of himself; it's a side I find just as attractive. 'I haven't ever had a serious girlfriend,' he'd confessed to me last weekend. It was Sunday morning, when we were in bed. 'Don't get me wrong, I had loads of flings at uni, but I was more into studying and having a good time, didn't want to be tied down. My longest relationship's been four months. You?'

I told him about my relationship with Christian. It had made him laugh, especially the part about the mother locking the fridge. That day I'd managed to drag Dan round the shops to help me buy a dress for one of our author's book launches. 'I can't believe you're making me give up my Sunday sport to do this,' he'd said, before pushing me into the changing cubicle and sliding the curtain shut. 'Come on, J, there have to be some perks,' he'd said before we kissed.

I stop running, a tsunami of sickness hitting me as I stagger to the side of the road, towards a bin. 'Are you all right, love?' asks a woman with a black Staffordshire bull terrier, a chunky stick in its mouth. I recover my breath, the sickness subsiding as quickly as it came. 'I'm fine. Must have been something I ate last night,' I say. But I know that's not true and I'm worried.

'You're back early,' calls Lizzie as she slopes into the kitchen in her shorts and T-shirt, with messy bed hair and a purple silk eye mask pushed high against her forehead. 'Everything all right?' she asks. Yet I can't stop thinking about that one weekend when I went back to Cornwall to see my grand-parents, returning early on the Monday morning. I forgot to take the pill; I missed two days. I followed the directions and took two pills in one day and finished off the rest of the pack as normal, but it did warn that protection against pregnancy could be affected, and how important it was to use extra protection for the next week. I have an uneasy feeling that there was this one time when we didn't use a condom. 'I've just made a pot of coffee,' Lizzie tells me. I pour myself a glass of water, before the smell of coffee beans makes me clutch my stomach and rush out of the kitchen. I make it to the bathroom just in time.

Lizzie kneels down beside me as I stay close to the loo.

She rests a hand on my back. 'Are you thinking what I'm thinking?' she says.

It's early evening on a Thursday and I'm on my way to meet Dan for drinks after work. I haven't told anyone yet that I'm pregnant, not even Granny. Lizzie is the only person who knows because she bought me the test and stayed with me as we both watched the line turn blue. Apart from Lizzie, I want Dan to be the first person to know.

I didn't get any sleep last night; kept on going over and over in my head what his reaction might be. I know he's not going to be exactly happy about it, it's too soon and this wasn't planned, but maybe, given time he might come round. I want to have this baby; at least I think I do. The trouble is, what choice do I have? The other option feels unimaginable. I can't swat a fly, let alone . . .

'Don't panic about what he might or might not say,' Lizzie had said, after finding me in the kitchen in the middle of the night, drinking a hot chocolate, scribbling down all the things I was going to say to him if he said this or that.

'I'm scared,' I'd said to her scrunching the piece of paper into a ball. 'He won't want a baby.'

'Well, I'll raise the kid with you if I have to. Two women and a baby.'

Finally I'd smiled, thinking of our neighbour from hell. 'Now, that *would* shock Morag.'

I'm brought back to reality when I arrive at the bar in

Notting Hill, a ten-minute walk from my office. People are sitting outside, enjoying the early-evening sunshine. I should have picked somewhere more secluded, I think to myself, as I nab the only table left in the corner, close to the doors. My heart skips a beat each time someone arrives. Dan is late. With a trembling hand I send him a text. A text comes back almost immediately. '*Sorry, running late. Got some exciting news! Something to ask you! Be with you soon. D x.*'

Exciting news? Great. He'll be in a good mood. I text him back. '*I've got some news too. See you soon. J x.*'

While I wait I try to read one of my scripts, but can't focus on the words. Do I tell him straightaway or do I give him time to unwind and have a couple of drinks?

'January,' I hear someone saying five minutes later. He bends down, kisses me on the cheek. He looks tired but happy as he sits down next to me and picks up the drinks menu. 'Really sorry I'm late.'

'Don't worry, I've been reading.' I gesture to my script. He scans the wine list.

'So what's this news?' I ask.

'Let's get a bottle of fizz first.'

'I've got a bit of a headache. But you order something.'

'I tell you the office was full-on today. We had to pull a piece at the last minute because we'd get sued if we used it. You need a degree in law in this job.' I notice him scratching his right hand; it looks raw and pink.

A pretty Spanish-looking waitress approaches our table, asking if we're ready to order. 'Sorry, did you say you didn't want anything, Jan?'

'Just a lime and soda, thanks.'

'Really?'

I nod, my heart beating like a drum. 'So come on, tell me your news.'

He looks at me curiously. 'Tell me yours first.'

'No, you go.'

'J? Are you sure you're all right?'

'Yes! I mean, no, I mean, I don't know.'

'Is it bad news? Have you lost your job? Are you ill?'

'I don't know how to say this.'

Dan looks uncomfortable. 'It can't be that bad.'

'OK, well the thing is . . .the thing is . . . tell me your news first.'

'Jan!'

I take a deep breath and try to look happy. 'I'm pregnant.'

'You're pregnant.' He smiles, as if he's hoping I'm going to tell him it's a joke, but I can see fear beginning to cloud his face. 'You're pregnant,' he repeats, this time more slowly. 'How? How did this happen?' He looks around the bar, a helpless look in his eyes, as if he wants to find someone to give this problem to. 'I thought we were being careful.'

'We were, I am!'

The waitress returns with a beer and glass of water. Dan's eyes remain on mine.

'But there was that one time,' I remind him quietly, 'when we didn't, you know . . .' I told Dan about missing the pill over a weekend and that we had to be extra careful to use condoms over the next seven days, but in the heat of the moment it's easy to forget the advice; besides, you never think it's going to happen to you.

We sit in silence.

'Listen, I'm as shocked as you,' I say finally.

Dan takes my hand. 'We'll get through this. I'll support you.'

I drop my shoulders and grip his hand. 'You don't know how relieved that makes me feel.'

'I can ask around, find the best place to go.'

'What?'

'It's going to be all right, J. We'll deal with it.'

'Dan, I think I want . . .'

He scratches his hand, bites his thumbnail. 'What'll it cost?'

'What do you mean?'

He looks at me. 'You know, a . . .' He can't bring himself to say the word.

'I don't want an abortion,' I fight back, finally realising how much I want to keep this baby. 'It's not that simple, Dan.'

'Think about it, J. We're really young. This isn't our fault, but let's face it, neither one of us is ready to be parents yet, are we?' When I don't reply he continues, 'I know I'm not. I'm nowhere near.'

'I don't think we should rush our decision.'

'I'm twenty-two,' he stresses, 'nappies, mortgages, trips to the park, that's a long way off. I want to travel, see the world, have a career. I think it's important to be honest, here.'

'Well it's not just about you,' I say, unable to keep the hurt out of my voice.

'I don't want to be a dad!' He raises his voice for the first time. 'This can't be happening.'

I'm painfully aware of people at the next-door table listening.

I lean towards him, say quietly, 'I know it's a shock, but with time—'

He makes a fist with his hand. 'But it shouldn't have happened! Let's be sensible about this. We have options. I like you, January—'

'You like me, oh wow, Dan, thanks. I'm touched.'

'I do,' he says, trying to remain calm, 'and maybe at some stage . . .'

'But life doesn't work like that, you can't plan—'

'I don't want us to end, but can't you see I'm nowhere near ready for this?'

'Nor am I! But—'

'Well then,' he cuts me off. 'We know what to do. It's the *right* thing to do, Jan.'

'I can't. I can't do it.'

Dan polishes off his beer. Anger clouds his face now. 'You

have to. It's either that or you have the baby on your own. I'm serious, J. I don't want a kid and I can't believe you're even considering it.' He gets up.

'Dan! Wait!'

He returns. We stare at one another; suddenly we're on opposite sides.

'I'm sorry,' he says. 'I can't do this.' I watch as he chucks a ten-pound note on to the table and leaves and a voice tells me not to go after him, it will only make it worse.

Back at the flat, I stab at the buttons once more. Please answer, please answer. I pray that Granny has just walked through the front door. It clicks into their machine again. 'Timothy and Patricia aren't here to take your call so please leave us a message . . .'

'Granny, it's me,' I say, yearning to hear her voice. 'Ring me the moment you get this.'

Alone in the flat, I pace the corridor, unable to think straight or sit still. I stare at my mobile, wondering, hoping, praying that Dan might call to say that he overreacted. He'll suggest coming round tomorrow to talk it through more calmly. Or maybe he won't call this evening. He'll sleep on it. I've had time to get my head round the idea of having a baby. He hasn't. He'll wake up tomorrow feeling different.

I lean against the wall, sink down to the ground and throw my mobile on to the floor. I place my head on my knees. How can it be that a couple of weeks ago I felt like the luckiest woman alive with my entire future ahead of me? Deep down I know Dan won't call me. I can't see him ever changing his mind. Clearly he hates the idea of being pinned down with a child so soon. In many ways I don't blame him.

What was his news? What did he want to ask me? Surely Dan will call? If he doesn't I'll ring him tomorrow. He can't throw us away just like that. I feel lost and scared too, not sure which way to turn. Maybe I should listen to him? Maybe I *should* get rid of it. I touch my stomach. I feel like a child who has run out into a busy road without looking left or right. Horns are screeching. Drivers are shouting at me to get out of their way. I stand paralysed in the middle of the road. My mother is scolding me for not looking before I stepped out on to the road. This is how lives are lost, January. But she takes my hand firmly in hers and guides me safely to the other side of the road.

I crawl across the floor to retrieve my mobile. I ring home again, wishing I were back in my blue bedroom, looking out to the sea and hearing the sound of the waves. What will Granny think? Will she be angry? Even worse, disappointed? All I want is to feel her arms around me. I take a steadying breath and wipe my eyes with my shirtsleeve. I'm in trouble. Real trouble. Please answer. It rings and it rings, before I hear her familiar voice on the answering machine again. I hang up. 'I want my mum,' I say, rocking backwards and forwards. 'I want my mum.'

I don't move until Lizzie comes home. 'It's over,' I say to her. 'Dan doesn't want to know.' I'm grateful she asks me no questions. My body aches with tiredness, drained of every single emotion. Lizzie helps me up and slowly walks me to my bedroom. Carefully she takes off my clothes and my shoes and helps me into bed. 'We'll get through this. You're strong, January,' she says, before switching off my bedside light and gently shutting the door.

13

2014

It's Friday, late morning. Ward is at a pitch with the head of the Sevenoaks office. Graham and Lucie are discussing one of our clients who is looking for a house in Devon with a 'nice long driveway'. I am finding it hard concentrating on my brochure when all I can think about is meeting Dan's girlfriend tomorrow. 'Who doesn't want a nice long driveway?' says Graham. 'I'd like one, but hey, dream on.'

'She also wants a wreck,' Lucie reminds him.

Graham looks as if he's playing the memory-card game. The houses registered with us along with our applicants are all cards faced down, Graham is thinking hard before he turns two over, hoping to find a matching pair. 'I've got it!' he pronounces, swivelling round in his chair to face her. 'How about that pigsty of a place in Suffolk?'

Lucie and Graham high five before Lucie makes a telephone call.

Ten minutes later we discover our applicant doesn't want the pigsty in Suffolk. 'You see, when a person says they want a banana,' says Graham, peeling his own, 'they want a banana. Not a fig.'

'But what you don't ask you'll never find out,' quotes Nadine in her sing-a-long voice, before sticking her head round the door to see if we want anything for lunch from the deli round the corner. 'I've discovered a delicious bean-sprout salad,' she says with peculiar excitement.

Later that day I take Mrs Roberts upstairs to the boardroom. Mrs Roberts is one of our new clients, here to discuss the forthcoming brochure of her five-bedroom house in St Albans. She's rake-thin, dyed blonde hair held back with a claw clip. She's wearing a chic cream shirt with a navy jacket, but her fifty-something-year-old skin is more lined than it should be, either from heavy smoking or too much worrying.

'Thank you for meeting me,' she says as we sit down. 'I feel the brochure has to be perfect.'

'I couldn't agree more, but I think it's looking promising so far.' As I lay the designs out on the table, Mrs Roberts puts on her glasses and scrunches her nose in concentration, before tapping my arm. 'Why isn't my greenhouse in the floor plan?'

I know Mrs Roberts is an avid gardener. The few times I have called, she's always just come in from her greenhouse where she tells me she's been transplanting her seedlings.

'Well, technically we don't need to include—'

'But it's a lovely greenhouse.' She produces a brown envelope from her handbag and out spills a selection of matte photographs. 'My husband printed these out on his new printer. They really capture the evening light and the apple blossom, don't you think?'

I take a look and try to disguise my concern. 'They're lovely.'

'Aren't they. A close up of the apple blossom could look perfect on the front of the brochure, don't you think?' She speaks quickly, as if everything is a matter of urgency. 'And then on the back we could have a shot of the greenhouse in the morning light.'

I hear footsteps coming upstairs and catch a glimpse of Ward. 'You OK?' he mouths.

Discreetly I nod before addressing Mrs Roberts. 'They're great, but in my view, the photos we already have sell your house more.' The photographer had warned me that Mrs Roberts had been particularly tricky when he'd visited, in fact 'neurotic' was the word he'd used. She hadn't liked the invasion one little bit, was cross that he hadn't taken off his shoes inside, had objected to all his unnecessary equipment and told him off for 'snooping around'.

I compose myself. 'I can see why you want to show off your garden and your greenhouse.' I tell her about my grandmother's kitchen garden in Cornwall, her pride and joy, but if Granddad wanted to sell up, the shot we'd want is of the front of the house looking out to the sea. 'That's what people will fall in love with.' I point to the professional shot taken of the outside of her house. 'This will make people put in an offer.'

'On to the blurb,' Mrs Roberts says almost an hour later, when she has finally conceded that perhaps the professional shots should be used rather than her own, although her husband will be disappointed. Out of her handbag now come pages and pages of single-line text that could be excellent additional material for the brochure, she says. When I see footnotes I start losing the will to live.

'People won't read this,' I say, catching Ward hovering outside, confusion on his face as to why this meeting is taking so long. He knocks on the door, introduces himself to Mrs Roberts. 'Do you mind?' He takes a seat.

Don't stuff it up now, I think to myself, aware his presence makes me want to impress him. I continue, 'Mrs Roberts, there are only three people who will read your brochure line by line.'

'Only three?' she says, crestfallen, looking over to Ward to contradict me. He nods.

'The agent will because he or she is paid to write it. So that's me. The client,' I gesture to her, 'because it's your home, finally, the purchaser *after* they've bought it. The only thing that counts is this: your home is stunning, you live within easy commuting distance to London, you have five bedrooms and a conservatory, three acres, you're near good schools, it's Grade 2 listed and you have a lovely green-house, which I am sure I can somehow fit into the blurb,' I conclude, hoping for a smile; not expecting Mrs Roberts to burst into tears.

'I have a wonderful greenhouse,' she tells Ward, who is now looking decidedly uncomfortable. 'My son built it for me. You see, he died four years ago.'

It's six o'clock. Mrs Roberts left five minutes ago and Ward and I are the only two left in the office. I have spent the last half an hour holding Mary's hand (we're on first-name terms now) and listening to her tell me all about her son. I couldn't let her leave so distressed. As I'm about to stick my head round Ward's door to tell him I'm off I hear him on the telephone. 'I'm not sure what time I'll be back. Marina, don't be so unreasonable.'

I decide not to disturb him, instead I head back down-stairs with Spud, mulling over what to cook for supper tonight.

'January! Wait!'

I turn and see Ward standing at the top of the stairs. 'I should think you need a strong drink after that?' When he clocks my hesitation he says, 'Unless you have to rush off?'

*

Ward opens one of the cupboards in his office, and produces a bottle of red wine along with a couple of glasses. As he pours me a glass I notice a faded scar on his right hand.

'How did you get that?'

'This? Er, a stupid accident when I was a kid. Burnt myself on the radiator. I thought you handled Mary really well.'

I tell Ward that she'd raised her son, George, in their family home, and when the photographer had come round it had felt too real, too final for her. Deep down she was looking for ways to delay the selling process. 'Silly really,' she'd said, blowing her nose.

'Her son was only thirty-one, Ward. He died of a brain tumour leaving a wife and little boy behind. Her grandson played in their garden, helped her pick tomatoes in the greenhouse.' Self-conscious and not wanting any awkward silences I continue, 'She said her husband can't talk to her about it. She's struggled all this time, alone. Her garden was her only sanctuary.'

'I guess people deal with grief in different ways.'

'A house is never just a house, is it? It's like a memory box, each room telling a story.'

'But when you do move, it's as if you never lived there in the first place,' Ward reflects. 'You don't drive down that road again. It's gone, forever.'

'That's exactly what scares her.'

*

'Why did I become an estate agent?' Ward repeats my question twenty minutes later, topping up my glass but not his own. 'Since I was a boy I always wanted to work in property. Mum could leave me for hours building Lego houses. Strange. Most kids want to play football or rugby, but this nerd,' he laughs at himself, 'wanted to visit a National Trust House. If I tell you this, you won't use it against me, will you?'

'Carry on,' I say, enjoying seeing a more relaxed side to him.

'In the school holidays I used to visit loads of estate agencies because they let me go through their brochure drawer. It was like tucking into a jar of sweets. You think I'm weird,' he says, a twinkle in his eye. 'How about you, January? Why did you want to work in property?'

'I didn't. I kind of fell into this job really. My daughter had started primary school and I was looking for work, this came up. I wasn't sure at first, you know, about the "estate agent" thing.'

'I can understand that. I still hate going to dinner parties. I've never enjoyed them at the best of times, but the moment I say, "I'm an estate agent" I can almost feel the waves of antipathy around the table. I should think a tax lawyer is preferable to one of us.'

'Or a traffic warden.'

'We're probably on a par with them. Sometimes I consider pretending I'm a doctor, but then fear that, knowing my luck, someone will faint or get a lump of meat trapped in their throat and I'll be expected to perform the abdominal thrusts – what's so funny?'

'I'm just remembering my granny. She was at a WI conference held over lunch and swallowed a Brussels sprout whole.' I giggle. 'It went down the wrong way, Granny said tears were streaming down her face, she thought she was going to die. She couldn't breathe.'

'You cannot be killed by a Brussels sprout,' Ward states, and just the way he says it makes me laugh even more.

'Tell you what, why don't you say you're a vet? That saves you from having to do the abdominal thrusts.'

'A vet's even worse!' He gestures to Spud lying down at my feet, his face turned away from Ward. He still hasn't forgiven him for not being allowed in the boardroom. 'People care much more about their pets than their partners.'

I shrug. 'Animals are much more loyal.'

'Exactly. Imagine if I couldn't resuscitate Fifi the poodle.'

I laugh again. 'OK, so maybe it's best to stick to the truth. You say, "I'm an estate agent, get over it."' I register that the framed photograph of his wife that used to be on his bookshelf has disappeared.

'After the expense scandals at least we're more popular than politicians.'

'True,' I say.

'I tell you what makes me so angry though. It's that everyone paints us with the same brush. I admit I've worked with the boys – and women actually – who think time is money, take shortcuts, are late, have sloppy manners, can't even be bothered to do their homework.'

I nod, telling Ward it reminds me of Alex, the agent who had shown me a series of houses when I was heavily pregnant with Isla, before finally I found the right place.

'I'll never forget this one flat.' I sigh. 'Priory Road. So he says, "Okey-dokey."'

'Okey-dokey?'

'Exactly. Bad start. "Okey-dokey, this is the kitchen." I say—'

'No shit, Sherlock?'

I laugh. 'I wanted to say that, but instead I ask, "How many years are left on the lease?"'

'Sensible question.'

'He says, "Not sure. This is the fridge."'

Ward laughs now. 'They don't care about anything but the commission. I'm guilty of that. Not so much the money, although of course that's great, but sometimes I forget the bigger picture. But these boys, who drag our reputation down, they'd never be able to speak to Mrs Roberts the way you did, January.'

'It was nothing.' I catch him looking at me, as if an idea is brewing.

'Have you ever considered coming on a few pitches?'

'I'm usually too busy running my boss's life.'

'Oh him. That little shit.'

We both look at one another and smile, something unexpectedly changing between us in that moment, a glimpse of promise that we might become good friends.

'I'll give you a lift,' Ward suggests again when I tell him I need to get going. Ruki will be wondering where I am, although she was only too happy to stay with Isla tonight because I think she believed or more like prayed I was on a Friday-night date.

Ward grabs his keys off the desk, helps me on with my jacket. 'Don't worry. Spud and I are happy on the tube.'

'But I only live round the corner.' Ward and his wife live in Brook Green. 'Come on,' he insists, pointing out that he's only had one glass.

On the way home Ward turns on the radio and asks me what I'm up to this weekend. After a couple of drinks I find myself confiding that I'm meeting Isla's dad's new girlfriend for the first time.

'Awkward on all sides,' Ward says. 'If you don't mind me asking, when did you separate?'

'The moment I told him I was pregnant.'

He glances at me.

'He wasn't ready; we were young.'

'So when did he decide he was ready to be a dad?' There's anger in Ward's voice.

'It's a long story,' I say, relieved we're nearly home. 'You take a right here, and then I'm just over the road. Anywhere here is fine.'

Ward still seems preoccupied by Dan. 'Where's your house?'

'This is great.'

Ward drives slowly down my road. 'What number are you?'

Reluctantly I say, 'Thirty-two.' Finally he parks right outside my house. The lights are on in the sitting room. A tub of what looks like fried chicken is splattered outside my front door.

Ward leaves the engine running as I unclick my seat belt and thank him for the lift. 'I'll see you on Monday,' I say, shutting the passenger door and yanking Spud away from the food on the pavement. I try to find my house keys that are, of course, hiding in the bottom of my bag. I wish Ward would go.

But then I hear a window being wound down. 'January,' he calls out.

I turn.

'You'll be fine. Remember, she'll be just as nervous as you, if not more.'

14

The following morning Isla is watching television. I am rushing around the house in a cleaning frenzy while Spud yaps at the hoover. Suddenly the hoover makes an ominous conking-out sound that makes me groan and Spud duck under one of the armchairs. I try to get it to work but it won't start. It's dead. Fuck. This is when I could really do with another person around to fix things. I wheel my sickly hoover into the cupboard under the stairs, cursing its lousy timing. Next I'm on my hands and knees making sure there's nothing dodgy lurking underneath the sofas, especially not one of Spud's half-eaten rubber balls or chews. I throw Isla's DVDs into the cupboard underneath the television.

'Can you tidy your room before they arrive?'

'Bear with,' she says, her eyes still fixed on the television screen. She's watching *Don't Tell the Bride*. 'It's, like, totes amazing.'

I switch the TV off, quietly amused at the teen language

she must have recently picked up at school. 'And make your bed.'

'Mum! Why do I have to do it right now?'

'Don't ask why. Just do it.'

'But Dad won't be here for ages.'

'And get changed too.'

I watch Isla lurch across the room, feet soon stomping up the stairs. 'Your swimming towel's hanging over the bath,' I call after her.

I tackle the kitchen next, clearing up our breakfast plates. Earlier this morning Isla and I went to our local Tesco Express to buy some croissants and chocolate spread. I also ended up buying some rather tired-looking pink tulips, but they're better than nothing, I think, placing the vase in the middle of the kitchen table, along with a couple of glossy fashion magazines. There. Much better. I can do this. Stay calm. Show maturity and be civil. Maintain eye contact. I chuck the plastic wrapping that came with the flowers into my white pedal bin, which is now full to the brim, topped off with last night's fried chicken and rice that I'd scooped off the pavement along with the empty can of Red Bull. I lift the bag out deciding now is as good a time as any to empty it. On my way out I catch Isla halfway down the stairs, wearing her white and navy spotted party dress. Her long hair is swished into a bun; Ruki's style is clearly rubbing off on her. 'Isla, why don't you save your dress for later?' I suggest, trying not to sound impatient. 'You need to wear your splints too.' She's wearing a pair of matching navy pumps, no tights.

'But Mum . . .'

'Please. Wear your tracksuit.'

'But if I wear my tracksuit my legs will get all sticky after swimming.'

My arm is aching from holding the bin bag, plus it smells. Deep breath. 'That dress is too smart for swimming and you can't wear your splints with those pumps.' I head outside with the bulging bin bag before stopping dead when I see a car parking outside. It's Dan's black VW Golf. What are they doing here so early? Quickly I shove the bag into the dustbin and squash the lid down. I haven't even had time to change out of my leggings and T-shirt and I'm standing by a stinky dustbin. 'Hi!' I say over-cheerfully when they approach the gate. 'Wow, you're here!'

'I called,' Dan says. 'Didn't you get my message?'

I picture my mobile on my bed, used as my alarm clock. 'Yes, yes I did.' I look at Fiona. Dan knows I'm pretending.

'January.' He touches my shoulder. 'This is Fiona.'

We shake hands. She's petite, olive-skinned, with short dark hair tucked behind neat ears that show off diamond stud earrings. I wonder if Dan gave them to her? Stop staring, January. Act normal. Step away from the dustbin.

'Well, come in, come in. Just doing all my boring old chores, as you can see.' That they don't need to hear about,

I berate myself as they follow me inside. 'Isla! They're here!' I call loudly when she's only right in front of me.

'There's my girl!' Dan gives Isla a hug.

'Hello, Daddy.'

'I'm sorry we're early,' Fiona turns to me hesitantly, 'but we checked the timetable at the leisure park . . .'

'And the slides shut at midday for the adult lanes so we thought we'd better get a move on,' Dan finishes off her sentence, ruffling Isla's hair before introducing her to Fiona.

Isla gazes at her, a finger pressed to her mouth.

'What a pretty dress,' Fiona exclaims, 'and such lovely shoes.'

'Dan tells me you're a teacher,' I say to Fiona, switching the kettle on. Unfortunately he said they had time for a quick coffee. I can't stop staring at her. She's dressed in skinny jeans and a sloppy grey mohair jumper that shows off a pale-pink swimming strap underneath.

'That's right,' Fiona says, 'I teach primary kids, for my sins.' A pause. 'And Dan tells me you're an estate agent?'

I am reminded of Ward and our drinks last night and for a moment it makes me feel brighter. 'That's right.' I grab some mugs. 'For my sins, for my sins.' I hate that phrase and somehow I've managed to say it twice.

'Well,' we all say at the same time, the kettle taking an interminably long time to boil.

'I've heard the weather's not too bad over the weekend,' is the best I can do, looking out of the window.

'May is such a beautiful time of year,' says Fiona self-consciously, 'when it's getting much warmer with summer only round the corner.' The telephone rings next door just as the kettle boils.

'Take it!' both Dan and Fiona urge.

I hesitate, before leaving it, wanting to get the coffee over and done with. 'Probably a scam.'

'I'm going to big school this autumn, Fiona,' Isla says coyly.

The telephone clicks into the answer machine. 'January, it's me.' It's Granddad. 'You're probably out walking Spud. I know it's the dreaded meeting later on this morning.'

Stop talking, Granddad.

'Hope it's not too awkward,' he continues. 'Call me later.'

Fiona's cheeks redden. 'Dan tells me you're a brilliant artist and photographer too, Isla. And who's this gorgeous little chap?' She bends down to stroke Spud, not wanting to look at me.

'You know what,' Dan glances at his watch, 'we'd better shoot.'

After I have waved them goodbye I walk back inside, pick Spud up and carry him on to the sofa, demanding he gives me a giant cuddle. Spud rests his head on my knee, looks up at me with his soulful brown eyes, then jumps up and licks my face when I begin to cry. 'I'm being so silly, Spud. I knew the day would come when Dan met someone, but it doesn't make it any easier, you know?' He looks at me as if he knows exactly what I mean; I swear dogs understand more than humans. I scratch him under the chin. He lies down again, rests his head on my thigh. I take my locket off, open it to look at my mother and father, then close it, telling myself not to feel like this. I pick up the controls, turn on the television; it's some cooking show. Before Dan came back into our lives, I used to fantasise about a weekend to myself, going to the shops, reading a book. When did I last read a book without interruption? But now that I've got the time I don't feel like it. The house is uncharacteristically tidy, leaving me with nothing to do except call someone out to fix the hoover. I hope Fiona doesn't let Isla run too fast around the pool and they must be careful going up the steps to the slides. Dan must have told her all about her CP.

Just as I'm about to take Spud for a walk, the telephone rings. I decide to screen.

'Hi, Jan, it's Lucas.'

I pick up.

'Oh hi,' he says, 'you're there.'

'What do you want?' I ask, before regretting sounding so harsh. But it has to be said, Lucas rarely rings for a chat.

'Love you too.'

'Sorry. It hasn't been the best morning.' When I tell him about Fiona and Dan he remains quiet. Lucas can't do emotion. I remember Granny saying how alike he and my father were, that Mum had been clever at bringing out Dad's softer, more human side.

'Sorry, that can't be easy.' Long pause. 'But you'll meet someone, Jan,' he adds almost with affection.

I soften. 'Do you want to pop over? I could do with some company. We could grab a takeaway—'

'I can't, sorry.' Lucas never elaborates on his plans. Who knows what he gets up to or whom he sees? He coughs awkwardly. 'Anyway, the reason I was calling is I need a witness for a signature, some legal document, so can I drop by later?'

'Sure,' I reply, resigned to Lucas never changing, before we hang up. The doorbell rings, making Spud bark. 'It's only me, Spuds,' Lizzie calls through the letterbox.

My heart lifts when standing in front of me is Lizzie carrying two cups of coffee and an overnight bag. 'I've got films, magazines, chocolate, booze, anti-ageing face masks and a toothbrush.' She dumps her bag on the sofa. 'But first things first, go and get changed, I'm taking us all out for a slap-up lunch. You too, Spud, get your coat on. I checked with the pub. They love dogs.'

Later that night Lizzie and I watch a film, share a bottle of wine and sit side by side with our broccoli-coloured face masks on, saying we'd give any burglar a scare. I imagine Dan, Fiona and Isla's day; they probably spoilt Isla rotten and let her eat dough balls as well as pizza for lunch. I imagine Isla telling Fiona all about school and home and how her boring old mum nags her to wear her splints.

Lizzie switches off the television, turns to me. 'You're thinking about them, aren't you?'

I get up and walk over to my bookshelf. I pick up a photograph of Isla as a baby.

'You don't need to feel threatened by Fiona,' Lizzie reassures me.

'I'm trying to get my head round it, but . . .'

'Don't panic, Jan, it's early days.'

Seeing Lizzie with her mushy green face looking so serious makes me smile. 'Thank you for being my 3 a.m. friend,' I say, returning to the sofa and clutching her hand.

'And thank you for being mine. You never know, Jan, Fiona might be a really positive person to have around.'

She turns the film back on and I pretend to watch, but I'm anywhere but in this room. I'm back with Isla when she was a baby. Lizzie is right. We have been through so much together that we have become a team, which is exactly why it's hard letting other people come on to our side.

15

2004

It's seven o'clock. Isla is thirteen months old and finally, after her warm milk and bath, she's asleep.

Lizzie and I spent the day out with friends and she's staying over tonight. 'To do my godmotherly duties and give you a night off,' she had suggested, 'before I go back to all my moaning guests.'

Lizzie still works for the travel agency in South Kensington, the same job she'd found when I was dating Dan. While I was pregnant she spent nine months in the London office, before they sent her out last year to Greece, from April to October, to be the island rep on Paxos. She's in charge of all the villas and guests. Despite the memories of her doomed relationship with the married man, Lizzie loves to travel so it seemed too good to be true to be paid to do it. Besides, she wasn't going to let a rotten old cheat stand in the way of her love affair with the island. However, as she discovered, it wasn't all floppy sunhats, olives, cocktails, white sand and turquoise sea. 'I earn every penny,' she said to me, roughly four months into the job. 'You wouldn't believe the guests and their questions, Jan. "When will the sea be calm?" As if I'm psychic. "Can you tell the donkeys to stop braying."' Lizzie's accommodation is a rundown cottage in an olive grove, surrounded by goats and chickens. 'If the weather is bad, it's my fault,' she'd continued. 'If there's turbulence, it's my fault. But I have to smile all the time, and if the disco music kept them awake last night . . .'

'It's your fault,' I'd said.

During my first year with Isla, Lizzie and I would call one another regularly. I missed her desperately, Dan's disappearance and his rejection was still raw. Whereas my news was limited to walking Isla to the park, the health visitor visiting or staying with my grandparents in Cornwall, Lizzie would always have a hairy-moment story to tell about a villa not being ready on time or a boat that had crashed into the harbour the night before, right outside one of the bars because someone had forgotten to throw the anchor out. 'Oh, and Jan, you should see the single girls in floods of tears when they leave. They believe they've had this perfect holiday romance, just as I did. Then I watch as their Greek gods wave them goodbye before they're back on the pull when the next lot of tourists arrive.'

I'll miss Lizzie when she goes back to Greece. The truth is, as much as I love Isla, I'm finding it lonely being a mother.

I miss my job at the literary agency and miss my salary, but if I did work, as I'd originally planned, I'd calculated that virtually all of it would be spent on a child minder. And besides, I haven't found Isla's first year as easy as I'd hoped. I've had to remortgage the house. I keep on telling myself I'm lucky to have a home. Money will be tight being a single mum, but it's tight for everyone. Millions are worse off. Daily I have to remind myself that I made this choice.

Lizzie breaks into my thoughts as she says, as only a best friend can say, that I look knackered, so she demands I have a lie down while she opens a bottle of wine. I'm not breastfeeding anymore. I step round the toys and books on the floor and collapse on to the sofa. I close my eyes and enjoy getting the weight off my feet, trying to put aside my worries about Isla. Throughout her first year I've been back and forth to the GP. Isla wasn't sitting up properly like other babies her age, then her hips weren't abducting, but more than anything it's the tightness in her legs that worries me.

Isla was born on 31 January 2003. It was agony. She was stuck in the birth canal, sliding back and forward, the pain making me understand how some mothers used to die in childbirth. I thought *I* was going to die. Isla came out with a bump on her head, but the moment I held her in my arms, all that pain was taken away. She looked so lovely and pink, and when the nurse told me all was well, that she was breathing normally, my heart filled with relief and joy. I have never been happier than lying in that hospital bed, exhausted but exhilarated, holding a miracle in my arms. For a moment I'd thought about Dan and felt tearful. I recall how she'd gripped her little fingers around mine and I knew then, beyond a shadow of a doubt, that even if I was alone, I had made the right decision. Granny had popped her head round the curtain and joined us. She sat on the bed, watching Isla and me, no need for words until finally, she said, 'Your mother would have been so proud.'

I thought back to my childhood, a confused five-year-old asking Granny, 'Shall I call you Mum?'

She had held both my hands. 'You could, but I'm your granny. Timothy is your grandfather. I think we should keep the order of the family, don't you?'

I rocked Isla in my arms. 'But *you* are my mother, *Granny*,' I said tearfully. I thought of the last six months, and how she and Granddad had done nothing but support me with no judgement, only deep-rooted resentment towards Dan that they did their best to hide, but was impossible not to see in Granddad's eyes. Men didn't behave that way. This Dan, he might be the father to my child, but he was no gentleman.

A few days after Dan and I had met in the bar on that fateful night in Notting Hill, after Dan had made his views so clear on the subject of having, or not having a child, I'd called him, hoping we could try and work it out. His mobile number wasn't recognised. I visited his flat off the North End Road. 'He's gone,' his gormless flatmate said.

'Gone where?'

'Abroad, I think.'

'Abroad!'

'Yeah, well I saw him looking for his passport.' He'd shrugged.

'What else did he say?'

'Nothing much, just left a month's rent on the table. He seemed pretty keen to go actually.'

I called Dan's old office, but in vain. No one knew; it seemed no one cared. Dan clearly had let his boss down. I reread his old texts. 'Sorry, running late. Got some exciting news! Something to ask you! Be with you soon. D x'.

I'm certain now that this news had something to do with his career. I looked up top journalism courses abroad, but it was hard to know where to begin when I didn't even have a country to go on. I realised then that Dan was going to tell me that night about some amazing opportunity that he had been given; maybe he was going to ask me to move abroad with him. His extreme reaction made more sense now. All he could think about was not only how much he didn't want a baby, but a baby getting in the way of his dreams. 'I like you, January . . . maybe at some stage . . .' Over the next few months, each time I thought about him, it reopened the wound and questioned my belief that I could have a child on my own. I even went so far as booking an abortion. Lizzie had offered to come with me, she would take the morning off work, but I cancelled the appointment the next day. 'There's your answer,' she had said. So I made my decision, knowing that Dan wasn't coming back. He didn't want to be found. He had done everything in his power to obliterate us from his memory.

Isla is a happy baby. She laughs a lot, as if someone has just told her the funniest joke about bogeymen. I remember her first smile; she must have been about six weeks old. It was a real proper smile, not a wind one. Her whole face had lit up, the smile reaching her dark-blue eyes. I saw something of Dan in that smile and for the first time I felt sorry for the bastard. He was the one missing out, not me.

I am jolted from my thoughts when Lizzie comes in with a glass of wine, medicine at the end of the day. She says she'll put on the potatoes for the cottage pie. 'Will you marry me?' I say.

'Have a rest, dear,' she jokes. 'Put your feet up. I'll call when it's ready.'

I take a large sip of wine. And another. Maybe I'm worrying too much. Isla is eating well and it is true that some children develop later than others, and the tightness, well . . . 'Babies need to cry, it's good for their lungs,' Granny had kept on reassuring me in the early months when I used to call saying she wouldn't stop. At eight months old, Isla had a hip scan, but of course the results came back normal, and by nine months old she was sitting upright in her chair. 'She's eating well,' my GP had said. 'Everything is on track.'

His promise felt good at the time, but over the next few months I began to worry again. Worry is like ivy; it keeps on creeping up on you until it reaches the point when it becomes uncontrollable. Only today I was with a group of mothers I'd met during my antenatal classes. At Isla's age children don't really play together, they sit side-by-side doing their own thing. One was stacking colourful bricks into a pile; another was playing with a baby shop till. I kept on watching Isla, willing her to slot the pieces of her animal puzzle into the right places. I am sure her movements are delayed, it's as if she is one step behind the beat. 'Isn't she beautiful,' said one of my friends as I watched her staring ahead, almost as if she were in a trance, or an outsider, observing.

It's not right. It's not right. I take my glass of wine and join Lizzie in the kitchen, deciding to confide in her about Isla's playgroup today. 'I was the strangest child,' she says, mashing the potatoes as I grate some cheese. 'I never wanted to play. All I wanted to do was sleep and eat. Mum said I was the easiest baby in the world. As long as I had my pasta and my blanket I was happy.'

I remain quiet.

'Every child is different, Jan, don't worry.'

The following morning I feel brighter, deciding Lizzie is right. Doctors must get so fed up with neurotic first-time mothers beating themselves up over the tiniest detail and wanting unnecessary tests for this and that. I head into Isla's bedroom. She looks so peaceful, content. I lift her out of her cot. 'Wake up, sleepyhead,' I say, holding her close, before wrinkling my nose. Lizzie enters the room in her stripy pyjamas and cardigan, hair scooped into a messy ponytail. 'Do your godmother duties extend to changing her nappy?'

'Nah, I think I'll leave that to the expert. I'll stick the kettle on.'

As I lay Isla on her changing mat I look down at her leg again. One is definitely a fraction longer than the other.

'Mumma.' Isla wriggles.

'This won't take long.' I reach for a nappy on the shelf underneath.

The tightness in Isla's legs doesn't make life easy when changing nappies. Surely it shouldn't be this hard? She looks up at me with those innocent eyes as if she wants to tell me something.

Why can't I shake this feeling? Something is wrong. I *know* it is. It's wrong and no one is going to convince me otherwise. Not Lizzie, not Granny and certainly not my GP. I'm taking her back to the doctor's first thing on Monday, and I won't leave until they tell me what it is troubling my little girl.

16

2014

It's early June and Lizzie and I are eating out at my local Thai; Ruki is at home with Isla. I left them building a Roman home out of an old cardboard box.

'How's the new job going?' I ask, helping myself to another prawn cracker. Lizzie set up a decluttering company a year ago. 'You're setting up *a what?*' I'd asked when she told me.

It's far from full-time since she still works for the travel agency, but she has cut down to four days a week to give her a chance to grow the business. The idea came to her when one of her work colleagues was going through a divorce. Lizzie had visited her one weekend and was so shocked by the squalor that she had to do something about it. Like the angel she is, she sacrificed almost her entire weekend sorting out the mess. 'I've moved around so much, Jan,' she'd said when explaining why she wanted to do it. 'I have a first-class degree in travelling, packing and organising, so I can't help thinking I can earn a wage doing it for others.'

'You still can't get your head round it, can you?' she says, watching my face dissolve into a smile when she tells me she has just joined the Association of Declutterers, which has an excellent website.

'I think it's fantastic,' I say, meaning every word. I admit to being sceptical at the beginning, along with many others who couldn't understand anyone paying someone to sort out their rubbish. But finally I realised how valuable her work was when she'd told me about one of her older clients, in her eighties, who lived alone, needing help to prepare her house for when she died. 'Let's face it, I'm in the departure lounge,' she had said to Lizzie with a wry smile. In many ways it reminded me of Granddad and the way he says he doesn't want Lucas and me to be left with so much clutter when he dies. This client didn't want her children to be burdened with the task because they all had full-time jobs. And yet she couldn't do it on her own. She was old and had severe back pain that didn't go well with heavy lifting. Together they had catalogued paintings, books and plays, and sent clothes and china to various charities. Lizzie had helped her auction the furniture that none of her children wanted. This client had been an actress, and like my grandfather, had worked in the theatre and travelled round the world. The two of them had laughed and cried sharing stories and by the end of the job, had learned much from one another and become firm friends.

Lizzie tells me she had a terrible experience today. She gives me the background as our food arrives. She was at a house in Barnes. Secretly the wife had called her to say she couldn't stand her husband's mess anymore. 'There are piles of ancient newspapers everywhere,' she'd said, 'that he won't throw away and food that is years past its sell-by-date. I feel as if I'm living in a skip. Forget that! A skip would be insulted.'

'Poor woman,' I say, thoroughly agreeing with Lizzie that this was indeed a time when a professional declutterer needed to come in on the case.

'You know my three rules for this job, Jan.' Lizzie tucks into her chicken curry. 'No children around, no mobiles and no husbands until coming-home time.'

'Uh-huh,' I say, sensing a disaster.

'The husband knew I was doing the job; I'd made him agree before I began. I don't want to be some secret declutterer, snooping around the house in camouflage with my bin liner. Stop laughing, Jan.'

'Well stop being so funny.'

'Both sides have to be happy. So the wife and I are getting along fine, she's lovely, and we've made a start in his study. Some of his paperwork dated back to 1974, before us old cronies were born.'

'You're kidding. So what happened?' I top up Lizzie's wine glass.

'He comes home early, turns up around four, storms outside the house going through every single dustbin liner like an addict, empties all his rubbish on to the driveway, shouting at us both, telling us we've ruined his life.'

'What did you do?' I ask, thinking how straightforward my day at the office had been.

'There wasn't much I could do. I tried gently to explain that he had agreed to this. We showed him round the house. I talked to him, wanted to make him see the improvement, but in the end I had to leave. I just pray he's not giving her a hard time tonight. She's terrified of him.'

'So how's it left?'

'I'll call her tomorrow. Do you know what the moral of the story is?'

'Go on.'

'Never get married.' She shrugs. 'Don't get me wrong, being single has its problems, but you get married and you're only swapping one set of problems for another, aren't you?'

As Lizzie and I walk home she asks me about Sherwoods. 'How's Ward? Have you had any more secret Friday-night drinks with him?'

'No.' Ward has now been working at Sherwoods for two months.

'Oh, shame.'

'He's married.'

'True. It's just Graham isn't an option and you keep on rejecting Spencer, although I don't see why you can't carry on having a hot affair.'

'Lizzie, gorgeous as he is, Spencer chats up anyone in a skirt with a heartbeat.'

'Well that only leaves Ward.'

'Who's married so that's not an option either. Anyway, even if he were single, he's not my type. He's too . . .' I think of him, one moment funny, thoughtful, even kind, the way he'd wished me good luck meeting Dan's new girlfriend; the other telling me to shut the door on my way out before I've barely stepped into his office, 'unpredictable.'

'Oh, but we like that.'

'Compared to Jeremy . . .'

'You can't compare.'

'I know. All I was going to say is Jeremy was straightforward. With Ward, I sense there's a lot going on in his head.'

'You know what, Jan? I doubt it. People always try to impose interesting qualities on quiet people. "He's so enigmatic" or, "he's so artistic", when the truth is he's probably dull. No one would try and impose anything on me. What you see is what you get. I'm too cheerful to be mysterious.'

'Ward isn't dull.'

'OK, so what sort of things do you reckon go on in his mysterious head?'

'Don't know. There's something not right. Maybe . . .' I

loop my arm through Lizzie's, 'his house needs a good old detox.'

'Ah, yes! It could liberate him, free his mind and make him nicer in the office.'

'I'll suggest it at our meeting tomorrow.'

'You do that. Tell him I can offer mate's rates.'

'I think I'm getting a stye,' Graham says in the boardroom, shoving his face too close to mine. I peer into his eye. 'Can't see anything.'

Lucie tuts. 'Because there's nothing to see.'

Ward strides into the room, and sits down at the table. Nadine mentioned he'd been here since seven and has been leaving the office late most nights; there have been empty take-away cartons left on his desk.

Halfway through the meeting Ward fills us in on the new houses we have recently been instructed on before we move on to other properties. 'Clayhurst?'

'In theory we should exchange next Monday,' Graham replies.

'Keep on it, Graham. The Farmhouse?'

'She thanked us for the flowers,' I report. 'Said her husband tried to take the credit.'

Graham laughs as he clicks his thumbs back, they crack like splintered wood. 'Arthritis.' He pulls a pained face.

'I'm surprised you're still alive, Graham,' Ward says. 'Mrs Roberts?'

'Advert was in *Country Life*,' I say, 'Lots of viewings. Someone's going round for the second time.'

'When? Today, tomorrow, next year?'

'This afternoon,' I reply.

'Good. If they offer let's close it fast because at the rate we're going we soon won't have an office in Mayfair. No news yet on Sittingbourne Park, the one Spencer pitched for too.'

'She's taking her time,' says Lucie.

Ward writes a note in his diary. 'It's beautiful: Queen Anne.'

'I know the house,' I say. 'I took—'

'I don't want Andersons,' Ward cuts me off, 'and I definitely do not want B & G to get this one. This place could attract a bidding war. It's got the right proportions, nice lake, fifty acres – I'd live there if I could.'

I agree. 'She has created this incredible wild meadow and—'

'This is ours, OK?' Ward interrupts me again. 'Mr Callaghan, Toad Hall?' This is the house practically on the M25.

'You'll never guess,' exclaims Lucie. 'I've found someone potentially interested.'

'I don't believe it.' Graham hits the table. 'You've done some work.'

'Sod off, Graham.'

There's that glimmer of a smile from Ward. He gives them out sparingly, teases us with them.

Lucie continues, 'The M25 traffic doesn't bother him. He's obsessed with lorries.'

Ward gets straight to the point. 'Is he going to offer?'

She crosses her fingers. 'I should hear today.'

'How did you find him?'

Lucie looks delighted to be asked, as if she's been hoping for that question from Ward all morning. 'Let's just say I thought about the kind of person who might want to live by a motorway and then became a member of one of the most elite lorry-spotting clubs in the world.'

'That's genius,' Ward says, much to Lucie's delight, just as Nadine enters the boardroom. 'Lucie, it's the lorry man on the phone.'

'Take it in my office,' Ward instructs.

Minutes later she returns.

We wait. It's more painful than waiting to hear if her boyfriend has proposed.

'We've got an offer!'

I jump up; clap my hands. Graham hugs me. Nadine dances around the table.

'How much?' Ward asks, remaining calm.

'Well, it's not the asking price.'

'Mr Callaghan should be *paying* someone to live there,' Graham says.

'How much?' Ward repeats.

'A hundred grand less.'

Ward nods. 'If Mr Callaghan has half a brain cell he'll

accept immediately. Call him, close it.' He wraps up the meeting. 'This is what I mean, team, lateral thinking. Well done, Lucie. Goes to show there is a house out there for everyone and there's a little bit of a lorry spotter in everyone too.'

Later on that afternoon, despite the good news, I'm still thinking about the way Ward cut me off twice in the meeting. I know I shouldn't care, it's business, he cuts everyone off, but if I'm to bust a gut getting Isla off to school just so I can sit around that table at eight in the bloody morning I wouldn't mind being able to finish my sentence once in a while. Distracted, I go online to take a look at the website that shows off some of the best gardens in the country, including Sittingbourne Park. The house is in Derbyshire and the gardens are open to the public. The owner, Mrs Harman, in her late sixties, is passionate about orchids and wild flowers. Isla and I took Granny there for her birthday, a year before she died. I look back nostalgically to that day. 'Look at these, Granny!' Isla had said, mesmerised. 'They are like little bees on pink petals.' She'd been standing in the midst of the most striking orchids in a field of wild flowers.

'They're called bee orchids,' Granny said. 'Aren't they something? Fascinating story behind them too.'

Granny had a story behind every flower and plant, showing both Isla and me how they all had private lives.

'They are cunning, deceptive old flowers, Isla. Do you want to know why? I hope she's not too young for this,' Granny had whispered, saying sorry in advance.

'It's too late now,' I said, Isla demanding to hear the story even more.

'Well, these petals, they mimic the female wasp so that they can con the male wasp into pollinating them. They give off the most irresistible perfume that makes the male get all excited, thinking he's going to get a sensational treat. So he buzzes over and tries it on, covering himself in pollen, but soon realises with frustration he's not getting anywhere, so off he goes and tries his luck elsewhere, depositing pollen on another bogus female which is just what the orchid needs, you see, Isla.'

Isla had looked entranced, although I'm not sure how much she'd understood.

I think of Granny dressed in her big straw sunhat with a wide navy ribbon tied round the brim. I see her taking Lucas and me around show gardens, Lucas trailing behind as if being dragged through mud. At the end of our visit Granny would fill the car boot with pots of plants and reward Lucas and me with an ice cream for being so patient. She used to do the same with Isla. A trip to see a garden was never such a bad thing if it meant a double mint choc chip in a cone and a story about naughty flowers.

I'm awoken from my thoughts when my telephone rings.

'Hello, it's Marina.'

I jolt hearing her voice. 'Oh hi, it's January.'

'Is he there? I can't get through on his line.'

I glance at the red button. 'I'm afraid he's on another call right now. Can I get him to phone you back?'

'Yes. It's urgent.' She hangs up. They are well suited. I picture them at home snapping at each other like terriers. She can probably never finish her sentence either.

When I see Ward is off the line I'm about to buzz him, but then see a brochure on my desk that needs his approval so decide to go to his office. 'Sorry,' I mouth, backing out of his room when I see he's on the telephone again, but he glances at the brochure and beckons me to stay.

'I completely understand, Mrs Harman. Barker & Goulding are very good too.'

My heart sinks. I fear Spencer has won the pitch for Sittingbourne Park.

'Life does get busy . . . no, I understand you can't make a decision without your husband.'

Oh. Maybe we haven't lost the pitch yet.

Ward clears his throat. 'If there's anything more we can do, please ask. We'd love to represent you and of course the summer is a great time to launch your house.'

I rush over to Ward's desk, lean over him for a pen, scribble in his diary since it's the only paper I can see.

'Absolutely, Mrs Harman,' says Ward, 'we'll be in touch.'

I nudge him, pointing to my note, 'TELL HER bee orchids amazing June.'

Ward reads it. Hesitates. 'Just before you go, I had a thought. Your bee orchids will be looking their best in June for the photos.' There's a long pause as I'm scribbling another idea down. 'Yes, I love gardening, am very green-fingered, me.' Ward reads my next note, glances at me in disbelief.

'SAY IT,' I mouth.

'And the pink willow herb and . . .'

'SAY IT.'

'. . . and the snake's heads . . .'

He looks at me anxiously. I stick my thumbs up. His shoulders relax as he says, 'My mother grew them, Mrs Harman. It's rubbed off on me . . . Yes!' He laughs. 'It's about the only good thing that has . . .' Long pause. Ward grabs his pen. Jots something down in his diary. 'Really? No, I'm sure your husband won't mind. My wife makes all the decisions. Mrs Harman, you won't regret going with us. Nor will your husband.'

The phone slams down. Ward stares at me before a small smile creeps on to his face. 'You are amazing, January Wild,' he says. It's only then that I realise Ward has a certain power. I might not like him most of the time, but I care about what he thinks of me, and right now I feel as if I've won an Oscar. 'Grab your coat,' he orders. 'It's not often we have a good day.' Ward flings on his jacket, heads downstairs, announcing that it's drinks in the pub. 'January has just won us the Sittingbourne pitch.'

'As long as you know the boss always buys the first round,' chirps Nadine, gathering her jacket and handbag, acting as if it's payday already.

'To Sherwoods,' says Ward, holding up his pint of beer. We all raise our glasses, sitting round a table in the corner of our local pub, which is fairly empty late in the afternoon. It's an old-fashioned pub with swirly carpets, the walls painted in an unattractive mustard colour, the bar mahogany. It's pretty dark, even on a summer's day. 'To January,' Ward adds resting his eyes on mine. 'And to snake's heads and bee orchids.'

'Snake's heads and bee orchids,' we all say, receiving strange looks from behind the bar.

'Do you know the best thing about winning?' Ward asks. 'It didn't go to Barker & Goulding.'

We cheer. Spud barks and jumps up against my legs, wanting to be in on the action. I pick him up and let him perch proudly on my knee as Nadine gives him a stroke and scratch around the ears. 'Let's face it. The only thing that counts is beating our opponents,' Ward continues. He really means Spencer.

Another cheer, all of us are caught up in the excitement, anticipating a possible bidding war. It's been a long time since we won a house like Sittingbourne Park. Today reminds me of the good old days with Jeremy, when we were winning pitches more often than losing them. In so many ways Jeremy influenced me today. He always used to say selling a house wasn't just about facts and figures and negotiating commission fees. It was about engagement. If he knew the breed of a potential client's dog or that their beloved car in the garage was an Aston Martin, it showed an interest in the same things. Suddenly you had a connection that bonded you, and with a little help that's exactly what happened with Ward and Mrs Harman.

After a couple of rounds of drinks it's too late to go back to the office. Lucie is meeting her boyfriend in town; Graham has to shoot off to Paddington. Nadine lives in east London, leaving Ward and me sharing a cab home, Spud sitting on the floor between us, watching our every move. Ward loosens his tie. 'How do you know about snake's heads? What do they look like? I'd better swot up before she discovers I'm a fraud.'

I show him a picture on my mobile of the bell-shaped flowers that hang down like pendants. 'Ah, I see, their petals look like snake skins.'

'The majority come out in spring, but I always remember seeing them at Sittingbourne. My grandmother was fanatical about flowers.'

Ward peers closer to the picture again. 'Hang on, the petals are checked.'

'Uh-huh. Their name comes from the Latin word *fritillus*, a dice-box.' I stop before I sound too like my grandmother.

He raises an eyebrow. 'You're showing off now. You sound close to your granny.'

'I was. She's not around anymore.'

'I'm sorry.'

'She raised me. My parents died when I was little.'

Ward is stuck for words. 'I'm sorry,' he says again.

'It was a long time ago. My grandfather is still alive, he lives in Cornwall.' I find myself telling Ward briefly about my childhood, Granddad sitting in his study reading scripts and eating chocolates, one by one, out of a two-tiered box. 'I used to eat them too and then substitute a stone from the garden for an orange cream, wrap it up in its gold foil and put it back in the box.' Ward laughs with me, saying he'll never bring chocolates into the office.

'How about you, Ward?'

'I'm an only child. Father dead,' he says with little emotion. 'My mother lives too close for comfort. Only round the corner from us to be specific. She'd give Graham a run for his money in the hypochondria department. She's lonely, you see, with Dad gone. She was never happy with my father, but he was at least a presence in the house and could nip out to pick up her prescriptions.'

His mobile rings. I see Marina's name on the screen and gasp, realising I forgot to pass on the message. 'Hi . . . Sorry, I was in a meeting.' He glances my way. 'I can't talk right now, Marina. I'll be home soon.'

He sounds cold. Distant. I stroke Spud, look out of the window; anything to suggest I'm not listening or interested in their domestic life.

'Can we not argue about this right now?' Ward is tapping one foot on the floor repeatedly. 'Later, OK?' He's fighting to keep his voice calm.

After the call ends, I say, 'I'm so sorry, I forgot to . . . '

'It's fine.'

'What with . . .'

'January, it's fine.' Ward chucks his mobile into his brief-case, snapping the lid shut with unnecessary force. 'By the way, I've been meaning to ask how that weekend went, meeting the new girlfriend?' he says, his mind clearly still on Marina. I imagine they are going to have an enormous row when he gets home. Has he had an affair? I picture her cutting up his suits and flinging his belongings out of a window.

'It was fine.' That weekend was over two weeks ago.

He looks at me, almost smiles. 'Fine never means fine, does it?'

'She was lovely,' I concede.

Isla had come home saying she'd had the best time ever. 'She's so much fun, Mummy, you'd really like her.' They had experimented with hairstyles on one another, Isla showing me the evidence on her mobile. After swimming they'd baked some custard tarts and Fiona had packaged the remaining uneaten ones beautifully in a lined box for Isla to take home. Isla had discovered she'd been seeing Dad for over a year. Dan has told me that he's going to ask Fiona to move in with him, assuring me that it won't make any difference to our routine. He still wants Isla every other weekend.

'Must be hard,' Ward says, reading my mind. 'You want Isla to get on with her, but at the same time there's this part of you that hopes she looks like Shrek.'

I sigh with relief. 'Exactly. Silly, really.'

'Human.'

'Pull in anywhere here, thanks,' I say to the cab driver.

'It's been a good day,' Ward says, reaching across me to open the door, and I catch the scent of lemon and basil mixed with beer, strangely seductive. I stop when I see her face at the window.

'That must be Isla,' Ward says.

She waves at us. 'Here,' I say, offering Ward some money and wanting to get inside quickly. He refuses my change. Just as the taxi is about to pull away the front door swings open and Isla sways towards us carrying a plate laden with cupcakes. I glance at Ward aware he has noticed the way she walks.

'Look, Mum.' Ruki follows, her blonde hair pinned up and she's wearing a miniskirt with wedge espadrilles. She tells Isla to be careful not to trip, 'We've already had one disaster today.'

'I fell over in the kitchen, Mum,' Isla says, 'when I was pulling the cakes out of the oven.' She laughs and taps Ward's window, offering him a cake. Surprised, Ward opens the door. I introduce them. Isla hunches her shoulders, tilts her head to one side. 'You're the bossy boss.' She giggles.

'Isla!' Ruki and I say at the same time.

Ward, clearly intrigued by her, says, 'That's probably a polite way of putting it.'

Isla thrusts the plate at him. 'They dropped on the floor but they still taste fine.'

'Fine never means fine, does it?' I mutter his way. Trying not to laugh he makes delicious sounding noises before he watches Isla stagger round to the driver's window, offering him one too. 'They're lemon and cream.'

'That's your tip,' Ward tells the driver, still watching Isla carefully before his gaze returns to me as if to say, 'You didn't tell me . . . ?'

As Isla and I walk back inside, I sense Ward watching us as the cab pulls away. I feel as if he has peeled off a layer of my private life, a layer I wasn't ready to show him yet, if at all. I don't want him to feel sorry for me; think of me as this single mum raising a child with a disability. I don't want to imagine him going home and saying to his wife, 'Poor woman, her parents died, she was raised by her flower-mad granny *and* her kid can't walk properly. Our problems don't seem nearly so bad anymore.' I used to hate that. Nursery mothers saying that whenever they had a bad day they only had to think of Isla and me. I told Lizzie that if she ever said that I'd slap her. I've never sought pity; I don't need any. Isla makes me so happy. Isla *is* happy.

'She made them all on her own,' says Ruki. 'Isla is the next Mary Berry.'

'Are you proud of me, Mum?' Isla may be eleven but she hasn't lost that yearning to seek approval. Do we ever lose it?

'Very proud.' I wrap an arm around her shoulder, before grabbing the biggest cake off the plate and taking an enormous mouthful, making all of us laugh.

Late that night I'm still tossing and turning, sleep seeming an impossible goal to reach. I'm thinking about Ward's surprised face as he said hello to Isla. Next my mind is taking me back to when I was twenty-seven. Isla was three. 'What are you doing?' I'd asked Lizzie. I was going out on a date that night and we were in my sitting room, Lizzie piling bags and a rucksack on to my back and shoulders. 'Feel all this weight, right?'

'I can't move.'

'Exactly. I want you to go out tonight and forget all your baggage,' she said, taking the rucksack off my back. Slowly the weight eased around my shoulders. 'It's time to let your hair down and be twenty-seven, be the old January who loves to dance and party.' Lizzie was in a serious relationship at this stage, with someone she'd met online, and she'd encouraged me to go on to the same website. Tonight would be the first date I'd had since Isla was born.

'But . . .'

'No buts! Go and have a bath, shave those legs, doll yourself up. Don't talk about cerebral palsy or hospital appointments. Don't mention the word splints. Not sexy, Jan.'

Only Lizzie could get away with saying that.

'Don't call me every five minutes,' she continued, 'wondering if Isla is all right. If you do, I won't answer. Forget about everything for one night and have some fun, right? Who knows where it might lead.' I'd turned to her, wondering how she'd become such a wise counsel. 'My parents taught me the art of letting go, but we didn't just forget our troubles for a night. We moved away from them.'

I close my eyes again, turn over in bed, trying to forget that night, but the memory still haunts me.

On the way home my date and I had kissed in the cab, his hand grazing the inside of my thigh. To my surprise I'd enjoyed myself. It felt good to flirt and drink with a man. I'd also forgotten how much I loved to be kissed. I wished the cab driver could take us to the other end of the world or we could be stuck for hours in gridlocked traffic. Who cared if the meter was running? Who cared if time stood still? All I wanted was to be desired, to be held; to feel *sexy*.

When we returned home Lizzie had slipped away discreetly, clearly sensing love was in the air. Or sex.

We skipped the coffee, moving straight to the sofa. He'd climbed on top of me, both of us ripping off our clothes clumsily. Soon we were semi-naked, bare skin on bare skin. I breathed in his smell of sweat and aftershave, even loved the taste of beer on his lips. He unhooked the strap of my bra, I coiled my legs around his, he murmured my name; I wanted him inside me. I want . . . I want . . . I want . . . don't stop . . . don't stop . . . don't stop.

'Mummy?'

'Hurry,' I said, praying I'd imagined that little voice.

'Mummy.' Her voice was louder, getting nearer. 'Mummy?'

He withdrew, frustration in his voice as he said, 'Go.'

I hesitated, not wanting the moment to be killed, then muttered, 'Sorry, won't be a sec.'

'Mummy.'

I slipped out from underneath him. 'Coming!' I grabbed my top off the floor and shoved it back on without bothering to do up all the buttons. Quickly I put on my jeans. 'Isla,' I gasped, racing upstairs. She was too close to the top step and the stair gate wasn't shut. Lizzie must have forgotten. 'Mummy,' she repeated, even more unsteady on her feet without her walker frame. 'Don't move! Stay there!'

'Everything all right?' I heard him calling.

'Fine.'

I grabbed Isla and slowly guided her back to her bedroom; she gripped on to my arm, her knees turned inwards and knocking together as she walked.

'Good girl,' I said, as we reached her bedroom door and switched on the light. I stopped cold when I heard his footsteps behind mine. I turned, Isla by my side. He was dressed only in his jeans and I noticed the tyre of fat around his middle. 'What's wrong with her?' he asked, staring blankly at us both. 'Why does she walk like that?'

I open my eyes and switch on the bedside light, catching my breath. *What's wrong with her?* I saw that look in Ward's eyes too; he was just too polite to say so. I'd told my date to go, the moment well and truly killed. 'What the fuck?' he'd said as I'd pushed him away. 'Just go, get out,' I kept on saying.

'Weird,' he'd muttered, gathering his clothes and jacket.

I locked the door, slid the chain across, safely knowing that was the end of his phone calls and texts. I rushed back upstairs and had a shower before tiptoeing into Isla's bedroom. I lifted the duvet, slipped into bed beside her. I held her close, her body so tiny and fragile. That was the last time I was going to try to pretend I was normal. Nothing about our lives was normal. It hadn't been since that day in hospital, when the doctor confirmed my deepest fear that Isla had CP. I stroked her hair in the darkness, trying to let go of my anger. It wasn't until lightness came and the birds started to sing that finally I drifted off to sleep, still in Isla's bed.

17

2004

Isla is eighteen months old and about to be assessed by a community paediatrician. We have a 10 a.m. appointment and we're in the hospital waiting room, Isla is playing with two other children about the same age. As I watch her crawling to keep up with them, I have to remind myself not to compare. I imagine all mums do it, especially first-time ones. We enter this pressured race, whether we like it or not, or even know it. Subconsciously we are always looking around like spies, noting down what other children can or can't do, doubt creeping in or complacency that our little one is advanced.

The good news is Isla *is* walking a little now. She can pull herself up into the standing position and when she's on her own, or just with me, she will walk from one side of the room to another. However, when she's in a room filled with toddlers, she slips back into crawling, like a dieter going back to comfort food. Her language is limited to the odd word, like 'up' or 'juice'. If I say 'toothpaste' she can repeat it, but she'll never say it again. Other children her age can link two or three words together – there I go again, comparing.

Isla isn't that interested in toys or books and she's not bothered by the television. The one thing she truly loves, however, besides food, is swimming. She never looks happier than when she is in her bright orange armbands and pink costume, splashing me in the pool, saying, 'Ha ha!' She gets prettier by the day with her chestnut curls that have been passed down the line, and her blue eyes that laugh. My thoughts are interrupted when our names are called.

The paediatrician, Dr Fry, is plain and stocky with a determined chin. Her hair is short; she wears no make-up, only glasses; a no-nonsense kind of doctor. I tell Isla to sit still, but already she's kicking her legs up and down restlessly. Dr Fry launches straight in, shoving a piece of paper in front of Isla, drawing a circle and asking if she can copy her with no hint of a smile. Perhaps what she lacks in the bedside manner department she makes up for in her work. Isla slithers down her chair, staring at Dr Fry, that unnerving stare children do when they're not sure who you are or if they like you. Dr Fry points to the piece of paper. 'Come on.'

I rummage in my handbag, produce a piece of dried fruit out of a packet. 'Can you draw the nice doctor a circle?' I say.

'We haven't got all day, have we?' Dr Fry adds.

Desperate, I encourage Isla to pick up the crayon. 'A circle is like the sun, isn't it, or the moon. Remember we can have a nice slice of cake after.'

'Cake,' Isla repeats, taking the crayon and scribbling across the piece of paper and on to Dr Fry's desk. 'Ha ha!' Her little shoulders are going up and down as she laughs.

Dr Fry casts her eye down to one pink scrawl across the page and I apologise for the mark on her desk, saying I'm sure it'll come out. Next she's showing Isla some animal books. 'What's this, Isla?'

I'm willing her to say cow. She knows it's a cow, but . . .

'What noise does a cow make?' Dr Fry is taking notes.

Silence.

'Cake,' she says, looking at me.

Another silence. 'You know the sound a cow makes,' I say, nodding my head vigorously at Isla. 'They go m, m mo . . .'

Dr Fry is taking more notes. No doubt not in our favour.

Isla's face crumples. She pushes the book away. Dr Fry looks up. 'What's she crying for?'

'It's my fault. She's hungry. I shouldn't have mentioned cake.' I give Isla another chunk of dried pineapple.

Next Dr Fry stacks three coloured bricks one on top of the other, dismantles them and asks Isla to do the same. 'We're doing these tests to see if she's at the milestones of a normal child,' Dr Fry explains to me.

Isla throws a brick on to the floor.

'She's hungry,' I explain. 'Normally she can do all this, she really can.'

Irritated, Dr Fry attaches her notes to a clipboard before telling us that the only thing left to do is a physical examination. Somehow I manage to get Isla kicking and screaming on to the bed in the corner of the room. I help her off with her clothes and soon Isla is lying down with only her nappy on. She looks so vulnerable, her legs wafer thin.

'No!' she protests when Dr Fry holds on to her legs. I can see how frustrated she is at not being able to express how much she hates being touched.

'Is that it?' I say, when we're shown to the door abruptly. 'Dr Fry? What happens next?'

'She needs to be referred to a surgeon, her hips aren't abducting and I'm going to refer her to the Child Development Centre for further tests.' She gives me no indication of what she believes could be wrong. As she's about to call in the next person I rest a hand on her arm. 'Dr Fry,' I say quietly, 'do you think it could be' – I pause – 'cerebral palsy?'

'Let's not jump to conclusions, now, shall we? Mrs Porter?' She scans the waiting room.

'But I've read up a little about it and Isla has—'

'I'm sorry, Miss Wild, my clinic is running late.'

Two months later, day by day Isla's movement is becoming significantly worse and it's impossible not to worry.

Even friends and family are no longer trying to reassure me. Granny is concerned. I can feel her anxiety at the end of the telephone line. I find myself on my laptop most nights, researching cerebral palsy. I mention it to my GP, praying he'll tell me I'm wrong. I don't want to connect Isla with those ugly, frightening words. He suggests we wait until Isla has had further tests. Like Dr Fry, he gives nothing away.

Just before Isla turns two, we take part in a four-week assessment at the Child Development Centre of our local hospital. Each Friday we are in a spacious open-plan room with other parents and their children, along with an army of medical people in uniform: physiotherapists, occupational and speech therapists, and a doctor. We have had three Friday sessions already and today is our last, when the doctor will set aside some time for each parent, to discuss conclusions that have been made; basically it's the day we receive the diagnosis.

I scan the room. Each corner is filled with toys, a wooden bench, blue play mats and small square tables littered with playdough, books, paper and colouring pens. Initially Isla didn't enjoy being surrounded by such a big group: she was so overwhelmed by the noise that she'd kept on looking over to me for reassurance. The only thing she has enjoyed is making as much mess as possible with the playdough.

A few fathers are here today, which makes me think of Dan. Rarely a day goes by when I don't wonder where he is and what he is doing. Sometimes I feel bursts of anger towards him; other times just a sadness that Isla is the one missing out. When mothers ask me about Isla's dad, it's hard to know what to say, so I just say we've separated. I wish Lucas and I were closer and that he could be a more hands-on uncle. Last time he popped over briefly for tea on a Sunday he'd looked terrified when Isla sat on his knee and in pain when he watched her walk.

Isla is with a physio right now, her poor old legs being pulled and pushed about again.

I think about Lucas again. Ever since he left home aged eighteen, he's been determined to lead his own life. He rarely visits our grandparents. It's as if they remind him of our past, a past he wants to erase. I thought having Isla would perhaps bring us closer together but if anything it's had the opposite effect. Whereas my grandparents supported my decision to be a single mother, I sensed Lucas understood Dan's point of view much more. I recall a time when the four of us were having a meal in a French restaurant close to Leicester Square. I was six months pregnant and my grandparents were up in London for a long weekend. Granny had stressed that everyone was here for me, 'Isn't that right?' she'd said, Lucas remaining ominously quiet. I could almost hear him thinking, 'In a way I don't blame Dan. You're young, you hardly knew him so why go ahead with this when he's done a runner and there are other options?' He didn't have to say it, it was written all across his face. Like Dan, Lucas is ambitious. He works long hours in the City and has little time for anything else except going to the gym and socialising with clients. I have no idea if Lucas has ever had a serious girlfriend. He is as private as I am open. I imagine women find him wildly attractive, this tall, dark-haired man who gives little away, a man who, with the right woman, could surely be transformed. After Isla's birth Lucas remained indifferent. The times when I have tried to include him, calling him on the telephone if anxious about Isla, he'd say, 'You're always worrying, Jan. All I hear from you and Granny these days is Isla this, Isla that. Poor kid! She's probably fine!' There was hostility in his tone.

Lucas's anger still follows him around like a shadow.

Yet I can't blame Lucas for not being here. The one person who really should be standing by my side today is Isla's father.

I am brought back to the moment when I hear someone say, 'Time for a drink, everyone.' There's an orange table laid out with jugs of water and squash.

'Wine!' Isla shouts out, making everyone laugh and look at me.

'I could do with a glass,' mutters one of the parents to me, as the session draws to a close and we're told in what order we're to see the doctor.

The doctor is a tall distinguished-looking man with wispy brown hair and glasses. He's taken off his white coat and is dressed in a blue shirt and striped tie, a stethoscope around his neck. I take a seat opposite him. Isla is crawling towards the weighing scales by the examination bed. Next she's tugging the floral curtain. 'Leave her,' he says, glancing at his notes. 'Well, needless to say, we've really enjoyed working with Isla.'

'Thank you.' My heart is racing.

'She can certainly crawl at a pace. She'd give Jenson Button a run for his money.'

I'm grateful he's kind and human, but inside I'm screaming, 'Just tell me, get it over with.'

The doctor looks at the empty chair next to mine, clearly used to talking to couples in this scenario. 'Isla has cerebral palsy.'

'Cerebral palsy,' I repeat, in a voice so quiet I can barely hear myself.

'I'm very sorry. I imagine it's a shock.'

I knew all along.

'Do you have support? I know it's a lot to take in.'

'I'm on my own, but I have family.'

He nods, before explaining what CP means, but I'm unable to listen. All I can think is this cannot be happening, it can't be true.

At the end of our meeting the doctor hands me a blue information pack. 'It's all the basics about the condition, along with help lines and support groups,' he says.

Numbly I put it into my handbag, but want to chuck it straight into his bin or better still, throw it against the wall and scream, 'Why didn't anyone ever listen to me?'

18

2014

It's Thursday morning and I'm on the tube, watching the woman opposite me applying mascara. She looks at herself in the small mirror of her compact, puckers her lips. Next to her is a man reading the papers, a shiny black suitcase in front of him. I wonder where he's going. To my right is a woman, maybe in her mid-fifties, who is gossiping to her neighbour, rare for this time of morning. She looks like a Hell's Angel, her arms covered in tattoos. Maybe she's coming home after an all-night bender. I am drawn to a dolphin tattoo on her right arm, with the name 'David' above it. An old lover? She must catch me staring at it. 'David,' she says, 'loved dolphins, had them everywhere in his bedroom, he did. Dreamed of swimming with them. I lost him when he was seven.'

The man looks up from his paper. The woman snaps the lid of her compact.

'He saw a heart specialist, but they sent us away, told me it was nothing. All the doctors said I was neurotic. I kept on asking them to do tests. There was something wrong with his lungs and his joints were swelling up. "Test for meningitis," I begged 'em. Then he had a rash on his feet that went up his legs within a day. I rushed him into hospital, soon he was having trouble breathing, needed an oxygen mask. The poor little devil was screaming when the nurses stuck needles in him. I was so angry by then, my little boy in agony. The nurse goes to me, "He's so starved of oxygen we don't know if he will ever speak again," and I say, "I don't care if he won't speak, just get him out of that bloody pain." A nurse then says, "David has meningococcal meningitis." His last words were, "Mum, I feel ever so tired and sleepy." He died on the third of February.'

Finally everyone in the carriage breathes.

'I'm so sorry,' I say, noticing the woman opposite me dabbing her eye with a tissue, and the man next to her shifting awkwardly in his seat.

'I'm going to visit him this morning.' She gestures to some flowers in her bag that I hadn't noticed. 'I visit him most days.'

As she steps off the tube, I can't help saying, 'He's probably swimming with dolphins now.'

She waves at me. 'Bless you, love.'

As the train rattles on I can't stop thinking of how unimaginable that would have been, to see your seven-year-old boy die so suddenly and in all that pain. Then I think about Isla and me and the day we'd received the bombshell diagnosis from the doctor. I didn't want Isla to pick up on my fear and anger. If anyone had seen or watched us chatting on the bus on our way home from the hospital, they would have seen what appeared to be a normal mother and child talking about banana smoothies. We never know what goes on behind closed doors, do we?

With only one stop left I picture Ward meeting Isla last week. We haven't mentioned it since, probably because he's been in and out of the office most days, although I sense he's avoided the subject too. I feel as if there is a ladder between us, neither one daring to step on and climb.

When Graham arrives on time, Lucie, Ward and I sit poised with our mugs of coffee, waiting to hear his latest trial on the train or how his tinnitus had kept him awake last night. Fresh-faced, he glances at us. 'Problem?'

'No,' we all say in unison.

Yet I sense Lucie, and even Ward, misses Graham's dramas almost as much as I do.

'You lot really shouldn't take life too seriously,' he says with a twinkle in his eye. 'Let's face it, none of us are going to get out of it alive.'

Ward coughs. 'Right, let's crack on. Sittingbourne Park. Lucie?'

'Text done.'

'Photographer?'

'This morning.'

'Perfect. Her bee orchids will look lovely.' Lucie notices him winking at me. '*Country Life*?'

I nod. 'As soon as I get the photos.'

'Toad Hall?' Ward's eyes remain on mine.

'Sales memo done. Paperwork with solicitors.'

'Good, we want to exchange in the next few weeks.' I see the competitiveness in Ward's eyes and body language when we go through the next five properties on the spread-sheet. Working with Jeremy during his last year was like lying in a soft comfy chair in the sunshine, listening to *The Archers*. With Ward, it's like being in a racing car, tearing round bends and hoping the car doesn't burst into flames.

We hear Nadine letting someone in and Spud barking downstairs. It's probably the postman.

'Graham: Broadhurst, Hants?'

'They're going through a divorce. Owner didn't want to let on, you know what clients are like, they reckon we'll think they're desperate to sell.'

'Which they are,' Lucie says.

'Her husband lost all their money gambling on the horses. We had a good old chat about it over scones and—'

Ward interrupts, 'What did you value it at?'

'Two million. I'm being optimistic and taking your advice.'

'The most sensible thing you've said since I arrived, Graham.'

'The letters are on my desk, one for him and her; they're incommunicado.'

Ward asks, 'Anyone else pitching?'

'B & G, Andersons, Dunn & Cox, but I think she'll instruct us. We really bonded, poor love, she's hitting the menopause—'

'Keep me posted, Graham,' Ward says, nipping that conversation in the bud. 'Mrs Roberts, St Albans?' Mrs Roberts is the greenhouse lover.

'We've had an offer, but she's dithering.' I think of the woman with the dolphin tattoo again. 'I'll talk to her.'

Ward accepts this, and we exchange a look of understanding. 'OK, we're done. Good work, guys.'

'Was that a compliment from Ward?' Graham whispers when we're the only two left in the boardroom. 'And if I'm not mistaken, I think our boss has a little crush on a certain person.'

'Don't be daft.'

'You can be married but still have crushes, Jan.'

'Yeah, but . . .'

'We're only human. I fancy other men all the time but that doesn't mean I don't love my Nick and—'

Graham stops when we hear shouting coming from downstairs.

'Out,' Ward is saying. 'Now!'

'But Ward,' Spencer says, 'I was only passing by.'

The door slams.

Graham and I jump up and head out of the room only to see Nadine cowering behind her desk as Ward continues shouting, 'You know you don't invite him in and give him free run of the office!'

'But he's always popping in to see Jan.'

'How long's he been here?'

'Not long. He left some croissants for us.' She holds up a brown paper bag, stained with grease.

'How long! Five minutes? An hour?'

'Ward,' I call from the top of the stairs.

He doesn't turn round, just raises a hand, as if to warn me not to say another word or come any nearer.

Colour drains from Nadine's face. She is scared. I think we all are.

'So basically he was here long enough to do some damage,' concludes Ward, storming into our office.

'I'm sure he wouldn't . . .' Nadine's voice falters. She looks at me helplessly, almost in tears. I head downstairs. 'Don't worry,' I say, touching her shoulder before following Ward.

I watch as he tosses brochures aside and picks up pieces of paper, desperately searching for anything Spencer can use against us. 'Ward, I think you're overreacting.'

'After everything he's done, I'm overreacting, am I?'

'That was one instance. He's never done it before.'

'How do you know?' Ward throws some more of my brochures on to the floor, goes through my in tray, as Spud quivers under my desk. He's acting like some crazed husband who won't rest until he finds evidence of his wife's adultery.

'Ward, what's going on?'

Nadine comes into the room. 'I didn't know,' she swears. 'Didn't know he couldn't come in without an appointment.'

'This is my fault, Nadine,' I assure her.

Ward locates the letters on Graham's desk addressed individually to the divorcing couple, his valuation for Broadhurst, clearly marked as two million. 'We've probably lost this pitch now.' He scrunches the letter into a ball.

'I'm sorry,' Nadine says, her voice trembling.

I prise the paper from his hand and stand in front of him while Nadine, Lucie and Graham hover by the door. 'You need to calm down. If anyone is to blame it's me, Ward. I should have made it clear about Spencer, but do you know what? It's just a house. One pitch.'

'One more pitch we can't afford to lose.'

Ward and I are standing close now, face-to-face.

He stares at me as he says slowly, 'I am trying to get this company up and running again.'

'I know, but mistakes happen.' I stare back. 'This . . .' I wave the paper at him. 'This is *not* life or death. Some perspective would help here.'

'Your perspective and mine are clearly different.'

'I spoke to a woman on the tube today who lost her son. He was seven. He died of meningitis.'

Ward is about to speak; he says nothing.

'At the end of the day,' I continue, 'all we do is sell houses. We are not saving the world.'

There's a long painful silence. 'I'm sorry,' is all he says, before leaving our office. Lucie, Graham and Nadine keep their heads down as he pushes past them, Nadine's confidence is shattered. I untie Spud's lead from the leg of my chair and leave, unsure if I want ever to go back.

19

The following afternoon I'm back in the office. I can't afford not to be. I can't lose my job.

Yesterday, after taking a virtually empty tube back home, Spud and I went for a walk in Chiswick Park. I needed to clear my head. I felt like my mum, playing truant. I thought a lot about her yesterday. My grandparents more than filled the void of losing my parents, but there will always be a small wound that remains, a cut that will never quite heal. Would we have been close? Enjoyed shopping trips and met in cafes to put the world to rights? Would my father have read stories to Lucas and me? Taught us to ride a bike? Would he have been as good a doctor to Lucas and me as he was to his patients? How I would have loved to talk to him about Isla's CP. Would I have watched Dad shave on a Sunday morning? I remember Granddad's round wooden box of shaving soap with his old-fashioned brush. I loved to kiss Granddad after he'd shaved; his skin was as soft as silk.

After lunch (I'd watched *Neighbours* but didn't recognise

half the cast) I'd called Ruki to let her know I'd taken the day off work and would pick Isla up at school. Seeing Isla's face light up in surprise when she saw me waiting behind the school gates with Spud and her purple scooter was the highlight of my day. We went for a swim and Isla did her homework at the kitchen table while I cooked spaghetti. When she mentioned that Dan and Fiona want to buy her an iPad for big school this autumn, I felt a twinge of irritation, perhaps jealousy, that I tried to disguise.

Lizzie came round straight after work and joined us for supper. When Isla went to bed, we opened a bottle of wine.

'Of course you go back tomorrow,' she said after I'd explained the day's events, 'and let Ward do the talking, Jan. Aren't you fascinated to know what's going on behind closed doors, because believe me, there's a story.' And of course I agreed with her. His reaction went way beyond losing a pitch; any fool could see that.

At the end of the evening Lizzie told me she'd met someone. His name is Dave. 'A right old bachelor,' she said. They met when he became a client. She'd visited his dark cluttered flat in Islington and over the following month had helped him to get his life back together. 'He works in risk management, or something like that. He's lovely, J, funny, eccentric – you know me, I need someone a bit eccentric.' I'm so happy for her. We talked about the forthcoming summer holidays. Lizzie wants Isla and me to visit her in Paxos. She's working out there for a month and could get me a cheap deal on flights and accommodation. 'And how about throwing in a Greek god,' I'd asked.

I pick up the telephone, the atmosphere in the office is subdued. I'm relieved Ward is visiting the Winchester and Salisbury offices today. I look over at Lucie and Graham; both of them are quiet. We don't take part in the Friday afternoon online general knowledge quiz, as we often do. Nadine doesn't sing down the telephone or stick her head round the door to take any lunch orders, nor does she sneak in any choccy bics. I talked to her this morning, over a coffee across the road. I filled her in on Spencer and how he'd stolen a pitch from us by reading one of our letters. 'He may well have done it before too, Nadine. Perhaps we've all been gullible, Jeremy included.' She told me that after I had left, Ward kept on asking where I was and if I was coming back.

Nadine's desk is adorned with a vase of pale-pink roses, an apology gift from Ward.

When five thirty comes everyone packs up to leave for the weekend, keen to scarper just in case Ward returns to the office. If only Jeremy could see us now. We might be getting more business, but our morale is at rock bottom. My mobile rings. I pick up.

'That's so weird,' I say. 'I was just thinking about you.'

'I hope nice thoughts,' Jeremy says. 'I'm coming to London next week, Jan, and wondered if I could take you out to lunch.'

'I'd love that.' We settle for next Wednesday.

'How's it going?' he asks.

'You've left a monster in charge.'

'What?'

I hesitate, unsure whether to tell Jeremy about Ward's behaviour yesterday. But then out it all comes, every single detail, even down to how I'd brought up the woman losing her son.

'January, go easy on him. Sometimes things aren't so black and white.'

'Meaning?'

Silence.

'Is there something I should know?'

'No.'

Jeremy can't lie.

'Jeremy?'

'I can't tell you.'

'Please.'

'I can't say a word,' he repeats, this time more forcefully.

'Spencer slept with his wife?'

'No.'

'It makes sense. Spencer sleeps with everyone.' Including me, I don't add.

'January, it's not my place to say, but *please* give Ward a chance. We all have tough days when we lash out but I promise you he's the right man for the job.'

*

Alone, I tidy up my desk. I can't stop thinking about what Jeremy said. What is this secret? As I'm about to leave Mrs Roberts returns my call. I hesitate, looking longingly at the front door.

'That's right,' I say reassuringly to Mrs Roberts five minutes later on the telephone. 'Your son would want you to move forward. No, he wouldn't blame you. Your husband's new job is a wonderful opportunity . . . Exactly, a fresh start.' I listen. 'Oh, that's great, I'll let them know their offer's been accepted.'

We finish the conversation firm friends, and I'm touched she thanked me. I decide to make one more quick call. I want to let the buyers know. I freeze when I hear the front door opening. Quietly I hang up, hoping Ward will walk on by and head upstairs. I hold my breath, praying Spud won't bark. But he does. He barks all right.

'January.' Ward stands at the door.

'I was just leaving.' I untie Spud, my heart beating fast. 'We've had a good day, Mrs Roberts accepted the offer and . . .'

'Don't go.'

I pretend I didn't hear him, walk past, wishing him a good weekend. He grabs my arm and keeps his hand firmly on it. 'We need to talk.'

'I'm running late.'

'Give me five minutes.'

*

As Ward leads me upstairs and into his office I remain quiet, determined not to feel awkward. As Lizzie had said, he's the one with the explaining to do.

'I wanted to say sorry,' he says at last. 'Please sit down. Yesterday was, well, it was unforgiveable.'

'It was frightening.'

'I shouldn't have let Spencer get to me, nor taken it out on Nadine, or you.'

'Is that all it was about? Spencer getting to you?'

'Yes.' He's a bad liar too.

'Is there anything else going on, Ward?'

'What do you mean?'

'You can trust me.'

'No, there's nothing. I saw red, that's all. As I said, it won't happen again.'

'But . . .'

'So Mrs Roberts has agreed to the offer?'

'Yep. I'll call the buyers.'

'I'm sure she appreciated—'

'Ward, I really need to go.' I get up to leave.

'I thought I'd lost you.'

I stop. Turn. There is something in his voice that compels me to stay.

He runs a hand through his hair, as if torn about how much to confide in me. 'I'm under a lot of pressure to get this company back on track and – well, the truth is . . .'

I wait.

'The truth is . . . I can't afford to lose you. You keep this office together. Jeremy made me promise I'd look after you and . . . Oh listen, I'm useless at all this stuff. You know, no one's ever stood up to me like that before.' He dares to smile. 'You're quite frightening too.'

'I've had a few battles. I'm used to fighting.'

'You mean with Isla?'

It's the first time he's mentioned her name since she offered him a lemon cupcake.

'You noticed,' I say.

'You don't have to talk to me about her, not if you don't want to.'

Ironically that makes me want to talk even more. 'Why wouldn't I want to?'

'Of course. I didn't mean—'

'If you want to stick a label on it, she has cerebral palsy.'

'I don't. I really don't.'

'But to me she's just Isla with her wobbly legs. There's nothing she can't do – nothing.' Why am I feeling so emotional in front of him? To my surprise I find myself telling Ward about her birth and the two years leading to her diagnosis.

'Forgive me if I'm being foolish but I always imagined people with her condition in a wheelchair.'

'Not always. There are different types, different degrees. Having CP doesn't mean you can't be independent or get married, have children, or lead a normal life,' I say, all the things I dream of Isla having, things I've discussed with her hospital team. 'There's no cure, but it can be treated and she does her physio twice a day or at least *most* days. Sometimes I'm too bloody tired to bother after work.'

'I can imagine. I'm sorry.'

'You don't need to be,' I reply, jumpy again. I understand what Ward is trying to say, but I loathe pity. Isla would hate pity too. She's as stubborn as I am and doesn't like to think there's anything she can't do, or any reason why she can't succeed.

Ward opens one of his cupboards and produces a bottle of red. He doesn't ask if I want a glass, just pours us both one. My mobile rings. I tell Ward it's Isla's father, before taking the call outside his office.

When I return, Ward says, 'Why did Dan come back?'

He's a good listener, I'll give him that. 'Long story.'

'I'm in no hurry. How about some takeaway?' He rummages in his desk drawer. 'Chinese, Thai?'

'Hang on, don't you have a home to go to?' I feel we're crossing some line here. I'm confused. One moment I'm angry with him, I don't like him, the next I'm drinking wine in his office. Ward apologised, I accepted, we should both be going home. Me to Isla; Ward to his wife.

'Stay. Tell me more.'

'Why? You tell me nothing about you.'

'There's nothing to tell.'

He's lying. 'Don't you have to go home to your wife?'

'She's away.'

'Really?'

'Blimey, what's with all the questions?'

'You can talk.'

'Fair point. Look, I understand if you need to get home for Isla.'

Briefly I mention Ruki.

'Well, I'm going to stay here and finish off a few bits and pieces and grab some takeaway, so if you're not going out tonight on a hot date and fancy some company . . .'

I hesitate, before hearing Lizzie's voice again, 'Aren't you fascinated to know what is going on behind closed doors, because believe me, there's a story.' And now I know from Jeremy that Lizzie is right.

I call Ruki to see if she can stay on. When I say something's cropped up at work I sense she's convinced I'm on another date with a mystery man.

'I'll tell you about Dan on two conditions,' I say when I hang up. 'One, you tell me what's really going on between you and Spencer.'

'And two?'

'I want Thai.'

He smiles. 'Sure. But I asked you first. What made Dan come back?'

20

2006

Isla is three. I hold her up to the window as we wait for Rosie, our friend from the portage team to arrive. We've been seeing Rosie for over a year now, she visits us once a week. People like Rosie want to encourage a child's development by playing, communicating and learning in a fun interactive way. I was sceptical at first; the idea of someone coming round to teach me how to play with my child felt awkward, insulting even. However, I was wrong; it's not like this at all.

The first time Rosie visited us, she burst into our sitting room, a bundle of energy, carrying a box bulging with toys. She was dressed in a red tracksuit, long black hair scooped into a high ponytail. Isla had clung on to my legs saying, 'Don't want her here.' She'd probably feared it was yet another of those physios who was about to pull her legs. When I asked Rosie if she wanted a cup of tea, Isla followed me into the kitchen, crawling on all fours, telling me to make her go away. But Rosie quickly won her over.

'Yay!' Isla waves when Rosie parks outside our house, beeping the horn in honour of her arrival. 'Toot toot.' Isla giggles. 'Orange car!'

Soon Rosie and Isla are playing in the sitting room. 'Do you want to look in my box, Isla?' Isla plunges her hand deep inside. When she lifts her hand out it's covered in foam. 'Ha ha ha!'

'There are lots of special things in the box,' Rosie continues.

Isla puts her hand in again, clearly enjoying the sensation of foam against her skin. She pulls out a rubber snake, throws it across the room. 'Hiss hiss,' she says, 'ha ha!'

Next Rosie puts up a little washing line that extends from the top of the television to the armchair. As I rejoin them with a tray of tea and squash, I watch as Isla takes a peg from the basket and wobbles her way to the line to hang up a pair of stripy socks. A part of me dies inside every time I see her walk. When we are out and about she needs a small walker frame, similar to a zimmer frame, only it works back to front. Isla can't walk at all with feet flat on the ground because her knees and feet roll inwards too much; instead she moves on tiptoe, the rest of her foot almost curling into a ball and her hips swing because her muscles are so tight. Sometimes the nerves in her legs spasm and Isla wallops her leg with frustration, as if to say, 'You're not to do that!' It breaks my heart the way she looks at me as if to say, 'Make it go away, Mummy.'

Rosie stands close behind, watching as Isla zigzags across the room, clinging on to furniture and anything else she can grab, to steady herself. 'What happened here?' Rosie asks Isla, pointing to her lip, which is cut.

'Fell,' Isla says, giggling. 'Splat!'

Isla crawls so fast now, that often she falls flat – 'splat' we call it – on the ground. She has a blackened front tooth from a previous fall.

'Oh look at you!' I say, when she turns to me, the socks now hung wonkily on the line.

'Proud, Mummy?'

'Very proud.' When she smiles I catch a glimpse of Dan. I don't want to, I can't bear to be reminded of him, yet Isla is becoming more like her father every day.

Isla and Rosie are now playing with an animal puzzle. 'Baaaaa!' she says when Rosie holds up the sheep. Gently she places her hand over Isla's and together they fit the piece into the right slot.

As they carry on playing with the puzzle, my mind drifts to the conversation I had with Granny last night. I'd told her about an operation I'd researched on the internet. 'They do it in America. Missouri. It's called a selective dorsal rhizotomy. They cut the nerves in the spine, the nerves that are sending the wrong messages to Isla's muscles.'

'It sounds interesting,' Granny had said cautiously.

'I've read all these stories of children who can now take part in sport, they can walk, run, dance.'

Granny stopped me. 'And what happens if it doesn't work?'

'That won't happen.'

'January?' Granny's voice was quiet, but firm. 'Supposing they cut into the wrong nerve?'

'She wouldn't be able to walk again,' I said quietly.

Granny had asked me to spell out the name of the procedure again. I could hear her writing it down, no doubt to discuss with Granddad. They would look it up on their computer. She'd promised to call me the following evening, i.e. tonight.

I'm still thinking about this when I hear, 'The dog's tail!' Isla claps her hands. They are on the last piece of the wooden puzzle.

'The dog's tail,' Rosie repeats. 'And what does a tail do, Isla?'

'It goes waggy, wag, wag!'

Rosie says they can play on the ball as a treat for finishing the puzzle. Rosie has a bright blue birthing ball and what is so clever is that when Isla leans against it or rolls over it she's doing her exercises without realising. Nothing is a task with Rosie. That's why she can step through our front door any time.

Later that evening, when Isla is tucked up in bed, I sit, curled up on the sofa with a glass of wine, waiting for Granny to call. I'm terrified she'll say it's too much of a risk, but what's the alternative? That I watch Isla get worse and worse, to the point where she can no longer walk, not even on her frame, or have any kind of independence? Of course I'm not sure Isla even qualifies for the surgery. If I'm serious about this procedure I'd need to send all her medical notes to the hospital, along with an up-to-date MRI scan, a spinal and hip X-ray and video footage of Isla walking, kneeling and sitting. Not every child is suitable. There's the money to consider too. The surgery costs thousands of pounds. This is probably why my doctor has never mentioned it; he's only suggested Botox treatment that is effective but doesn't last long before the tightness in her legs returns. The money Lucas and I inherited after our parents' death has been enough to give us a roof over our heads; I know how fortunate I am. 'But I have *parents*,' Lizzie had once said to me when I told her I felt guilty that she was struggling to pay her rent. Yet I'm in no position to pay for this. Plus, it's not only the surgery. It's the intensive care and rehabilitation, the travel, the ongoing check-ups. I've been jotting down ideas as to how to raise the cash. Lizzie and I are going to do a sponsored run; I could sell cakes and biscuits at Isla's nursery; I could pawn all my gold. I touch my gold locket. I'll sell it if I have to. But I can't. I can't sell it. It's the only thing that makes me feel close to my parents. My brother is the obvious solution; he earns a fortune in the City. This would dent his income, but by no means bankrupt him, and Isla is his niece. We might not be close, but he'd want to help, wouldn't he? I'd reinforce the fact that it was a loan. But then again, realistically how would I ever pay him back? I think I'd rather sell my house than ask my brother. This is what I'll have to do. Sell up and rent further out of London. I'll live in a tin hut if I have to.

The telephone rings. I give myself time to have another gulp of wine before picking up, my heart beating fast.

'January,' Granny says, 'we've talked about it. It is a risk. Whatever the outcome, Isla's life will never be the same.'

'I know.'

'The way we look at it is you either take Isla on a trip to America, or you invest in the most expensive fancy wheelchair.'

I laugh and cry in relief as Granny continues. 'We need to get the money together. You can't travel on your own. I'm coming with you. We can sell some pictures, flog some furniture and Granddad and I will ration baths to twice a week. Only joking. We'll do as much as we can, but we can't raise it all.'

'I'll sell the house.'

'Over my dead body. It's the one and only bit of security you have, January. Let's see if she qualifies for the surgery first. If she does, we say a prayer to win the lottery or we ask Lucas. One way or another we'll raise the money.'

Three months later, while Isla is at nursery, Lucas and I meet in a cafe in the City, close to his office in Cornhill.

I buy the coffees. Lucas asks for a slice of millionaire's shortbread too. As I wait to be served I glance over at him, sitting at the table with his BlackBerry that he's surgically attached to. I long to feel a connection that binds us together. Lucas is tall and broad-shouldered with light-brown hair and blue eyes. He works out in the gym each morning before work; he's on his bike at the weekend. Every inch of him is disciplined and he's handsome in a sporty, fit kind of way. He dresses conservatively, his hair is cut short, his tie is always straight. He wants no nonsense, no fuss; everything in his life needs to be kept simple and controlled. I place the millionaire's shortbread in front of him, along with his black coffee. 'Thanks,' he murmurs, still tapping on his BlackBerry.

'What's this all about, Jan?' he asks after he's fired off a message. He tucks into his biscuit.

I twist the packet of sugar in my fingers, unsure how to begin. 'It's about Isla,' I say, my stomach clenched with nerves. I can see the letter from the hospital, sent to me a week ago. 'Thank you for sending Isla's video tape and medical information . . . We feel she is an excellent candidate . . .'

I didn't scream or shout, or wave the letter in the air. My feelings were mixed. Part of me had wanted them to turn us down; then I wouldn't have a choice, I wouldn't be able to roll the dice and play with Isla's life. We could muddle on. We'd established a good routine. Yet when I read, 'If she has this surgery we expect that her sitting, standing, walking and level of comfort will improve,' I was in the other camp, the other part of me happy, clinging on to the only piece of hope we'd had since the diagnosis.

'What about Isla?' Lucas prompts me.

'I want to take her to America.'

'Right. For a holiday?'

'Not exactly. I've researched a treatment that might help her walking.' I tell him that Lizzie and I had filmed Isla in her swimming costume sitting on a stool, kneeling down and walking on her frame, all the movements the doctor needed to see to determine if she qualified for the treatment. 'Isla didn't know what was going on. We played music, anything to try and make her relax, poor thing she was shivering in her costume, you know how freezing cold she gets.'

'Jan, I can't be too long.'

'Well, as I was saying I've researched this treatment in America, and she's been accepted. But it's expensive.'

'Right.'

I give him the figure.

He doesn't blink.

Ask him.

'What do you get for that?'

After briefly explaining the procedure he remains quiet. Just for once I wish he'd say something.

I clear my throat. 'So I was wondering . . .'

He knows what I'm wondering, but still he doesn't make it easy.

'I, er, well, I wondered if you could lend me the money?' I daren't look at his face or wait for an answer. 'Granny is going to come with me and—'

'Of course she is.'

I can't help noticing the sting in his voice. I look up. 'I'm sorry?'

'It's always about you, isn't it, Jan?'

Confused, I say, 'Sorry, what do you mean?'

'You have no idea, do you? Why did we move to Cornwall? Because of you, Jan. I once overheard our grandparents say that if you couldn't settle at school, if you were bullied again, we'd move. It didn't matter what I wanted, did it?'

'Lucas, that's not true, they always thought about us!'

He shakes his head, his skin reddening. 'No, Jan, not once did they think how I might be missing my friends in London. They never asked if I was happy at school or—'

'But you were fine, weren't you?'

'I had to be. Had no choice. It didn't matter anyway, as long as *you* were all right. I remember Granny saying all the time how much you looked like your mother, it's not difficult to see why you were the favourite.'

'I wasn't the favourite,' I say, uncomfortably. 'I'm not . . .'

'Don't pretend, Jan. You're the daughter she lost. She can't help loving you more.'

'But Lucas, she loves you, of course she—'

'And then you get into this mess with Dan and it's all about you again, isn't it?'

'Do you think I want all of this?' I raise my voice for the first time.

'All they can talk about is January this, January that. I get the same old pep talk, "We have to support you." They have no idea who I am or what I need.'

'Because you don't let them in. You're so closed off from us.'

'And then with Isla.'

'You think I want Isla to have to go through this? You think I love all this drama, because let me tell you—'

'Just ask Lucas for the cash,' he cuts me off. 'I bet that's what you and Granny said. He won't mind. He earns enough.'

I reach for his hand, but he pulls his away. 'Lucas, that's not what I thought and it's far from easy asking you. I wish I didn't have to, but I'd pay you back, every single penny.'

'The answer's no,' he says, standing up, grabbing his jacket and walking away. 'The three of you can sort it out on your own, just like you always do.'

'Lucas, wait!'

He turns, comes back to our table. 'I've never felt part of our family.' I am shocked to see tears in his eyes. 'I've always been second best to them and I won't have it. I won't have it anymore.'

He slams the door of the cafe, walks away without as much as a glance over his shoulder.

Alone, I dry my eyes with the napkin. I realise this argument has nothing to do with the loan. I had no idea his jealousy was this deep-rooted, that he had harboured such resentment against us all for so many years. I kept on hoping that one day we would become friends. I didn't want to believe that I had lost my brother a long time ago.

Later that day, when I call Granny to let her know how my meeting went with Lucas, she is furious. 'I'll ring him! Didn't you say we'd pay him back, how can he—?'

'Granny, don't! Leave him be. I'll think of something else, another way to get Isla to America.'

'But you shouldn't have to! Sometimes I wonder if that boy has any feelings.'

I see the tears in Lucas's eyes and hear the anger in his voice. 'He does,' I say quietly. I can't bring myself to tell her what else he had said. It would upset her too much. 'Please, Granny, let me work this out. Don't blame him.'

When the telephone rings only minutes later, 'Granny,' I say, picking up, 'this is my problem, it's not fair to expect Lucas to—'

'Jan, it's me.'

My heart beats fast. 'Lucas . . .'

'I'm sorry.'

'No, I'm sorry. It was a huge amount to ask of you. I'll remortgage the house or I'll sell, or I'll get a loan from my bank.'

'If this is going to fix the problem . . .'

'It won't fix it but . . .'

'But it could help her to walk better?'

'Yes.'

'I can lend you the money.'

'Lucas, you don't have to,' I say, a lump in my throat.

'I hope the operation works, Jan.'

'I don't know what to say. You don't understand what this means.'

'I think I do.'

'About the other things you said,' I broach tentatively.

'Please don't tell Granny. I was angry and it was unkind, unfair.'

'I won't, but Lucas, she'd understand. I completely understand. I feel terrible.'

'When do you need the money by?' he asks, clearly not wanting to talk about it.

'I want to take her to the States late December.' That's in three months' time. 'Lucas, I had no idea you felt . . .'

'Please forget what I said.'

'I can't.'

'I was tired, I didn't mean half of it.'

I know he's pretending. The truth is, it was easier for my grandparents to love me because I needed them. Yet Lucas, in a different way, needed them too. 'But I feel guilty, bad that—'

'Jan, enough. I'm glad I can help.' He pauses. 'Mum and Dad would have wanted me to help you too.'

There's another long silence. I'm fighting hard not to

cry. There are so many things I want to say to him, if only there wasn't such a barrier between us.

'It's a brave decision,' he says finally. 'I admire you for bringing her up on your own. I know I couldn't do it.'

I take a deep breath. 'Thanks Lucas, that means a lot.'

'You've always had courage, J, much more than me.'

'Lucas, I can't thank you enough, I—'

'I'll sort out the cash this week,' he says before I hear the click of the receiver.

Isla, Granny and I are due to fly to Chicago tomorrow morning, before we transfer on to a flight for St Louis. I have told Isla that we are going on a Christmas holiday but we will see a doctor too, who might help fix her wobbly legs. Rosie had advised me not to tell her too much too soon. 'One day at a time,' is our motto. Granny is arriving later on today. She has been ringing regularly, often to discuss the clothes she's packing. I can imagine she's had her suitcase, passport, dollars and clothes laid out in one of the spare rooms for days, weeks even. 'I'm taking my winter coat, I should think it will be nippy although they always keep hospitals beautifully warm.' I think both of us are excited, but at the same time, completely and utterly terrified. It's as if we have been pushed, blindfolded, on to a diving board, and when we jump in, we have no idea how deep the water is.

Isla and I are on the tube late that afternoon, coming home from Covent Garden after doing some last-minute shopping. I bought a couple of paperbacks for the journey, along with Christmas presents: a reindeer jumper for Isla, fleece pyjamas, slippers and hair accessories. It's odd to think we'll be four thousand miles away from home on Christmas day, eating lunch in a hotel. The operation will be behind us.

I try to put the surgery out of my mind, instead thinking about Lucas again. 'Oh he cares all right, Jan,' Granny had said, changing her tune when I'd called to tell her the news. She was proud that he'd changed his mind, adding that sometimes it takes time to think things through. 'He's got many demons, that boy, but deep down he's a good man.' At Earls Court the doors slide open and hurriedly I reverse the buggy out of the carriage, a passenger taking pity and helping me with my bags and Isla's walking frame. As we make our way towards the escalators that lead us to the District Line I'm wondering why I thought this was such a good idea. Tubes are a nightmare at the best of times.

Somehow, with the help of another Good Samaritan passenger, we manage to get ourselves and all our clobber on to the escalators. I watch people travelling down; a couple kiss passionately. I have no desire to be with anyone right now. Most of the time I'm too bloody tired for sex.

Suddenly, I see him.

He's dressed in a suit. Has he seen me? He's with another man. He turns, his eyes following mine. I stop breathing. I feel as if the entire escalator has come to a grinding halt and we are the only two remaining on it. I turn away, catching my breath, panic racing through my chest. What do I do? Do I pretend I didn't see him? Shall I turn round and find him? I glance over my shoulder. He's still there, looking up at me.

'Mummy!' Isla says as we reach the top. I step off just in time and retrieve the frame from the kind man in front of us, still in a daze.

I don't know how many seconds or minutes go by. It was him. It was Dan. Did he see Isla? Should I try to find him?

'It *is* you,' he says walking through the throng and pulling me to one side. 'I knew it was you.'

The sound of his voice sends shivers down my spine. My past is standing right in front of me.

Dan looks at me and then down to Isla's buggy, colour visibly draining from his skin. 'How are you?' he asks.

'Fine.' Long pause. 'You?'

'Good. Hello,' he says to Isla. 'How old is she?' Dan stares at me now.

'Three.'

Deal with it. I'm sorry. I can't do this. I'm not ready.

Determined to get away, 'We need to . . .'

'When's her birthday?'

I'm twenty-two. Nappies, mortgages, trips to the park, that's a long way off.

I walk on, my hands trembling.

'She's mine, isn't she?'

In that second I have the choice to carry on and don't

look back, or turn round. I'm scared of what I'll do and of how much I want to punish him.

I'll look into costs. I could take out a loan . . .

I carry on, weaving myself through the crowds. I can't look back. Soon I'm standing on the platform, the train to Ealing Broadway will arrive in three minutes. It's the longest three minutes ever. Come on. Come on.

I feel someone gripping my arm. It hurts.

'Dan, let go of me.'

'You didn't tell me!'

Rage now courses through my veins. 'You disappeared! You made your views very clear.'

Dan repeats, as if in shock, 'You didn't tell me. You should have told me.'

'How exactly? I tried to track you down.'

'Well you didn't try hard enough! We have a child!'

I back away from him, aware people on the platform are staring, but I don't care anymore. 'What would you have done? Changed your plans and become the doting father?'

'I thought you'd dealt with it,' he murmurs.

'That's what you wanted me to do. Where did you go?'

'New York,' he says, his skin reddening. 'I won a place on this journalism course. I've just got back.' He stops.

'You were going to tell me that night, weren't you?'

'I was going to ask you to come with me.'

'But then I broke the news and ruined it all.'

He glances at Isla. 'I'm sorry.'

'You're sorry! One *fucking* lousy sorry? Actually, I didn't ruin it, because you went anyway. You made your choice and just hoped I wouldn't go ahead so you wouldn't feel guilty.'

When the train approaches Dan stands in front of me, helpless. To think I have imagined this moment so many times; how I have longed to make him pay for his weakness.

'Choosing to keep Isla was one of the hardest decisions I've ever made, but I had her. The only thing I regret is I had her with you.'

'Mummy?' Isla is trying to turn to me. 'Who?' She's pointing to Dan. 'Funny man.'

He runs a hand through his hair, despair in his eyes. 'January, whatever has happened between us – no, don't get on – wait,' he urges, pulling me back. 'Can we talk, can we . . . I was young, I didn't deal with it well, but I am her father.'

'A father who wasn't there at her birth, who didn't see her first smile or watch as she struggled to walk,' I say registering him looking at Isla's walker frame. 'A father who was living it up in New York on the day I was told Isla had cerebral palsy! I tried to track you down many times, I thought her father should know.'

Dan looks at Isla and back to me. 'She has cerebral—'

'You're nothing but a selfish bastard, Dan. Isla doesn't

need you and nor do I.' Desperate and fighting for breath, I watch the Ealing Broadway train leave.

'Mummy,' Isla says, clearly picking up on my anxiety.

'I can't believe this,' Dan is saying, looking as if he's been punched in the stomach. 'I can't believe it.'

'Well believe it and then go back to your old life.'

'Can't we meet up, talk about this when we're alone?' Dan says quietly, gesturing to Isla. 'How about tomorrow?'

I shake my head, determined to get on to the next train.

'The day after tomorrow?'

'No.'

'January, please, you owe me— '

Anger flares in my chest again. 'I owe you nothing.'

'Nothing,' Isla repeats.

'This weekend?'

When I shake my head Dan turns away, exasperated.

'We're going to America,' I tell him, his back still facing me.

'Holiday,' Isla says. 'A doctor fix my legs.'

Dan turns round, looks at me with concern. 'How long for?'

'Chrissmass!' says Isla.

'Can I have your number?' He feels in his pocket, produces a business card. He hands me a pen, glances down at Isla again. She looks up at him curiously, kicking her legs. I clock him noticing her trainer-type boots, big enough to allow room for her splints.

He kneels down and smiles as he says, 'Hello, Isla, what a pretty name.'

I turn away, unable to watch. I grip the pen. Do I make up a number?

Later that day, before I've barely arrived home and put the kettle on, my mobile rings.

'What's this about America?' says Dan.

I fill him in on the whole story. In a way I want him to know what has happened; I long for him to understand what we have been through, what Isla, his daughter, struggles with day after day. I tell him we'll be on the BA6945 flight to Chicago tomorrow morning. I give him every single detail of our lives, making sure he understands the risk involved, making sure he realises that he has no part in this. Dan doesn't interrupt me once. As I'm about to hang up he says, 'I'm coming,' and before I can protest, 'You can't stop me.'

I glance through the kitchen door, towards Isla. 'You're a stranger to her.'

'Say I'm an old friend.'

'No. Dan you can't just—'

'This is a massive deal. She might never walk again, she's my child.'

'A child you never wanted.'

The doorbell rings, making me jolt. 'Granny!' says Isla.

I hang up. When my mobile rings again I reject his call.

Shaken, I let her in. Granny opens her arms. 'Hello!' She stops when she sees my face. 'What's wrong?' In the midst of all this, there was one person I forgot. 'January?' She pushes her cases inside, grabs my hand. 'What's happened?'

'He won't come,' Granny whispers after I have recounted our meeting. 'He'll let you down.' I can hear the tremor in her voice, the fear that she is trying to hide. 'I don't want that man anywhere near us,' she blurts out now, unable to suppress her feelings. 'He *can't* come.'

The following day, as Granny and I are about to hand our passports over to security one final time before boarding the plane, I feel a mixture of enormous relief but also acute disappointment that Granny is right. What was I thinking believing him?

'Thank you,' the attendant says, ushering us through alongside all the other families with children.

Granny, Isla and I enter the plane and locate our seats. I help Granny put her bags in the overhead lockers. She wants to keep hold of the paper to do the crossword. Isla wants to keep her special pink heart fleece cushion that travels everywhere she goes.

He hasn't come. He's woken up and decided to keep his life simple. People don't change.

A stream of passengers boards now. Granny unwraps a packet of mints, offers one to me.

I settle back into my seat and close my eyes, exhausted

from lack of sleep. I try to catch one minute of rest before Isla demands something.

'Funny man, ha ha,' she says.

Immediately I open my eyes. Granny has never met him, but she knows, just from the way he is walking towards us, that it's him. I catch the daggers look in her eye.

I didn't think anything could scare me more than Isla's operation, but the thought of Dan coming back into my life comes close.

21

2014

It's mid-September and as the tube rattles to Green Park I think about the past couple of months. Sherwoods was quiet over the summer. The property world always goes to sleep during August. However, in early July we did have the excitement of a bidding war with Sittingbourne Park. Graham, Nadine and I were on tenterhooks as Ward and Lucie reported back after their telephone conversations with each bidder. It was like watching the Grand National, not knowing who was going to fall or cross the line first.

We exchanged on Toad Hall. Mr Callaghan, despite his grumbles, was secretly delighted and sent us a thank-you gnome. 'You keep it,' Graham had insisted to Lucie.

'Oh no, I'd hate to deprive you,' she'd replied, thrusting it back into his hands. In the end Nadine took it for her garden.

We also exchanged on Mrs Roberts' house. She sent me a

kind thank-you letter, saying how I had made her see sense about letting go of the past. I wish I could be such a wise counsel to my own life.

The atmosphere in our office has definitely improved. It's a mixture of winning more pitches and settling in with Ward, who has been at Sherwoods for almost six months now. Nadine and Ward get on particularly well especially since I advised her not to be scared of him. As for Ward and me, after our Thai takeaway that Friday evening we have become friends. He'd listened intently to me talking about Dan, had held his breath when I'd described the escalator moment. 'He's lucky you gave him a second chance,' he said. 'If someone wrongs me, that's it.'

I tried to encourage him to stick to his side of the bargain and open up more about his own life and his attitude towards Spencer, but he'd simply reinforced that he and Spencer had had a major falling-out over a work issue. But Jeremy has sown a seed. He's party to the secret troubling Ward, and I don't understand why I care so much to find out.

In a way I'm relieved Ward is aware of Isla. Often he asks after her, which is touching. She's started secondary school in Brook Green, and last week he'd wanted to know how her first day had gone. Her uniform is a black knee-length skirt and a yellow jumper with a yellow-and-red striped tie. We laugh each morning, putting her tie on. Her coordination isn't the best, her tie always looking tipsy. 'It's had a late night out,' I suggest.

The tube stops at Hyde Park Corner, only one stop to go. My mind drifts back to Ward. Since our Thai, we haven't had much of a chance to chat again, mainly because of the summer holidays. I took two weeks off and Isla and I visited Lizzie in Greece during August. I met Lizzie's new boyfriend, Dave, and liked him instantly. He's kind, fun, loved fooling around with Isla in the sea, but most of all he is besotted with Lizzie, and who can blame him for that? Ward was in Portugal for a fortnight in July. He'd called the office most days, Nadine getting huffy. 'Stop calling us and spend time with your wife.'

I have also kept my distance. He's married and I don't want to blur the lines or become too attached. Who knows how I feel, deep down, for him, but if I'm honest with myself I missed work while I was in Greece, and I wasn't thinking about brochures. On my last night in Greece, I kissed a Greek god, letting my inhibitions go since I knew I was flying home the next day. I can't even remember his name; just recall his touch. I enjoyed every single moment dancing with him; I haven't laughed so much on a holiday in years. Yet I am aware Ward crept into my thoughts. He shouldn't have done, but he did.

Graham coughs as he takes a seat at the boardroom table. Lucie and I stare at him, waiting.

'Air pollution,' he says finally.

Ward taps some keys on his laptop. 'Let's crack on. Looks

like we're on track to sell Broadhurst. Graham?' Despite Spencer possibly seeing Graham's letter to the divorcing couple, with his valuation of the property, thankfully they have decided to go with us.

'Under offer.'

We all wait for a comment about the owner's scones, but nothing. 'Great. Keep me posted,' Ward says. 'Sutton Park House?'

'Under offer,' Graham says again.

'Survey?'

'Today.'

We wait, hopefully, for a guess from Graham on what might go wrong in the survey.

Ward scrolls down the list of properties. 'Uley Manor, Gloucestershire?'

'Twelve thirty,' I tell him.

'And you're coming with me, January.'

I sit up. 'What? I am?'

'About time you came on a pitch.'

'But I've got so much to do.' I'm sensing Lucie's surprise too. Not once did Jeremy take me on a pitch.

'Everyone needs to get out of the office,' Ward says.

'Can I come?' Nadine totters in with a tray of coffee and biscuits. 'I'll get me coat.'

'Yes! Nadine can go,' I suggest.

'I want you to see some of these houses for yourself, January, not just the brochure.'

As coffees are being passed round, all I can think about is the two and a half hour drive with Ward. In fact I'll be spending five hours in his car. What are we going to talk about?

'The Farmhouse,' Ward continues. This is the pitch we lost to Spencer, who'd bumped up his valuation after seeing our letter. Ward looks as if he has won the lottery when he says, 'B & G can't sell it.'

'Ha ha,' I say, sounding like Isla, though my mind is still on that car journey.

'Ha ha,' Ward agrees. 'Flowers paid off as they want us back on board.'

I make a note to call the photographer.

'The convent hasn't sold either.' He looks at Graham. 'Sister Mary's prayers aren't working,' he suggests with a hint of a smile.

At the end of the meeting he wraps it up with, 'Keep up the good work. We've got a lot of properties coming up over the next few months, we're beginning to get just as many if not more than B & G.'

'And let's face it,' says Graham, grabbing the last biscuit off the plate, 'that's all that counts.'

'Mint?' Ward offers me a silver tin.

'Thanks.'

He taps the postcode into his satnav. 'Are you cold?'

'I'm fine.'

'How about your seat warmed up?'

'I'm . . . Oh, go on then.'

Ward presses another switch. 'Music? Radio?'

'Either, I don't mind.' Are we *ever* going to get going?

'I prefer Radio 4 these days, shows my age.' Finally he pulls out of the parking slot.

It's *Woman's Hour*. They're talking about the history of the vagina. I want to die. I want to *die*. I turn round to check on Spud, perched on the back seat. 'Hello, Spudster,' I say, catching the words 'cervical mucus'. Oh lord, it's almost as bad as watching a sex scene on television with Granddad.

Ward switches it off as quickly as he switched it on. 'Can maybe do without that.'

'Maybe.' I laugh nervously.

He settles for Radio 2.

'You must feel like you live in a car,' I say, already wishing I were back in the office with my faithful old box of brochures and my comforting list of things I have to do, ticking them off as the day goes by.

We hit the M4, neither of us having spoken much, except the odd comment on the weather and Ward taking a couple of telephone calls from the office. My bottom feels like toast now.

'So,' we both say at the same time, almost as if we've been aware of the long silence between us.

'You go,' we both say.

I clear my throat. 'I was just going to say Graham is quieter than usual.'

'I've noticed.'

Another awkward silence. 'So, what's your tip for the perfect pitch?' Anything to get a conversation going.

'Be on time. If you're over fifteen minutes late I reckon you've lost the pitch before it's even begun. Other than that, keep it simple. Let them show off the house. Make all the right noises when they show you a bedroom with purple woodchip paper. Love the chintz and the pink jacuzzi.' He smiles. 'Actually if I can't fall in love with a house just a little bit, I can't take it on.'

'Even if that means giving it to Spencer?'

He glances at me, knowing I'm still digging for the truth. 'January? Can I ask you something?'

'Depends what.'

'Has anything ever happened between you two?'

'You can't ask me that. No,' I add, lightly crossing my fingers. 'Why?'

'Well, I don't think he pops round to see Graham, do you?'

'He likes Spud.'

He raises an eyebrow. 'He likes beautiful women.'

I turn away, unsure how to react to his compliment, knowing I liked it a little too much.

After stopping for a coffee and Danish pastry at a service station, and Spud has had a couple of pees, I feel more comfortable, especially since we're closer to Uley. We're now heading through Tetbury, a small market town in the Cotswolds, the street lined with antique shops. I'm looking forward to seeing the house now and watching Ward in action. My list of things to do seems a world away.

'Most memorable pitch?' I ask Ward.

He taps the steering wheel. 'There was one time when I drove away with Felix the cat. Almost got home before I saw him sprawled on my back seat.'

'Oh shit. What did you do?'

'What do you think I did?' There's something flirtatious in his tone.

'You turned round.'

'Chucked him in the hedge.'

'You didn't!' I hit him on the arm.

Spud barks in agreement.

'If I'd only been a mile or so away, then maybe, but I was longing to get home, put my feet up, pour myself a large drink.'

'Ward, please tell me you didn't chuck Felix in a hedge.'

He hits me back, saying 'I can't believe you asked.' His hand rests on my arm a moment too long and I feel a shot of energy or electricity, something I haven't experienced for a long time, race through me.

To try and distract myself from his closeness, I tell Ward about some of the pitches Jeremy went on, including the one where he was shooed off the property, mistaken for being drunk. Ward finds this insanely funny. 'I do remember one time feeling badly hungover and the owner insisting he take me out for a spin around their estate. Driving over their bumpy fields.' He pulls a queasy face.

'Jeremy once had to buy some mousetraps for a client who was away.'

'You get some weird requests.'

'You get some weird people.'

'I once walked in on two people in bed and they weren't sleeping.'

'A vibrator in the airing cupboard, the most enormous you have *ever* seen, according to Graham.'

'Who never exaggerates,' says Ward.

'Never.'

Ward takes a sharp turn to the right, down a narrow road with fields on both sides. We head down a steeper hill, the road twisting and turning. The satnav tells us to turn at the T-junction into Uley. There's a church on the left, a pub on the right. Two horses trot in front of us, so we make slow progress up the hill before seeing a handsome Georgian house on the edge of the village. Ward and I guess it was built around 1780, Cotswold stone, with a pale-green door and pillars on either side. We fork right and drive through a gate, parking in front of the house. A balustrade and stone steps lead down into their back garden with its sweeping lawn and small pond. 'This looks great,' says Ward.

A man with snow-white hair, wearing a tweed cap,

cords and boots comes out of the front door with a sandy-coloured greyhound. Ward introduces us. 'Call me Thomas,' he says when I shake his hand. I ask if I can let my dog out into their garden. Ward had explained earlier this morning that he'd be bringing along his assistant, but could he also bring Spud? That had been my condition; I'll come if Spud can come too. 'Of course, Willow is very friendly,' Thomas says, gesturing to his dog.

'Are you sure Spud won't get eaten by that thing?' Ward mutters to me.

'It's more likely the other way round,' I say, as Spud jumps out of the car and hurtles towards Willow as if to say I might be small but don't mess with me. Thomas takes us inside while the dogs play in the garden.

'Well, this is the kitchen,' he says, and I catch Ward's eye.

'No shit, Sherlock,' he mouths.

The kitchen is a cosy cluttered room, cactus plants and flowers on the windowledge, an old black cooker and shelf of spices next to it holding some eighty bottles.

'Dread to think how old those herbs are,' Thomas says, noticing me looking at them. 'Probably as ancient as me.'

I laugh, asking if he enjoys cooking.

'I'm exceptional at taking things out of a packet,' he says.

Thomas's wife arrives minutes later. She's learning to play the piano and has just had a lesson. Her name is Penny. She's medium height, with layered, soft chestnut hair, olive skin and brown eyes. She shakes hands with

Ward, who mentions that his mother has also taken up the piano.

'Oh, how exciting. What grade is she on?'

'Five.'

'Is that true?' I whisper as we begin the grand tour.

'Shush. Grade One,' he says.

Uley Manor is like a rabbit warren, each room full of character. Paintings line the walls and I am fascinated by the many sculptures in each room; a pair of horses with their jockeys, a cobra, a dog, a camel, a rhino, a fish jumping out of a river, a pair of lovers. The movement and expression in each piece is breathtaking. When Ward and I discover Thomas did them, we lavish praise on him.

Upstairs in the sitting room are photographs of their children. When Ward asks why they want to move, they explain that they want to be closer to their two children who live in London, and besides, the house and garden are too big for them now. 'But I will miss it here,' confides Penny. 'When we first visited this house fifteen years ago I knew it was perfect for us. I'd stopped in this room, right here,' she says, standing by the window with a view out to an apple orchard. She goes on to describe the village. 'There's a gardening club, painting groups, I joined a society that knits clothes for African babies and blankets for refugees.'

Penny shows Ward a black-and-white picture of the two of them on their wedding day. She is beautiful and he looks so happy. Next to this photograph is a recent picture of them arm-in-arm. 'Don't know who leans on who now.' Penny laughs.

'I'm in awe,' Ward says.

'Are you married?' she asks him.

He nods, before moving swiftly on.

We take a look around the bedrooms, making all the right encouraging noises, until finally we are in a nursery on the top floor, a couple of checked blankets hanging over a cot. 'My son has just had a little girl,' says Penny.

I notice Ward staring out of the window. 'I have a little girl,' I tell her, making up for his silence. 'Well, she's not so little now. Eleven.'

'Oh, a lovely age.'

'Yes,' I agree, waiting for Ward to say something, but he seems lost in his own world. I touch his arm lightly.

He turns. 'I've got a fair picture now, so may we take a quick look around the grounds?'

Penny and Thomas take Ward and me into the garden. Willow sprints across the lawn like an athlete; Spud waddles in his middle age. They tell us about the wonderful walks in this area. Often they take Willow up on the Bury, an Iron Age hill fort. I talk to Penny about the flowers, admiring her cosmos, roses and mauve tree hydrangeas. She seems impressed, so I describe my grandmother's garden in Cornwall. When we reach the bottom, we turn left by the small pond down a narrow path that leads us into another open space with exotic-looking trees. 'Come and meet our funny boys in the orchard,' says Penny. In front of us, behind a gated field, is a group of alpacas, all different colours. In a frenzy of excitement Spud tries to squeeze underneath the gate, unsure what these peculiar camel-like creatures are. Penny assures me Spud will be fine, the alpacas only hate black dogs. Ward and I lean against the gate, our legs touching and neither of us edges away. 'Do they have a pecking order?' I ask Penny, watching Thomas feeding them.

'Oh yes, Big Brown is the boss.' She points to the caramel-coloured one.

'And if you're the boss what does that entitle you to?' asks Ward, nudging me. We're still standing unnecessarily close. Being so close to him reminds me of how I used to feel with Dan. Only this time I know it's dangerous. I edge away.

'First go at the hay for starters,' she replies, as we watch Big Brown chewing and munching from a bale.

'Remember that, Wild. I get first go at the choccy bics.' He touches my arm again, and I'm ashamed to say I like it, whatever 'it' is.

When Penny is out of earshot, helping Thomas feed the others, Ward leans against the gate. 'Quickly,' he murmurs, his face so close to mine that for a brief insane second I wonder what it would be like to kiss him. 'How much did that place round the corner go for?'

I whisper the figure before forcing myself to walk away, aware that Ward is watching me.

On the way home I decide to keep the conversation strictly to work. 'They seemed happy with the price, didn't they? I reckon that went pretty well. Thanks for bringing me. You were right, you know, it was good to get out of the office, nice to have a change of—'

'Jeremy underused you,' Ward interrupts. 'You know that, don't you, Wild?'

'What's with all this *Wild*?' I ask, deflecting his compliment. 'We're not at boarding school.'

'It's shorter than January and I'm not keen on Jan.'

My mobile rings. I dig around in my handbag, alarmed when I see Ruki's name on the screen. She never rings unless there's a problem. Has she lost Isla? Isla is one person amongst nine hundred pupils. How can teachers monitor nine hundred people leaving the school grounds safely?

'Everything OK?'

'Yes, fine,' Ruki says, although she doesn't sound it.

'What's happened?'

'Isla fell.' Isla trips over all the time. 'She says she was pushed.'

'Who pushed her?'

'Gemma Sanders.'

I know Isla doesn't get on with this girl.

'Is she hurt?' I catch Ward looking at me.

'No, just a little shaky, so I wanted to warn you.'

'I understand. Tell her I'll be home as soon as I can.'

'Please don't worry. She's fine.'

After the call I tell Ward what happened, knowing Isla wouldn't lie, she wouldn't be *capable* of it. Deep down I fear this might not be the last incident with Gemma. I stare out of the window recalling my own days at school, seeing Toby Brown and his friends pinning my arms back after lessons one afternoon and taking it in turns to punch me in the stomach. 'Harder!' they'd shouted. When Granny saw the evidence of a broken rib she promised never to send me back into the clutches of this thug. 'I dread Isla being singled out,' I confess to Ward.

'Bullied?'

I nod, telling Ward briefly what had happened to me and how at secondary school Granny had advised me to not to tell anyone about my parents dying, that what they didn't know couldn't hurt me.

'Did that work?'

'For a while, but then I was stupid enough to trust Amanda Young and she told the whole school.'

'Funny how you always remember their names.'

'Amanda Young said in front of the whole class that her parents had said I must have done something wicked in a past life to end up with no mum and dad. Up until then I'd always gone down the ignore them route, but something snapped. I went up to her' – it's as if I am back in that classroom, I can see her face; Amanda had fine blonde hair and cold blue eyes – 'and slapped her across the cheek.'

I see myself in my navy uniform, shouting, 'If you ever come near me or say anything about my mum and dad again I will hit you again, do you understand?' Most of the class had gathered around Amanda, except for one girl who stood by my side: Lizzie.

'Sorry, this is really depressing. Isla isn't hurt; that's all that matters.'

Ward puts his foot down, promising he'll get me home soon. We drive some distance without talking until he breaks the silence. 'You see this scar?'

It's the scar I have noticed before, on his left hand.

I nod.

'We were in the cloakroom after games. They held me down against the bench and burnt my hand with a cigarette lighter. I screamed inside but didn't cry. My father used to say only wimps cried. He wasn't a cosy man, January. If I came second in a test he used to think nothing of giving me a beating and he'd hurt me even more if I cried, so I got used to just, well, keeping it all inside me.' He exhales deeply.

'Oh, Ward. Why did they do it to you?' He seems the most unlikely of people to be bullied, but then again, sometimes it doesn't work like that.

'They have to target someone, Jan. I was quiet, hard-working, didn't dare not to be with my dad. Remember I told you I loved National Trust houses, visiting old castles and ruins? Well, none of the other boys were into that. They wanted to smoke and kiss girls. I wanted to do that too.' He looks at me with that half smile before laughing sadly. 'I couldn't take part in as much sport as I would have liked either, which didn't help my cause. I had terrible asthma. The teacher used to make me do circuits around the sports field until I could hardly stand up straight or breathe.'

'How long did the bullying go on for?'

'Three years. I used to spend a lot of time with my grandparents in the school holidays. My father was a barrister, spent all his time in court so my mum packed me off to Devon. My granddad had this sailing chart in his shed. He used to say that there was treasure hidden under the ocean, pots of gold. He kept loads of wood in his shed too, and I used to dream of building a boat in there and sailing away. I had it all worked out. I could push the boat into a local brook and then into a stream, and out I'd go into a river, and then I'd be alone on the high seas, just me in the boat with a box of sandwiches, surviving on choppy waters, looking for that treasure.'

It's the first time Ward has truly opened up to me and I look at him, wondering what it would feel like to run my hand over his cheek or through his hair. 'So what happened? Please don't tell me those boys got away with it.'

'They did that time. My mother talked to the teachers, but it was hard telling Dad. Mum was soft, kind, she hated the way my father treated me, but she was scared of him too. She pushed Dad to wake up to what was going on, but he refused to believe it could happen to his son. A year after that incident I'd had enough. Mum told me to stand up for myself and if that meant hitting back, then fine. One decisive strike, target neutralised.' Ward smiles, but I can see the pain behind his eyes. 'If ever I had a child now . . .' He takes another deep breath, 'My advice would be to walk away at first, but if they don't leave you alone, stick on that George W. Bush hat and launch a missile.'

'But what if you can't?' I ask, thinking of how vulnerable Isla would be to the likes of Toby Brown. Tears sting my eyes. It's unthinkable and I'm thankful we're nearly home. I want to see my baby girl.

But before I know it Ward has pulled over into a layby. 'She'll be all right,' he says gently. 'Don't underestimate Isla. Like her mother, she's had many battles, but she's come through them.'

I glance down to his hand and want to touch it, stroke his painful memories away with my own.

'We need to go,' I say, but when I look up again, Ward's eyes still rest on mine and I can't turn away. Something has changed between us. I catch that look in his eye and understand he's asking me if I feel the same. With his thumb he wipes a tear from my eye. I don't move. I know I should but . . . He touches my cheek with his hand as he says, 'It's not just about physical strength. It's about strength of spirit.'

Our foreheads are now touching, his lips close to mine.

'What are we doing?' I whisper, but he doesn't answer. He kisses me and I kiss him back, a slow deep kiss, but soon his arms are around me, my shirt is coming loose, I feel his hand brush against my bare skin. I kiss him back more urgently, passionately, lost in this man; I am lost in his arms, in his touch. His telephone rings. His telephone keeps on ringing. It's getting louder. I pull away. 'Take it,' I urge him, looking out of the window. What *am* I doing?

'Hi.' Long pause. 'Marina, can we . . .'

I shudder with guilt when I hear her name.

'I'm in the car,' Ward continues, clearly desperate to finish the conversation. 'We'll talk later.' He hangs up.

I'm unable to face him.

He touches my arm. 'January, listen, I—'

I snatch my arm away. 'Drive. Ward, please drive. I need to get home.'

'Let me explain.'

'Explain what? That you're married? I gathered that.'

'I'm not happy.'

'Oh poor you! I don't know what I was thinking! What were *you* thinking, Ward?' I know, deep down, it's my fault too, and that's why I hate myself. Why do I fall for men who will only hurt me? 'We can't do this to Marina. And not only are you married, you're my boss.'

'I know, I know, but will you let me—'

'No. Drive.'

'I've been wanting to kiss you—'

'Stop.'

'Things aren't straightforward between my wife and me.'

Finally I turn to him. 'Don't you feel guilty?'

He nods. 'We shouldn't have, I *shouldn't* have kissed you but . . .'

'Just drive!' I feel so ashamed of myself. 'Or let me out, now.'

'January, please.' He reaches across, places a hand over mine to stop me from trying to unlock the door. 'I'm sorry, but—'

I withdraw my hand from his, stare out of the window again. 'Please, Ward. I need to get home.'

When I return home I find Isla curled up on the sofa. Spud jumps up and covers her with licks, making her giggle. She then wraps her arms round me and I hold her close. 'Do you want to talk to me?' I ask her softly when we pull apart. Ruki joins us from the kitchen. 'Do you want to tell Mum what happened?'

'Gemma was cross that I talked to some of her friends. She said, "You're leaving me out. If I moved school none of you would care."'

'She said that?'

Isla nods. 'We had maths last, with Miss Bunting.' Isla loves Miss Bunting. 'When the bell rang and I stood up Gemma pushed me. She pushed me and I fell, Mum, with all my books.'

'And no one saw her do it?' I stroke her hair.

Isla shakes her head. 'She waited for me, Mum. She doesn't like me. She said I'm handicapped.'

Ruki and I exchange looks, in an understanding that we feel the same way. 'When people say horrible things, Isla,' I tell her, 'it usually comes from an unhappy place. Gemma is probably unhappy so she is trying to make you feel that way too and that's wrong. Do you understand, Isla? None of this is your fault.'

After Ruki has gone, Isla and I have supper together, but I worry when she barely touches her food.

My mobile rings. Thank goodness it's Dan, not Ward. 'I was going to call you,' I say, leaving the kitchen to take the call in private. When I tell him what happened, he asks, 'What did the teacher say?'

'No one knows yet. This isn't going to end here, Dan. Gemma called her handicapped.'

Dan is quiet, but I can feel his anger down the telephone line. 'Do you know what she needs to do?' he says at last. 'Isla needs to say something really kind back, do something this girl doesn't expect, to unnerve her.'

It feels good to talk to Dan, it reminds me that I'm not alone and nor is Isla.

'I'm not sure if I should call the school, have a meeting or what?'

'Talk to Fiona.' Clocking my hesitation he adds, 'She's right here and used to dealing with this kind of stuff.'

I tell myself that I'd rather be in a dinghy with Isla heading towards an iceberg, but I don't say so.

Fiona listens carefully before advising me to write a letter to Isla's form teacher to let them know Isla's side of the story. 'Whatever you do, January, don't try and take the matter into your hands. I've seen parents challenging other parents and it can turn into a war. One more thing. It's so important that Isla tells a teacher. Zero tolerance is all well and good, but if children don't report the incident, we know where that can lead.'

I know too well. It was only when the physical evidence began to show that Granny had realised I was in serious trouble. For Toby, his bullying finally led to an official warning from the police and a period of exclusion from school. It led to our family moving to Cornwall and Lucas deeply resenting my grandparents and me for the change.

Isla and I sit huddled together in our pyjamas on the sofa watching *Mamma Mia!* I'm so relieved when I hear her laughing and singing along with Pierce Brosnan.

'Who is it, Mum?' Isla asks when my mobile rings, alerting me to a text message.

'No one, darling.'

'*I'm sorry. We need to talk. Call me. Ward.*'

Flustered, I turn my mobile off. It was a moment of

weakness and stupidity. It's a road leading to nowhere. I'm not even going to tell Lizzie about it. The office can never find out. Imagine if Jeremy knew!

As Isla and I continue to watch the movie, desperately I try to block Ward out of my mind, but soon I feel his lips on mine, the palm of his hand touching my cheek, his fingers wiping away my tears. I feel the warmth in his voice as he'd told me Isla would be all right, that it's her strength of spirit that counts. I'm ashamed by how much I'd wanted him to kiss me. Guilty, so guilty I can't tell a soul. I huddle close to Isla.

I need to switch Ward off.

'This bit's so funny, Mum.' Isla points to the screen.

Switch him off and pretend it never happened.

I can do that.

Of course I can.

How hard can it be?

That evening, when I kiss Isla goodnight, I see her certificate of bravery framed on her bedroom wall. The kind doctor in America had given it to her, after her surgery.

I think back to that time. If we can get through that, I can surely deal with one mistaken kiss and I can take on Gemma Sanders. Isla and I can get through anything, I tell myself, shutting the door behind me.

22

2006

Before the plane takes off, Granny pretends to be absorbed in the safety manual with its picture of a woman attaching an oxygen mask. I have turned all my attention to Isla.

'Who is funny man?' she asks again as I'm helping her with her seatbelt.

'Exactly,' Granny mutters, her face like a thundercloud.

My stomach is in knots. Hurry up with the drinks trolley. 'He's, he's an old family friend.'

'Right,' Granny tuts, now opening the British Airways magazine and flicking through the pages.

'Why he coming?' Isla looks at me with those large innocent eyes.

Keep your voice calm. 'Well, you know we're seeing a nice doctor.'

'Going on big holiday to fix my leggies,' she says, swinging them up and down.

'That's right. Well, Dan wants to be with us.'

'Why?'

Granny unbuckles her belt saying she needs the loo. I daren't turn around to see if she's going to talk to Dan, only six rows behind us, to ask him exactly the same question.

An hour into the flight, Granny remains quiet. I understand her disbelief and anger at Dan's intrusion. Of course she doesn't want him here; this trip, as frightening as it is, was something intimate that only the three of us were going to share. 'Granny,' I whisper.

'Um.'

'I can't believe he's here either, but whatever we feel about Dan . . .'

She stiffens at the sound of his name.

'This is about Isla.'

'I know.' She stares ahead.

Clearly Granny doesn't trust Dan or his intentions, and neither do I.

Two hours into the flight I'm still thinking about him. What was I thinking allowing him back in so easily? He doesn't deserve to be a part of his daughter's life. I think back to all those hospital appointments and scans, Dan's absence had been a thorn in my side. Looking round flats and houses, fielding awkward questions from the estate agent about my growing bump and would my partner join us to view the property? The mothers at Isla's nursery asking me what my husband did and the nurses enquiring if I had support. Getting up in the early hours of the morning to see to Isla and not being able to get back to sleep, all my fears and concerns for the future haunting me, my state of mind as black as the night sky. I know we were both young, it might not have worked out between us, but it was his inability to see it from any other side but his own.

I unbuckle my belt, unfortunately needing the loo. I glance behind me, noting there is no queue. Quickly I walk down the aisle, making sure to avoid eye contact with Dan, but my attempt to ignore him is in vain. 'Jan.' He hops up from his seat and follows me. 'Wait!' He pulls me back. 'Listen, I know you don't want me here, and nor does your grandmother.'

'Too right.'

'I don't blame you, but try to understand.'

'Dan, this isn't going to work,' I say, staring at the occupied sign on the loo door, willing whoever it is inside to hurry up.

'I'm not saying it's going to be easy, but—'

I turn to him. 'Why now? Why do you care?' The door to the loo unlocks and a young woman emerges from the cubicle. Distracted, Dan allows her past.

'Please, Jan, give me a second chance, let me get to know my daughter,' he says before I shut the door in his face.

I lean against the small basin, trying to compose myself. I can't stop Dan from being here. I know, more than anyone, how stubborn he is. Once he's made up his mind to do something, that's it. But if he thinks I'm going to let him back into our lives just like that he is truly mistaken. Dan has one marathon of a climb before Isla knows he's her father.

It's dark when we land in Missouri, but it doesn't matter since I'm in no mood to admire the view. Isla is the merriest member of our party, chuffed that the captain spoke to her before we got off the plane. Isla had graciously accepted her present, a pair of airline toy wings, as if it were quite right that she should be singled out and told she was brave. With CP comes attention, both good and bad.

Sitting in a cab, Dan is jittery, tapping his foot against the floor. I catch him gazing at Isla, absorbing her features as if taking her in for the first time. I sense he is trying to make out if he can see a tiny part of himself in her. When he looks at me, hoping maybe for a gesture of reassurance, I turn away. Granny has turned all her attention to Isla, who is pointing at the flashing lights of cars speeding past us on the highway. 'You guys come to see the Arch?' the driver asks us.

He means the Gateway Arch, the most famous monument in St Louis.

Tomorrow we'll be in the hospital, it's Isla's pre-operation day.

'It's a must-see folks!' he continues. 'You can take a ride

273

up the top, see awesome views of downtown St Louis as well as across the river to Illinois. But you need to go early, avoid the queues,' he advises, no doubt wondering why we are such a gloomy old bunch, but then again, we are British.

Finally we are in the hotel reception lobby with its marbled floor and fountain. Dan has booked himself a single room, thankfully three floors below us. 'Jan.' He pulls me aside. 'Can we talk?'

'I'm tired.'

Aware of Granny standing protectively beside me, he doesn't push. 'Sure,' he says, hands deep in his pockets. 'We could all do with a decent sleep.'

Awkwardly we wish one another good night, before agreeing to meet for breakfast at eight o'clock. 'Sharp,' Granny adds, treating him to another dagger stare.

The following morning, the mini-shuttle bus drops us off outside the main entrance of the St Louis Children's Hospital. Isla says, 'Wow,' as each of us takes in the tall building, the archway, the elephant characters outside and the garden area adorned with brightly coloured Christmas decorations. It's a relief to see Isla smile since up until now she has been unusually quiet. The hotel had a selection of bacon, eggs, pancakes and even muffins that you could make for yourself by putting the mixture into a cooking mould and setting the timer, but Isla wasn't interested. I don't think she trusts that we are going on a big holiday anymore.

Carefully I help Isla out of the bus and hand the walking frame to her.

'I can manage,' Granny says to Dan, resisting his help. Like me, he looks as if he didn't sleep at all last night. Over breakfast I saw him hiding a book in his rucksack before Granny, Isla and I had joined him, Granny ignoring his question, 'How was your night?' While he was helping himself to another cup of black coffee I took a quick look. It was called, *Everything You Need to Know about Cerebral Palsy*. There were numerous pencil marks on each page, including a lot of questions with words underlined.

It's cold, but the sun is shining. Slowly we make our way through the hospital entrance doors and into a huge reception area decorated with more tinsel and fish tanks. I catch Dan watching Isla walk; he's trying not to wince as she stumbles on, dragging her left foot behind her. I still react physically, as if someone is twisting a knife in my heart. A security guard approaches us with a beaming smile. 'Hi there, folks, where are you from?' He says we are very welcome to St Louis, before asking which floor we need. We tell him we need Floor 4, Neurosurgery. 'Hi there, sweetie,' he says to Isla as he presses a button on the lift. 'Aren't you the cutest little thing! You look just like your daddy.'

I feel sick. This is agonising.

'He's not my dada, ha ha. He's funny man!' Isla says.

Granny looks away. I turn to Dan, lost for words, hating

him for making this even more harrowing than it needed to be.

Floor 4 is another flash of colour with murals on every wall and from here we can look down to the canteen on the ground floor, a large room with glass walls and big stripy hot-air balloons coming down from the ceiling like something out of Disney. After a meeting with the rhizotomy coordinator, Jane, who takes us through all the basics of the procedure, she says that the doctor who is performing the surgery is waiting for us.

When I enter the room I like him immediately, a relief given my emotional state. He might be in his white coat but he appears at once human, kindness in his eyes as he shakes our hands and greets Isla like a friend. 'And you are?' He looks inquisitively at Dan.

'A family friend,' I announce with my best smile before anyone else can say a word.

We all sit down. I notice framed pictures of previous patients on the walls, no doubt all success stories. The doctor asks Isla if she can hold her arms up, 'Like this.' He raises his arms above his head. Isla copies him with a big smile.

'Your arms are in good shape.' He then wheels himself towards Isla on his swivel stool before testing her reflexes, tapping her knees in turn. 'She's better with her right leg.' He examines her feet. Finally he watches her walk up and down the room on her frame, and by mistake she runs over my foot, making me squeal. 'Ha ha ha,' Isla giggles, breaking the ice.

'Good. She can take a few steps,' he comments, looking from Dan to me. I sense Granny feels elbowed out of the room; she's nothing more than a spare part now that Dan, a father figure, is around. 'But we want Isla to be able to walk with a flat foot, straight knees and by herself.'

We all nod.

'As you will know from your meeting with Jane, I will be exposing the sensory nerves at the lower end of the spinal cord – the nerves that control feeling in Isla's legs.' Dan is scribbling something down in his notepad. 'Then I will separate the nerves one by one, and cut any that are hyperactive and sending the faulty signal from the brain to the spine, causing the tightness in the legs.'

While Isla is distracted with some toys, we watch this procedure briefly on film. It's almost impossible watching the doctor snip the nerves. They look like slimy white- and red-veined bands. One mistake is disastrous. When the film is over, Dan says, 'And what happens if you cut through a wrong nerve?'

'Well, there is always that risk. In any type of surgery.'

'Yes, but what happens?'

I shift in my seat. He *knows* what happens. Jane mentioned the risks to us.

'If the lower end of the spinal cord is damaged that causes paralysis,' the doctor replies.

'What are the stats?' he continues, the journalist coming out in him. 'There are no guarantees this will work, are there?'

'Let me stress, this isn't an experimental procedure. It's been around in this country for over twenty years and I've had terrific success.'

'But you still can't guarantee . . .'

'Dan!' I urge. 'Leave it.'

After our meeting I ask Granny if she can take Isla to the canteen. I beg her with my eyes to take my daughter away.

Alone with Dan he says sheepishly, 'What?' but I know he knows.

I hit him. I hit him across the cheek with all the strength I have.

Dan clutches one side of his face as I say, 'You need to respect that I have made the decision.'

'But if it goes wrong . . .'

'You have no right to question me.'

'I'm sorry, listen, I'm sorry. I just want us to be fully informed.'

'There is no "us". You can't sweep in overnight and have a say, Dan, father or not. Don't you get that? If it goes wrong I will never forgive myself, but if I do nothing, then what? I can't sit and watch my daughter, *my* daughter, struggle anymore. Nearly four years, Dan. You've known Isla for *three days*. If you can't support us, walk away now and don't come back.'

I'm glad yesterday is behind us. It was an exhausting day for my girl with all the endless physiotherapy assessments and appointments with the anaesthetist. Isla now knows something is up, that we're not exactly on a seaside holiday. She loved playing games with Molly, the hospital dog, but the moment the word 'physio' was mentioned again, she'd withdraw into herself.

It's now 7 a.m., the day of the operation. Isla is in her hospital gown. She's had her medication to make her sleepy. This is it, I think, carrying her to the doors of the operating theatre still pretending it's all one big adventure when dread clenches my stomach. Dan is by my side. I sense he wants to reach out and touch her. Granny walks a few steps behind us, carrying Isla's favourite teddy and her pink heart fleece cushion. When a woman in a blue gown approaches me, I kiss Isla again and again until reluctantly I have to let go. Dan is pushed aside as Granny holds me. Isla looks at us all with such trust in her eyes before she is taken away.

I wave, fighting with all my strength not to rush after them and snatch her back. If this does go wrong and Isla never walks again, will she hate me? She's so little. Despite all the reassurances the hospital team has given, what if Isla is the one case that goes wrong? The doctors and nurses in their coats walk past the lifts and through the double doors. When they are out of sight Granny hands me a tissue. Dan touches my arm. I pull away from him, running the opposite way down the corridor, needing to be on my own.

Twenty minutes later, I'm about to head into the small room where we are to sit and chew our nails waiting for updates. I stop outside the door when I overhear Granny and Dan talking.

'I won't disappear again,' Dan says. 'She's my daughter.'

'You never wanted this child, so what's changed?'

'I've grown up.'

'Well done you. January had to grow up years ago.'

'What I did – I was selfish back then. I wanted my career more. I'd won a place on one of the best journalism courses.'

'In New York. She told me. So off you skipped.'

'I'm – I'm not proud of myself, OK? I was scared.'

'It was always about you, wasn't it? When my daughter died my husband and I looked after Jan and her brother, Lucas. We were *terrified*, we were grieving, but we knew we had to face up to our responsibilities. I don't regret it, Dan. Being such a big part of Jan's life has been a blessing and I love my grandchildren and Isla, with all my heart. These are the things you do for love, Dan, and I'd do them all over again if I had to. You don't run and hide when the going gets tough or when things don't suit you.'

There's a long silence, then Dan eventually says, 'I'm

sorry for everything I've put you through and I understand why you hate me. I was weak.'

Granny grunts. 'Why should I believe a word you've said?'

'Last year my older brother had a cancer scare. He was lucky enough to survive but, well, it taught me something, that none of us knows what's round the corner so it shouldn't all be about work, earning cash and climbing the career ladder. It's about people. I have a daughter.' He sounds tearful now. 'When I left Jan, I made myself believe she wouldn't go through with it. I forced myself to think there was no child. But when I saw Isla's face, when she smiled at me . . . I understand why you're protective.'

'Protective? I'd *die* for that girl and for Isla. January has had enough hurt and pain in her life, enough disappointment. I swear, Dan, if you hurt her again—'

'I won't. You have my word. I'm home now. I've got interviews lined up with papers. I'll get a decent job. I want to support them. I'll pay Lucas back for helping us. I swear on my life I won't let you down again.'

There's another long silence. 'If you go back on that word I'll cut your balls off.'

I place a hand over my mouth, smiling and almost crying.

'I can see where January gets her strength from,' Dan says, for the first time a touch of humour in his voice.

After three harrowing hours Dan, Granny and I are in the recovery ward, standing by Isla's bed, a machine beeping beside her. Isla is drowsy, with various tubes attached to her and her teddy and heart cushion are by her side. It's too early to say if the operation has been a success. This may be wishful thinking, but I am sure she was moving her feet better in intensive care. For the first time since her diagnosis I feel hope that this operation might give her a better future. When Isla opens her eyes she looks at me and says, 'I'm hungry, Mummy.'

I reassure her she can have some toast and juice soon. I stroke her hair, kiss her cheek, overwhelmed with relief that it's over. Granny tells her what a brave girl she is. Dan is standing back, but looking at Isla tenderly, his eyes watering. Praying that I'm not going to regret this, I walk over to him and say, 'Do you want to . . . ?'

'Can I?'

I nod.

Tentatively he steps forward, crouches down by Isla's bedside and kisses his daughter.

23

2014

I sit at the corner table of my local pub, waiting for Lucas to arrive. As Isla is with Dan and Fiona, I'd called to see what he was up to this weekend. To my surprise he'd suggested supper on Saturday night. Since our conversation about the loan, over five years ago, when Lucas's resentment boiled to the surface, I have worked hard at our friendship. Lucas still keeps his cards close to his chest, but we are certainly more honest with one another and make more of an effort to meet regularly. I wouldn't go so far as to say he's a doting uncle, but Isla likes him and understands he played a part in helping her go to America. Lucas made me promise never to confide in our grandparents about his feelings. He accepted that they had done the best possible job in raising us, and that he hadn't been entirely fair on them, or on me. 'I know you didn't ask to be bullied or have all the stress with Isla. I'm sure if it had been the other way round, Granny would have done the same for me.' He does feel guilty that he didn't thank her enough for sacrificing her retirement. Each time I try to encourage him to make it up to Granddad, to open up more, I can only push him so far before the eyes harden and the barrier comes down. Lucas is a law unto himself. I'm not sure I'll ever be able to read him, but I am glad he is a part of my life. Our family is small. We need one another.

Lucas sends me a text, saying he's running late. As I wait, my mind drifts to Ward. I haven't been able to settle back at work since we kissed just over three weeks ago. How can I forget about it when I see him almost every day? I tap the menu against the table. I didn't choose to be attracted to Ward, but I can choose how to deal with it: avoidance. I have become an expert. If I sense Ward wants to talk I've become masterly at diverting his attempts with trips out for coffee or an urgent need to rush to the bathroom. I time my trips upstairs to place documents on his desk just as Ward heads outside to take a private call. Nadine asks me why I always seem to be in such a hurry when I fly down the stairs and race back to the safety of my desk. I don't hang around in the evenings. On the one occasion that Ward did find me on my own he'd wanted to let me know we'd won the instruction for Uley. 'Great,' I'd said, pretending I had urgent filing to attend to. I could sense him staring at me. Ward's presence is so strong; he fills a room even if he's only sitting in one corner of it.

'How's Isla?' he asked.

Briefly I told him that I'd written to the school to report the incident.

Ward approached me slowly. 'About the other day . . .'

'Great we won the pitch! I'll put a picture of Big Brown on the back of the brochure,' I said, avoiding eye contact before backing away and leaving the room.

It was one stupid kiss. The trouble is what would have happened if Marina hadn't called? What might that kiss have led to? I know we both wanted more. I have to keep on thinking of his wife and how wrong it is. When she rings the office I am overwhelmed with guilt on hearing her voice. I won't be that person who wrecks a marriage. I couldn't live with myself. But my feelings for Ward have woken me up to the fact that as much as I love Isla, something is missing. I think of Dan and how he has moved on and I want that too.

After Isla's operation trust slowly began to build between us. He reinforced the fact that he had no intention of flying home, that he was in this for the long run. Isla was more important than any job interview. Over the next four weeks she had intensive physiotherapy and we watched her gain strength and mobility day by day. We knew then that the operation had been a success. Dan and Granny began to tolerate one another too. When Isla was strong enough to leave the hospital Dan had suggested we all watch the Harlem Globe Trotters. 'What are they?' Isla had asked, screwing up her face. 'A basketball team,' he'd replied, trying not to smile. I was unsure if I wanted to go, I felt it was far too soon to play happy family, but Isla had pleaded with me to go, and after everything she had been through, how could I refuse? She had loved the atmosphere of the stadium and I had enjoyed watching Granny out of her natural environment clapping and waving her arms like a cheerleader. Dan had been right. It had helped us to relax and unwind after so much tension. On Christmas Day our motley crew opened our presents and watched a Walt Disney movie, Isla still calling Dan 'the funny man'. Granny and I had called Lucas. We'd kept in touch regularly since arriving in America and had asked if he'd wanted to join us for Christmas, an offer he declined, saying he was having a quiet one with friends. The build-up leading to Isla's operation, plus Dan's reappearance, made me even more tearful than usual as I'd said to him, 'If it weren't for you, Lucas, we might not be here.'

I'm so deep in thought that I don't notice Lucas entering the pub until he sits down opposite me. He's wearing a dark jacket with a stripy blue scarf and I catch a hint of his aftershave. 'You look as if you're trying to solve all the problems of the world, J,' he says.

'Just one,' I reply, with a sudden urge to confess everything to Lucas. I need someone to know. I'm going mad keeping this secret. Perhaps a male perspective is exactly what I need?

Lucas orders a beer, before saying, 'Shall we order? I'm starving.'

I discover Lucas went on a twelve-mile cycle ride today. His discipline puts me to shame. Spud and I only did a circuit of Ravenscourt Park, quickly followed by a croissant and coffee.

Lucas orders the fish pie. I go for a chicken salad. I scan the crowded pub to make sure I don't know anyone here.

'What's up?' Lucas looks at me curiously. 'You look like a spy.'

'I kissed Ward.'

He smiles as if I'm making it up.

'Lucas, it's not funny.'

'Right. Not what I was expecting.' He breathes deeply, as if gearing himself up for the conversation. 'So, I'm guessing you're worried because he's your boss?'

'He's married.'

'Ah. I see.'

Lucas's expression gives nothing away. It's as if I've just told him I hate carrots.

'I know I shouldn't have, but the thing is, it happened in his car, I was really upset and Ward . . .'

Lucas stops me. 'Spare me the detail, Jan, I'm not about to judge. I've slept with a married woman.'

Again he says it as if he's just told me he hates carrots. I frown. Maybe this was a bad idea. 'So that makes it OK for me, then?'

'I'm not proud of it, but I let it carry on because the arrangement suited us. Her husband was always away on business and I wasn't up for a committed relationship. No one was getting hurt.'

'Except the husband, maybe?'

'He didn't know.' Lucas shrugs as if it's no big deal.

'That's not the point! Didn't you feel guilty?'

'No. Well maybe,' he admits, 'a little.'

'When did it end?'

'The moment I realised I, well, I had feelings for her. It started off as fun, but I fell—'

'You fell in love?'

'Don't sound so shocked.'

My heart softens when Lucas shows any vulnerability. 'So you never saw her again?'

He shakes his head.

'I'm sorry, Lucas.'

'My fault.'

'So, do you want to meet someone?' I ask, hopefully. Granny and I used to talk about Lucas, Granny claiming that the right woman could be the making of him. 'She'd have to be a strong character, mind,' Granny would add, 'to put up with his moods.'

'Maybe.' He changes the subject with, 'Enough about me. Do you like this Ward?'

'I wish I didn't.'

'Don't start something you can't finish. Stay well clear.'

'I am. I'm avoiding his texts, I'm doing everything in my

power not to be on my own with him, but it's not easy, not when I'm his PA.'

'Get another job then.'

'I can't, I mean I don't want to. I enjoy my work. Anyway, why should I? I'm not the one who's married.'

'Fine. Date someone else.' Lucas makes it sound so simple.

'Got any decent men up your sleeve?'

'In fact I have. Ralph. Works with me. Good mate. I'll set you up. In fact I think you could be a pretty good match,' he decides as our food arrives, and I don't protest. Perhaps Lucas is on to something. The only way to stop thinking about Ward is to meet someone else.

The following Thursday morning Graham, Lucie and I sit in the boardroom waiting for Ward, who is surprisingly late. 'Do you think Jim might pop the question this weekend, Luce?' Graham asks. Lucie and her boyfriend are spending the weekend with her parents to celebrate their ruby wedding anniversary.

'Doubt it. He wouldn't want to overshadow them.'

'Another excuse.' Graham rolls his eyes.

'Why don't *you* ask *him*?' Nadine suggests, popping down the tray of coffee.

'I'm old-fashioned.'

'Oh bugger,' sighs Graham, 'we *so* need some romance

in this office to spice things up! How's your love life, Jan?'

'Non-existent.'

'Oh for goodness sake, what's wrong with the pair of you?'

'I'm going on a date tonight,' I reveal.

'I knew something was up! Spill.'

Lucas had kept his word and called Ralph after our supper, promising he'd make me sound irresistible. 'It's nothing major, Graham, just drinks round the corner.'

Ward enters the room. 'Our Jan's going on a hot date tonight,' he tells him. Why does Graham blurt out whatever he's thinking? Does he have no filter?

Ward doesn't react. 'Let's crack on.'

Graham nudges me. 'Come on, who's the lucky man?'

'Just this guy,' I whisper, finally catching Ward's eye before looking away.

'Mr Ivy, Oxford,' Ward says towards the end of the meeting, 'has instructed Spencer to work with us.'

A famous architect designed Mr Ivy's ultra-modern house, which has been on the market for three months now, with no bites. 'This place should be picked up and plonked in LA,' says Ward, and I know exactly what he means. The house has high security because his wife is a renowned actress, but the couple are now going through a pretty ugly and public divorce. 'Maybe another agent will take the pressure off because I've pretty much exhausted my contacts.' Ward looks exhausted himself, as he says, 'January, can you fix an appointment with Spencer for this afternoon?'

'Will do,' I keep my head down, writing overly long notes on my square Sherwoods pad.

'Uley Lodge. January?'

'Yes, um . . . fine.' The stupid kiss was almost a month ago, Jan, why can't you forget about it? I'm sure Ward has.

'What's up with you?' Graham asks after the meeting. 'You need to seriously perk up for your date, missy. Dead people are more warmed up than you.'

After lunch Nadine staggers in with a heavy box of brochures. I hop up to help her.

'Thanks, darling. Choccy bic?' she asks as I grab a pair of scissors and cut through the parcel tape.

'I'm fine.'

Graham swings round in his chair, 'Are you coming down with something, J?'

'That's your department, G.'

'At last, she smiles.' He helps me open the box. 'You would tell me if something was wrong though, wouldn't you? I'm a good listener.'

'Thanks.' Touched, I kiss his cheek. 'Honestly I'm fine.'

'Scout's honour fine?'

'Scout's honour fine.'

The buzzer rings. I glance at my watch. Spencer isn't due for another half hour.

'Come in,' Nadine says, before calling out, 'Guys! It's Marina!'

I freeze.

'This should be interesting,' says Graham, venturing out into the reception area.

'You must be Nadine. We've talked many times on the phone.' Her voice is strong and confident with a warm tone.

'Graham. We met briefly at Jeremy's party. I'm the one Ward hates.'

'Pay no attention to him, Marina,' Nadine chuckles. 'Is Ward expecting you?'

'You know what he's like, probably forgot to mention it.' She laughs. 'Can I go on up?'

I tiptoe to the edge of the door, catch a glimpse of her wearing a stylish black coat that shows off her slim waist, her natural fair hair glossy and straight, as if it's just been ironed. When Graham returns to the office I pretend to be engrossed in my brochure.

'Stunning. She could be a model,' he says.

'Really?' Acting uninterested, I turn another page.

'But she's almost *too* perfect if you know what I mean.'

I don't. If I were going to take up smoking now would be a good time, I think, heading outside with Spud for some fresh air, which wouldn't be quite so fresh if I did smoke. Oh, January, calm down and breathe.

I pace up and down the road, almost tempted to go into that expensive shoe shop, or I could nip into Jigsaw and buy something for my date tonight. Sod work. I touch my locket, thinking I may be more like my mother than I'd realised. 'Oh, Mum,' I whisper, 'I wish I'd had the chance to get to know you.'

Half an hour later I emerge from Jigsaw, clutching a brown carrier bag with an emerald-green top and a pair of skinny jeans inside, trying not to feel guilty that I have overdone it on the credit card. I stop when I see Marina walking towards me. I pretend to concentrate on the shop window. Graham is right. She is breathtakingly beautiful. She is the kind of woman who would never have to rummage in her handbag for keys or trip over in public or ladder her tights. She walks on by and I catch a wave of citrus scent. Without thinking I turn, and just as I do, she glances over her shoulder, as if aware she's being watched. She must be used to being admired. She's now heading towards me. Soon she's right by my side. 'You're January, right?' She stares into my eyes.

'Hi, Marina! How are you? Just been out shopping. Naughty of me.' Shut up, January.

'I don't know how to say this,' she says.

Don't say it then. Please don't.

She rubs her lips together. 'You spend a lot of time with my husband.'

I nod, gingerly. There is a deep sadness haunting her eyes.

I want to tell her how sorry I am, that I wasn't thinking and that the last thing in the world I want to do is come between them. I'm a nice person, honest I am.

'I'm just going to have to come out and say this.'

Please don't. It was a terrible mistake.

'Is Ward having an affair with Lucie?'

When I return to Sherwoods I sit down in a crumpled heap at my desk, hearing myself saying to Marina, 'No! Lucie? No! Why, I mean what would make you think that?'

'I know this is awkward, but I'm asking you, woman to woman,' she'd said, making me feel even worse. 'He's been working late in the office and—'

'I promise you nothing is going on. Lucie has a serious boyfriend.' I felt wretched, like I was lying to her.

She turned and walked away. I don't think she believed a word I'd just said.

I hesitate whether or not to show Ward the Uley Lodge brochure. I look at my cluttered in tray, work I don't want to do. I need to sort out Ward's pitch in Marlborough tomorrow. What time was it? I'll confirm it all later. Restless, I get up and talk to Nadine. 'Wasn't she amazing?' Nadine coos from behind her desk. 'Some people are just born in another league, aren't they, Jan? I bet their kids are going to be right old stunners,' she whispers before the telephone rings. 'Hello, Sherwoods, Nadine speaking, how can I *help* you?'

I go to sit down at my desk again and check the messages on my mobile. Oh good, there's a text message from Ralph. I'm determined to let my hair down tonight, enjoy myself and take advantage of Ruki babysitting. *'Going to have to take a rain check this eve, something at work has come up* ☹. *Can we rearrange?'*

It's late afternoon. I'm outside Ward's door, debating whether I should interrupt the meeting with Spencer. All I need to do is go over Ward's travel arrangements for tomorrow. I could leave them with Nadine . . .

'It's cutting-edge style, Ward,' I overhear Spencer say. 'I'm amazed you haven't been able to sell this pad.'

'Not everyone wants an indoor infinity pool, heated by solar panels, and a cinema room with a screen as large as a football pitch, Spencer.'

'Why the fuck not? It's state of the art. Tell you what, Jan can redo the brochure with better photos, we'll do the advertising.'

'Thanks. Give us the hard work and steal all the credit.'

'Now now, don't sulk. You'll get a little mention in the right-hand corner.'

'Tell you what, how about this?' Ward retaliates. 'We'll do the advertising and you can redo the brochure and we'll have as little to do with one another as possible.'

'Oh Ward, I thought we'd moved on. How's your home life these days?'

'Business only.'

I knock on the door and can't fail to register the ice-cold atmosphere between them. 'Let's toss for it,' suggests Spencer. 'Ah, January, just in the nick of time.'

I place some paperwork on Ward's desk. 'Details for tomorrow.'

'Ah yes,' chips in Spencer, doing his "let's read upside down" trick again, 'I'm pitching for that place in Marlborough too. May the best man win.'

'Right, I'm off.'

'Before you go, can you toss?' Ward asks me.

Spencer winks as he hands me the coin, giving it a little kiss beforehand.

'Heads or tails?'

'Heads,' Ward says.

The coin lands in my palm before I turn it over. 'Sorry, tails.'

'Well, well,' Spencer gloats, 'I win again.'

As I'm clearing my desk, Spencer joins me after his meeting, saying hello to Spud before taking a peek into my Jigsaw bag. He lifts the top out, holds it against his chest, posing.

I snatch it off him.

'Put it on,' he suggests.

'Fuck off, Spencer.'

'What is it with you and Ward? All you do is hurl insults at me.'

'Maybe you deserve them.'

'You both need a holiday.'

'Yep, away from you.'

'Harsh. I'm hurt.' He looks at the green top again. 'What's the occasion?'

'I was meant to be going on a date.'

'Meant?'

'He cancelled. He has to work.'

'That old chestnut.' He laughs. 'Sorry, you know my teasing is a sign of undying affection.'

'Whatever, Spencer,' I say, my nerves on edge.

'Well, seeing as you're not doing anything now, why don't you and me—'

'Not falling for it again.'

'You don't know what I was about to say.'

'Go out for a drink?'

'I was going to say have hot sex on the desk.' He taps it.

'Tempting, but no.'

'Oh come on, J. I've had a pig of a day and could do with a laugh and I don't see why that top should suffer by staying in the bag because some jerk stood up the most beautiful girl in town – in the country – in the world.' He grins. 'So what do you say?'

My mobile rings. It's Lucas. I hesitate. Should I screen, but he so rarely calls me. What if something's happened to him or to Granddad?

Spencer waits as I stare at my phone. 'My offer is going . . .' he backs away, 'going . . . gone.' He blows me a kiss goodbye.

'Hope tonight goes well,' Lucas says when I pick up.

'He has to work.'

'Oh. Sorry, Jan. I know he was looking forward to it.'

'These things happen.' I bite my lip. 'It's just annoying because I sorted out the babysitter and . . .'

'Well, you should still go out.'

I'm about to say it doesn't matter and that I fancy an early night but – what the hell! After we say goodbye I gather Spud's lead calling, 'Spencer! Wait!'

Spencer is ordering drinks in one of the only bars in this part of town that doesn't mind dogs. It's heaving on a Thursday night, jazz music playing in the background. Everyone appears to be in a good mood, the taste of the weekend in the air. I'm sitting at a table by the window. I've let my hair down and am wearing my new top and jeans. I changed into them quickly in the office while Spencer waited for me, asking to give him a shout if I needed a hand with any zips. 'So, Jan, what's the gossip?' he says when he joins me with a bottle of white wine, two glasses and a couple of packets of dry-roasted peanuts. 'How are you getting on with stiff old Ward?'

'Why do you ask?'

'Whoa. I was only making conversation.'

'Sorry.' Act normal. I reach down to stroke Spud, his

head warming my feet. 'It's fine.' Fine never means fine, I hear Ward saying.

'I hate to admit it, but Sherwoods is very much the topic of conversation in our boardroom these days. You're doing pretty well.'

It's true. We're currently winning about 80 per cent of our pitches.

'Jan, we're friends. Something's wrong, I can tell.'

I look at Spencer, knowing I can't confide in him about Ward. He must never find out.

'You can trust me.'

I circle the rim of my glass, almost empty now. 'I feel stuck in a rut,' is all I say.

'Don't we all.'

'Do you, Spence?'

'Sometimes. I've been doing the same old job and living in the same old flat for years. A lot of my friends are settling down now, moving out of London, having kids.'

'You don't want that?'

'With the right woman, yes.' He looks at me.

'I've been thinking about trying to find a job in publishing again.'

'Why? You're so good at what you do.' Spencer tops up my glass. I like men who notice when a glass needs refilling.

'I need a change.'

'That's all very well, but jobs are hard to come by these days. If you seriously want change, come and work for us.'

'I can't do that.'

'Why not? Get away from Ward.'

'Why do you hate each other so much?'

'He's a difficult sod.'

I think of Ward's overreaction to Spencer arriving un-announced, can still see the fury in his eyes. 'What exactly happened between you two?'

Spencer puts on a camp expression. 'We had an affair. He cheated on me.'

'Oh be serious.'

'You're thirsty tonight.' He picks up the bottle.

'I don't get out much. Tell me.'

'It's way too boring to go into,' he insists. 'The thing is, I'm willing to put it all behind us. I'm prepared to be the bigger man. Ward isn't.'

I recall Ward saying, 'When someone wrongs me that's it,' before noticing yet another woman pass our table and stare at Spencer before strutting off with a flick of her hair. He leans towards me. 'I didn't bring you out to talk about Ward. Let's change the subject to you and how hot you look in that top.'

'Spence, if you want to sleep with me . . .'

He grins suggestively, 'Again.'

'You need way more original lines than "you look hot" because that's what you say to anyone in a skirt.' The wine is slipping down nicely now.

He crosses his arms, gives me another flirtatious grin

that reminds me of when I'd first met Dan. There is a playfulness in Spencer's eyes that is undeniably attractive and I'm beginning to wonder what harm there could be just having a fling, no strings. At least I know Spencer; there wouldn't be any shy or awkward scenes in the bedroom, no stripping off in front of a stranger. And let's face it: I need some distraction.

'What I like about you, Jan, is that you challenge me. This is the first time I've managed to drag you out for a drink, just the two of us.'

'And Spud.'

Spud sits up, looks at Spencer, hoping for another peanut.

'If I'm honest, all I have to do is click.' He clicks his fingers. Spud jumps up, paws on Spencer's thigh, eyeballing the packet of peanuts.

'I'm not that well trained, Spence.'

'But with you . . .'

'So it's all about the chase. But when you get your wicked way, what happens next?'

'Well, let's see, shall we?'

I don't stop him from ordering a second bottle.

'Sometimes, Spence, just sometimes,' I hiccup, 'I think I missed out on my twenties.'

'Doing the mum thing.'

'Don't get me wrong, I gained a lot too, I wouldn't change anything, but . . .'

Spencer takes my hand. 'You feel you missed out on being young, free and single, travelling the world and following your dreams? Too much responsibility too soon, right? You know what, Jan? It's not all that it's cracked up to be. What you've got with Isla is real.'

I nod. 'I'm lucky. I know I am.' The room is beginning to spin. 'But sometimes all I want to do is get up on this table and dance.'

'Go ahead.'

I laugh. 'Or learn to fly or bungee jump off the highest cliff, sing naked in the rain.'

'I'll buy a ticket for that. Listen, J, if you want a change, a new job then cool, do it. I can ask around too, see if there's anything going at B & G.'

I can't work there, but I'm flattered. 'You'd do that, for me?' I am feeling light-headed and Spencer is becoming more and more attractive by the minute, by the second.

'I'd do anything for you.'

'No strings attached.'

'I'd prefer strings attached.'

I smile at him, lapping up the attention now. 'I've got dreams.' I lean my elbows against the table. 'Don't you? You have dreams, right?'

Spencer nods. 'My philosophy is to live each day to the full because we never know if it's our last. So here we are, J, both single – both lonely, in different ways. I'm attracted to you, I know you are to me.' Spencer takes my hand again, kisses it.

Oh, so what? Why must I always do the right thing? Although I didn't do the right thing kissing Ward, did I? I squeeze my eyes shut. Forget about him. I lean towards Spencer; he leans towards me, his lips are on mine.

'January!' The familiar voice makes me jump and pull away.

'Look who's here,' says Spencer.

I turn. Ward is approaching our table. Spud barks.

'What's going on?' Ward stares at us.

My heart sinks. How did he know where I was? Then I remember that Graham had asked me, right in front of Ward, where my date was taking me.

Spencer stares back. 'What's it to you, mate?'

'I'm not your *mate*.'

He shrugs. 'I'm with January, as you can see.'

Ward glances at the empty wine bottles. 'This is your date?' he asks me, disappointment in his tone.

'If you don't mind,' Spencer says, 'we were kind of in the middle of something, weren't we, J?'

Ward is looking at me as if I am his child who has let him down, told him I'd be home by eleven and it's now past midnight. 'I do mind,' he says. 'I mind a lot.'

'Why?' I protest. 'It's just a drink.' I'm aware we've attracted an audience, the people at the next-door table doing their best to pretend they're not eavesdropping.

'January, what are you doing?' There's that disappointment again. Who is he to judge? 'You told me nothing was going on between you.'

'Fuck off, Ward. Jan and I go back a long way, don't we?'

Ward shakes his head. 'January, tell me you're not—'

'I don't have to tell you anything. What I do, who I see, what I do.' Have I already said that? I hiccup again. 'It's *my* business.'

'Stay away from him,' Ward demands. 'You don't know what he's like.'

'Oh yes I do.' I laugh. 'I know exactly what he's like. What you see is what you get with Spencer. He's fun and charming, he's single and we're having fun, fun, OK? We're going to have sex,' I say drunkenly. 'Sex.' I shoo Ward away.

'You need a strong coffee,' Ward says when I top up my glass.

'No wonder she wants to find a new job,' mutters Spencer.

'I'm sorry?' Ward turns to Spencer.

'She's looking for a new job.'

'Is this true?' Ward asks me.

'Maybe, no . . . I don't know.'

'She might come and work for B & G.'

'I'm not! I'm not doing that, Spencer.' I shoot him a warning look.

Ward takes the bottle from my hand. 'I think you've had enough.'

'Oh fuck off, Dad.' Spencer stands up to face Ward. 'It's no wonder your wife—'

But before Spencer can finish the sentence Ward punches him, right in the jaw, to gasps from people around the bar area, including me. Spud barks again, pulling at his lead. Spencer staggers back into a table, knocking over some empty glasses, before lunging at Ward, who punches him again, this time harder, cutting his lip and drawing blood. Soon they're in a rugby tackle; they want to kill one another. They *are* going to kill one another. 'Stop it!' I screech. 'Stop it! Stop it now!'

The bar owner barges between them, says she'll call the cops if they don't take their business outside. 'And everyone, you can stop staring, fight's over,' she says, addressing the room before asking a member of staff to sweep up the broken glass.

'I'm sorry you had to see that, January,' Ward says in that calm composed way of his, while Spencer covers his bleeding mouth with his hand. 'But it felt good.'

I grab my handbag and coat. Funny how sober I feel now. All I want to do is get home and see Isla. Spencer urges me to stay. 'Don't let him ruin our night.'

'You've both done that.'

Ward picks up his briefcase and follows Spud and me. I turn on him. 'You too! Leave me alone! Both of you!'

'He slept with my wife,' Ward calls out to me.

I stop. Turn. Spencer is slumped in his chair as he says, 'It takes two to tango. Remember that.'

Ward looks at me, his eyes wounded. 'You can do so much better than him, January. Spencer doesn't care who he hurts and the last person I want him to hurt is you.'

24

The following morning I have a sore head. Serves me right. Isla is disappointed it's not raining. Not raining means double games this afternoon. 'Why do they always pick me last?' she asks, playing with her toast.

'Someone has to come last,' I say, a little too impatiently since I've heard it all before.

She drops her knife; it clatters on to the plate. 'But why me?'

'I wasn't any good at sport either. You'd be picked first if—'

'No I wouldn't! No one ever picks me first!'

'Oh Isla!' I snap, my head pounding. 'It doesn't matter!' But I know it does. Of course it does, and whatever I say isn't going to convince her otherwise.

When I drop her off at the school gates I see a couple of girls from Isla's class walking towards the front entrance, past the netball courts. I recognise Gemma with her long blonde hair scooped up in a high ponytail. She's huddled closely together with her friends, as if discussing something important. They appear much more grown-up than Isla. I can imagine they're into fashion and make-up already and it won't be long before boys aren't quite as revolting as they used to be either. Isla is eating less and less. She hasn't been herself since the incident with Gemma. She turns to me, waves. I feel guilty for being such a cow this morning. Her games bag looks heavy on her slight shoulder as she walks on. It kills me when I see Gemma and the girls laugh at her and talk in whispers.

I keep my head down in the office. Thankfully Ward is out. He has the twelve thirty pitch in Marlborough. He shouldn't be back until about three. Graham and Lucie are away, leaving me in peace. My head still feels like one giant fur ball. Going out midweek is not a good idea. At least Ward's anger and resentment makes sense now. *He slept with my wife.* Why? How long ago? And then I think of Marina demanding if Ward had slept with Lucie. She has lost a fair bit of ground playing the wounded wife. Why didn't Jeremy tell me when I'd asked him outright? Maybe he didn't know. Maybe there's something else going on with Ward too, on top of Spencer and Marina. So many questions remain unanswered . . . but to think I was going to sleep with Spencer again. Spencer is not the solution to my problems.

*

An hour later Graham and I are debating what to have for lunch. For Graham it's a toss-up between an egg- or tuna-mayo sandwich.

'Not egg,' I groan, wrinkling my nose and polishing off another bottle of water.

'I used to work with a woman who ate nothing but boiled eggs,' Graham tells me, perching himself on the corner of my desk. 'There was a rather unfortunate smell that lingered in the office.'

When I laugh it hurts my head.

'A shame you and your date didn't hit it off,' Graham says. 'Even with the beer goggles on, he was still unattractive?'

'It was a disaster.'

'I didn't expect you back so soon,' Nadine says as Ward strides past our office calling, 'January, a minute.'

I panic. What's happened?

'I'll grab us both a sarnie,' Graham says, before wishing me good luck in the lion's den.

I sit down opposite Ward. The night before hangs heavy between us. 'How did the pitch go?'

'It didn't.' He pours himself a glass of water.

'It didn't?'

'I was late, January. I was meant to be there at *ten* thirty, not twelve thirty.'

I feel sick. 'What? No, I'm sure they said—'

'They called me and asked where I was. I urged them to wait, that it was a misunderstanding.'

'So you saw the house?' I ask, praying he managed to resolve the situation despite my colossal mistake.

'Oh yes, I saw the house all right. It was pink and white, with a view to die for, an estate with two hundred acres and three large cottages. We get these kinds of houses about three times a year *if we're lucky*. The thing is, January, to say they were unimpressed is an understatement. When I left, Spencer had arrived and it's pretty obvious the owners aren't going to instruct us now, isn't it?'

'I'm so sorry.'

'It's no use saying sorry! You know how I feel about being late! It's unacceptable.'

'I know, I know.'

'You've probably lost us thousands of pounds.'

My head drops.

'We can't afford to make mistakes like this!'

I stand up, pace the room. 'What more can I say, Ward? I've messed up! I have lost the company a huge fee. My stupid mistake has cost the entire office. You should sack me.' I stand in front of him, as if it all makes sense now.

He takes off his glasses, rubs his eyes. 'I don't want to sack you.'

'If you don't sack me I'll leave.'

'And go and work for Spencer?'

'Sack me.'

There's a long silence. There's nothing I can say to put

this right so I don't say anything at all. 'We need to talk about last night,' Ward says finally, in a calmer voice.

I sit down. 'Oh Ward, if I'd known about Spencer sleeping with your wife, I wouldn't have . . . ' I stop, unsure what to say next. 'I'm not dating him, we're not together.'

'It's not about him, not really. It's about me; the way I reacted. I had no right to interfere in your evening but when I saw you with that man . . . There's more, January, more I need to tell you.'

I hear someone coming upstairs. 'Tell me then,' I urge. There's a knock. '*Tell* me.'

'J, Isla's teacher is on the line,' Nadine calls, before sticking her head round the door. 'Miss Miles?' She clocks the tense atmosphere. 'Sorry to interrupt, but she says it's urgent.'

Ward gestures to take the call in his office.

'What's happened?' I ask anxiously down the phone.

'We've had an incident with Isla. She wanted to run away from school this afternoon. You need to get here, as soon as possible.'

'Go,' Ward says when I put the telephone down. 'Isla needs you.'

Never before has a tube journey taken so long. The train, of course, has to stop at various stations, with yet another apology for the delay, due to a signal failure.

I hail a cab from Hammersmith down to Brook Green. I shove a note into the driver's hand and don't bother to wait for the change. I race across the school grounds, towards the double front doors, into a hallway, left towards the headmistress's office. A few children are walking up and down the corridors, books in their hands. I knock on Miss Miles's door, open it before she can say, 'Come in.'

'Where is she?' I ask.

Miss Miles approaches me, shakes my hand. 'Isla's fine, she's with a member of staff.' Miss Miles has short dark hair, a warm open face and a soft Scottish accent. 'I wanted to have a word with you before I call her in.'

I establish from Miss Miles that Gemma was furious that Isla had sent a text message to one of Gemma's best friends, asking her over for tea. Miss Miles shows me the message Gemma had sent back to Isla: *'Don't come near my friends or text them or else, you crippel.'*

'That's awful,' I say, my voice flaring. 'It's unkind, it's . . .'

'Miss Wild, we agree. We do not tolerate bullying or discrimination in any shape or form.'

'So what are you going to do about it?'

'I'll come on to that in a minute.' Miss Miles goes on to tell me that during netball Isla had fallen over just as she was about to attempt to shoot the ball through the net. She had tripped up over her laces. Gemma had jeered and pointed at her, encouraging the others on her team to do the same, saying, 'You see, she *is* handicapped!'

'Where was the teacher?' I demand.

'This all happened in a matter of seconds, Miss Wild.

Have no doubt, we will be informing Gemma's parents of the incident and telling them why she is getting some time in isolation.'

'Is that all? Time off lessons? Sounds like a reward.'

'She will be given a long period of isolation to think about what she has done. Our letter will be a written warning telling them that if she ever does this again, there will be severe consequences, but at this stage we want to talk to Gemma to help her to understand that what she's saying to Isla is wrong and hurtful.'

When Isla is called in to Miss Miles's office, she's tearful.

'Isla, I was telling your mother that we are taking this matter seriously because we want to ensure it doesn't happen again. Do you understand?'

Isla nods.

Everything that happened between Ward and me, my disaster of a day pales into insignificance when Isla clings on to me, a frightened girl who doesn't want to let me go. And I won't let her go. For a split second I feel close to tears, missing Granny and her support desperately, but also my mother, whose absence in my life has left me feeling never quite whole.

25

Later that night Lizzie comes over for supper. While Isla is massaging her shoulders in our kitchen, a tactic to stay up later, I am making fish pie.

As I mash the potato, I think about this afternoon. After our meeting with Miss Miles, we'd come home and made ourselves a mug of hot chocolate before watching some television snuggled up together with Spud. She seemed happier when I told her that we were going to Granddad's for the weekend. While I packed, Isla had a bath in her swimming costume. It was the first time she hadn't wanted me to see her naked. I'd imagined it was partly due to an awareness that her body is slowly changing, but I also sensed, deep down, it had something to do with games lessons and Gemma. Gently pushed, Isla confided that Gemma and her friends keep on telling her that she's flat. 'Here, Mummy,' she'd said, touching her chest. 'Like a pancake.' It had reminded me of the days when I'd stuffed socks down my cotton bra. 'You have plenty of time, Isla,' I'd assured her, wanting to throttle that girl now. 'Don't let the things Gemma says worry you. If she ever says something nasty again think of your favourite song, or your favourite place and take yourself there. But if she upsets you always, *always*, tell a teacher and me.'

I'm brought back to the moment when my oven timer rings. Isla is telling Lizzie that she has decided she wants to run a massage and hairdressing salon when she's older. 'That feels great,' Lizzie sighs with pretend pleasure. 'Now I'm sure it's Mum's turn for a back rub.'

'Can I do your hair, Lizzie?'

Before Lizzie can reply Isla is brushing her hair, Lizzie trying hard not to squeal as her head is yanked back, the brush caught on tangles.

When Lizzie's hair is plaited to death, along with a pigtail sticking out at both sides because Isla became frustrated with how long it was all taking, Lizzie looks in the mirror and turns from one side to another. 'I could go on a date with George Clooney,' she says, trying not to laugh. But it's too late. She does laugh. And so do I. And so does Isla. We can't stop laughing and after the day we've had, it's a golden moment.

Later that night, Lizzie leans against Isla's bedroom door, watching as I kneel down by her bed and stroke her hair. Isla has been tearful again, partly because she didn't want to go to bed; mainly because she feels sad and lonely because of what's happening to her at school. I don't want

Isla to dread putting on her uniform; I don't want her to fear Monday mornings just as I used to. I want her to feel happy, safe, loved.

'I am different, aren't I, Mum?' She looks at me with those large innocent blue eyes. 'I'm handicapped.'

'No, no you're not. You're Isla and if we were all the same that would be very boring. Your CP makes you the girl you are and that is a brave and kind one who makes her old mum so happy.'

Lizzie joins me. 'Godmum Lizzie thinks the same. Your legs are wobbly, Isla, that's all. My ears are far too big and flappy.' She wiggles them, but Isla still doesn't smile.

'Gemma laughs at me. She says I can't walk in a straight line.'

'Well,' I say, 'you tell her it doesn't matter because you're never going to be a tightrope artist, ha ha.'

A small smile creeps on to her face.

'You might not walk in a straight line, but in my eyes bravery counts for more.' I kiss her cheek.

Lizzie kisses her too. 'Your mum's right. You are different. I'm different too. That's what makes the world go round.'

Over supper I demand that Lizzie distracts me with her news. She fills me in on her boyfriend, Dave. She is over the moon happy; he is her soulmate. Next she tells me a decluttering story. Over the last four weeks she has visited a grossly overweight and depressed woman in her thirties.

'Her house was so bad I couldn't get through the front door,' Lizzie says, grinding pepper on to her food. 'Can't think how *she* does. Even her shower cubicle was filled with rubbish.'

'It's terrible, but in an awful way this is cheering me up,' I tell Lizzie with a dry smile.

'I know what you mean. She made my life seem so straightforward. Oh Jan, she's lost her way, like we all do. I can't begin to cure her, but we did make a start. I have never worked so hard; we cleared out her entire house. I had to battle with her to throw away an old receipt for a pint of milk, so imagine going through her wardrobe. But she did it and she's promised me she'll go and see a counsellor.'

'You know, you should become one yourself. You're so good at this stuff.'

She plays with her food. 'It's funny you say that. I've been looking into taking a degree. I might save up, take a course next autumn.'

'You should. You have a gift.'

'How are you doing? After today?'

'It hasn't been the best week.'

'Jan?' Lizzie can see right through me. Trying to hide something from her is like trying to hide an elephant in the room.

So I end up telling her everything, from the pitch, to the kiss, to bumping into Ward's wife in the street, to the punch up with Spencer, to Spencer sleeping with Marina and finally to my colossal mistake getting the time wrong for Ward's pitch.

'Crikey, you *have* been busy.'

I laugh at that. 'Everything was so simple when I worked for Jeremy.'

'Why didn't you tell me about Ward before?'

'I'm ashamed. I don't feel that proud of kissing a married man.'

'Spencer and Ward were fighting over you.' She refills our glasses.

'No they weren't.'

'Spencer is easy to work out. He's an opportunist, but why did Ward even turn up that night when he knew you were on a date? Imagine if you had been with this Ralph guy? What would Ward have done then?'

I have thought about this. 'I don't know.'

'He was jealous, J.'

'He has no right to be.' But I felt for him when I saw that hurt look in his eyes, the hurt and anger that Spencer had slept with his wife. I care. I want to make it better. I care. Oh, why do I care so much?

'Course Ward doesn't have a right to be jealous, but us humans, we don't follow the rules. I'm sure he does have feelings for you, clearly he does, but . . . Oh who am I to give advice given my affair with a married man?'

'That was years ago, and anyhow, you didn't know he was married.'

'All I'd say is be careful. The only person here that's going to get hurt is you.'

I nod. 'Thanks. Anyway, back to Dave.'

'You've fallen in love with Ward, haven't you?'

I get up to clear the plates.

'Oh, Jan.' There's a long silence. 'What are you going to do?'

It's a good question, one I have been thinking about all day, in between worrying about Isla.

I put the dishes into the sink. 'I know exactly what I have to do.' I turn to her. 'I'm handing in my notice, first thing Monday.'

26

'Whoever sees the sea first gets an ice cream,' says Granny's voice inside my head as Isla and I set off in the car to Grand-dad's. He said he'd buy some sausages and spuds and make up the twin beds. 'But you must bring some warm clothes, it's freezing, January,' he warned me. 'These days I sleep in a pair of old salopettes and a woolly hat.'

I feel better the moment we head out of London. It's a beautiful crisp autumnal morning, cold, but with the sun already shining bright and lifting our spirits. We talk only briefly about yesterday. Miss Miles had assured Isla and me that Gemma will apologise. All this emotion brings back memories of Granny. She'd always wanted to understand why a bully does what a bully does. I also think of Ward and the trouble he'd had. Was Toby Brown or the culprit at Ward's school acting out what was happening at home? Did he have attachment problems or was he just plain attention-seeking? If Gemma continues to hurt Isla, Miss Miles needs to delve deeper. An apology, a detention and time in isolation is all very well, but not if she'll only go and do it again.

The further we drive, the more relaxed Isla becomes. We talk about the enormous box of praline chocolates we have bought for Granddad, and Isla wants to make sure I packed the bottle of Reggae Reggae sauce. She likes to splash it on to her sausages. 'It tastes so nice, I had to name it twice,' she sings to Spud in a Jamaican accent, a different girl to the one yesterday just from knowing we're going to see Granddad.

Soon I'm turning on the music and we're singing along to Katy Perry and Taylor Swift. Isla tells me about a photography competition that she's going to enter at school. She has to take a series of photographs that tell a story. It's open to all the years, and the deadline is in two weeks; the winner will be announced at the end of the Christmas term.

After over four hours driving, we turn left, towards Porthpean beach.

'I can see it!' Isla calls out.

I love turning down this winding road and catching a view of the sea and the headland. In the depths of winter it is dark and desolate, no families trekking down to the beach with their toys and picnics. We're almost into November now, a time when I worry about Granddad being in a large cold house on his own. My favourite time is the spring when this road is lined with brightly coloured camellia bushes. Granny's kitchen garden is planted with asparagus, baby carrots, neat rows of lettuces, radishes and shallots. Isla toots the horn for me as we turn round another sharp, blind bend. The road gets narrower and narrower, me praying not to meet another car coming the other way. We turn left through a green wooden gate and I toot the horn again. When I see the white house, the small stone bench on the lawn and the blanket of blue sea in the distance, my heart fills with joy.

I am home.

After lunch and lucky old Granddad being treated to the Reggae Reggae sauce song many times, Granddad, Spud, Isla and I totter down to the beach to catch the last of the sunlight, wrapped in jumpers, hats and coats. Isla is determined to walk Spud on the lead. Off she stomps in her blue beret. 'Keep your feet flat on the ground,' I call out to her. 'No dragging that left foot!'

'You're so slow you two, like snails, ha ha,' she says, glancing over her shoulder before carrying on, stomp, stomp, Spud trotting by her side.

'Cheeky monkey,' Granddad says, clutching on to my arm. We don't venture down the higgledy-piggledy garden path leading from the house; instead we make our way gingerly down the steep coastal path, past the sailing club. The air smells of salt, seaweed and the sea. At the end of the path I help Granddad down on to the beach. The small hut that is a cafe during the spring and summer months is closed, but I only have to shut my eyes to see Granny buying Lucas and me each an ice cream from this hut after our long car journeys from London. 'Can I have a lick?' she'd ask, chasing us on the sand. Lucas would snatch his ice cream back, saying, 'You said a lick, Granny, not a bite!' all of us laughing.

A few boats are in the distance and the sunlight glitters on the sea. It's magical. 'It looks like there are lots of silver birds,' says Isla, taking a picture with the new digital camera Dan gave her for her birthday. We watch a young woman wearing a pink fleece walk her heavy-breathing black pug. 'He's old,' she says when Isla bends down to stroke him. 'But he still likes to come out for some fresh air.'

'Sounds rather like me,' Granddad says.

The tide is out so an elderly couple are helping one another across the rock pools, where Lucas and I used to take our nets in search of the odd crab, starfish and shrimp. I also used to collect shells, and Granddad and Granny would ooh and ah when I brought them back into the house. I smile thinking how I now ooh and ah when Isla shows me anything she's found. Granddad tells me he never tires of the beauty of this beach with its small sheltered bay and soft sand. Most days, before breakfast, he comes here for a walk and listens to the sound of the waves.

After our walk Granddad puts me to work with a list of things to do, while I insist he has a rest. I've noticed he's more doddery than usual, his walking increasingly unsteady.

Bella, his actress friend and neighbour, who often helps Granddad with any chores, has been away for a few weeks so the list has mounted up. Over the next couple of hours I am a hive of industry, sewing a button on to one of Granddad's ancient dark pink cardigans, given to him by Granny. He likes to wear it with his dapper red trousers. I sew a leather patch on to the elbow of his old tweed jacket. Granddad also shows me a section of the kitchen floor, near the sink area, where the lino is peeling away and in need of urgent sticking-down attention. We'd laughed at his broken tooth mug, Granddad wondering if I could fix it with a steady hand and a spot of superglue. Finally I'm in the old dining room, where Granny and Granddad used to serve breakfast to their B & B clients or produce fabulous suppers for their friends, especially the actors Granddad had met through the theatre. The old Belling, used for heating plates and dishes, is now rusty and home to a few cobwebs. I hop up on to a rickety chair and hook the lopsided curtain back on to its ring. The curtain, an old-fashioned chintz, weighs a ton. By the end of the afternoon I need a strong gin and tonic.

Granddad passes round the box of chocolates and we watch *Strictly Come Dancing*. 'How's work?' he asks, peering at me from behind his glasses, a question I was dreading him asking almost as much as how is my love life.

Before I have time to answer Isla gets up, saying, 'Ward's like this, OK! You ready, Grandpa?'

He nods.

She puckers her lips and points at us in turn. 'Right you guys let's crack on! We need to sell much more, much more, much MORE!' She jumps up and down, almost falling over in her excitement. 'And the best person gets a promotion.'

I find myself smiling.

'You!' She points at me again. 'What you laughing at? Are you dissin' me?' She stands, hands on hips and says, now in an American accent, 'Go sell that kitchen.'

Granddad laughs.

'And you!' Isla looks right into his face. 'I got my eye on you. You need to step up your game otherwise you're in the bin.'

'In the bin?' Granddad cowers. 'But I'm trying so hard, boss.'

'Not hard enough, old man!'

We all laugh again, the stress of the week melting away.

'And you!' She turns to me. 'You're fired!'

When Isla is in bed Granddad and I can talk properly. I fill him in on what's been happening at school. He listens patiently before reassuring me that there is nothing more I can do at this stage. The school are right to give Gemma a chance, although he understands how much I hate the thought of Isla having to see her day after day. Perhaps the problem has been caught in time. 'Children are often cruel through ignorance, just as adults can be.' I mention that

Dan and Fiona have been exceptionally supportive, Fiona explaining late last night that if the school didn't deal with it properly, my next port of call would be one of the school's governors, the police liaison officer or local authority. With any luck it won't reach that stage, but with her advice at least I feel more in control.

Granddad puts down his paper. 'When I was at school, many moons ago, there was a young boy called Ned. He was a handsome, ambitious lad, but he had a birthmark across his face that would make any boy self-conscious. But what was criminal was a teacher ridiculing him in front of the class and encouraging us children to call him names. I'm glad to say I was having none of it, January, but the weaker boys did as they were told. So often it's the cowards that bully because, well, in this case, this wretched teacher had probably failed in all other areas of his life. I was in touch with Ned recently, on Facebook. He'd seen my name, sent me a message. It was rather moving. He'd had a successful career in law – human rights. The point is, it was a deeply unpleasant phase in his life, but no doubt he'd grown from the experience, just as you did, January.'

'I'm hardly a success, not like Lucas.'

'Flying first class and making a lot of money doesn't always mean success.'

'I'm not happy at work, Granddad.' I bite my lip, trying hard not to cry. 'I'm going to hand in my notice.'

Granddad peers at me again, like a wise old owl. 'January,

I understand I'm a poor substitute for your grandmother but I'm here for you, if you want to talk.'

'Oh Granddad . . .'

'Are you having man trouble?' he asks, and for some reason it makes me smile.

'You could call it that.'

'It's not all about Spencer. It's about me,' Ward had said, *'and the way I reacted. I had no right to interfere in your evening but when I saw you with him . . . There's more, January, more I need to tell you.'*

'Put the kettle on,' Granddad suggests.

27

I type into my search engine, 'How to find a new job fast', only minutes before our boardroom meeting. Since my weekend with Granddad I have taken on board his advice not to be impulsive and hand in my notice, despite the situation with Ward. He was right. I have bills to pay and Isla to consider. 'But start looking,' he'd said. 'It's always easier finding a new job *in* employment rather than out.'

'January, no!' Graham exclaims. I hadn't even noticed he'd crept up on me. 'You can't leave us. I won't let you. You can't.'

Nadine rushes into our office. 'What's this? You're not leaving, are you, Jan?'

'Shush,' I urge them when Ward joins us with a mug of coffee, but it's too late.

'Who's leaving?' he asks, staring at me.

'Let's crack on.' Ward fires up his laptop.

As Ward goes through the list of properties I tune out,

instead thinking about Isla's week so far at school. On Monday Miss Miles had a meeting with Gemma and Isla during break time. Gemma shook hands with Isla and said she was sorry. Gemma's friends also shook Isla's hand and everyone has agreed to be kind and respect one another. Who knows if it will work? The good thing is Isla didn't need dragging out of bed and she ate her breakfast and played with Spud this morning. Ruki tells me she's been brighter, more talkative at the end of the day. The baking cases and tins have come out of the cupboard again. Yesterday I came home to the welcoming smell of warm syrup sponge.

After my weekend in Cornwall I have felt much stronger. As Granny used to say, only I can change my life. Life doesn't owe me anything; it's up to me to be happy. I have one job interview tomorrow at noon. It's at a literary agency in Soho. I've pretended to Nadine that I have a dentist appointment, trouble in the root-canal department that means a series of appointments. The role is a PA one, but I want to do more; I want to learn the business side of the job, but I'll only get there by working my way up the ladder. There will be many applicants. I touch my locket. 'Believe in yourself,' Granddad had said to me.

'January?' Ward is waiting for me to say something.

'Sorry, what was that?'

'You're coming to Cornwall with me.'

'*What?*' I'm listening now.

'I'm pitching for a place in St Mawes tomorrow, south

coast, not far from your grandparent's home. It's a fantastic location, right on the sea, close to the castle. You know the countryside.'

'I'll come,' Lucie pipes up when she sees my face. 'I know the area too, Ward.'

'Great,' I say, as if that's decided. 'Thanks, Lucie.'

Ward shakes his head. Graham and Lucie look at Ward and then at me, confused.

'I have a dentist appointment tomorrow,' I say. 'I'm in a lot of pain.'

'You never said a word, Jan.' Graham is sniffing the air curiously. Any old fool can feel the atmosphere is strained.

'I told Nadine. It's agony. Root-canal.' I pull a pained face.

'That settles it then,' announces Lucie. 'I'm going with you, Ward.'

Ward calls me into his office after the boardroom meeting. I take a deep breath as I sit down opposite him.

'I used to have many dentist appointments when I was unhappy at work,' he begins in that maddeningly calm way. 'I tell you one excuse I once used when I had a job interview. I told them I had a funeral to go to in three weeks' time. "So your friend hasn't died *quite* yet?" my boss said.' When Ward sees a flicker of a smile he says, 'Can I at least make you an offer?'

'I can't work here any longer, Ward,' I reply, thinking he's about to up my salary.

He nods, as if he understands things are complicated between us. 'If you do have a painful tooth which is in urgent need of root-canal treatment, I'd hate you not to go. There is nothing worse than toothache. I have two crowns.' He taps one of his back teeth, followed by the other. 'But if you're not in agony, can I take you on one last pitch?'

'Ward . . .' I don't know what to do. I'm torn. Can I really go on ignoring my feelings for the man sitting in front of me? But then again, I have this job interview tomorrow and I swore I'd stay away from him.

'One last pitch,' he says.

28

It's twelve noon when I call Granddad from Ward's car. The line rings, and it rings. If he's out he usually puts the answer machine on. Come on, Granddad. I don't like to think of him getting older and deafer.

I watch Ward entering the cafe to buy us some coffee. We parked in front of the beach at St Mawes. We left London at the crack of dawn to be at the pitch by eleven o'clock. I'm still not sure what I'm doing here, but at least I managed to rearrange my job interview for Monday. I told them I had urgent root-canal treatment.

The pitch went well – a pretty pale-blue house with white-framed windows, set back from the coastal road, with stunning views. I talked to the elderly owners about my grandparents and how they had been so happy down here and that living by the sea was good for the soul.

The car journey wasn't too awkward. We talked a lot about Ward's childhood. He grew up in Sussex. His parents didn't have a happy marriage. Mum was creative, bohemian; Dad was a disciplinarian. 'Mum and I would go out on long walks along the Sussex Downs just to get away from him.' Often he wonders how they fell in love in the first place. 'Wouldn't you love to be a fly on the wall and see their first encounter or their first date?' he'd asked. 'I can't imagine my father ever being romantic. He was as dry as an old bone.'

I found myself telling Ward about Lucas. Sometimes I feel deep love for him. Other times I could throttle him for remaining so distant with my granddad. 'He finds any kind of intimacy hard,' I explained, understanding why, in a way, he'd had an affair with a married woman. He didn't have to commit. It wasn't daunting because he didn't believe it would lead to anything. However, Lucas was terrified when it exposed him, when he realised that he did have feelings. 'I know he cares, he's just not that good at expressing himself.'

'Like the entire male sex,' suggested Ward. 'Do you think he's closed off partly because you lost your parents?'

'I guess so. I know we all deal with grief differently.'

Ward has a younger sister who lives in Canada, married with three boys. 'She has her hands full.' He'd wanted to know about my childhood in Cornwall and I'd told him how this part of the world would always be my home. London is a place where I work; Porthpean is where I feel close to my parents and my grandparents. I feel Granny's presence every time I visit Granddad. I think he does too, which is partly why he doesn't want to move, not until he has to. When I go for walks along the beach I tell her what's going on in my life, as though she can hear me. 'Change the lights, Trisha,' Granddad always says when we approach a red traffic light and it seems, almost instantly, to turn green, Granddad thanking Granny as he drives on.

Spud barks when Ward gets in the car. 'Any luck getting through?' he asks me when I hang up. I shake my head, worried. 'Let's go anyway. He's probably just asleep.'

As I direct Ward to Beach House my mobile rings and I pray it's Granddad. It's Ralph. He tells me he's booked a table in a French restaurant on Marylebone Lane. 'L'Entre-côte,' I repeat, jotting the name down in my diary. 'Great. See you tomorrow.'

When I hang up I'm aware Ward is watching. 'A date?'

'Um,' is all I say, unable to meet his eye.

We drive on in silence.

When we reach the narrow road leading to our house Spud sits up on the back seat, knowing exactly where we are. I hop out to open the gate and also let Spud out of the car.

I hurry to open the front door. 'Hello!' Ward follows me inside. I rush into the kitchen, hoping he'll be having lunch, but there's no sign of him. 'Granddad?' I call again, heading into the sitting room.

'Oh Granddad,' I say when I see him lying on the floor by the fireplace. Ward helps me lift him up.

He mumbles, disorientated, 'What time is it? Is it supper?' He looks at Ward. 'Who are you?'

'Granddad, it's me, January,' I say as Ward and I settle him into his armchair. I kneel down beside him. 'I've been trying to call you. What happened?'

His watery eyes look into mine. 'Darling.' Slowly he comes round, clutching my hand. 'I must have taken a tumble.' He glances at Ward, still confused.

'This is Ward,' I tell him, keeping my hand firmly in his. 'We did a pitch locally, so we thought we'd drop by.'

Ward approaches us. 'Hello,' he says with warmth. 'I hope you're not hurt?'

Granddad waves an arm. 'I'm fine, quite all right. I came in here to do the crossword, I must have ... I can't remember what.' He scratches his head, muddled.

'Doesn't matter, the main thing is you're OK. How about I make us all a cup of tea and something for lunch?' I say, catching Granddad taking in this tall figure in front of him with thick dark hair, dressed in a suit. 'Stay put, Granddad,' I say, but he insists on getting up to help me make the tea and dig out the treacle biscuits.

'What's he doing selling houses?' he whispers, leaning heavily on my arm. 'He could be a film star.'

After tea and a toasted cheese sandwich Granddad insists he feels better, so before it gets dark Ward asks if he can take a walk round the garden and maybe head down to the beach. Ward gazes out of the sitting-room window, towards the dark grey sea. 'January told me the view was special, but it's not until you see it that you understand.'

'Bad luck,' Granddad says with a twinkle in his eye. 'It's not for sale.'

Minutes later Granddad puts on his coat and picks up his stick and we take Ward out through the kitchen door that leads to the back of the house. Slowly and carefully we walk up a few steps and through a gate. Ward notices the letters P and T carved on the gate, along with a date. 'Patricia, my wife and me, Timothy,' Granddad says as we approach Granny's kitchen garden and her greenhouse.

'January can vouch for my ignorance when it comes to gardening,' Ward says, before he tells Granddad about the time I'd won him a pitch because I knew about snake's heads and bee orchids. 'The only flowers I've heard of are roses and daisies,' Ward continues, making Granddad chuckle.

Winter doesn't show this space at its best. Instead I imagine it in the spring, with neat rows of vegetables pushing up, divided into sections, along with the handsome and bold artichoke plant, towering above the young plants like a sil-very-green fountain. I tell Ward how Granny had introduced me to gardening when I was ten. 'I was a professional raker of leaves by eleven.' I see myself in my flowery pink-and-yellow coat and navy gumboots, pushing my wheelbarrow filled with carrots, potatoes and lettuces. I tell Ward how much I loved being in her greenhouse, sunlight beaming through the windows. I could still hear the sound of bumble-bees against the glass. 'Granny's greenhouse smelt of growth, of earth, goodness and heat. There was a chair here,' I point, 'where she'd often take a nap or do the crossword.' I see her dressed in her faithful old gardening trousers, hair tied back in a headscarf, pricking out her seedlings. 'People need light and warmth, then they flourish just like these plants,' she'd say, before touching her herbs or tomatoes, saying, 'these are doing nicely,' or 'I'm very proud of my peas, January. Come and take a look.' I recall the excitement of growing my own basil and mint, and of planting tulips in the autumn and seeing them grow in the spring.

Next we take Ward around the main garden. Granddad says he needs to take some wood in from the shed. Ward offers to do it for him. The old red swing is still suspended from the shed's rafters. 'Isla used to play on it,' I tell him.

There are many hidden paths in this garden. 'It must have been a great place for hide-and-seek,' says Ward, as we cross the lawn, where my school friends and I used to play French cricket. We head out of the gate, towards the beach. Granddad tells Ward that our house was built in 1792 and that the road leading down to the coast used to be nothing more than a grassy lane.

On the way to the beach I point out to Ward the beach car park. 'Granny used to put Lucas and me on car park duty to make sure people put their pound coin into the honesty box.'

'And did they?' Ward asks, amused.

'If they didn't they had Lucas to answer to,' I say. 'He'd chase them across the car park, shouting, "Cough up!"'

Granddad laughs at that, saying with affection that Lucas hasn't changed.

After our walk, I show Ward the rest of the house, self-conscious at being alone with him again. 'It needs some attention,' I say when we come into the nursery, where Lucas and I used to watch television. In one corner, by the glass doors that open out into the garden, there's still the pale-pink doll's house that Granny bought for Isla. I walk over to the bookshelf and take out a copy of Daphne du Maurier's *Rebecca*, blowing dust off the top. 'I remember Granddad telling me about Daphne du Maurier after we moved here. He used to read her books to me by the fire. Her spirit remains everywhere on the coastline.'

Upstairs, I hover by my bedroom door, not wanting Ward to enter, but he walks straight past me.

'This place has so much charm,' he says, looking out of the window towards the sea. Tentatively I approach.

'I was fascinated by the sea and how it changed all the time. Even in the winter, when it was usually grey, it still had this power over me.'

Ward picks up a silver-framed photograph of my mother on my old dressing table. She's the spitting image of a young Granny with her chestnut hair tied back in a scarf, a baby in a white shawl in her arms.

'Is this you?' he asks.

I nod. My head rests against her shoulders, my face turned towards her. My mother's eyes are closed; I'm fast asleep, so content. I wish I could remember that moment, but I feel it instead, breathing in her vanilla scent, hearing her heart beat close to mine. Tearful, I nod again. 'That's my mum.'

Ward looks at me. 'She was beautiful,' he says. 'Like you.'

This time I don't turn away.

'I mean it, Jan. You're beautiful.'

'Why won't it start?' I say to Ward as he turns on the engine again but it splutters to nothing.

'It's been a bit temperamental lately.'

'Now you tell me.'

Ward attempts to start the engine once more, Granddad waiting patiently to wave us off. Nothing happens.

'I think the battery's dead.'

'I don't understand,' I say irritably. 'It was fine earlier.'

'Not helpful, January.'

I wind down the window. 'Granddad, don't get cold,' I say, determined we will set off any minute.

Next thing I know, Ward has his head in the bonnet, but clearly he doesn't have a clue what to do. He looks up, oil smeared on his hands. 'Is there a garage nearby?'

It's Friday evening and Ward and I have no other option but to stay the night with Granddad. We need a new battery and of course it has to be ordered so we can't get one until late tomorrow morning. Arrangements have been made. Thankfully Isla is spending the weekend with Dan and Fiona.

'Do you need to call your wife?' asks Granddad, observing him like a hawk as we sit by the roaring fire in the sitting room.

I hop up. 'I'll fix us all something for supper.'

Over fishcakes and vegetables, Ward asks Granddad about his career in the theatre. He tells us about the opening nights, the most exciting of events, as long as the actors didn't forget their lines. 'Oh, I got nervous all right,' Granddad says. 'Before every rehearsal, as I'd turn the corner to the theatre, a part of me hoped to see the building in flames.'

Ward smiles.

'You need to feel nervous, Ward. If you're not nervous surely that means you don't care.'

'I often get nervous before a pitch.'

'You don't show it,' I say.

Ward looks at me as he says, 'I hide my feelings well.'

'Right, you two,' Granddad says, after watching the ten o'clock news with coffee and chocolates. 'Bed. Don't stay up too late,' he says, throwing me a warning look. I kiss him on both cheeks, his skin so soft and fragile.

Ward stands up, thanking him for the evening. 'I've put a towel in the spare room,' Granddad says. 'And blankets on your beds. It's darn chilly.'

When Ward and I are left alone I exaggerate a yawn, saying I might head upstairs too. As I get up from the floor where I've been sitting, he grips my arm.

'Wait.'

'Ward, I don't know what you want from me.'

'There are things that need to be said,' he says, 'things I need to explain to you. Why do you think I wanted you to come on the pitch, January?'

I sit back down on the floor, in front of the fire and hug my knees to my chest. Ward sits down next to me. I edge away, certain that if he comes any closer I will want him to kiss me again, finish off what we began.

'January, it's over.'

'It's over?'

'My marriage.'

'Your marriage,' I repeat, giving myself time to digest it.

'These last six months we've been on a trial separation.'

I work out that that's practically since he began working for Sherwoods. All this time they haven't been together? 'What? How? I mean, why didn't you tell me?'

'I couldn't. It was between us. Marina didn't want anyone to know our business while we tried to work things out and I had to respect that. The only person who knew was Jeremy. When we were in talks over the new job, he happened to overhear a conversation between us and he'd asked me, quite rightly, if it would affect my work. I made him promise not to say a word to anyone at Sherwoods, that it was personal. But then, when you and I began to get close, I wanted to tell you, but I couldn't. It was all so unexpected too, Jan, my feelings for you. I was confused and felt just as guilty as you. But I can be honest now because Marina and I are getting a divorce, and it's out in the open among our friends. We're sad, but we've agreed it's the right decision. If we're honest, our marriage was over a long time ago.'

'Because of Spencer?'

Ward shakes his head. 'He didn't help, but . . .' He runs a hand through his hair. 'Marina and I, we lost a child eighteen months ago, our baby.'

I look at him, understanding now that look of loss in his eyes when I saw him in the nursery at Uley Lodge, gazing out into the garden, trapped in his own world of pain.

'Marina gave birth to a little girl who had to be put into a ventilator immediately. I didn't have time to hold her,' he says, his voice breaking. 'Didn't have time to introduce myself. We lost the baby only hours later.'

I touch his arm. 'You know what it's like, Jan, losing someone. You know more than anyone. It rips you into pieces. Her death broke me in two; sometimes it only feels like yesterday. Instead of Marina and I coming together, working through our grief, she decided I'd failed her. It was my fault. Spencer isn't the only man she's slept with; there have been a string of them. We've tried to work through it. We saw a counsellor. I wasn't very good at that,' he says with a tiny glimmer of a smile. 'I kept on being told I needed to let go; I needed to cry. The thing is, from my schooldays, by my father it's been ingrained in me not to cry. Marina took it as coldness, as not caring, which is why she sought out other men for comfort. But it was quite the opposite, if only I could have shown it. In the end I had to accept it wasn't working. Our love wasn't strong enough to overcome this. I only have to be here, to hear your grandfather talk about your granny, to understand what we had wasn't a patch on their relationship.'

I touch his arm again only this time I keep my hand there.

'I didn't get to say hello or goodbye to my little girl,' he says, looking at me with such sorrow in his eyes, before bowing his head, and soon I'm holding him in my arms, rocking him like a child, as he cries his way through unshed tears.

'I'm sorry,' Ward says, when finally we pull apart, 'but you have this way of making me . . .' He shrugs, 'I don't know, be myself. I feel like you know me, you understand me.'

'I feel the same about you,' I say, thinking of all those times that I've opened up to Ward about Isla or my school days. I have shared fears with him that I wouldn't even share with my friends, let alone my boss.

'I know we don't know one another that well.'

Ward is right. In so many ways our friendship is like a book. We have turned a few pages, a few chapters perhaps, but there's still a long way to go. And it's true to say that since our kiss I have done as much as I can to distance myself, to stop turning the pages, scared of where the end might lead. 'But I was wondering if you'd like to spend some time with me,' he asks, 'some time outside of the office to see if you like the Ward who isn't your boss? I don't know what the situation is with this other man, but . . .'

I nod.

'Is that a yes?' he asks, a small smile beginning to spread across his face.

We edge closer to one another. 'It's a yes. A big yes.'

Ward takes my face into his hands and kisses me.

We do no more talking that night. Ward sleeps in the blue room with me, with the sound of the waves outside our window.

All those years of loneliness melt away at his touch.

In the middle of the night, I wake up, naked and wrapped in his arms. It takes me a moment to remember our evening, but when I do I close my eyes and drift into a deep sleep.

The following morning Granddad notices the change of mood round the breakfast table, me pouring Ward a coffee, both of us unable to wipe the smiles off our faces. I'm bursting to tell Granddad the news. Ward had wanted me to tell him when we were alone. 'He thinks I'm married,' he had said. 'Which, technically, I still am.'

'I'll explain,' I reassured him. 'I'll tell him, if that's OK?'

Ward had nodded, before kissing me again.

When Ward is outside with the garage mechanic I

mention I'm taking a walk with Granddad. We're going for a stroll along the beach and won't be long. I know his smile is wishing me good luck.

I take Granddad's arm. 'How are you feeling?' I ask him. 'Bella told me you've—'

'Don't listen to Bella.'

'She told me you've had a few falls, Granddad.'

He dismisses my concern. 'I'm old, it's normal.'

'Yes, but—'

'Stop fussing, Jan. I'm quite all right. Now, what's going on with you and Ward?'

'He's been on a trial separation, which explains so much. He and Marina are getting a divorce. Oh Granddad, we talked all night.' I tell him about Ward and his wife losing their baby. He remains quiet, but there is no better person to understand Ward's pain than Granddad. 'Please don't worry.' I turn to him. 'We're going to take it slow and keep it quiet, until his divorce papers are signed, until that's over, but I do trust him and I promise you can trust him too.'

Granddad clutches my hand. 'Well, if you're happy, so am I. I liked him the moment we met. I was wary, of course I was, but I can see he's a good man.'

We walk along the empty beach. I ask Granddad what he's doing for the rest of the weekend, and he tells me Bella is joining him for supper tonight, she's buying some fish from the fish man as a treat. When he asks me the same question, I mention that Ward had suggested we go out on our first official date. 'He's taking me out for dinner.'

'How romantic.' Granddad sighs, as if remembering the times when he and Granny dated. 'I know your grandmother would have liked Ward. She'd have given him a grilling, mind.'

'And threatened to cut his balls off if he hurt me.'

'Most likely.'

'She'd probably be saying *about time too.*'

He clutches my hand. 'No, she wouldn't be saying that. Life hasn't been straightforward for you, January. She'd say that there is a time to be happy and to be sad, a time to be alone and to grieve, but also a time to find love again.'

29

These past few weeks have been *incredible*. I don't know how to describe how happy I am. It's as if my life over the past five years has been coasting along just fine, but now I'm sailing in this glorious sunshine and swimming in clear turquoise sea, washing the loneliness away. Ward and I have decided to keep our relationship private; we don't want the office to know yet, not until his divorce is finalised. But everyone at Sherwoods is aware that Ward has been separated for the past six months and is now in the process of a divorce. 'There will be regular calls and meetings with the lawyer so it's best to be open about it all,' he'd said, and I'd agreed.

'Jan!' Nadine calls as I rush past her desk and towards the stairs. I turn to her. 'Yep?'

'You're in a hurry again.'

I wave a file in her direction. 'For Ward.'

'Really?' I ignore that playful look in her eye.

'So scatty,' I say, before trying to go upstairs slowly and

professionally, before almost tripping over the last step and hearing Nadine chuckle.

I shut Ward's door firmly behind me, wishing it had a lock and key. 'Jan,' he says, getting up, 'you only came up five minutes ago.' We're walking towards one another, big grins across our faces. 'I'll never get any work . . .' Before he can say 'done' we're kissing, my file falling on to the floor, paper scattering everywhere.

As I'm unbuttoning Ward's shirt we hear a knock on the door. Ward presses a finger across my lips. I want to bite it.

'Ward?' Graham says and I know crafty old Nadine has sent him up to investigate.

'Hang on,' Ward calls back, tucking his shirt back into his trousers. 'I'm kind of in the middle of something.'

We both laugh quietly. 'Can you come back in five?'

'Five?' I mouth, unimpressed. 'Make it at least ten.'

'Afraid not. It's rather urgent,' Graham says before we hear the door opening. I rush over to Ward's desk and crouch underneath it, trying hard not to laugh.

'What is it, Graham?' asks Ward. My heart is pounding.

'Have you seen Jan?'

'How would I know where she is?' Ward asks. 'That's what's urgent?'

I'm about to sneeze. Oh no. Please don't. Please don't.

'Anything else, Graham?'

It's coming. 'Atishoo!'

I crawl out from my hiding place. 'It's magic!' exclaims

Graham before raising an eyebrow at me. 'What have you been doing underneath Ward's desk, or don't I want to know?'

'All right, all right, but let's keep it between us,' Ward suggests.

Nadine enters the office now. 'Oh Ward, everyone knows, we weren't born yesterday.' She looks at me. 'Urgent file, my foot.'

'I think it's great,' Graham states. 'But just so you know, I worked you two out a long time ago.'

Nadine hits his arm. 'No you didn't. You had no idea.' They continue arguing as though Ward and I aren't in the room.

'Let's crack on,' Ward says the following day as Nadine enters the boardroom with a tray of coffee and biscuits. 'Uley Lodge.'

'Exchanged,' Lucie says. 'No hitches.'

We all clap. 'Where's the champers?' asks Graham. I catch Ward's eye and he smiles at me in a way that suggests the sooner he can get this meeting out of the way, the sooner he can shut the door and we can have a minute to ourselves.

I gaze at him, thinking how lovely it is to be in a relationship. Ward can't sleep over at my place yet during the week or the weekends when Isla is at home. I need to introduce him to her slowly, but they did meet, finally, last weekend. To begin with Isla was shy. She didn't want to chat and stuck close to my side, while Ward was careful not to be too demonstrative towards me. He was there to pay lots of attention to her, to make Isla feel comfortable. By the end of the afternoon Isla was showing Ward her bedroom, her photographs, her paintings and drawings and the certificate she'd been awarded in America for her courage, framed and hanging over her desk. We cooked bangers and mash for supper, and Isla showed off her apron and chef's hat as she made cupcakes. Ward even did the washing up, but not before having had a tea towel play fight with Isla when she said she didn't want to do it. I remembered Granny's words of wisdom all those years ago, '*A man who washes up is a goodie.*' Ward was clearly a hit, Isla asking if he was going to spend Christmas Day with us, now only six weeks away, the adverts already played to death on television.

Outside work, Ward is remarkably relaxed. He puts it down to the relief of making a decision about his marriage. 'I knew it was over, too much damage had been done,' Ward had told me the weekend we'd returned from Cornwall, when Isla was staying with Dan and Fiona. We were lying in bed on Sunday morning, Ward stroking my arm that rested across his chest. 'But I didn't want to give up. I could still hear my father's voice saying I mustn't quit, that quitting was for losers. But I don't want to listen to that voice anymore, Jan. All I'm doing is making a choice not to stay in a marriage that was making *both* of us unhappy. I met Marina when she was in her late thirties. She was a make-up artist, successful, worked on many films and television shows. She wanted a child and I wanted one too. She was beautiful; my friends were crazy with jealousy. I got swept along in this madness. We were engaged within weeks and trying for a child, Marina saying it could take some time. She became pregnant almost immediately. When we lost our baby . . . well she wanted to try for another one straightaway, but I . . . I wasn't ready. She wasn't ready either; she was trying to fix our problem, our sadness overnight. When I said I needed time she looked elsewhere. I know I became distant. I hid my feelings from her. She felt alone and so did I. She needed comfort. I don't blame her.' I'd wrapped my arm more tightly around him. 'Anyway, all this led me to you,' he'd said. 'Wonderful you.'

We'd spent the rest of the morning in bed. Ward had cooked us scrambled eggs, warning me that that's about all he can cook. We went for a pub lunch and took Spud for a walk along the river, spending hours sharing stories about our past, knowing with certainty that we were one another's future.

Surely, any moment, someone will wake me up and tell me that it's a dream?

'January,' Ward says, waking me up with a start.

'*Dearest*,' Graham adds.

I scrunch my piece of paper into a ball and throw it at him.

'It's so nice to have some gossip at last,' Graham continues.

'Actually I have some news,' says Lucie, thankfully nipping that conversation in the bud. 'Jim and I—'

'You're not?' Graham interrupts.

'Oh my God!' I gasp. 'Are you?'

Lucie nods.

We all cheer as if we've just won a multi-billion pitch. Nadine joins us, Spud scuttling into the room too to get in on the action. 'Where's the ring?' she asks, grabbing her hand.

'We're choosing one this weekend.'

'How did he propose?' asks Nadine, wanting all the gossip.

'In Asda,' says Lucie, 'we were in the frozen veg aisle. He said he wanted to do it when I least expected it.'

'Well he certainly did that! This is marvellous, love is in the air!' proclaims Graham. 'Surely we can have some champers now?'

30

When Nadine transfers a call to me from Bella, first thing Monday morning, immediately I sense something's wrong. Bella rarely calls me at work and never at this time of day. 'It's your granddad,' she says breathlessly before even saying hello. 'He's had a stroke. He's in hospital. You need to get here as soon as you can.' She gives me the details of the ward. 'I'll call Lucas too. Just jump in a car, Jan. He's confused. He's been calling out for you all.'

An hour and a half later I'm in Ward's car, Isla sitting in the back. Ward had contacted her school to let them know we were picking her up. I was determined that Isla should have the chance to see him too. Ward's driving fast, his foot pressed hard down.

This is when I wish with all my heart Cornwall wasn't so far away from London, but Ward gets me to the hospital in record time, brakes screeching as he parks the car right outside the entrance, behind an ambulance.

'Go!' he demands, unlocking the doors. 'I'll find you. Go!'

Isla and I stagger down the corridor, me dragging her by the hand, trying to run as fast as we can to get to Granddad's ward. We take a lift, frowning when the doors reopen to let in an elderly couple, one of them pushing the other in a wheelchair. The carer reverses the chair into the lift at a snail's pace. 'Here, let me give you a hand,' I say, and gratefully they accept before I press the up arrow.

'Come on, come on,' I mutter, waiting for the doors to shut.

As we run down another set of corridors, Isla trips over a shoelace that's come undone.

Finally, on Granddad's ward I rush to the reception desk. A nurse is talking on the phone while a fair-haired doctor in a white coat fills out paperwork. She looks up.

'Can I help?' she asks.

'My granddad! Timothy Wild. He was admitted—'

'Bed twenty-eight. I'll take you there.'

Isla and I follow her through the men's ward. Granddad is in the corner bed. I have to fight back tears when I see him, asleep, wearing his old pyjamas, a drip attached to his frail arm. Bella is sitting on a chair by his side. She gets up and hugs us both. The doctor fills me in briefly on the medication they have administered to Granddad, along with the drip for dehydration. 'I'm afraid his condition is critical,' she says, 'but I'll give you a couple of minutes to yourselves.'

I nod, before turning to Bella. 'Thank you,' I say, 'for being there for him.'

'That's all right. Lucas is on his way too,' she reassures me.

The moment I touch Granddad's hand, he slowly opens his eyes and smiles weakly at me. 'Oh January,' he says. 'Little Isla.'

Isla comes forward and kisses him softly on the cheek. 'Hello Great-grandpops,' she says tearfully, before Bella takes her hand and says, 'Let's give your mother a little moment on her own.' They leave the ward, Bella telling me they'll find the canteen and get some coffee and a juice for Isla. I sit down next to Granddad, my hand still clasping his. He grips it with as much strength as he has. 'Not feeling – my – best,' he says, his speech is slurred and his beautiful face twisted, attempting a smile.

'Shush. Rest.' I stroke his hand, not wanting him to exert himself. It's enough to be by his side.

'January,' he battles on. 'Soon I can . . . I can be with them.'

I squeeze his hand.

'It's one of the hardest things.' Long pause. 'Losing a child.' He's fighting for breath.

'Oh Granddad.'

'But we gained you. I am so . . .' He gulps. 'So very proud.'

I rest my head gently against his chest, my tears dampening his pyjama top. 'I love you. I love you so much and won't ever forget what you did for Lucas and me. I love you with all my heart. Don't go yet. Please don't go. Thank you, thank you for being the best. I might not have had my parents, but I had you and Granny and that made me the luckiest girl in the world.'

'Thank . . . you,' Granddad says weakly. 'Lucas?'

'He's coming, he's coming Granddad.'

Granddad makes only a sound now, but I know he understands.

When I lift my head his eyes are closed. He looks peaceful.

'Granddad?'

'Granddad!' Lucas rushes over to us. 'How is he, Jan?'

I move aside. 'Not good.'

Lucas sits beside him. 'Granddad? It's me.'

Slowly Granddad opens his eyes. 'My boy.'

Lucas presses a hand against his forehead, clearly in turmoil and unable to believe his health has deteriorated so quickly. 'Don't leave us,' Lucas says, his voice merely a whisper. 'Please don't go.'

'You'll be . . . fine.'

Lucas shakes his head. 'I haven't been a good son, I've never thanked you enough for everything you've done for me, but that doesn't mean . . . that doesn't mean I don't . . . I don't . . .'

Granddad taps his hand. 'I love . . . you.' He closes his eyes.

'I love you too.' There is a long silence. 'Granddad, I'll never forget the time you taught me to drive and all the fun we had playing chess – and that time when you stripped off and swam in the sea – Granddad?' Lucas touches his arm. 'Granddad?'

I rush to the other side of the bed, take Granddad's limp hand. He can't be – I'm not ready. Lucas presses the buzzer, 'Granddad!' he calls out. 'Nurse! Nurse! Granddad!' My brother turns to me. 'He's gone' he says, his voice choked. 'Oh, January, he's gone.'

But I press the buzzer again. I keep on pressing it until Lucas pulls me away and takes me into his arms.

A week later the tiny church in Porthpean is packed, with people having to stand at the back. Many of Granddad's theatre friends are here, some as old and frail as he was, and then there are younger actors who had worked with him in London. All the locals are here too. Granny and Granddad had been at the heart of this community, always inviting friends for lunch and tea on the lawn and Granny had got to know so many neighbours and friends by selling her home-grown vegetables in the beach car park and at the front of the house.

Dan wanted to be here. He's sitting behind me, with Fiona. He'd also come to Granny's funeral. 'I'm really fond of the old dragon,' he'd once said. 'Since having Isla I understand now the lengths you'll go to, to protect your child.'

For the past few days I have been with Bella, helping to arrange the funeral and the tea afterwards. Lucas stayed for a couple of days, before having to return to work, but I encouraged Ward to go back to London, and to take Isla with him, arranging for her to return to school and stay with Dan. Bella and I had so much to do that I felt there was little point in him hanging around. Also, as much as I'm grateful to Ward for all his support, I wanted to be alone to talk to Bella about Granddad's last few days. Bella had told me that she'd popped by first thing in the morning to give him his newspaper. Normally he'd be in the kitchen eating breakfast with the radio on, or he'd be in the sitting room. He wasn't in either. She'd called and she'd called, fearing he might have had another fall, before rushing upstairs to find him in bed. He knew she was there but he couldn't move, his right-hand side was paralysed. She'd called an ambulance. It was then that he'd managed to murmur Granny's name, followed by mine and Lucas's. Bella had done everything she could to keep him calm. 'I told him you and Lucas were on your way, Jan. He waited for you.'

Bella and I have organised drinks, tea and cake after the funeral, and also worked on a photograph display to celebrate Granddad's life. There are some black-and-white shots of him as a child, some pictures of him on stage with his actors, along with some photos of Lucas, Granny and me on Porthpean beach, all of us in shorts and T-shirts. There's a lovely image of Granddad pushing Isla up and down on his homemade wooden swing.

It's been so odd and sad sleeping in the house without him; it's cold and empty. I haven't been able to stop crying at night, hugging my pillow. It hurts physically to think he has gone, that I will never see his face again or have his wise counsel. I am so relieved that I managed to spend that precious time with him when Ward's car broke down. I think of our lovely walk on the beach. I grip the service sheet. I was meant to see Granddad this weekend. Ward, Isla and I were going to go down and stay. Granddad had already planned the meals. He was going to buy some cod in batter for Friday. But I keep on reminding myself how lucky I was to reach him in time to go down and say goodbye. Had it not been for Ward . . . I turn to him and he clutches my hand. It's as if I am saying goodbye to Granny all over again, and it brings up the loss of my parents too, who should be here. They always should have been here. I'm relieved Ward hasn't seen me in pieces, but his telephone call at the end of the day has meant the world to me. I feel a little nudge. When Isla hands me her small pink heart fleece cushion my heart bursts with love.

As we sing the first hymn I glance towards Lucas, sitting at the end of our row. He's staring at Granddad's coffin. I am so relieved for him, and for Granddad, that he'd managed to say goodbye. I am also glad that he had the chance to say he loved Granddad. 'But did he hear me, Jan?' Lucas had asked, distressed. 'I don't know if . . .'

'He did. He knew you loved him.'

Yet Lucas had looked unconvinced, as if he'd done too little, too late.

After the service guests mill outside before heading back down the steep hill to Beach House for tea. I am talking to Dan and Fiona, Isla holding my hand tightly. Ward has walked on ahead with Bella. 'He seems lovely,' Dan says to me, gesturing to him. When Lucas approaches he asks, 'Is that Ward Metcalfe, your boss?'

I nod. 'I'll introduce you.'

'That would be great.'

'Ward is Mum's new boyfriend, Uncle Lucas,' says Isla.

'Right.'

'It's early days,' I say, biting my lip.

'We probably ought to set up a meeting,' Lucas continues, staring ahead, bottled anger in his voice.

'A meeting?'

Dan and Fiona are deathly quiet. Discreetly they walk on ahead.

'Well, we need to sell Beach House and I'm sure Ward would reduce the fee, wouldn't he?' When I say nothing he goes on, 'There have got to be some perks for being an estate agent.'

I turn to him, shocked and more angry than I can say. 'What's the matter with you?'

'Being practical, because someone has to be.'

'By talking about selling up when he's barely in his

grave?' I shout. 'Don't you dare take your anger out on me, Lucas! Why don't you just grow up and accept that what happened to our mum and dad happened to both of us!'

Ward tries to intervene.

'I'm OK,' I say, concentrating on Lucas. Pain is etched on my brother's face, his eyes clouding with tears.

'I'm sorry,' he says. 'I didn't mean it, Jan, you know I didn't. I failed him. I failed. There were so many things I didn't say. Oh Jan, I'm sorry.'

But his apology is too late. 'Some things aren't for sale,' I say, grabbing Isla's hand and running as fast as I can, away from everyone.

31

It's a late Friday afternoon in early December, two and half weeks since the funeral, and I'm back at work. If possible, I feel even sadder about Granddad. Now that the funeral is over, it feels so final. I don't know what I would have done without Lizzie taking some time off to help me go through all his belongings. She has been gentle but firm, and slowly we have been clearing out Beach House. Granddad left lots of precious things for me. On my mantelpiece at home is his French carriage clock decorated with flowers, a butterfly and birds. I wanted to keep so many photographs, including the picture of my mother holding me as a baby. I haven't seen Lucas since the funeral, only spoken to him on the telephone. He apologised again and we've cleared the air, but he is still intent on selling the house as quickly as possible. 'We have to be realistic. I'm not doing this to punish you, I swear I'm not, but we can't afford to keep it.'

But I still can't give my consent.

Lucie, Graham and Nadine have all been wonderful.

Nadine makes sure to pop an extra sugar in my tea or coffee and nags me to go out at lunchtime, insisting the fresh air and break will do me good. She escorts me to the cafe over the road or the deli round the corner to make sure I'm eating. Graham tries to make me laugh with his jokes and because they are often so bad, his trick works. Lucie is sensitive enough not to flash her ring and be over the moon happy right now, despite me telling her she mustn't worry. Instead the office is subdued but warm and I can see more clearly than ever that my colleagues aren't my colleagues, they're my friends and when or if I ever leave Sherwoods, I will miss them. Even Spencer sent me some flowers and a brief note saying he was thinking of me. Since finding out what Spencer did to Ward, Spencer's visits have thankfully been less frequent. I find it difficult to see him, especially when Spencer acts as if nothing has happened. Ward didn't want me to tell anyone in the office about the affair; understandably he doesn't want the property world to know his business.

Ward has been incredible and, if anything, this has made our relationship even stronger. He appears to understand the position with Lucas and has promised me he won't do a thing without my consent, and I trust him.

As I head upstairs to Ward's office, Graham is heading down with a mug of coffee. 'He's on the phone, Jan,' Graham warns me, 'to your brother again,' he whispers.

'To my brother? Are you sure?'

Graham nods. 'Why?'

'Nothing,' I say, confused. As I'm about to open Ward's door I stop when I hear him saying, 'It's about time she saw sense. It's completely irrational.' I wait, my hand resting on the doorknob. 'I agree. I'll see what I can do. I'm sure with time she'll come round. Yep, we could just go ahead.' Long pause. In shock I back away, but then lean closer into the door again. 'Of course she can't. I don't know – when people are grieving they're all over the place.' Another pause. 'It's a lot of money. I'll talk to her, don't worry, leave it with me.'

I turn away, head back downstairs. How *could* he?

'Sweetie,' says Graham, watching me clear my desk with grim determination and put Spud on the lead, 'are you all right?'

'No.'

'What's happened?'

'Tell Ward it's over, will you?' I say, my hands shaking.

'Over?'

'Tell him I heard him talking to Lucas.'

'Jan, calm down,' says Graham, who hates confrontation and arguments.

'Just tell him,' I say, leaving the office. 'He'll know what I mean.'

32

I'm standing on the doorstep of Jeremy's house in Richmond, Spud by my side. Lizzie is away on business and the only other person I could think of, the only person I wanted to see was Jeremy.

'What's the matter?' I fly into his arms. 'January, what's happened?'

I don't know how long he holds me, but finally, when we part, Jeremy's wife, Emma, ushers us inside, saying she'll put the kettle on. 'Take her into your office,' she tells him, deeply concerned. 'It's nice and warm in there.'

Jeremy sits in his armchair listening. His office is cosy, a real fire burning, shelves lined with books, Christmas cards and family photographs. I tell him everything, in great detail, out it all comes like a flowing tap. Jeremy doesn't say a word until I look at him, saying, 'Can you believe Ward went behind my back?'

Jeremy hands me one of his handkerchiefs. 'No,' he says simply. 'I can't.'

'I trusted him.'

'I can't believe he did that because I'm certain there has been a misunderstanding. Ward wouldn't go back on his word.'

'But . . .'

'Don't you think you should have waited to talk to him?' he asks gently but firmly. 'Could Graham have maybe got it wrong? Let's face it he does often get the wrong end of the stick. Doesn't Ward at least deserve the benefit of the doubt?'

'But he was talking to Lucas about the house, the money.' Wasn't he? I try to recall the conversation again. '*I don't know, when people are grieving they're all over the place.*'

'January, you know how much I love you as a friend and former colleague, don't you?'

I nod, blowing my nose.

'I'm only saying this because I care. Why did you run away? Why didn't you try to talk to Ward?'

I inhale deeply. 'Because . . .' I press my lips together. 'I don't know, Jeremy. I'm so confused.'

'Could it be because you love this man and sometimes the easiest thing to do is to run a mile at the first sign of trouble?'

'No. That's not it, not at all.'

'You're scared of being happy. You've been alone for a long time and then suddenly here is a man who loves you and you love him, but boy, isn't that frightening as well as truly magical? When I fell for Emma I was so terrified I couldn't think straight. I thought it was the end of my freedom, the end of the life I'd known before, but I had to take a giant leap of faith and go with it, and I'm so glad I did. Of course it wasn't the end of anything, it was the beginning of a new and wonderful life. Loving someone makes us vulnerable, but we owe it to ourselves to take that chance.'

Suddenly my mobile rings and Ward's name lights up my screen.

He urges me to take the call. 'Don't ruin something before it's even begun.'

I meet Ward in a pub local to my home and close to Ward's flat in Brook Green.

He hands me a glass of wine, anger burning in his eyes. 'You didn't think to wait, to find out who I was talking to?'

'I got it wrong,' I admit. 'I know now. I called Lucas.'

'You called Lucas?'

'He told me he'd been in meetings all day.' As I say it I know it sounds bad, so foolish of me not to talk to Ward first. 'He reassured me he won't do anything without my consent, he understands I need time.'

'You calling him makes it even worse!' He lowers his voice. 'All you had to do was talk to *me*.'

'I know. And I'm so sorry,' I say, ashamed of myself.

'If you really want to know, I was talking to *Luke*, my solicitor. I was talking about Marina. I thought we could do the divorce thing in a civilised way, but apparently not.'

'I'm sorry,' I say, reaching for his hand, but he withdraws it immediately.

'Do you know what really hurts, Jan? That you were so ready to believe, to think the worst of me.'

'I'm . . .' There's no excuse. I lean towards him again, but he edges even further away.

'After everything we have been through, do you honestly think I'm the kind of man who'd do that to you?'

'No. I don't know what—'

'You think I'd have a cosy old chat with your brother to get you on side, just so I can earn a fat commission? If that's what you think of me, you and I have no chance,' he says, getting up and grabbing his coat from the back of his chair. 'And Lucas deserves better. He gave you his word not to go ahead without your consent and you should have trusted him too. That day, when you ran off, Lucas was in pieces. He knew he'd taken his pain and anger out on you and was truly sorry. He was in tears, Jan. You're right, he's bottled a lot up over the years; you aren't the only one who's suffering.'

'Ward! Wait! Please don't go.'

He turns to me. 'If that's what you think of me,' he repeats, 'it's best we end it right now.'

I rush home and throw some clothes into a case. Isla is furious with me. She doesn't want to get in the car yet again and go to Cornwall for the weekend, especially not when Great-grandpops isn't there. 'I want to work on my photography competition!' She and Ruki had been busy going over her images on the computer.

'There's no point arguing!'

'I have rights!' she shouts back at me. 'I should be able to choose what I want to do sometimes. My teacher said—'

'Enough! You do as I say, Isla.'

Ruki touches my arm. 'Are you sure you're safe to drive?'

'I'm fine,' I say, feeling anything but. I have blown it with Ward. I have shattered the trust between us and it's all my fault.

I can't even remember driving out of London or getting on to the motorway. I can't even remember arriving at Beach House.

It's the early hours of this morning. I'm exhausted from the long drive, but still can't switch off. I turn my bedside light on and send Ward a message. '*I'm so sorry,*' I type. '*I didn't mean to hurt you. I should have trusted you. Please forgive me.*' I press 'Send' wishing I could tell him how much I love him. Never before have I felt this way. I realise my feelings for Dan didn't even come close to how I am feeling now. I felt scared when Dan broke up with me because I was having his child and didn't want to be alone. I didn't love him, not in the way that I love Ward, a love so strong I would do anything to put this right.

The following morning, the moment I wake up, I check my messages on my mobile, but my heart sinks when I haven't had a response.

After breakfast we head down to the beach. Isla takes Spud's lead and walks him across the sand, looking for shells or anything else interesting. The beach is deserted. Both Isla and I are wrapped up in many layers. Winter seems so much colder in Cornwall. I sit on the wall by the closed cafe and watch the sea, listening to the sound of the waves and trying to work out my next move with Ward. Granddad used to say that the waves often gave him an answer to his problems. I wait. I'll write him a letter, that's what I'll do. I'll tell him exactly how I feel. I will keep on calling him. I'll knock on his door; I'll bash it down if I have to. I won't let our relationship die. I won't. I close my eyes, and hear Granddad's voice saying, 'That's my girl. You fight.'

I open them when I hear another voice.

'I'm scared too,' he says, 'but I want this to work.' Ward sits down next to me, dressed in a thick coat and stripy scarf.

'How did you know I was here?' I ask, amazed, touching his arm, wanting to make sure I'm not dreaming.

'Ruki called me. She was worried about you, told me you were in a pretty bad way last night.'

Wonderful Ruki. I want to throw my arms round Ward, never let him go again. It takes all my restraint to sit still.

'I'd never do anything behind your back.' He stares out to the sea. 'You know I'm on your side.'

'I do, I really do, and I can't tell you how sorry I am for jumping to the wrong conclusion. Ward, I . . .'

Isla waves at us. 'Hello, Ward!' she says, as if it's completely natural that he has appeared out of nowhere to join us. He waves back, before turning to me. 'Can I put my work hat on for just a minute?'

'Go on.'

'Lucas's timing was lousy, he knows that, but he has a point. Unless you want to move here, you do need to think about selling. The house is too run down to let, you'd need to spend thousands renovating it and I imagine that's money you don't have.'

I nod. 'Lucas has, but he's not emotionally invested in Beach House, not like I am. I know it wouldn't work keeping it, but I can't imagine not being here. This has been my home for over thirty years.' I touch my locket.

'I'm saying this as Ward now, not an agent, OK? I know how much you love it here, how much it means to you, but a home is never the same without the people in it.'

I turn to him, tears in my eyes.

'Can you imagine being here without your grand-parents?' he asks. 'Because they are what made it your home. And do you know where their home is now? It's in here,' he says, touching my heart, before touching my locket. 'We can sell the house, anyone can, but we can't sell them or your memories. They will remain with you forever.'

I rest my head against his shoulder. 'I love you, Metcalfe.'

'You know what, Wild? I love you too.'

I lift my head and throw my arms around him. Restraint is so overrated. 'I love you,' I repeat, taking his face into my hands and kissing him.

33

It's a week before Christmas and Ward, Ruki, Godmother Lizzie and I are at Isla's school, looking at all the entries for the photography competition that line the corridors outside the classrooms. I asked Lucas if he could be here too, but unfortunately he had to work. Isla is busy chatting with her friends, pretending she doesn't know us. Ruki French-plaited her hair and she's wearing a pale-pink cardigan with a fabric rose pinned in one corner over a simple navy dress with matching navy shoes. I told her she didn't have to wear her splints tonight.

There are forty-five entries in total and each entry consists of a series of photos that tell a story. I stop beside some photographs of a child running across a lawn, before sitting in a crumpled heap, laughing, leaves in her hair. There are other pictures of farm animals, travels in Africa; Lizzie points to an image of a child with a meerkat on his head, saying, 'Dave would love that one.' There's a seaside resort with a child eating a chocolate ice cream, sticky brown mixture dribbling down his chin and a big grin on his face. There is a series of someone looking bored as they wait for a bus, before dancing when a bus approaches. Finally we all gather in front of Isla's. She has taken a selection of pictures of Porthpean beach; there are photographs of Granddad in his old tweed cap looking out to the sailing boats bobbing on the horizon, another image of Granddad and me walking arm-in-arm, our backs facing the camera, a reflection of our shadows on the sand. There's Spud flying across the beach, ears pinned back in the wind, and finally a sunset, capturing the most beautiful light across the sea. She'd kept her pictures a secret. I'd had no idea she'd taken that shot of Granddad and me together, I think, proudly looking at the image.

Finally Dan catches up with us, coat still on, car keys in his hand. He's on his own tonight because Fiona couldn't make it. 'Wow,' he says, standing back. 'She's good.'

'They're all good,' I say.

'But Isla's is the best, right? Not that we're biased.' Dan grins.

'Of course not.' I grin back. 'We're not biased at all.'

All the parents are sitting in the main hall, waiting for the presentation. Isla is sandwiched between Dan and me; she keeps on fiddling with her rose. Ward is sitting on my other side.

As we wait, I think about the past fortnight. I've had an interview with a literary agency in Marylebone. As happy as I am with Ward, I don't want to be his PA anymore, I don't think it would be healthy for our relationship. Nor am I sure how long I can cope with Graham's teasing at the boardroom table. I will miss working in property. How wrong I was all those years ago to dislike estate agents. I've worked with some of the best, people I'm proud to call my friends, but I'm ready for a change.

I'll find out tomorrow if I've got the job. I think the interview went well. I didn't gabble and I didn't cry. I think of Jeremy and smile. I sent him a box of his favourite vanilla fudge with a little note saying that Ward and I were back together, all thanks to him and Ward forgiving me. I'd finished my note with, '*And I promise, no more tears, love, Jan xxx.*' I also let him know that Ward would be putting Beach House up for sale early next year. I couldn't bear the idea of handing it over to Spencer.

Ward was right about what makes a home. It's the people. Beach House, without my grandparents, isn't the same. Ward has promised to try and find the perfect family for it. He's staying with Isla and me on Christmas Eve and we're visiting Dan and Fiona on Christmas Day. Ward wants me to meet his mother over Christmas too. I have also invited Lucas, although he hasn't replied yet. I have to keep on hoping and believing that maybe, one day, Lucas will want to be a larger part of our lives.

I watch the judge and headmistress fuss around on the stage, before playing with their microphones, adjusting the sound. There's a table mounted with a silver trophy and other prizes. The winner's name is engraved on the cup each year. Isla keeps on saying it doesn't matter if she doesn't win.

'Exactly,' Dan reinforces. 'I'm proud that you got this far.'

'So am I,' Ruki and I say at the same time. Isla didn't have to enter this competition. It's open to the whole school, but it wasn't compulsory. Ruki tells me she has worked hard on her shots after school, putting much time and thought into them.

'Right,' the headmistress begins, hushing the audience. 'Thank you all very much for coming tonight. It's been an exceptionally high standard this year, but without further ado, over to the judge, Mr Simpson, for the results.'

Mr Simpson is young with dark hair and round spectacles, wearing jeans and a casual red checked shirt. He's an ex-pupil and now making a name for himself as a freelance photographer. He explains that each entry was judged on technical difficulty, content and style. He opens a small brown envelope. 'So, guys, in third place . . .'

Isla keeps her head down, touches her rose again.

It's Mark Williams, fourteen years old, who took photographs of his family holiday in Africa. Everyone claps as he shakes Mr Simpson's hand.

'In second place . . .' Mr Simpson smiles before saying a name, enjoying keeping us in suspense. 'I loved these images. They made me laugh. The photographer really captures the joy of running about and being a child. Amy Morris.'

There's lots of clapping as fifteen-year-old Amy Morris

struts down the hall and up the steps, before she shakes the judge's hand.

'In first place . . .' The audience is silent as we wait for the envelope to be opened. Ruki crosses her fingers. Isla stares at her shoes. 'I chose this entry because it shows extraordinary talent for detail and light,' Mr Simpson says. 'I think this person has real potential.' Slowly he unfolds the piece of paper. 'The winner of the Christmas 2014 Young Photographer of the Year Award goes to . . .'

'Doesn't matter,' Isla shrugs looking at me and then to Dan. 'Whatever.'

'. . . Isla Wild.'

Mr Simpson searches for Isla in the audience.

'It's you!' Ward, Dan, Lizzie, Ruki and I say all at once to Isla who's still glued to her chair, as if she hasn't heard. I nudge and push her. 'You've done it! Isla, go!' We all scrape our chairs back to allow room for her to get past. I kiss Ward. 'She's done it, she's done it!'

'She must get it from me,' Dan jokes.

I watch Isla stagger up to the front of the hall, towards the stage. But then, just before she reaches the steps, she trips, crashing down on to the floor. There are gasps from the audience. I leap out of my seat, but Ward pushes me back down. 'It's fine,' he says, 'look.'

Someone in her class is helping her. She's a tall blonde girl with a ponytail. I watch as Isla stands up and this girl repositions her rose to make sure it's straight. They shake hands. Ruki and I exchange glances before I say quietly to Ward, Lizzie and Dan, 'That's Gemma.'

I feel so proud as Isla tackles those steps, one by one, gripping the rail. The audience cheers like mad.

'Uncle Lucas,' she calls, waving. 'Look! I won!'

Surprised, I turn to see my brother standing at the back of the hall. He smiles at me and I smile back, willing him to come and join us. Ward makes room, taking Isla's empty seat, allowing Lucas to sit next to me.

'You came,' I say, surprised.

He stares ahead. 'I thought to myself, why am I working when I could be here? Jan, I've been a mess for so long, unable to enjoy the things that are right in front of me. I don't want to go through life scared anymore. Scared to love, terrified of failure. If I can't let love in, then I can't give it back, can I? I'd love to spend Christmas Day with you, if you'll still have me?'

I reach for his hand. 'Oh Lucas, Isla and me, we'd love that.'

Lucas watches Mr Simpson present Isla with the silver cup. 'Look at her, Jan, you must be so proud. She's quite a girl.' Finally he turns to me. 'Like her mother.'

Tearful, I watch as Isla shakes the cup in the air with the biggest grin on her face.

Someone jumps up from her chair. She shouts and whoops for joy. She's one of those really embarrassing mums, someone who doesn't know when to stop.

That someone is me.

ACKNOWLEDGEMENTS

Firstly, I'd like to thank a lot of estate agents. One of my closest friends happens to be one and, I have to say, every agent I met was charming and not a patch like the stereotype, Alex Whyte, in the prologue. Masses of thanks go to Tim Harriss, Simon North, Guy Welchman and Henrietta Redgrave for inspiring so many of the stories in this book and for giving me such a good insight into the job and the atmosphere of the boardroom. I have of course used a lot of artistic licence but what certainly came through was your enthusiasm for selling houses and also how much you care about your clients.

There are many other people who helped me research my characters. I'd like to thank the creative and passionate Giles Havergal for telling me about his experiences as a theatre director. Huge thanks also to Emma Fletcher for giving me such a colourful account of her job as a professional declutterer.

Thanks to www.grandparentsplus.org.uk, who kindly put me in touch with Jenny Harris, who was open to telling me about raising her granddaughter. Jenny tragically lost her son to cancer and found herself responsible for caring for his daughter, Sophie. Jenny has supported her grandchild through many tough times and continues to do so. They have also shared great happiness. I found Jenny's story touching and admire her enormously.

My niece and nephew, Emily and Billy Noel. Thank you for all your funny stories and for just being the best. I have three little words to say to you: Reggae Reggae sauce!

Thanks to Tim Powell for allowing me to base one of the houses on his own, with the funny old alpacas. Thanks also to Carole White for sharing a story about her son. To the lovely Delia Macarie – thank you so much for your help with the book.

Much thanks to Charlotte Petherick, for allowing me to stay with you when I was researching Cornwall.

To my mother and father – as always – for your unconditional love and support. To all my family for their support – I couldn't write without it.

To Diana Beaumont, my new agent and old friend. Your advice, editing and constant support over the years have meant a huge amount to me. What an exciting future we have in books.

To Jane Wood, at Quercus – thank you for your infinitely wise and skilful editing. It is always a joy to work with you. Many thanks also to Therese Keating for all your involvement in this book.

Finally, *The Things We Do for Love* could not have been written without Kim and Steve Edwards and their daughter, Charlotte. Kim read *Monday to Friday Man* a few years ago and wrote to me saying how much she had liked the disability angle. She went on to tell me how her eight-year-old daughter had Cerebral Palsy (CP) and that if I ever wanted to know more about her, I was welcome to get in touch. Out of curiosity, I wrote back and visited. This was the beginning of Kim telling me exactly what it is like to be the mother of a child with CP. She told me so many stories, some funny, others sad, but all of them moving. Kim and Steve also made the brave decision to take Charlotte to America for life-changing surgery, which has transformed her life. Charlotte came to visit me at my parents' home. We had a lovely time together, Charlotte telling me about her school, her boring old physio and exercises, and she completely fell in love with my dog – who wouldn't? – Darcy, insisting we take him for a walk after lunch. I watched as she stomped off with Darcy, determined to walk faster than the rest of us. She had spirit, a sense of fun and a beautiful smile. Thank you so much, Charlotte, Kim and Steve for letting me into your lives and allowing me to draw on your experiences.

And finally, finally: to SJ, my cousin, for giving me the idea in the first place to write about the world of property. SJ is the most special estate agent and friend you could ever hope to have in your life. I cannot thank you enough for being so supportive of me and my writing and I look forward so much to celebrating this book with you.